PRAISE FOR *ALL THE BROKEN PLACES*

Winner of the 2016 Paranormal Romance Guild Reviewer's Choice Award for Best Paranormal Romance/Suspense Series

"...Those with an interest in parapsychology will be fascinated by this artfully written series starter."

—*Publishers Weekly*

"With the introduction of a charismatic group of alternative healers, Eden creates a unique world that readers will find fascinating."

—*RT Book Reviews*

PRAISE FOR *ALL THE WOUNDS IN SHADOW*

"Anise Eden's *All the Wounds in Shadow* is the continuation of a remarkable journey. Peopled with engaging characters and filled with intrigue, this book will delight readers of paranormal romance. This series occupies a special place at the top of my favorites list and I can't wait to see what Ms. Eden brings us next."

—Rosanna Leo, author of the Gemini Island Shifters series

All The Light There Is

THE HEALING EDGE - BOOK THREE

ANISE EDEN

DIVERSIONBOOKS

Books by Anise Eden

THE HEALING EDGE SERIES

All the Broken Places

All the Wounds in Shadow

All the Light There Is

Diversion Books
A Division of Diversion Publishing Corp.
443 Park Avenue South, Suite 1008
New York, New York 10016
www.DiversionBooks.com

For more information, email info@diversionbooks.com

First Diversion Books edition September 2017.
Print ISBN: 978-1-63576-164-1
eBook ISBN: 978-1-62681-702-9

LSIDB/1708

To Mom and Dad, my best friends and real-life heroes,
for your unconditional love, support, and faith.

Chapter One

ParaTrain Internship, Day Six

It's just a meeting. Nothing to be nervous about. I wiped my damp palms on my skirt and ordered my brain to focus on something else. *Like the Jag,* I thought. *Focus on the fact that you're finally getting a ride in the Jag.*

And not just any Jag—the British 1936 Jaguar SS100 Ben had restored. He'd found the car in a barn in Pennsylvania, sitting on blocks and covered in hay bales. Now, it looked like it had just left the showroom. My fingertips roamed across the soft leather seat as I admired each piece of shining chrome and the deep glow of the wood on the dash. The car's transformation was a testament to Ben's workmanship—not to mention to his patience and tenacity when it came to the things he loved.

The things—and the people, I thought, smiling down at my ring. I hadn't exactly made things easy for Ben, but now, two gold birds were wrapped around my finger, holding a lustrous piece of Scottish agate between their wings. He'd wanted to give me a tangible reminder of how he felt, a talisman to guard against anxiety and doubt.

I stole a glance at Ben. He was completely in his element, left hand loosely holding the steering wheel, right elbow propped up on the door. Everything about him was solid and squared-off, from the angle of his jaw to the way he carried his shoulders. These qualities were augmented by his charcoal gray suit and crisp white shirt—worn sans tie, as usual. I marveled that no matter what internal battles he might be fighting, Ben always exuded a quiet confidence.

"Enjoying yourself?" he asked.

"Completely." I closed my eyes and inhaled my new favorite

scent—a mixture of fine wool, cotton, and vintage leather that clung to Ben like an olfactory tattoo. "My mom would have loved this, you know."

His light brown eyes softened. "You think so?"

"Absolutely." Every summer when I was a kid, she had taken me to the local car shows. Back then, we could only look, never touch. Riding along with Ben, I felt like a glamorous movie star. I struck my best Hollywood pose, and he smiled.

It was such a pleasure—not to mention a relief—to see Ben relax after the nonstop drama of the past two weeks. There had been too many life-and-death situations, too much tension. And more than anyone, Ben had earned a vacation. With that in mind, after our meeting at the Smithsonian, we planned to spend the rest of the weekend on the Eastern Shore. That evening, we had a dinner date with my mother's cousin, Ardis, and a reservation at a nice bed-and-breakfast. Sunday's schedule was still open. I thought we might head to the ocean; I loved the beach in the fall. Or we could take the ferry to Smith Island, wander around St. Michaels, go sailing… As I considered the possibilities, I nearly forgot to be nervous.

Then we entered downtown D.C. I sobered as stately suburban homes gave way to modern office buildings and massive structures of chiseled granite. Before long, the Smithsonian office building came into view—ten stories of tinted glass reflecting the cloudless blue sky like a darkened mirror. It took up half a city block.

Ben caught me biting my lip. "You know there's nothing to be nervous about, right?"

"I know," I lied. The truth was, I couldn't believe we were actually *there.* It had been less than twenty-four hours since Ben told his mother, Dr. MacGregor, about our group's experience with the double kheir ritual. Now we were on our way to meet with her world-class paranormal research team—and not just to exchange information. We'd been asked to give a demonstration, as well.

I had dressed up for the occasion, wearing a dove gray pencil skirt and a wine-colored cashmere sweater my mother had given me one Christmas. Still, I couldn't shake the feeling that I didn't belong at the Smithsonian—not as anything more than a tourist, anyway.

"Well, just in case," he said, "let me remind you that you have nothing to prove here. None of us do. My mother already told her colleagues what happened with our ritual, and they're keen to know more. But they don't have any definite expectations; after all, half of them still think the double kheir is just a myth." In a conspiratorial tone, he added, "Think of it this way. I know you have a lot of questions. Today, you can ask anything you like."

"Hmm." I bit the tip of my finger. "Anything?"

"Sure."

"Like whether *The Da Vinci Code* was based in fact? And whether they're all members of the Illuminati?"

He chuckled as we pulled into the underground parking garage. "If you ask them *those* questions, I'll make sure you get a substantial year-end bonus."

"Deal," I said, smiling tentatively. I was still getting used to the idea that my new boyfriend was also my new boss.

Ben was the manager of the MacGregor Group, an alternative healing clinic founded by his mother and housed in a repurposed church. I first met him when my former employer, Dr. Nelson, sent me to the MacGregor Group for treatment. My mother's recent suicide had left me in pieces, unable to function. As close as she and I had been, somehow I hadn't seen that my mother was in crisis. Her shocking loss had debilitated me, and I could barely leave my house, let alone return to my job as a psychotherapist. What Dr. Nelson *hadn't* told me was that Dr. MacGregor was a psychiatrist who specialized in paranormal gifts, and that instead of "treating" me, she and Ben were enrolling me in ParaTrain, a paranormal skills training program. My first lesson had been to learn the definition of an empath—and that I *was* one.

Since then, my life had changed so dramatically that it was unrecognizable. Dr. Nelson, Dr. MacGregor, and Ben had all worked hard to convince me that because I was an empath, the key to maintaining my mental health was to leave my job as a therapist and go to work for the MacGregor Group. The idea of leaving my beloved therapy clients was nothing short of heartrending. But after due consideration and several persuasive paranormal experiences, I had agreed to take their advice. Before I could officially start my new job, though, I had to complete a three-week training program: one week of preparation, followed by a two-week internship.

My time in ParaTrain had flown by. Although I was starting my final week of the internship, I still didn't feel anywhere near ready to take on my new role as an empath healer. Before I met the MacGregors, I hadn't even known that empaths existed, so I was still struggling to find my bearings. And the unexpected romance between Ben and me was keeping me permanently off-balance. Add in the mind-blowing experience we'd had with the double kheir the previous week, and... Well, I didn't even know what had *happened* there, so I was fairly certain that I'd make a fool of myself trying to describe it to the Smithsonian research team.

That thought had me wiping my palms on my skirt again. "I am nervous, though, about this demonstration we're supposed to give. The researchers may not have any definite expectations, but surely they're hoping to see *something*. And unlike the rest of you, I have no idea what I'm doing."

"You'll be fine, Cate," Ben reassured me as we pulled into a parking space. "Kai's got it all figured out. He said he has something simple and easy planned, so just follow his instructions. Even if nothing interesting happens, that's still useful information for my mother's team. They're scientists, remember? In an experiment, even a negative result is valuable."

I had no reason to doubt Kai. He was a highly capable expert in ancient rituals, among other things. But when it came to the paranormal, I had a track record of unintentionally messing things up. "What if I forget our instructions and start reading people's emotions?"

Dr. MacGregor had passed on a request from her project director that we refrain from using our paranormal gifts on the members of the research team without their specific permission.

Apparently, they were much more comfortable observing others than being observed themselves.

"The fact that you're already worrying about that means it's highly unlikely you'll forget," he said. "And even if you do, who's going to know?"

Only everyone, I thought. My poker face was nonexistent. I buried my face in my hands. "I'm just afraid that I'm going to embarrass myself. And you. And your mother. And disappoint everyone."

Ben turned off the ignition. I felt him lean towards me and gently tuck an escaped strand of hair into my braid. "That's not possible."

His optimism was endearing, if ill-founded. "Oh, I assure you, it's possible."

"I'll tell you what." He rested his hands on my shoulders. "If you start to feel uncomfortable, give me a thumbs-down sign, and I'll do something so humiliating that it will draw the focus off of you completely."

I couldn't help it; I was intrigued. Pulling my hands away from my face, I asked, "Like what?"

He paused for a moment, considering. "I could drop my pants."

That was just about the most un-Ben-like thing I could imagine. I pressed my lips together to keep from smiling. "Well *that* wouldn't help."

"Why not?"

"Because then I'd be uncomfortable for a whole new reason."

His eyebrow arched. "*You'd* be uncomfortable?"

"Of course! I'd probably start thinking all sorts of inappropriate thoughts—which Asa could easily pick up." I was confident that Asa, our group's resident telepath, would have zero interest in knowing the intimate contents of my head, especially when it came to Ben.

"Oh, I see." Ben leaned back in his seat and smiled roguishly. "You're right; we wouldn't want to scandalize Asa. Well, if the need arises, I promise I'll think of something."

"And you always keep your promises." That Ben could be

counted upon was one of the things I'd learned for certain over the past couple of weeks.

"Yes, ma'am." Ben got out, then came around and opened my door for me. "I promised you a ride in the Jag, didn't I? And here we are."

In spite of my nerves, Ben had managed to make me smile again. "Even if I'm not feeling uncomfortable, I may give you the thumbs-down sign at some point, just to see what happens."

He took my hand and helped me out of the car. "Just another example of why 'Trouble' is the perfect nickname for you."

I shot him a glare. I'd hoped Ben would forget that annoying and only partially valid moniker. But when I opened my mouth to object, he swooped in for a kiss that was firm enough to silence me, but gentle enough to leave my lipstick in place. *Dammit,* I thought as my knees went weak—right before the most intimidating meeting of my life.

• • •

We passed through three security checkpoints before making it up to the fourth floor lobby. Dr. MacGregor was waiting for us there, neatly stylish as usual in a mint green, fitted suit. She was petite and wiry, and her red-framed reading glasses hung from a beaded chain around her neck. How I wished Ben and I were at her house, having a nice, quiet lunch. That had been our original plan for the day—until the Smithsonian meeting was called.

"There you are!" She smiled warmly as we stepped off of the elevator.

"Are we late?" I asked as my nerves began to jangle again.

"No, not at all! You're just the last ones here." She ushered us down the hallway. "This way."

Most of the doors we passed were closed, but the open ones revealed offices with an academic feel to them. They housed overflowing bookshelves, reams of file cabinets, and desks covered in computers, piles of papers, and more books. Near the end of the hallway, we followed Dr. MacGregor into a small conference room full of people.

"Here they are!" she announced, pointing Ben and me toward the remaining two vacant chairs. "My son, psychologist Benjamin MacGregor, and Miss Cathryn Duncan, clinical social worker."

There was a general murmur of greeting. I felt a wave of relief at the sight of our friends, the other members of the MacGregor Group. Then Dr. MacGregor introduced her colleagues.

"This is Dr. Morgan, the director of our research project," she said, nodding toward a tall woman with short blonde hair on the other side of the table. She was so well put-together that I imagined a whole team of stylists had been involved.

Dr. Morgan stood, greeting us warmly. "Welcome, and thank you so much for coming, especially on such short notice. We've heard quite a bit about you—especially you, Dr. MacGregor. Your mother is quite proud of the work you've been doing at the clinic."

"No need to get up. And please, just call me Ben," he said. "It's much less confusing that way."

"Yes, I imagine it is." Dr. Morgan smiled as we all took our seats. "All right then, Ben. We are very grateful to you and the rest of your group for being here."

"It's an honor," Ben replied. "My mother has told us great things about the research you're doing, and we're all anxious to hear more."

"And so you shall." A lanky man with rimless glasses and a bushy gray beard spoke. "I'm Dr. Byrne. My area is ancient history. Dr. Morgan and Dr. Singh are archaeologists, and Dr. Abera here is our expert in linguistics and anthropology."

"It's a pleasure to meet you," Dr. Abera said, her eyes alight. Tossing a long silk drape over her shoulder, she moved with the elegance of a dancer, leaning across the table to shake my hand and Ben's. "We're so excited to talk to you about the double kheir."

"We are indeed," Dr. Singh cheerfully agreed. He looked every inch the archaeologist in his khaki vest with multiple pockets, his hair curling down over the collar of a slightly rumpled shirt. "But first things first. It is Saturday morning, after all, and Dr. MacGregor has rousted us all from our beds. Does everyone have coffee or tea?"

I felt an immediate kinship with Dr. Singh, who clearly shared my priorities. We were given a few minutes to get our beverages from a table set up in the back of the room. I took advantage of the chance to say hello to the other members of our group.

I ran into Kai first. Only minimal makeup accentuated his strong Greek features, and his wardrobe was more understated than usual—leopard print leggings and a long black tunic. Even his usual high heels had been replaced with ankle boots. He smiled and arched an artfully shaped eyebrow. "Look at you, all dressed up!"

"Yeah, not too shabby, sis," said Pete. He called me "sis" because I reminded him of his little sister, Lydia. Pete slid his arm around Kai's waist. He had swapped out his blue jeans for black jeans, but otherwise he wore his usual button-down flannel shirt, cowboy boots, and ten-gallon hat.

Vani joined us, giving me a quick hug. "Yes, well, Cate clearly knows how to dress for a professional meeting," she said in her clipped London accent as she cast a disapproving eye toward Pete's hat.

"Excuse me, ma'am." Pete smiled, removed his hat, and placed it on the table.

Vani looked flawless as always. Her shining black hair was pulled into a French twist, and she wore a striking color-block sheath dress. Vani and Dr. Morgan both looked like they had either just stepped off of movie sets, or were about to step on.

"You want me somewhere on a Saturday morning, you get weekend causal," Kai said, flipping his hair back. "Those two obviously agree."

Kai pointed to the last two members of our group, Eve and Asa, who were making their way over to us. Eve wore her usual layers of torn, black fabric and sported multiple facial piercings. The only change was that her spiked hair was now tipped with fuchsia, instead of purple like the day before. Asa wore his customary khaki slacks and T-shirt, although it was a plain navy shirt, not his usual graphic tee. I guessed that was his way of acknowledging the seriousness of the meeting.

"They're still in college," Vani whispered. "They have an excuse."

Kai just shrugged as Asa and Eve approached us. "Isn't this awesome?" Eve asked, grinning. "The Smithsonian! I told my parents; they are so psyched."

"When did you all find out about this meeting?" I asked. Our group and Dr. MacGregor had been guests at a banquet in D.C. the day before, but Ben and I had left early and driven home to Baltimore. We were notified about the Smithsonian meeting in an early-morning phone call from his mother.

"Dr. MacGregor told us after the banquet yesterday," Vani said. "Since we all still had our suitcases packed, it made sense to just stay in town. She put us up in a place just a few blocks from here."

"Our hotel was *sick*!" Asa exclaimed gleefully.

"How would you know? You barely left the room—up all night playing video games!" Vani gave Eve and Asa a warning look. "You'd better not fall asleep during the ritual."

"Don't worry," Eve said. "We're too pumped to be tired!"

"Totally," Asa agreed. I was relieved to see that he was wearing the bracelet Kai had made for him, a piece of black obsidian woven into a hemp band. It was designed to protect Asa from unintentionally hearing others' thoughts—a phenomenon that disturbed him greatly, and also gave him migraines. Asa caught me eyeing the bracelet and gave me a thumbs-up sign, which I returned.

A series of crisp claps got our attention. "If you're all ready," Dr. MacGregor said, "we'd like to get started."

Ben met me back at our seats. "You look more relaxed."

"I am, I guess. The others don't seem nervous."

"Like I said." Ben reached under the table and took my hand. "Nothing to worry about."

But as the room fell silent, my stomach did a flip. "I'll hold you to that," I whispered.

Chapter Two

Dr. Abera spoke first. "Dr. MacGregor has asked me to summarize our research, just to be sure we're all on the same page. My apologies if this is repetitious for some of you."

She went to the dry-erase board at the front of the conference room and picked up a red marker. I had a flashback to the Parapsychology 101 class Vani and Kai had given me on my first day in ParaTrain. "There are two main theories about the origins of paranormal abilities," Dr. Abera said, drawing two dots. "One is evolutionary—the theory that these are traits that evolved naturally over time, like variations in hair and eye color." She wrote "evolution" under one of the dots. "Some call the second theory spiritual, some call it mystical—and some call it preposterous."

All of the researchers smiled at Dr. Byrne, who noisily cleared his throat.

"The spiritual theory says that paranormal abilities were gifted to select individuals in five Bronze Age civilizations by a divine force, and for a divine purpose," Dr. Abera continued. "Further, this theory holds that the gifts have been transmitted from one generation to the next via lineal descent. Over time, numerous branches of 'sensitives' have been created—our term for people with paranormal abilities. We've learned more about the spiritual theory since the recent discovery of the kheir tablets. They were found by Chinese archaeologists in an underground chamber near the Terracotta Army site."

"Whoa," Asa said, giving voice to the awe we were all feeling.

"Quite," Dr. Abera said. She drew the outline of a hand on the board. "I know you're all familiar with the concept of the 'kheir,' a term derived from an ancient Roman word for hand."

"Yes," Vani said, "and the belief that a kheir—five fingers, working together—can accomplish great things."

"And two hands can accomplish even more," Dr. Abera said, drawing a second hand. "A double kheir."

"This might be a good time to remind everyone who's who in our double kheir configuration," Dr. MacGregor said. "Ben, will you do the honors?"

"Of course," he said. "As you know, one hand represents the five categories of paranormal gifts, and the other represents the five civilizations to which those gifts were originally gifted—according to the spiritual theory, that is." Ben nodded at Dr. Byrne, who seemed to appreciate having his skepticism acknowledged. "All ten fingers, as it were, are present within the MacGregor Group. We know this in part because Vani has been specially trained to read sensitives' auras and identify from which of the five Bronze Age civilizations they are descended." Ben turned to us. "Would you like to introduce yourselves, or would you prefer…?"

"I'll go first," Vani offered, raising her hand. "I'm Vani. As an aura reader, I represent the gift of clairvoyance, and I'm descended from the Indus Valley civilization."

Sitting next to Vani, Asa went next. "I'm Asa, telepath. I represent Egypt."

Then Kai gave a graceful finger wave. "And I'm Kai. Mediumship, Mesopotamia."

"Eve!" Eve smiled brightly. "Precognition, China."

All eyes turned to me. I swallowed hard. "Um, you can call me Cate," I said. "I'm an empath, so I represent psychokinesis. And I'm descended from the Caledonian civilization, or so I'm told."

Vani piped up, "That's right. Caledonia, or ancient Scotland."

There was a moment of silence; no one seemed sure where to take the conversation next. To everyone's surprise, Pete stood up. "So, I'm Pete," he announced. "My tribe is the United States Marine

Corps. My special ability is wranglin' cattle, but nowadays I help Ben keep this double kheir in line."

Smiles broke out around the room. Ben and Pete had served in the Marines together. After Ben's father had died several years before, he'd left the Corps to help his mother get the MacGregor Group started. Pete had then accepted Ben's invitation to help run the clinic. Officially, he was in charge of operations and security, but he really did whatever needed doing.

"Thank you, Pete. Everyone," Dr. Morgan said. "As you're all aware, information about the double kheir has been hard to come by. What little we do know has been pieced together from various historical sites and archaeological digs. From what we gather, it seems that the double kheir is a rare configuration that could potentially give sensitives immediate and full knowledge of how to use their gifts. Researchers across the globe have been trying to figure out how to activate this rumored power to bestow instant knowledge. While several groups have noticed that their rituals in general are more potent when they have a double kheir configuration, experiences of this 'downloading,' as we're calling it, have not yet been reported—until yesterday, that is, when Ben told Dr. MacGregor about your recent experience."

Dr. Morgan focused in on me, and I felt my face start to flush. "Cate, we're told that you might have undergone this 'downloading' phenomenon during a ritual last week. We understand that the project you were working on is top secret, but we were hoping that you could tell us whatever you can about what happened."

"Top secret" was putting it mildly. Our group had spent the past week sequestered in a secure sub-basement under the National Institutes of Health. We had been called in to try to solve an attempted murder while being guarded by Yankee Company, Ben and Pete's former Marine Corps unit. We had all been sworn to secrecy about the mission, so I wasn't sure what, if anything, I was allowed to share.

Ben seemed to tune in to my dilemma. "It's okay, Cate," he

said softly. "Nothing about your experience with the ritual is confidential."

"Okay," I whispered, but then fell silent. I had no idea where to start.

Thankfully, Vani came to my rescue. In her smooth, professional voice, she said, "Since I designed and led the ritual in question, I can set the stage for everyone."

The researchers sat in rapt attention. Vani explained that someone we were treating had died. That trauma had caused the surfeit of toxic emotional energy within me to break loose from the psychic vessel I'd built to contain it. The toxic energy surrounded me, putting me into a state of complete paralysis.

As she spoke, I remembered the terror I'd felt, lying in the hospital bed, unable to move, speak, or even open my eyes, and listening to people talk about me as though I couldn't hear them. My throat tightened. Ben reached under the table, rested his hand on my leg, and began massaging gently. Leaning in close, he whispered, "Are you okay?"

His touch stopped the rise of the panic attack. "Just keep doing what you're doing," I whispered back.

"Gotcha."

As Ben redoubled his efforts, Vani described the ritual they'd designed to clear the toxic energy and cure my paralysis. Kai used meditation and Tibetan singing bowls to put Asa into a trance. Asa then read my mind, acting as a conduit and allowing me to speak through him. Meanwhile, Eve sat behind me performing acupuncture while Vani asked me to visualize the toxic energy like a balloon surrounding me, filling with air and expanding until it disappeared.

Eventually, I felt able to join the conversation. "But the ritual wasn't working," I explained. "Or it *was* working, to an extent, but I've never been very good at visualization. So after a certain point, I couldn't seem to push the balloon out any further. I felt like I was using all of my strength, but it wasn't helping."

"We decided to try forming a circle around Cate, holding hands," Vani explained.

"And then..." I cleared my throat. "Well, something happened."

Dr. MacGregor must have sensed my hesitation. "In your own words, dear," she said.

Ben gave my leg a reassuring squeeze.

"Okay." I said. "It was like the air in the room began to vibrate."

"We all felt it," Vani said.

"That's right," I said. "And then the inside of my body began to vibrate, like every atom in every object and person in the room was pulsating to the same rhythm. It was like we were all making music, and suddenly, I knew how to conduct. I don't know how else to explain it. All at once, I just knew exactly how to control the vibrations and direct the energy so that it would expand the balloon. Then, just when I felt like the pressure inside of the balloon was too great, it disappeared."

"Pop, and it was gone," Kai elaborated.

"That's incredible," Dr. Singh said, his excitement tempered with caution. "So then you were no longer paralyzed?"

"Well," Vani said, "it was a bit more complicated than that. We needed to do more work to cure the paralysis, but at the end of *this* ritual, she was free of toxic energy. We had to take care of that problem before any other interventions could even have a chance of helping her."

Each of the professors took turns politely picking our brains about the exact details, like what acupuncture points Eve had been using, and whether Asa could remember any part of the experience.

As Vani explained again how we had all been positioned, I prompted her, "Don't forget, Ben was there, too."

Dr. MacGregor said, "Well, we assumed Ben was there—"

"No," I clarified, "I mean when Vani decided they should all form a circle around me, Ben was in the circle, too."

The researchers exchanged puzzled glances. "Why was *Ben* in the circle?" Dr. Singh asked, sounding baffled. "Does he have a paranormal gift as well?"

"No, no special gifts," Ben said. "I just joined the circle because that's what Cate said she wanted."

"But...why?" Dr. Singh asked, turning to me.

"I don't know why," I said, "I just felt strongly that I wanted him in the circle, that it was important for him to be there."

"It may be relevant that Cate and Ben are a couple," Dr. MacGregor told her colleagues.

Dr. Abera shook her head. "I can't see how that would make any difference—paranormally, I mean—although I'm sure his presence was a comfort to Cate. But it has never been proposed that the relationships between kheir members matter, just the combination of their individual gifts."

"That may be," Kai said, "but it wasn't until after Ben joined the circle that the vibrations started. Isn't that right, Cate?"

"Yes."

"It's true," Vani said. "I remember."

"Well, that *is* interesting," Dr. Morgan said. "Ben, did you do anything in particular while you were in the circle?"

"No," Ben answered. "I just stood there."

"Fascinating," she replied. "Of course, without a comparable ritual *not* involving Ben, we have no idea whether his presence there had any significance. And even if it didn't, it is noteworthy, at least, that having a non-sensitive as part of the circle wasn't detrimental. I agree with Dr. Abera; it seems unlikely that the special relationship between Ben and Cate had anything to do with what happened. However, at this stage, we should keep an open mind."

Ben must love hearing that he's not detrimental, I thought. Sure enough, I glanced sideways to find Ben suppressing a smile.

"What about the palm?" Dr. Singh asked.

"What palm?" Kai asked.

Dr. MacGregor answered. "This is one of the puzzles we've been trying to solve with the terracotta kheir tablets," she said. "We've found some references to the kheir that describe not only the five fingers of the hand as being essential, but also the palm of the hand. So far, we've only found the palm referenced a few times, but it has been called the 'heart of the kheir' and 'the center.' If your double kheir didn't activate, so to speak, until Ben joined in, that could suggest that there is a role for a sixth person—even a non-sensitive—in this configuration."

"Or it could suggest nothing at all," Dr. Byrne said. "We've all agreed that the palm is most likely just a metaphor for something abstract, like a divine force."

"But it *worked!*" Dr. Singh said excitedly. "You can't dispute that whatever they did worked. They figured it out, Byrne. No one else has even come close."

"Whatever they did—that's the point," Byrne responded. "We don't know what aspects of their ritual made it work. Without controlled experiments—"

"I'm not saying we shouldn't replicate it," Dr. Singh said. "As soon as possible, preferably."

"Well, if you want to cook up an experiment," Kai said, "we've got all of the ingredients right here. We have a demonstration planned; there's no reason we couldn't try it with and without Ben, just to see what happens."

There was a moment of stunned silence, as though the researchers couldn't quite believe that this rare opportunity was being presented to them. "Yes, of course," Dr. Morgan finally said. "That's a wonderful suggestion, Kai. I'd like to thank all of you for sharing your experiences—especially you, Cate. It can't have been easy to relive something so harrowing."

"Thank you," I said, doing my best to smile.

"Shall we move on to the demonstration, then?" Dr. MacGregor suggested.

CHAPTER THREE

We were led to a large, open room, empty but for a couple of dozen chairs scattered about and a water cooler in the corner. The blinds had been drawn and some gym mats placed on the floor. I didn't know what I had been expecting—maybe a place like the basement of our church headquarters, decorated with warm colors and filled with New Age paraphernalia. At least Kai had brought some crystals and candles so we'd feel a bit more at home.

Dr. MacGregor explained that she and Kai had designed a demonstration that would give the researchers an idea of our "baseline," in terms of our abilities and how we worked together. In this case, it was a simple illumination ritual in which each of us would use our different gifts to discover things that were previously unseen or unknown. We decided to do the ritual first without Ben, then add him in to see if it made a difference.

Feeling a little bit like a circus freak, I tried to remind myself that we were taking part in a global research initiative at a respected institution. The five of us sensitives sat in a circle on the gym mats, while the researchers arranged chairs around us and sat poised with their notebooks. Ben and Pete stood outside the circle, offering thumbs-up signs. Kai arranged three rough, pointed crystals in a triangular formation in the middle of our circle, then put a few candles around the triangle and lit them. He then gestured for us all to hold hands.

Once we were ready, Kai began to speak, falling into a rhythmic tone and cadence. "I ask the gods and goddesses, spirit guides, and guardian angels, spirits from beyond the veil, and all those who wish to support us in this illumination ritual to be in attendance with us now."

In the pause that followed, I felt a soft flow of cold air blowing on the top of my head, just as I had during my first ritual in the church basement. So it *had* been spirit energy, after all, as Kai had said, and not an erratic air-conditioning vent. I looked around the circle and saw that everyone else had their eyes closed, so I closed mine as well.

"Dr. Byrne," Kai said, "your mother is here. May I have your permission to speak to Elba?"

I heard Dr. Byrne spit out a mouthful of what I guessed was his coffee.

"Sorry for the surprise," Kai said. "We never know who's going to come through in these things."

"It's fine, fine," Dr. Byrne sputtered. "Yes, you have my permission."

"You inherited her cat, Luna?" Kai asked.

"Ye—yes."

"Well, Elba is saying that you should stop feeding Luna those liver treats. She knows they're cheaper, but apparently some of the ingredients are carcinogenic. She wants you to buy the organic kind. Okay?"

I peeked at Dr. Byrne, who had gone as white as a sheet. "Organic. Yes, okay."

"Good. All right, Elba and the other spirits are pulling their energy back, but they'll stay nearby for now," Kai said. "As a medium, that was my offering to the illumination ritual. My gift has shared what it has to share. Everyone else, go ahead and share as you feel inspired, whatever your gift is giving you."

Vani spoke first, unable to conceal the concern in her voice. "Dr. Abera, I am feeling drawn to your aura. May I have your permission to read it?"

"Yes, go ahead," Dr. Abera said.

Vani paused for a moment, then continued, "I see something concerning—a blockage around your lungs. I want to say you're having trouble breathing, but the problem is in its early stages yet, and it can be managed. But I also sense some stubbornness around the blockage, as though you are reluctant to seek treatment. There is fear—fear that it won't get better. But it will. You just need to see a doctor."

We heard Dr. Abera mumble something. Kai said, "Can you validate what Vani said, Dr. Abera?"

"Yes, she's right," Dr. Abera reluctantly admitted. "I was diagnosed with refractory asthma, but I've been putting off my follow-up appointment. You know how it is; after a certain age, every time you go to the doctor, it's just more bad news."

"Well, time to stop procrastinating," Kai said. "Thank you for validating that. Anyone else?"

"I'm blocking out the research team as we agreed," Asa said, "but Dr. Singh, something you're thinking is transmitting so loudly, I can almost hear it without even trying. Is it okay if I read that thought?"

"By all means, share," Dr. Singh said.

Asa nodded. "The thought is, 'I'm so thirsty.'"

Dr. Singh chuckled. "Remarkable that you picked that up, Asa. That's absolutely right. A medication I'm taking causes dry mouth. It's quite distracting at times."

Kai said, "Then by all means! Pete, would you be so kind as to get Dr. Singh some water?"

"I'm on it," Pete drawled, and we heard his boots clomp towards the water cooler.

"Much appreciated," Dr. Singh said.

"Eve," Kai asked, "anything on your end?"

There was a pause before Eve replied, "Nothing—which isn't surprising, right? I mean, I'm not really doing my *thing*, here, I'm just supporting everyone as part of the double kheir."

"No, not surprising at all," Kai reassured. "I just thought I'd check in."

Dr. MacGregor explained to the other researchers, "Eve can

only access her precog abilities and look into the future when she's in a trance." There were murmurs of understanding.

Kai continued, "Okay, let's see what our newest member has for us. Cate?"

"Um…" I bit my lip. "What am I supposed to do again?"

"Don't force it," Kai said. "Just turn inward, tap into your empath gift, and see what comes up, if anything."

"Okay." As I turned my attention inward, I saw in my mind's eye the ever-present, tiny filaments of light rooted in my heart. They extended in all directions, connecting me to the people I cared about and allowing me to feel their emotions, no matter how far away they were. In my first week of training, I'd learned that those filaments were called portals, and that being able to open portals to other people was one of my paranormal abilities. But now, as my focus on my heart intensified, instead of discovering any new insights, I was overwhelmed by one thing, and one thing only.

"Um, Kai, I'm not sure I can contribute anything useful."

"Why not?"

"It's a little embarrassing." I sighed. "All I can sense are the feelings Ben and I have for each other. They're kind of pushing everything else out."

"Nothing wrong with that," Kai said cheerfully.

Dr. Singh chimed in, "Maybe that's your signal that it's time to bring Ben into the circle."

"That's what I was thinking," Vani said.

"Let's do it then!" We all opened our eyes.

"Wait!" Dr. MacGregor stood up. "Why don't we try it with Pete first?"

Pete peered out from under his hat. "What for?"

"Yes, I'm not following," Dr. Byrne said.

"Like Ben, Pete is an integral member of the group," Dr. MacGregor explained, "and he, too, is in a relationship with one of the sensitives."

Kai smiled and waved.

"Oh, well—an excellent suggestion, in that case," Dr. Singh said.

"That will help us determine whether or not the palm phenomenon is specific to Ben."

"Interesting." Dr. Abera eyed Pete. "Would you be willing to give it a try?"

The look on Pete's face indicated he was quite reluctant, but Ben appeared pleased with the idea. He turned to us. "Are you all okay with trying Pete out? And do you promise not to bite?"

We called out our encouragement, and Kai and Vani made a space for Pete in the circle.

Pete tried to conceal how awkward he felt as he sat down. We all joined hands again. "Okay," Kai said, "now we're going to repeat the exact same ritual. Close your eyes, everyone, and concentrate on listening to your gifts. If you feel moved to share, just jump in."

We all did as instructed. There was a period of silence. Then—nothing. I sensed no change at all in the room's energy, or within myself. I opened one eye and looked around. One by one, the rest of the group opened their eyes, as well.

"So?" Vani asked. "Did anyone notice anything?"

We all shrugged and shook our heads.

"No offense, Pete," Asa said with a grin, "but I think you're a dud."

Pete chuckled as he pushed himself up off the ground. "Nobody's happier to hear that than me. I'm not cut out for mumbo jumbo."

Kai smacked him playfully on the leg as he walked away from the circle. "I'll show you mumbo jumbo. Get over here, Big Dog."

Ben patted Pete sympathetically on the shoulder, then took his place in the circle, flashing me a quick smile.

"Don't distract her," Kai scolded. "Okay, everyone. One more time."

We closed our eyes and began to refocus. Gradually, I felt the air around me begin to vibrate—just as it had during our ritual the previous week. Once again, it felt like the molecules in my body and those in the room were drums beating together in a single pulse.

"Oh, wow," Asa said. "Does anybody else feel that?"

There was agreement around the circle.

"I'm not sure, but I'm think I'm seeing something," Vani said.

"What is it?" Kai asked.

"It's—I think—it's like I can see the auras of people elsewhere in the building, even some people outside," she said. "When I shift my focus into a certain direction, I can see all of the auras of the people there, see through the walls, floors, everything."

"Fascinating," Dr. Singh said. "Can you narrow your focus and tell us about a specific person? Maybe—" he consulted with the others briefly—"can you see a woman behind the desk at the main entrance? On the first floor. You didn't come in that way, but it's a large lobby, and she's usually the only one there."

There was another pause. Then Vani said excitedly, "I see her! Oh!" Her voice softened. "Her aura is heavy with grief. She's barely holding it together. She lost someone recently—her husband, maybe?"

"That's right!" Dr. Singh exclaimed. "That's Judy. She's been here for twenty-five years, and she was recently widowed."

"Oh my goodness," Vani said, awestruck. "There are so many… I've never experienced anything like this."

"It's crazy over here, too," Asa said. "I can hear dozens of thoughts transmitting from all over the building, even from outside. It's like a whole lot of radios turned on at once. But if I focus on one stream of thought, the others fade away so I can hear it more clearly—and my head doesn't hurt!" he declared, victorious. "Usually I get a migraine from listening to just *one* person's thoughts."

"Can you give us an example, Asa?" Dr. MacGregor asked. "Try reading me."

"Um—are you sure?"

"Yes, of course."

"Okay. I only ask because you're thinking something personal—that Ben and Cate seem to fit together well, and that they could be really good for each other."

Fortunately, Dr. MacGregor laughed. "You're right—that

thought did flit through my mind. I'm sorry if that made you uncomfortable, Cate, Benjamin."

"Not at all," Ben said.

I forced myself to smile, even though I could feel a deep blush heating up my cheeks. "Yes, it's fine."

"Wait your turn!" Kai said. "Not you all, the spirits. The top of my head has become like the door to a waiting room, and all of these people who have passed on are standing around in there, trying to tell me things. One at a time! Sheesh!" I opened my eyes and looked over at Kai, who had tilted his head back and was talking to the ceiling. "Usually one or two spirits come through at the most, and their speech is kind of muddled, but this time, I hear them loud and clear and they're all clamoring to get a word in. I'm sorry; I can't get to you all today. Choose a representative. One person. Okay." Kai cleared his throat. "Dr. Singh, your father is here. May I have your permission to speak with him?"

"Oh my!" Dr. Singh sounded awestruck. "Yes, you may speak with him."

"He's insisting—very loudly, by the way—that you wear the gray suit to your sister's wedding."

Dr. Singh guffawed. "Hah! He would say that; it was the suit he wore to *his* wedding!" His voice softened with emotion. "Thank you, Kai. I'm touched that he came through, and I will take his wishes under consideration."

"He says he's glad to hear that," Kai said. "Whoa. Okay, spirits, that's all I can do for today. We have to move on. Cate, Eve, tell us about you. What are you experiencing?"

"You go first, Cate," Eve said. "I think I'm getting something, but I can't make it out yet."

"Okay." I closed my eyes again, but this time, I was only able to focus on my own interior for a split second before I was propelled outside of myself. "I can see the filaments of light shooting outward from my heart, connecting me to every other heart in the building—like I've formed portals to all of them. But all of their hearts are connected to one another's, too, with the same light filaments. Now they're spreading—oh!" I gasped as my visual perspective zoomed outward at high speed. "The filaments are shooting out like vines, connecting everyone in the city. It looks like a web, now, spreading across the globe and pulsating with light."

"Fascinating," Dr. MacGregor said. "What do you make of it? Just intuitively, your first thought."

I opened up my empathic senses and tried to hold the vision in my mind. "The filaments look like portals that already exist, linking all of our hearts together. Perhaps empaths don't open or create portals, after all; we're just better at accessing them."

The researchers spoke softly but excitedly amongst themselves. Then Eve broke in.

"I see something, too," she whispered, her voice a rough whisper. "I'm not in a trance or anything, so this is weird for me. But I see a light originating at Ben's heart chakra. It's bright and warm, like the sun, and it's beaming out to the five of us, to our heart chakras, carrying some kind of energy—like a battery charging us. Ben," she asked, "are you feeling this?"

"I feel nothing out of the ordinary," he said.

"But the light—it's so *beautiful*," Eve said, her voice softening to a whisper.

"Okay," Kai said gently, "The spirits are pulling their energy away. That's our sign that we've done all we were meant to do for today. Thank you, everyone." We all released hands. I felt the vibrations stop abruptly, and the web of light disappeared. Eve collapsed to the floor—smiling, but with tears wetting her cheeks. We gathered around her, offering our support. After several minutes, she was able to stand.

The researchers invited us back to the first conference room to debrief. They'd had lunch brought in, so we had a few minutes to recover as we put our plates together and took our seats around the table.

Dr. Morgan cleared her throat, and the room fell silent. "I want to thank you all again for being here today, and for giving us that very impressive demonstration." Smiles were exchanged around the table. "Would anyone like to share their thoughts?"

"I was most intrigued by what you said, Eve, about the energy from Ben charging the group like a battery," Dr. Singh said.

"Yes, that's how it felt," Eve replied.

"That fits in with the theory that the palm activates the double kheir somehow." Dr. Singh examined Ben closely. "And you didn't feel anything at all that was unusual?"

Ben shook his head. "No, nothing."

"Well, I *am* a precog," Eve pointed out. "Maybe he's not charging us yet, but will in the future."

"That could be it," Dr. Abera said. "The control experiment with Pete certainly seems to indicate that there is something unique about you, Ben—something that makes you the key to this particular lock. But we're here to discover how the double kheir works, not to dictate it. This phenomenon has been around since the Bronze Age; it would be quite arrogant of us to superimpose our own expectations upon it. I am impressed with what we saw today, but I must say it raises more questions than it answers."

The other researchers murmured their agreement.

"I hope all of you won't mind coming back for more meetings like this," Dr. Morgan said. "You're unique in the world, as far as we know—the only ones who appear to have made the double kheir work the way it is meant to. I believe we can learn a tremendous amount from you."

Ben glanced around at our group members, all of whom nodded. "You can count on our cooperation, Dr. Morgan," he said. "It's an honor to be a part of your research."

"Well, I'm glad that's settled," Dr. MacGregor said. "Now let's finish up lunch. I know you all have places to be."

And since none of us ever argued with Dr. MacGregor, we all dutifully began to eat—including Ben, I was pleased to see. I knew he was still battling his childhood phobia of eating in front of other people, but if he was feeling nervous, he kept it under wraps. In my first week of training, he had let me try to help him using my empath healing abilities and some other therapeutic techniques. He'd improved steadily since then, but this was the first time I'd seen him break bread in front of such a large group of strangers. I tried not to let on that I was watching him, gauging his anxiety levels.

He picked up on it anyway. Leaning in close, he murmured, "Don't worry, doc. I'm doing fine—thanks to you."

"I can see that," I murmured back, resting my hand on his arm. "And don't you dare let go of my knee."

He chuckled and began gently massaging my knee. "Is this a new therapy technique? Making me eat with one hand?"

"Yes," I said with fake gravitas. "It's brand new, cutting edge."

"In that you just made it up."

I grinned. "Okay, you can have your hand back. For now."

"No, that's okay," he said, sliding his fingers a little farther up my leg. "I like a challenge."

And with that, my ability to form coherent thoughts flew away like a cloud of starlings. *Thank God the meeting is over,* I thought, my skin warming beneath Ben's stirring touch.

Chapter Four

After we left, our group hung out in the elevator lobby for a few minutes, talking in general terms about how well the meeting had gone. No one seemed quite ready to have a serious conversation about what had happened during the demonstration. It had been powerful and a bit shocking; my guess was that we all needed time to process. However, that didn't stop everyone from giving Ben a good-natured ribbing about his apparently secret power as a double kheir human battery pack. Superhero nicknames were bandied about; eventually, "The Energizer Benny" came out on top. Ben took the teasing with good grace.

Certainly, the whole experience had been overwhelming for me—starting with reliving my paralysis episode. I was eager to get back on the road with Ben and forget about everything for a while. Fortunately, he picked up on my impatience, and we said our goodbyes.

This time, Ben put the top down on the Jag. I closed my eyes and enjoyed the sensation of the air currents playing with my hair as he drove. The wind had blown my scarf off when we hit the highway, but my leather jacket was doing a pretty good job of keeping me warm. Still, I knew I'd look a little ragged by the time we got to the Eastern Shore, with my wavy brown hair being torn bit by bit out of its braid.

I took the opportunity to text my best friend, Simone. We had met while working together at Dr. Nelson's clinic, where she was my clinical supervisor. She had been there for me through my mother's suicide and the aftermath, so she had a tendency to worry about me. I let her know that Ben and I were going away for a few days—again.

She was happy for me, but disappointed that she would have to wait even longer to hear all about Ben. Then she freaked out when I told her that we were going to see my mother's cousin, Ardis, sure that something really serious must be going on between Ben and me if I was getting family involved. But I managed to convince her that it was just a coincidence—we were going to be in the same place at the same time—and that I didn't have anything to announce. She made me take a selfie to prove that I was alive and well and hadn't been kidnapped. I sent her a picture of Ben in the driver's seat, too. She conceded that he didn't look like a serial killer, texted me the smiley face with heart eyes emoji, and told me to do everything that she wouldn't do. I smiled to myself, relishing the idea of filling her in on my romance with Ben over a long meal when we got back.

An hour later, the Chesapeake Bay Bridge stretched out before us. I closed my eyes and tried to let the *clu-clunk, clu-clunk* sound of the metal seams beneath the tires lull me into a meditative state until we reached Kent Island.

Whatever tension we'd been feeling drained away as we headed east. The strip malls gave way to harvested cornfields and abandoned vegetable stands. Every gas station advertised "Live Bait," and we began to see more pickup trucks and bumper stickers declaring, "There's No Life West of the Chesapeake Bay." The flatness of the landscape meant the horizon was miles away. I found it a soothing change from the more constricted visual spaces of city living; from the look on Ben's face, he felt the same.

Ambient noise prevented much conversation, but we still pointed things out to each other: a tree that still had most of its fire-orange leaves, a formation of Canada geese flying overhead. I felt so light, as though the wind were blowing right through me. There we were, the two of us, driving along and taking in the landscape just like a normal couple.

Of course, we were anything but. Our meeting at the Smithsonian had driven that point home. But for the next little while, I pushed everything else out of my mind and soaked in the deliciousness of the experience.

My reverie was interrupted when we pulled up to the Tidewater Inn, a gorgeous, four-story historic building in downtown Easton. The valet whistled in appreciation at the Jag, thanking Ben as he took the keys.

As we stood on the sidewalk, I leaned in and gave Ben a quick kiss on the cheek. Then I took both of his hands and rested them on my hips as I beamed up at him. "That was an incredible ride. I think we should take the Jag out as often as possible."

Ben gave me a sideways grin. "You don't have to convince me. I'm glad you enjoyed it." He nodded towards the door of the inn and rubbed his hand gently up and down my arm. "You ready for this?"

"Yes, of course." After all, we'd come all that way just to meet Ardis, my mother's cousin. Ardis had called and asked me to meet her in Easton for dinner. I'd thought that it was odd, since she lived in Delaware, but she said she was going to be there visiting an old friend and that she wanted to talk to me about something important. I assumed it had something to do with my mother's effects or her last wishes. When, for the first time ever, her question about whether I was dating someone was answered with a yes, she'd insisted that I bring Ben too, so that she could "check him out." To my surprise, Ben was more than eager to meet my closest living family member, and didn't appear to be in the least bit nervous. I wondered for the hundredth time if he was really that self-assured, or if he was just a very good actor.

I did a quick repair job on my braid in the ladies' room and met Ben back in the lobby. I took his elbow, and we walked into the tavern. I gave the hostess Ardis's name, and she guided us through a series of elegantly furnished rooms. My heart swelled when I finally spotted Ardis half-standing out of her seat and waving to me.

"Ardis!" I called, approaching her with open arms—then stopping. And looking to my right. And freezing in place. Standing up from his seat at our table wearing a polo shirt and a sheepish expression was—no, it couldn't be…

"*Skeet?*" I barely whispered his name, certain that I must be hallucinating. Skeet was the head of the National Institutes of

Mental Health, or NIMH. He was also the man who had asked the MacGregor Group to spend the past week holed up in one of their sub-basements on our top-secret mission. For some reason, he had taken a liking to me, and had even come to my defense a couple of times. But he had also tried to recruit me to join paranormal research studies that used empathic abilities in ways that could potentially be coercive or intrusive, which had made me doubt his ethics. And there was absolutely no reason in *hell* why he should be at the Tidewater Inn in Easton having dinner with Ardis.

I felt Ben's whole body stiffen behind me. He stepped to my right and placed himself between the apparition and me. "Skeet, what a surprise," Ben said with forced politeness.

Ardis paled. "Oh, Cate, I'm sorry, honey," she said quickly. "I know you don't like surprises, but Skeet is the old friend I told you I was coming to visit, and when he told me that you all knew each other, I just thought…" Her voice cracked as she spoke. "I thought it would be fun."

Well, that settled that. I couldn't have Ardis feeling bad, not on my account. I jammed a smile onto my face, pulled her into an embrace, and hugged tightly. "Of course, I'm sorry!" I pulled away from her, looked her straight in the eye, and lied. "It's a wonderful surprise! I was just shocked for a second, you know, seeing Skeet out of context like this." Then I turned to my right. "Nice to see you, Skeet!"

"You too—both of you!" Skeet smiled apologetically, shaking Ben's hand, and then mine. "I'm glad this is okay."

Ardis's shoulders dropped with relief. "Me, too. I didn't want to upset you, sweetheart."

"Don't be silly!" My cheeks were burning with the effort of wearing my cheerful expression. "Ben, this is Ardis, my mother's cousin."

Ardis's eyebrows shot up as she looked him over. "It is certainly a pleasure to meet Cate's young man."

"It's wonderful to meet you, too." Ben's tone was warm as he shook her hand. "Cate has told me so much about you."

Ardis smiled and even blushed slightly. She was clearly charmed. "Well, make yourselves comfortable."

We all took our seats. Ben took the chair next to Skeet, while I sat next to Ardis and scanned the room for whatever rip in the fabric of the space-time continuum had led us all to that exact space, at that particular moment in time.

CHAPTER FIVE

There was an awkward silence, which the waitress mercifully broke by taking our drink orders. "So Cate, Ben," Ardis said, "Skeet tells me that you three worked together last week on some kind of secret project!"

"That's right," Ben said.

"Yes." I looked from Ardis to Skeet and back again. "I'm just amazed by this coincidence! How do you two know each other?"

They exchanged a glance, as though silently trying to decide who should answer my question. Ardis apparently drew the short straw. "Well, sweetheart, that's actually related to the thing I wanted to talk to you about."

It felt like all of the breath left my body in a *whoosh*. What on earth was going on? I pulled some air into my lungs and took a sip of water. "The *important* thing?"

"Yes, that." Ardis looked over at Skeet again. Both of their expressions were grave. He nodded at her, and she continued. "Skeet was good friends with your parents."

I gave my head a quick shake. I couldn't have heard correctly… could I? "My *parents*?"

He nodded. "Your father and I were fraternity brothers at George Washington University, and we started out together at NIMH. We met Rhona and Ardis at a barbecue—a mutual friend's house in St. Michaels. For a while, the four of us spent almost every weekend together."

"We sure did," Ardis said, her expression brightening at the memory. "Those were good times."

"I…I don't understand." I had no memories of my father,

who'd left before I was a year old. I'd always assumed that Ardis had known him, since she had always been close to Mom, but she'd never spoken about him—nor had my mother, for that matter. But discovering that *Skeet* had been friends with both of my parents? That was too bizarre—especially because in the week we'd worked together, he'd never mentioned it.

Suddenly, all of the sounds around me became muffled. I could see Ardis's mouth moving and hear her voice, but I couldn't make out what she was saying. My mouth went dry, and my pulse pounded loudly in my ears.

"Cate." I heard Ben calling me as though from a distance. He slid his arm around me and rubbed my shoulder briskly. My sense of hearing began to normalize. "Cate, are you okay?" he asked.

I leaned into him and inhaled slowly, trying to absorb some of his energy, his strength. I swallowed hard and nodded. "I'm sorry," I said to Ardis, "this just all comes as kind of a shock. I mean, Skeet, you never said anything."

"I know, and I'm sorry." Skeet smoothed out the linen tablecloth in front of him. "The Captain ordered me not to. He was afraid that any such personal revelations would distract you from your work."

Captain Abbott—the man in charge of Yankee Company, Ben and Pete's old Marine Corps unit. Yankee Company had handled security for our mission the week before. I turned quickly to look at Ben. If he had known about the situation and kept it from me… But it was clear by the look of suppressed anger on his face that he was as surprised as I was.

Ben's arm tightened around me. "You could have told her afterwards," he said coolly.

"Well, that's why I'm here now," Skeet said, smiling tentatively. "That's why Ardis invited me."

"That's right." Ardis reached over and gave my arm a reassuring rub. "I thought you would want to know. I'm sure you figured out that your mother forbade me to talk to you about your father. She wasn't thrilled about the fact that Skeet and I stayed in touch, either.

But since she's gone—" Ardis paused, pain flashing across her face. "Well, we can talk freely now."

"It's okay, Ardis." I took her hand and squeezed it. "Mom never talked to me about him, and since no one else did either, I just assumed she had you all under a gag order."

"I'm so glad you understand," she said, visibly relieved.

A strange thought flashed through my mind. "Skeet, did you know me when I was a baby?"

"Yes," he said, his eyes misting. "From the start, actually. I was in the waiting room with your father when you were born."

The more I learned, the weirder it got. "And you said you were at NIMH together?"

"Yes. Your father was a neuroscientist too. We worked in the same lab."

At least that explained why Skeet had acted so strangely familiar with me the week before, when as far as I knew we'd only just met—and why he'd said at one point that he was "proud" of me, which had seemed odd. Now I understood. I was his good friend's daughter; he must have felt some paternal inclination toward me.

"Wait a minute—*was* a neuroscientist?" A sudden chill passed through me. "What does that mean?"

"Sweetheart, I'm so sorry. This is the important thing I wanted to tell you." Ardis gripped my hand hard. "Your father passed away about a year and a half ago."

"What?" I said with a gasp.

Ben twisted around and looked at me directly, his worry lines hard set. He slid his chair closer to mine, reached down, and held my free hand. I gripped his fingers as I tried to absorb what I was hearing. I had lost both of my parents within a year and a half, and I hadn't even known it. And here were two people sitting in front of me who had known, but hadn't told me.

As though she'd read my mind, Ardis jumped in. "I wanted to tell you right after your mother's funeral, but you ran off before I got the chance, and then you weren't answering your phone... I thought it best to wait until I could tell you in person."

The pleading in her voice pricked me with guilt. She was right; for a while, I had avoided her calls, along with anything else that might remind me of my mother. "I'm so sorry, Ardis. I should have been in touch. It was just…"

"Too much. I know." She patted my arm. "You don't have to explain. I knew you were going through a lot. I'm just glad you're here now."

"Me too," I said, and I meant it. I only wished that Skeet hadn't joined us. His presence during such an intimate family conversation felt like a splinter under my skin. Still, I couldn't stop myself from asking, "How did my father die?"

Ardis looked to Skeet, who cleared his throat. "A hunting accident," he said.

"Oh god! How awful." My stomach clenched against a wave of nausea.

"Yes, it was a terrible tragedy," Skeet said.

"What…what happened?" I whispered.

"Witnesses said that he reached for his gun, and it accidentally discharged. You should know, though, that his death was instant. He didn't suffer."

"Oh." I clung to Ben to keep my balance as the room began to spin. Death was instant…didn't suffer… Still, I couldn't stop my mind from painting gruesome scenes. I forced myself to turn and gaze into Ben's face, my only solace. But he looked miserable, and I could tell how much he hated that he couldn't save me from everything I was hearing.

"I'm so sorry, Cate," Skeet said, and he sounded sincere.

It felt like an emotional black hole was trying to suck me in. I combatted it by reminding myself that I wasn't the only one who had lost people I cared about recently. Ardis had been very close to my mom. And the week before, our patient at NIMH, another friend of Skeet's, had spent days in a coma before finally succumbing to poisoning. "I'm sorry too," I said softly.

Ardis got up to embrace me. It was comforting to hold her. Ardis was so like Mom in many ways, and she had been a constant in my life, someone who loved me unconditionally. True, she had kept secrets from me, but I knew she had only been respecting my mother's wishes.

She pulled away from me, tears filling her eyes. I figured I should be crying as well, but it was as though the shock of the situation had knocked the tears right out of me.

We sat back down, and the waitress came to take our orders. I couldn't imagine anything tasting good to me in that moment, so I let Ardis order for me. Someone put a cup of coffee in front of me.

I sat on my hands so no one would see them trembling. It struck me as odd how close together my parents' deaths had been. I couldn't help but wonder if my father's tragic passing had contributed somehow to my mother's suicide. I turned to Ardis. "Did Mom know? About my father, I mean?"

"Yes," she said, sighing heavily and looking down at her hands. "She knew. Skeet told me, and I told her."

"How did she…react?"

"It's a little complicated," Ardis said. "I think it's best if we save that conversation for later."

She was right. I had no idea what kind of Pandora's box that question might open, and I had many more questions—none of which I wanted to get into with Skeet around.

We passed a few moments in silence. Ben wrapped his arm around my shoulders again and murmured in my ear, asking if I needed to get some air. But I didn't want to move. I was afraid that if I did, some strong emotion might break loose. On the other hand, if I sat perfectly still and concentrated on the sensation of Ben's arm around me, I might be able to keep myself under control.

"We erected a memorial to him not far from here if you'd like to visit," Skeet said.

"Where is it?" I asked absently, trying to keep another awkward silence at bay.

"About half an hour southwest, near our lodge."

"Your lodge?"

Skeet nodded. "After college, your father and I built a sporting lodge with some of our fraternity brothers. A group of us stayed in D.C. after graduation, and we needed a place to get away to on the weekends. It has a lot of outdoor recreational activities—fishing, paintball, archery…"

"And hunting," I said.

He cast his eyes down. "Yes."

Suddenly, holding up my end of the conversation became too exhausting. One glance at Ardis told me that she was still feeling too emotional to make small talk. I leaned my head to the side and rested it on Ben's shoulder, shooting him what I hoped was a subtle but pleading glance.

As always, he came to my aid. "Half an hour southwest—is it near Tilghman Island?" Ben asked.

Skeet appeared relieved that the conversation had moved into less emotional territory. "Yes. Are you familiar with the area?"

"A bit," Ben said. "One of my buddies, another Marine vet, lives in Neavitt. He's a mechanic, but he spends a lot of time on the water."

"Well, then, you've probably passed right by the lodge and not realized it. It's a good-sized compound, but it's hard to find behind the trees unless you know where to look."

"A compound?" Ben's eyebrows lifted.

"Well, it's grown over time," Skeet said with a note of pride. "There's the main lodge, some recreational facilities, a clubhouse, and various other buildings to support our agricultural and sporting activities. There are cabins too, for guests who like more privacy, and for some of our NIMH research subjects who come out regularly."

At "research subjects," Ardis seemed to regain interest in the conversation. "You mean the people you experiment on?"

Skeet gave a tight-lipped smile. "Come on, you know that's now how I look at things. Which reminds me, Ben. I wanted to invite you and Cate to come stay at the lodge this week—and the rest of your group, as well, if they like. It's not peak season, so there are plenty of empty rooms. I thought you all might enjoy some R&R, especially after how intense things were last week."

Ben's shoulders stiffened almost imperceptibly, but his tone remained friendly. "That's a tempting offer. But we were away from the clinic all last week, and our clients..."

"Of course." Skeet shook his head. "You have obligations. Maybe another time. I just thought it would be a good opportunity because two of the research subjects involved in a private project of mine will be there this week. I thought our people might enjoy comparing notes, maybe even give each other some tips."

"That is a good thought," Ben said. "You're working on a private project?"

"Yes," Skeet said. "Actually, it's something I've been wanting to talk to you and Cate about. I just didn't think today would be...well, the best time. For obvious reasons."

"Of course." I saw a muscle in Ben's jaw twitch. "I'll tell you what. Let me touch base with the clinic and see what this week looks like. We have a backup team who helped us out last week; they might be able to do some pinch-hitting. We probably can't spare our whole group for an entire week, but I agree, they've earned some time off, and the lodge sounds like a great place. Can I let you know tomorrow?"

What the hell...? Was Ben actually considering staying with Skeet for the week—and did he actually think *I* would want to as well? Slowly, I lifted my head and turned to look at him. As our eyes locked, I could see that there were many wheels turning beneath that casual demeanor of his. Clearly, he had reasons for not immediately rejecting Skeet's invitation. Ben gave me one of his charming half-smiles, then reached under the table and gave my knee a squeeze, confirming that some kind of plan was afoot. I mustered a weak smile. I would play along, but I would be looking for answers once we were alone together.

Skeet seemed to grow ten years younger in an instant. "Absolutely! We'd love to have you. All you need to bring is yourselves. We'll take care of everything else."

"That's great," Ben said. "We'll be in touch."

"Terrific!" Skeet was beaming when the waitress arrived with our food.

If we were really considering spending the week with Skeet, I was definitely going to need my strength. I plastered another cheek-aching smile on my face and attacked my enormous crab cake platter with gusto.

Chapter Six

We had found a bed-and-breakfast near St. Michaels that had two rooms available and convinced Ardis to spend the night as well. Once we arrived, the proprietor made us a pot of tea before retiring for the night. Ben went out on the front porch. He said he needed to make a phone call, but I knew that he was really trying to give me some time alone with Ardis. For that, I was deeply grateful.

She and I sat at the table in the kitchen of the converted farmhouse, at first admiring the way the owners had blended clean, modern decor with nostalgic items, like old cookie jars and tobacco ads from the 1940s and '50s. But then there was an unusually long silence, and I knew that Ardis was ready to have a serious talk. I sat quietly, staring at the steam rising from my cup, and waited.

"Cate, you have no idea how good it is to see you." She rested her hand on my arm.

"It's wonderful to see you, too," I said. "I'm sorry I was such a stranger after…"

She winced and held her hand up. "Enough. No more apologizing. You're sorry for that; I'm sorry for surprising you with Skeet and everything this afternoon. We could both apologize to each other forever. But we don't have all the time in the world, do we? And I have things to tell you."

I bit my lip as a grim shadow passed across her face. "About Mom?"

She nodded. "And your father."

I shivered. I had never allowed myself to feel anything toward my father but ice-cold anger, which I disguised as indifference. After all, he'd abandoned us. My mother only mentioned him once, when

I asked—and then, she simply said that he wasn't a part of our lives anymore. Meanwhile, my question upset her so much that I vowed never to bring him up again. I convinced myself that I didn't want to know anything about a man who had abandoned us and caused my mother so much pain. As far as I was concerned, the whole issue of my father was a closed book. But hearing Skeet and Ardis talk about him and learning of his death made me want to open that book up again. I steeled myself and gave Ardis a nod. "Okay. Go ahead."

"I guess I'll start at the beginning." She blew out a hard breath and clasped her hands together on the table. "Cate, I don't know how much your mother shared with you about this, but she had a special gift. She was a healer of sorts. She could tell how other people were feeling, even if they were far away. And if someone was upset—well, people sought her out to make them feel better. Emotionally, I mean. I know that must sound strange—unless you already knew about it, that is."

Tears stung the corners of my eyes. I blinked them back. "She never talked about that."

Not while she was alive, anyway. My mother's spirit had spoken through Kai during my initiation ritual two weeks before. That was the first time Mom had told me she was an empath, and that because of her gift, she had become emotionally overwhelmed by her work—a problem that ultimately led to her suicide. She had also confirmed that I was an empath too, and warned that I would be headed for a similar tragedy unless I accepted the support and guidance of the MacGregors. I decided against sharing any of that with Ardis, however. While she apparently was open-minded on the topic of alternative healers, I was unsure where she stood on psychic mediums.

"Well, I'm not surprised," Ardis said. "She wanted to forget about it most of the time, because it usually brought her nothing but grief. Like with your father, for instance. Well, you know now, he and Skeet worked together in the same lab. They did research on people like your mother, people with her kind of gifts. Once she told your father about her abilities, he kept trying to talk her into being part of their research projects, but she said she didn't want to be a guinea pig. She was afraid of what they might do to her. He insisted that she wouldn't come to any harm, of course, but I don't think she fully believed him—or maybe she thought it wouldn't be entirely up to him. Either way, it was an ongoing argument between them."

"Unbelievable," I whispered, incredulous.

"I wish it were," she said. "After you were born, though, everything was fine for a while. They had something else to focus on, something positive. But when you got to be around nine months old, you started acting a bit like your mom. If someone was sick or upset, it was like you just *knew*. You'd reach out for them and hug their neck and make this little humming sound. It was the sweetest thing."

My stomach began to churn. "So they thought I might have a gift like hers."

"Well, you were so young, no one could tell for sure, but they suspected," Ardis said. "Then, your father wanted to put *you* in his research project—for observation only, he said. He was all excited about doing a 'cradle-to-grave' study, as he called it. But your mother was too scared, especially with you being as little as you were. They had a huge fight, and she told him to leave and never come back and never to contact either one of you again. She exiled Skeet from your lives, too."

"Oh my god." I tried to imagine how she must have felt—so scared, so torn. "Poor Mom."

"I know," Ardis said. "It was terrible. We all liked your dad a lot, and he sure doted on the two of you. I've never seen a man so in love with his baby daughter. But for whatever reason, your mother was beyond terrified. Something spooked her, and she was convinced that she had to cut him out of your lives to keep you safe."

Ardis looked down at her teacup. "He offered to pay child support, but she refused to accept it. She said she didn't want to be under any obligation to him, because he could use it as leverage someday."

I struggled to absorb this new information. It seemed like

everything I'd believed about my father—and some of what I'd believed about my mother—wasn't true, after all. "So you're saying that he didn't abandon us."

"Not willingly, no."

"He didn't want to leave? He actually loved us?" I whispered, "Loved *me*?"

"Very much, sweetheart." Ardis looked pained. "One of the conditions he demanded in return for staying away from you was that he could contact you once you turned twenty-five—an age they settled on after a lot of negotiation. She wanted him to wait until you contacted him, but he was afraid that might never happen. He said a quarter of a century in the shadows was enough, and that by that time, you would be more than grown-up enough to make up your mind about whether you wanted to be in touch with him. Eventually, she came around, and they made an agreement. But as it turned out…"

The tears that had threatened earlier finally wet my cheeks. "He died before my twenty-fifth birthday."

She stood and walked around the table, wrapping her arms around me. "My poor girl. I'm so sorry."

I screwed my eyes shut as the tears streamed down. My father had wanted to know me, but my mother's fear had been so intense that she'd kept me from him. Why was she so afraid? I gripped Ardis's wrists.

"I don't understand why she didn't at least tell me when he *died*," I said softly. "Whatever she'd been afraid of, he couldn't hurt anyone at that point."

Ardis shrugged as she returned to her seat across the table from me. "Well, for a while, she was working through her own grief. Then, she was having trouble figuring out how to tell you, after all those years of not saying a word about him. Shortly before she died, she told me she'd finally made up her mind to talk to you about him the next time she saw you. But then…"

"She never got the chance."

Ardis nodded. We both looked down at the dwindling contents of our teacups.

Eventually, I broke the silence. “Can I ask you something?”

“Of course.”

“What was his name?”

Her shoulders dropped under a heavy sigh. “Joe. Joseph Robert Grant.”

“Joe.” I’d never known anyone named Joe. The name felt strange on my lips.

“I’m sorry, I should have told you that first thing.”

“No apologies, remember?” I gave her a mock-stern look, and she tried to smile. “Were he and Skeet friends all this time?”

“Sort of.” She shook her head. “Not long after your mom and dad separated, Joe and Skeet had a big argument—over what, I’m not sure. They stayed friends, and they still worked together, but Skeet said they were never really as close after that.”

Another falling out; another mystery. Had their argument been about my mother? I couldn’t help wondering.

“Your mother planned to tell you one day all about her and Joe,” Ardis said. “In fact, right after she made him leave, she asked me to promise that if anything ever happened to her, I would give you the whole story. Over the years, I told her several times that I thought you needed to know what happened. But she said the one time you’d asked about him, you were too young to hear the details. Since you never brought it up again, she told herself you weren’t interested in knowing more. I didn’t think there was any way that could be true. It seemed only natural to me that a girl would wonder about her father. I feared you might have assumed the worst about him.”

I didn’t want to make Ardis feel worse by telling her how right she’d been. “Yeah, well. As it was, I never knew *what* to think of him.”

“I know,” she said, “and I think that was a poor decision on your mother’s part. But Cate, you know she didn’t scare easily. She must have had her reasons, although she’d never tell me what they were. She said it was better if I didn’t know.” She slumped down in her chair. "Skeet has always told me that she didn't have anything to be afraid of, but she was certain she was doing what was necessary."

I nodded. That was the real question, wasn't it? The root of the whole thing. What was it about their research that had scared my mother so badly? And it was Skeet, Joe's friend and colleague, who would be able to answer that question.

Suddenly, I had a compelling reason for wanting to spend the week at Skeet's lodge. But I still didn't know what Ben's motivation was.

"By the way, Skeet asked me to tell you that he needs to speak to you in private sometime," Ardis added. "Something about an inheritance from your father. I don't know the details."

"Okay," I said absently. I had no idea what my father might have left to the daughter he never knew. A notebook full of answers, I hoped. But my brain was unable to process any more new information. Ardis caught me glancing at the front door of the house.

"That's all I've got for you, sweetie," she said gently. "You should go spend some time with Ben."

I felt my cheeks heat up. "I didn't mean—"

"No, go on. It's a nice night, and I'm sure he's wondering what we've been talking about."

"Probably." I smiled. "Ardis, thank you for telling me all of this. I can only imagine how hard it must have been for you, carrying these secrets around for so long."

"Harder on *you*, not knowing about your father. I'm just glad you finally do."

We stood and looked at each other, and I knew we were both thinking the same thing: we wished my parents were both still alive and there with us. We shared a hug heavy with grief. Eventually, she pulled away. "I'm off to bed."

"I'll be up in a while." Ardis and I were staying in a room with two twin beds, and Ben was in another room with a double.

"Well," she said, with a wink in her voice, "if you spend the night in Ben's room, I won't tell anybody."

"Ardis!" I said with forced indignation, as though I hadn't spent an indecent amount of time fantasizing about just that. "I'll be up in a while," I repeated firmly.

"Okay, whatever you say." She grinned and pointed to the front door. "Well, don't leave him hanging."

I waved her up the stairs. Then I took a moment to pull myself together. Everything Ardis had told me… It was almost too much. My body felt leaden, but my emotions rumbled like unstable elements, skating on the edge of control. I didn't know if I'd be able to repeat everything I'd learned to Ben, to physically get the words out.

In the quiet, I could hear Ben's voice. He really *was* talking on the phone. I winced as the screen door squeaked loudly and closed it carefully to make sure it didn't slam. With his cell to his ear, Ben waved me over to where he was sitting, a long wooden swing hanging from the porch ceiling. I sat next to him for a moment, then gave in to my overwhelming desire to lie down. I rested my head in his lap and curled my legs up on the swing. The cool night air was like a balm on my skin. I heard the sound of water lapping up against something nearby—a pier? A shoreline? Ben began to stroke my hair as he wrapped up his conversation.

"So you and Vani can be here Monday, and Kai, Asa, and Eve can come up on Tuesday? … Okay, that should work… Might as well bring everything… Kai can do that? … All right. Couldn't hurt… Right. I'll call to confirm." Ben pushed a button and slid his phone into his shirt pocket. Then he tucked his arm under my head, cradling it.

"Talking to Pete?" I guessed.

"Yeah," he said softly, moving his stroking fingers from my hair to my cheek. "You okay?"

I closed my eyes and tried to lose myself completely in the sensation of Ben's touch. "I am now." I knew he wanted to know how I was after my conversation with Ardis, but I wasn't quite ready to talk about it. "Hey, I've been meaning to tell you, I was pretty impressed that you ate in front of everyone at the meeting this morning, then with Skeet and Ardis."

"Thanks. I'm working on it." Ben brushed a strand of hair off of my forehead. "I don't want this phobia to hold me back anymore. It's getting easier all the time—especially when you're with me."

He leaned down and kissed me softly on the temple. A low note of pleasure vibrated through me, as though I were a bar on a xylophone that had just been struck. I felt myself melting into his lap and onto the swing. I didn't want to move or think or speak anymore, just dive into the sensation. Ben seemed to sense my reluctance to talk further. For a few blessed minutes, he just sat there, stroking my hair as I slipped further into bliss. But I knew it couldn't last. There were too many things pressing on us.

"So," he murmured, "how do you feel about spending the week at the lodge?"

I turned onto my back and looked up at him. Even with his face in shadow, I could see the worry lines forming. "It's not exactly my idea of a vacation, but I have my own reasons for wanting to go, now. And I know you have reasons, too, which I've been waiting to hear about."

"Right." Ben straightened up and shifted into businesslike mode. "Do you remember telling me last week that you felt ambivalent about Skeet, and had suspicions about his research ethics?"

"Yes, of course."

"Well, you're not alone in that," Ben said. "You know that we treat some of his research subjects at our clinic when they need help. There's more to that story that I was planning to tell you about—especially after Skeet tried to recruit you to join his experiments. Sometimes his participants come to us with problems they shouldn't be having, or *wouldn't* be having if they were cared for properly."

A shiver skidded down my back. "What kinds of problems?"

"Addiction issues, sleep and appetite disturbances. Less often, visual and auditory hallucinations, but you can imagine how confusing those are for telepaths, mediums—people who already hear and see things that others don't." Ben paused. "Of course, these could just be naturally occurring problems, unique to each individual client. Sensitives aren't immune to mental health issues, after all."

"You don't believe that, though?"

He blew out a hard breath. "I wish I could, but we've observed certain patterns that are concerning. These patterns suggest that questionable research methods are being used, but we've never had enough information to know for sure. Spending time at Skeet's lodge might be the opportunity we need to get answers, especially since some of his research subjects will be there too."

"Right, of course." It was chilling to think that Skeet could actually be harming sensitives. Ben had clearly decided that it was his job to find out and to fix the situation if necessary. His expansive sense of responsibility worried me at times, especially when it meant putting himself at risk for others—something he forbade anyone else to do. But Ben's determination to protect the vulnerable and the people he cared about was also one of the things about him that I loved and admired most. It seemed that having a real live hero as a boyfriend came with some unavoidable complications.

Ben looked at me quizzically as he helped pull me up into a sitting position. "Okay, your turn. You said you have reasons for wanting to go to the lodge now."

"Right, yes." I gripped the edge of the swing. "I do want to go, but not for R&R purposes, as Skeet suggested."

Ben draped his hand over mine. "It's about your father, then."

My throat closed, trapping my voice. I looked down at our hands.

"Cate." As he spoke my name, I could hear the depth of his caring and his urgent desire to make everything better. "Tell me."

I clutched his hand as though it were a life vest, the only thing keeping me from drowning. Slowly at first, then in a flood, the words spilled out of me. I told him everything Ardis had told me—including how my mother's fears had been so intense that she'd kept me away from a father who had loved me.

"But Ardis never did find out what scared my mother so badly,"

I said. Ben leaned in, wiping the tears from my cheeks before I realized that they'd fallen. "Skeet must know, though. That's why I want to go to the lodge—to find out. And to learn more about my father."

The more I spoke, the graver Ben's expression became. "I see." Frowning, he rubbed his jaw. "I'll be honest, Cate. I'm questioning the wisdom of you going to the lodge, now."

"What?" I jumped, pulling my hand away from his. "What are you talking about?"

"You and Ardis agree that your mother didn't scare easily," he replied. "If she was so worried about exposing you to whatever Skeet and Joe were doing, there could be more to this than any of us have suspected. Maybe Pete and I should go in first and check things out."

"Are you kidding me?" I gaped at him. "Forget it!"

Ben looked at me like I was a book written in some sort of impenetrable code. "I don't understand why you're objecting."

I threw my hands up. "Because this could be my only chance to get answers!"

"That seems unlikely." Ben's expression turned stony. "And even if that were true, your safety is non-negotiable."

Dammit. I knew how hard it was to reason with Ben once he'd gone into over-protective mode. I pushed off of the swing and began pacing. "Okay, look," I said. "Let's say you and Pete go in there and find out that something shady's going on. Obviously, you'd have to put a stop to it somehow—and probably destroy your relationship with Skeet in the process. Am I right?"

Ben remained stoic as I wore down the floorboards. "It could play out that way, yes."

"Well, I'm with *you*, now, and I'm part of the MacGregor Group," I argued. "So if it *did* play out that way, Skeet certainly wouldn't trust me anymore. He might never even speak to me again, let alone invite me back to the lodge. And whatever he had to tell me about my father's inheritance, I'd probably hear through a lawyer."

"That is a possibility."

"So you see my point."

"I do. Do you see mine?"

I stopped pacing and narrowed my eyes at him. "I'm going to the lodge, Ben."

Ben studied me for a moment, eyes glinting. "I thought we'd agreed last week to consult with one another before making important decisions."

My face flushed with indignation. "Yes, well, that's obviously moot!"

"What? Why?"

"I heard you on the phone with Pete, making plans. You two have already decided you're going to the lodge. You didn't bother talking to me about it first. You didn't even know whether I wanted to go!"

"Whoa, slow down." Ben held his hand up. "You misunderstood. Yes, we worked out a plan, but I told Pete not to act on it until I'd had a chance to talk to you."

I blinked. "Really?" Ben usually operated under the philosophy that it was easier to ask forgiveness than permission—or to just do what he thought was right and not ask for either. "You told him that?"

"Of course I did."

A telltale muscle in his jaw twitched, betraying the effort it had taken for Ben to wait to take action until after we'd spoken. I felt a rush of affection toward him. "I'm sorry," I said softly. "I shouldn't have jumped to conclusions."

He flashed me a half-smile. "In fairness, it wasn't exactly an unreasonable conclusion."

"That's true." I smiled back.

"So let's talk about this. As you yourself pointed out, you're part of the MacGregor Group now. And since our trip to the lodge is a job-related activity, it falls under my purview as clinic manager."

My eyes rolled heavenward. "How do you figure this is a job-related activity for *me*? I'm going to find out about my dad—an entirely personal matter."

"True, but Skeet has an ongoing professional arrangement with the MacGregor Group, and you first came in contact with him last week at NIMH as part of our work," Ben pointed out. "So it's both personal and professional. That muddies the waters a bit, but it doesn't make me any less responsible for your safety in this situation."

I planted my hands on my hips. "Meaning what, exactly?"

"Meaning, if we both go, I would be very grateful if you would agree to follow whatever security protocols I put into place while we're there."

While his whole "job-related" argument was absurd, at least he was asking politely for my agreement. Ben's jaw muscle ticked again. He was making a genuine effort; I could meet him halfway. I waved my hand through the air. "No problem."

Ben's brow formed a straight ridge. "I mean, *all* of the security protocols."

I fought back a smirk. "I got that."

"Consistently."

"Okay, look—"

"Cate." My name on his lips sounded like a supplication. "Nothing can happen to you."

I gasped sharply as suddenly, his emotions flooded into my heart—love, fear, and the certainty that if anything happened to me, it would destroy him.

The portal I'd opened to Ben was turning out to be unique. Usually, I had to focus on an individual portal to know what someone was feeling. But when I was with Ben, sometimes his emotions pushed through all on their own. This was one of those moments.

Tears pricked the corners of my eyes. I blinked them back. "Nothing will happen to me, I promise," I said. "I know I haven't always been the best at following instructions..."

With an artful arch of his brow, Ben conjured up the memory of each time over the past two weeks I'd thrown rules to the wind, usually with dire consequences. I'd put myself into cardiac arrest, then into a coma. I'd required rescuing, first from a criminal gang, then from rogue CIA thugs. And while I hadn't meant for any of those things to happen, I knew I'd made Ben sick with worry. I felt terrible about that, but there was nothing I could do to change it now. I could only reassure him that things would be different in the future—more specifically, in the coming week.

"You don't have to worry this time. I understand your concerns. To be honest, I'm nervous, too. But I trust that you know what to do to keep us safe. So yes, I'll follow your protocols. All of them. Consistently."

The silence that followed was tense and too long for my liking, but I held my nerve. Finally, Ben said, "All right, then. We'll go together."

I was surprised by how relieved I felt. In spite of all that had happened, Ben still had the capacity to trust me. He believed my promise—and I had meant it, every word.

I felt the impulse to thank him, but the words stuck in my craw. As glad as I was that we'd reached an agreement, I couldn't ignore the irritation buzzing inside of me. I felt compelled to clarify something. "You get that I wasn't asking your permission, right?"

"Yes," he said in his cool, managerial voice. "We simply talked things through until we came to an understanding."

"That's right—and not because of your laughable attempt to play the 'boss' card."

The gold flecks in his eyes shimmered with amusement. "Laughable, was it?"

"Mm-hmm."

Ben took a step closer and covered my hands with his. I inhaled deeply, taking in his scent. His gaze locked onto mine, holding me in place like a tractor beam. "Would *you* rather be in charge?"

Whether due to the rakish tone of his voice, his general nearness, or my overactive imagination, I found myself wondering if we were still talking about our trip to the lodge. A flash fever raised my temperature a few degrees. "As it happens, I'm too tired to take charge of anything at the moment, but I'll consider that a standing offer."

Ben smiled broadly. "Noted." He removed his hands from mine and splayed his fingers along either side of my waist. "Speaking of tired, we should probably go to bed. You've had quite a day."

That much was true. It had been an emotional roller coaster where even the highs were lows. But after such upheaval, all I wanted was to be close to Ben—to lose myself in him, and to feel nothing for the next few hours but his kiss, his touch. He wouldn't deny me that, would he? "It *has* been a really hard day," I whispered. I slid my hands under his and twined our fingers together. "Any chance I can spend the night in your room?"

He gripped my hands tightly and slid them around to the small of my back. As his eyes searched mine, the smile left his face. "There's nothing I would love more than to take you back to my room and distract you from all of this for a while, if that's what you're asking."

I swallowed, wide-eyed. Was he actually considering…?

"You have no idea how much I want that, Cate," he murmured. "But you know the program rules, and I have a feeling that if you came with me right now, we wouldn't be able to follow them for very long."

Frustration shot up through my body like a scalding geyser. "Goddamned rules!" Until I finished my internship with the MacGregor Group, I wasn't allowed to do certain things, such as eat red meat, drink alcohol—or have sex. Apparently, doing so would muck up my energetic aura and render me useless for certain rituals and training exercises. It had been hard enough for me to agree to follow those rules at the beginning of the program, just on principle. But the closer Ben and I became, the more oppressive the restrictions seemed. "Don't I even get a goodnight ki—"

Ben's lips on mine were firm, but gently apologetic. When he drew away, the intensity in his eyes showed without a doubt that he was telling the truth. He wanted more too. But clearly, nothing more was going to happen—not that night, at least. I sighed, turned on my heel, and headed for the screen door.

Ben beat me to it, opening the door for me. I did my best to act pulled together as I strode back into the house. He gestured for me to go up the stairs ahead of him, which I did—then blushed as I felt his eyes on me and imagined the view he must be getting as we climbed. I paused at the top of the stairs, having forgotten which room was mine.

"This way," Ben said, leading me to a familiar-looking door. "They serve breakfast at nine thirty. Do you want me to wake you at any particular time?"

"No," I grumped, turning away from him and putting my hand on the doorknob. "I'll set the alarm on my phone."

"All right then."

I wanted to reach out for one more touch, one more kiss, but I couldn't see Ben's expression in the dark, and I didn't want to face another rejection. I forced myself to step inside of my room as Ben whispered, "Goodnight, Trouble."

I almost smiled. "Goodnight," I whispered back, shutting the door quietly so as not to wake Ardis.

I leaned back against the door, mourning the loss of Ben's presence. I had a sinking feeling that this last week of training would be the longest week of my life.

Chapter Seven

ParaTrain Internship, Day Seven

Skeet had been right about one thing: the compound was well hidden. After turning off the main road at the sign for Mercier Lodge, we drove for more than a mile down a narrow private lane flanked on both sides by an endless forest of loblolly pines. Just when I began to wonder if there was anything there at all, the road ended at a circular driveway. Ben pulled over, saying that he wanted to take a look around and get his bearings.

When Skeet had described the lodge, I'd imagined a few cozy log cabins and modest outbuildings. Instead, I found myself gaping at the type of luxury sporting resort they'd feature on the TV show *Mega Mansions.*

We got out of the car and stood at the mouth of a sizeable clearing. The circular driveway alone must have covered an acre of land. Directly across from us was a building that appeared to be the main lodge. At its center, there was a vaulted entrance about four stories high, with three-story buildings stretching out on either side. Around the driveway stood four other buildings, each about half the size of the lodge. They were all Adirondack-style wood constructions, and about as upscale as they could be while still maintaining a rustic feel. Someone had clearly put a lot of thought into creating a getaway for people who were used to the finer things, but that also felt a world away from the city, blending into the natural environment.

On the other side of the lodge, I caught sight of a body of water, and a pier where a few skiffs were docked. Several other driveways led off of the circular one, winding away into the forest. I didn't see any other cars or a parking lot.

"Good grief," I whispered. "What is this place?"

"It's impressive," Ben said. "There are quite a few places like this tucked away around here, built for the D.C. crowd."

I scanned the clearing again, inhaling the sharp scents of the water and the pine trees. If we had to spend the week getting answers about Skeet, his research, and my father, at least we'd be doing it in a breathtaking setting.

"Cate! Ben!" The voice came from the lodge. Skeet had stepped out from the main entrance and was waving to us. "Over here!"

We got back into the Jag. Ben turned to me and took my hand, giving it a brief squeeze. "You ready for this?"

I didn't feel ready—but I also didn't feel that I had much of a choice. I forced myself to smile gamely. "Absolutely."

Ben shook his head. "I hope you only play poker *online*," he said as he shifted the car into gear.

I decided not to mention that I had played poker in person, since it had been *strip* poker with my friend Sid, back when he was a friend-with-benefits. Ben and Sid had met the previous week after Sid became involved in our mission, and their interactions so far had been nothing but positive. I certainly didn't want to rock that boat. I turned to look at Skeet so that nothing in my expression would invite further conversation on the subject.

There was a gentle crunching sound as the tires rolled over the driveway of crushed oyster shells. Skeet beamed at us as we pulled up to the wide staircase in front of the entrance to the main lodge. Two young men appeared out of nowhere, dressed in white button-down shirts and khakis. One of them got our bags out of the car, and the other took the keys from Ben and drove the Jag away.

"Don't worry, he'll take good care of it," Skeet reassured Ben. "I'll show you the garage when we take our tour of the grounds. Welcome to Mercier! I'm glad you could come."

My eyes couldn't stop roaming around as Ben and I navigated our way up the wide staircase and joined Skeet on the porch. The whole building was made of different types of wood, ranging in color from nearly black to deep red to light gray, each piece fitted together with flawless artistry. The floor was smooth, but the columns holding up the roof were made of trees left in their natural shapes, with rough bark and branches splaying upwards. Every surface had been treated with something that gave the wood a soft shine. As far as I was concerned, the lodge could have been a palace for wood nymphs in some kind of fairy tale.

As I took everything in, Skeet and Ben exchanged a brief handshake. I was used to dressing casually, but it was still an adjustment to see the two of them out of their usual business uniforms. Ben seemed just as comfortable in his worn jeans, Marine Corps T-shirt, and work boots as he normally did in his business suits. Skeet, on the other hand, had appeared much more at home in his lab coat than he did in his chamois shirt and chinos.

"Yes, I'm pleased we were able to work it out," Ben said. "Two of our crew are coming tomorrow, the rest on Tuesday."

"Great!" Skeet clapped his hands together. "Well, come on in!"

We followed him into a huge, circular foyer, where a wood sculpture of a deer dominated the center. More natural tree posts held up the vaulted ceiling, and the walls were decorated with hunting trophies—everything from ducks and geese made to look as though they were still in flight, to deer heads mounted on plaques. Even though the room had a rare beauty and bright sun filtered in through skylights, it felt oppressive to me—heavy with reminders of death. I was grateful when Ben slid his arm around my waist. He always seemed to know when I needed a physical reminder of his presence. I rested my hand atop his.

"This is the front desk," Skeet said, pointing to a recessed space in the wall by the door occupied by two more young people. They looked up from their computers to give us a wave. "Just let them know if you need anything at all."

"Thanks," Ben said. He appeared completely at ease, as though it was his normal weekend routine to visit eye-popping sporting resorts. But with his arm around me, I could feel a familiar tautness in his body. I knew he was on high alert and ready for anything, though he was doing a fantastic job of hiding it. Meanwhile, I was certain I looked like a gaping tourist.

Skeet pointed out various hallways leading off of the foyer. "These two lead to the residential wings. Your rooms are on the south side," he said, handing us key cards with our room numbers on them. "That opening in the back goes to the boathouse and pier. And the last two hallways go to the dining room and the conference wing. I'd like to take you on the grand tour, but why don't we get a cup of coffee first? Cate, you look like you could use one."

He gave me a friendly wink, presumably to reassure me that he wasn't mocking my incredulous reaction to the place. I picked my jaw up off of the floor and smiled. "I never turn down a cup of coffee."

Ben's arm squeezed me lightly. "Sounds good."

"This way." Skeet led us down a wide hallway, with arrangements of leather chairs and coffee tables on one side. The opposite wall was covered with photographs of people posing with the deer or wildfowl they'd killed, or holding up the fish they'd caught. I glanced at the photos as we walked by, wondering if my father was in any of the pictures.

The dining room was another sumptuous feast of wood colors and textures. Everything, including the tables and chairs, was meticulously designed with both style and comfort in mind. One entire wall was a window overlooking the water.

Another staff member appeared out of nowhere and led us to the table with the best view. Skeet murmured something to her, and she disappeared. Then he took in the water with a sweep of his hand. "And this is Mercier Cove. It leads out to Broad Creek, and from there you can reach the bay."

"It's beautiful," I said, almost to myself. There were no boats out that morning, and the water was smooth and placid. From where we sat, I could see it lapping gently against a couple of boats docked at the pier. We were surrounded by pine forest, but on either side of the narrow opening where the cove met the creek there were fields of tall grasses, and I could glimpse the watery horizon.

"I'm glad you like it." Skeet cleared his throat. "I mean, I'm particularly glad *you* like it, Cate, because part of it is yours."

In my reverie, I must have misheard him. "I'm sorry, what was that?"

"I said, part of this is yours. But I'm sorry, maybe this isn't the right time..." Skeet's eyes flickered over to Ben.

More secrets? I hated secrets. Skeet didn't know it, but he had turned his bellows on banked coals. With my irritation stoked, I straightened up in my chair and leaned forward. "Is this about my inheritance? Ardis mentioned that you wanted to talk to me privately about it, but anything you have to say to me, you can say in front of Ben."

Ben tensed for a moment, but the look on my face must have convinced him that I didn't need his assistance. He leaned back in his chair and watched.

"Okay, then," Skeet said, smiling nervously. "Well, Cate, you've inherited a one-tenth stake in Mercier from your father. He, I, and eight others all went in together as equal partners to build this place."

"One tenth—of this?" I gaped. When Skeet said part of it was mine, I thought he was referring to something of my father's that he'd kept at the lodge, like a trophy or a box of letters. I couldn't believe my father had left me something so...magnificent. My insides began to tremble. "I don't understand. What about—I mean, didn't he have other people...?"

Skeet shook his head. "Like you, he was an only child. His parents passed years ago, and he didn't produce any other heirs."

"Oh." I was glad that it hadn't yet occurred to me that I might have living grandparents or siblings out there. Otherwise, the news that I didn't would have added to my strange grief. "No other children?"

"No; he never married." Skeet nodded to the waitress, who came over and poured coffee for all of us. I welcomed the pause in the conversation and tried to absorb what I was hearing. Mercier, this incredible place—my father had gifted a part of it to me.

Ben reached over and squeezed my hand, and once again, I found the power of speech. "But my father died a year and a half ago. Why are you just telling me this now?"

Skeet looked down at the tablecloth. "At your mother's request, Joe left your inheritance in trust to her. Ardis said that Rhona kept wanting to tell you about it, but never found the right moment. After your mother passed, Ardis requested that *she* be the one to tell you, but as you know, she's had trouble reaching you..." He shrugged apologetically as his voice trailed off.

"No, of course," I said. "That makes sense, I guess."

"There's a small nest egg for you, as well, although Joe donated most of his assets to NIMH." Skeet reached across the table and took my free hand. "He was passionate about our research, Cate. He wanted you to be a part of it."

I froze, unsure how to handle that turn in the conversation.

Ben's smooth baritone voice eased its way between Skeet and me. "I'm sure we'll have plenty of time to talk about that this week."

Skeet took the hint, patting my hand before pulling his back. "Of course. And Joe's estate lawyer, Harris, will be here tomorrow; he's a founding member of the lodge, as well. He can go over all of the details of the will with you, if you like."

My throat had gone dry. I took a sip of coffee. "Okay, sure." The truth was, I knew next to nothing about wills and property, and certainly nothing about nest eggs. I'd never even needed the services of a lawyer before, and had no idea what to expect. I glanced over at Ben, who gave me a barely perceptible but reassuring nod.

I welcomed another pause in the conversation as we all sipped our coffee. I looked out over the water and felt a deep pull, a desire to go out to the edge of the cove and keep on walking. I found myself wondering if the water was deeper than I was tall. If I walked out along the bottom of the cove and let it cover me, would I meet them there? My mother, my father? Closing my eyes, I imagined them under the water, both finally at peace with themselves and each other, walking toward me, clothes and hair moving ghostlike on the undercurrents, inviting me to embrace the same peace. My heart strained with that longing, while at the same time cracking into brittle pieces at the thought of leaving my life behind—leaving Ben, and all of the possibilities I had begun to allow myself to hope for.

My hand floated up to touch my pendant, the beautifully carved circle of silver Kai had made to protect me from absorbing other people's energies. Then I touched the ring Ben had given me—a reminder that he was always with me, even when we were physically apart. Tears built up behind my eyes like water pressing against a dam. I knew that if I looked at Ben, the dam would break, so instead I reached under the table and squeezed his leg, hoping he would grasp what was happening.

Ben's hand was warm and heavy on mine. "Skeet, I know the plan is to take the grand tour, and we're looking forward to it. But is there a chance we could settle into our rooms first? I know Cate would probably like to freshen up."

I managed a smile and a nod.

"Yes, of course!" Skeet exclaimed. "And I apologize, Cate; I know this is a lot to take in. Take as long as you need. When you're ready for the tour, just come down to the lobby and tell the front desk staff."

"Thanks," I said. "We shouldn't be long."

Ben and I stood and followed Skeet back down the hallway to the foyer. He pointed down the hallway that had been on our right when we first came in. "South wing. About halfway down is the elevator bay. You're on the third floor. Your bags should already be up there."

"Thanks." Ben grasped my hand. "We'll see you shortly."

• • •

Ben dropped me off at my door, saying that he had to get something out of his bags. As I walked into my room, my mouth fell open as if its hinge had broken. Like the rest of the lodge, everything was made of sumptuous, hand-carved woods from floor to twenty-foot ceiling. A tall window faced the cove. The room was dominated by a huge four-poster bed on one end and a giant stone fireplace on the other. There was a couch flanked by two lounge chairs covered in deep green velvet, and a coffee table with part of a thick tree trunk as the stand. The tabletop itself was a horizontal slice out of an even bigger tree, every ring visible.

A door led to a private bathroom. I took a quick glance and saw that the whole room was lined with gray and white granite tiles, and a hot tub stood on an elevated platform in the corner. Recessed lighting gave the room a soft, cool glow.

By contrast, the bedroom itself was all warm colors and fabrics that invited touching. I fell backward onto the bed, ready to hash out everything that had happened over coffee. But when Ben came in, he held his finger over his mouth in a silencing gesture. He was carrying some kind of small device. It unfolded into the sort of metal sculpture you might see on an office desk. He placed it on the windowsill, concealed behind the curtain.

"What is that?" I mouthed when he turned back towards me.

"It's okay, we can talk now," he said. "It's a scrambler. It'll disrupt any attempts at surveillance in this room. We'll each have one."

"Seriously? You really think we're being bugged, or tapped, or something?"

"No," he said in a tone that sounded more like "probably." "Just erring on the side of caution."

I was shaking my head when a gauzy white canopy over the bed caught my eye. "Is that—*mosquito* netting?"

Ben reached up and rubbed the fabric between his fingers. "It is. Obviously, they're going for authenticity here."

For some reason, his dry tone made me giggle, and in spite of the fact that there was nothing funny about the situation, I found that I couldn't stop. I curled up on the bed, then stretched out spread-eagle as laughter overtook me. Ben just looked down at me, rubbing his jaw.

Between guffaws, I managed, "Don't you get how absurd all of this is? We come here to investigate whether Skeet's up to something sinister and find out I'm part owner of the Death Star! Oh!" Then the thought of another *Star Wars* comparison threw me into gales of laughter. "And my father might have been Darth Vader! Oh my god—and I dressed up as Princess Leia one Halloween!" I rolled onto my stomach, grabbing a pillow to laugh into so that the whole lodge wouldn't hear.

I felt the mattress sink beside me as Ben joined me on the bed. The waves of laughter gradually slowed until they were just occasional lurches. The outburst had drained the tension from my body, and I felt limp. I turned my head to look at Ben, who was half-reclining next to me. He reached out and rested his hand between my shoulder blades, then began to rub slow, wide circles on my back. The last of the jerky laughter stopped as my body entered a relaxed trance. "Mmm." My eyelids fell closed.

"Princess Leia, huh?"

"Yeah. My mom put my hair in those rolly side buns and everything."

"I should warn you, I had a crush on Leia back in the day."

I opened one eye and looked at him. "Really?"

"Absolutely." He arched an inquisitive eyebrow. "Any chance you had the hots for Han Solo?"

"Why?" As soon as I asked, it dawned on me. Ben's hand dropped away as I rolled onto my side and propped myself up on my elbow, grinning. "Did you dress up as *him*?"

Ben nodded solemnly. "My mother may have photographic evidence."

"Hah!" I loved the thought of little Ben trick-or-treating in a Han Solo costume. "I am *so* talking to your mother when we get home. I want to see every single photo album. But why didn't you dress up as your namesake, *Ben* Obi-Wan Kenobi?"

"You're disappointed?" Ben frowned. "You had a thing for Obi-Wan Kenobi?"

"Of course not! He was old enough to be my grandfather. I *much* preferred Han Solo."

He reached over and squeezed my hip, then ran his hand up over my waist until it came to rest on the side of my ribcage. I gasped, hoping beyond hope that his fingers would continue their journey upward… But no such luck. Instead, Ben just gave me a sideways smile and said, "At your service, Princess."

"If only." I reached up and stroked his hand, teasing the soft skin between his fingers. "You do realize that Leia gives the orders; she doesn't take them. And she doesn't take 'no' for an answer, either."

"Hmm." He lifted my hand to his lips and kissed me on the palm, sending a shiver through me. "This Leia sounds pretty headstrong. Good thing she has Han Solo to look out for her."

Although his tone was light, Ben's words called to mind each time over the past two weeks that he had, in fact, stepped in to protect me—even saving my life a few times. The gold flecks in his eyes flashed, and I knew that his subtle reminder hadn't been accidental.

But this week, we were honored guests at a luxury sporting resort, not trying to solve a top-secret murder under Marine Corps protection. "As I said before, you can relax, Rottie," I said, using his old Marine Corps nickname. "I promised to follow your safety protocols, remember?"

"I remember, but we haven't established what those are yet. Until we do, I want us to stick together, okay? No separating, no running off."

"I'm not going to *run off!*"

"Just making sure."

Hearing the undercurrent of pain in his voice, I kept my irritation in check. In fairness to Ben, I *had* sort of run off once before, even though it had been for a good reason. And I knew why he was so fixated on protecting those he loved. He felt guilty for failing to prevent his father's death, even though it had been due to an accidental overdose. But his father had struggled with alcoholism for years, and when Ben left home to join the Marines, his father began abusing painkillers, as well. Ben blamed himself for that, believing that if he had stayed home, his father would still be alive.

Between that guilt and being a member of Yankee Company—

his special Marine Corps unit dedicated to protecting whistleblowers from the government—Ben had developed an amplified sense of responsibility for protecting others. Unfortunately, the fact that I kept getting into life-threatening situations had only intensified his need to feel in control of things.

I squeezed his hand. "We'll stick together."

"Good." Ben released my hand and gently brushed a loose strand of hair from my cheek. "Now let's talk about you. You had me worried, back there in the dining room. How are you holding up?"

"I'm okay, I guess. The past twenty-four hours…it's been a lot to take in. I guess I just needed a minute to breathe."

"It *has* been a lot." He began stroking my hair. "You want to talk about it?"

I shrugged. I *had* been ready to talk things over, but suddenly, the idea seemed exhausting. Besides, until I found out what my father and Skeet had been up to, I wouldn't know whether to feel angry at my mother for keeping me from Joe, or grateful to her for protecting me. I also didn't know whether to respect Joe for going along with my mother's wishes, or to hate him for depriving me of a father for all those years. And until I learned more about who Joe was as a person…

At that point, there were just too many unknowns. I wouldn't even know in what direction to fall apart. All I knew was that there had been too much tragedy, and I wished everything had been different. Grief turned my heart to lead, and tears once again pressed against the back of my eyes. But I knew that if I let myself start to feel all of the emotions clamoring for attention inside of me, the tears would start and never stop. My time at the lodge would be a waste. I'd leave there a complete mess with nothing resolved—and I wasn't willing to risk that. It was too important.

I decided to try a visualization technique that had helped some of my therapy clients temporarily contain overwhelming thoughts and feelings. I closed my eyes and turned inward. I imagined a lockbox with its lid open, floating in the middle of my chest. Then, I pulled together every thread of willpower I could find and pushed all of those troubling emotions into the lockbox. With a final burst of effort, I pictured myself slamming the lid and affixing a padlock. I wouldn't open the lockbox again until I had everything I needed to deal with the feelings stored inside—not until I was ready.

But Ben was still waiting for an answer to his question. I took a deep breath and let it out slowly, focusing my attention on the sensation of his hand stroking my hair, soothing me. Finally, I reached a place of relative calm. "I'm not sure what to talk about right now, or how to feel—and I *won't* be, until I get the answers I'm looking for."

There was a long pause, and I could almost hear him arguing with himself, deciding whether to push me or leave it alone. "I understand," he finally said, but I could hear the uncertainty in his voice. He knew I wasn't telling him everything. "I'm amazed at how well you've been holding it together."

"Yeah, me too." If only Ben knew how tenuous my control was.

"Listen, whatever you need, I'll make sure you get it. And that includes answers. We won't leave here until you're satisfied."

Relief breathed through me. *That* was the Ben I wanted, the Ben I needed. Determined and focused on problem solving. "Thank you." I turned and kissed the palm of his hand. "I mean it."

He cradled my face in his hands and looked down at me, his eyes impossibly full of affection. "And when this is all over, whatever happens, you won't be dealing with it alone. I'll be there, and I'll take care of you. I'm in love with you, Cate, and I'm not going anywhere. Ever."

I swallowed hard as his words wound their way around my heart, sliding into every corner like the glow of firelight, blanketing me in warmth and comfort. I closed my eyes and nestled my face into his hand, never wanting to leave that exact spot.

"Do you want to postpone the grand tour?" he asked.

"No." I grasped his hand. "I really do want to see the rest of this place, and honestly, I think I could use the distraction."

"All right. But if you ever feel like you need a break, just say the word. And if you don't feel comfortable just bailing, let me know, and I'll find a way to get us out of whatever we're doing."

The heat of a blush pricked my cheeks. The last thing I wanted was to stoke Ben's overprotective tendencies by letting him think I was a helpless damsel in distress. "That goes both ways, you know. I can get you out of uncomfortable situations, too. Maybe we should come up with a code word we can use, like a universal distress signal."

"Hmm. That's not a bad thought. Any ideas?"

I scanned my brain and came up empty. "No, sorry."

Ben rubbed his jaw for a moment. Then his face lit up. "I know!"

"What?"

"'Help me, Obi-Wan Kenobi. You're my only hope.'"

It felt so good to have a real reason to smile. "But that's Leia's line!"

He cleared his throat and said in a tortured falsetto, "Then I'll say it in my Leia voice." Grinning, he eased himself up off of the bed. "Tell you what. I'll go unpack and let you get settled in. When you're ready, just let me know, and we'll head downstairs—unless you change your mind about the tour, that is."

"Okay." I felt the familiar tug on my heart as Ben left the room, even though I knew he was just going next door. Being with Ben was simply a far superior state than being without him. How I'd come to feel that way after just a few weeks, I didn't know, but it was useless to deny it. I knew I had to get used to being without him, though; we couldn't spend every minute together for the rest of our lives. I forced myself to unpack slowly and practice being alone.

CHAPTER EIGHT

Our grand tour proved to be eye opening. Skeet showed us the rest of the lodge, which was bigger than it appeared from the outside. In addition to the two sizeable residential wings, the sitting room and hallways, and the dining room, there was a recreation room with a pool table and video games; a living room with seating for twenty and a large screen for viewing movies; an office for general use, with computers, fax machines, scanners, and copiers; and a room filled entirely with decoys of various wildfowl. There was also a trophy room that housed awards lodge members had won in various sporting contests. As we walked around, we kept running into people, all of them on a first-name basis with Skeet. Mercier was a busy place, even in the off-season.

There were also several nicely appointed offices and meeting rooms, but the most interesting was an enormous, round conference room with a domed roof. There was a circular table in the middle that could seat at least twenty people comfortably. It was one of the few rooms with no nature-themed decorations; rather, world maps and paper and coin currencies from all over the globe were framed and hung on the dark wood walls. The room had no windows, and the floor was made of a synthetic material that muffled the sound of our footsteps. Skeet explained that was where the lodge owners gathered, and where special guests could hold meetings. He said that Mercier had become a favorite place for politicians and other D.C. heavyweights to bring important visitors from around the world to showcase the best of American sporting life and spend some informal time in a relaxed atmosphere—but they still had to attend to business on occasion.

That led Ben to ask about security. Skeet said that since many of their guests were high-profile individuals with safety and privacy concerns, Mercier was under armed guard 24/7, and the property was surrounded by a twelve-foot fence with motion sensor-activated cameras. Apparently, ninety-five percent of the time, the sensors were set off by wildlife, and the other five percent of the time, it was kids out exploring or young couples looking for someplace private. Even a front gate would draw too much attention to the property, which was why we hadn't seen one. But the security guards had been told to expect us; if they hadn't, Skeet explained, upon our arrival, a roadblock would have suddenly appeared. He was of the opinion that they didn't need nearly that much security, especially since most people didn't even know Mercier was there. But the guests expected it, he said, so they provided it.

Then Skeet took us down an elevator to the space below the round conference room. It turned out to be another round room of the same proportions, but with a lower, flat ceiling. The floor was covered with exercise mats, and the room smelled vaguely of candle wax and incense. Against the walls were stacks of folding chairs, and metal shelves holding all manner of things, from books to blankets to boxes. Skeet said the room was called "The Sanctuary," a dedicated space where his paranormal research subjects could practice using their gifts together. He said the MacGregor Group was welcome to use the space while we were there. We thanked him for the offer.

After touring the lodge, we were treated to a sumptuous lunch featuring the fresh catch of the day. Then we were loaded into a Jeep and taken around the rest of the property by the head groundskeeper, Owen. He was a local botanist who had jumped at the chance to work at Mercier once he heard how serious they were about nature conservation efforts. The hunting was done sustainably in cooperation with area authorities, and the lodge members had committed early on to doing what they could to preserve indigenous flora and fauna, and to keep the waterways in good shape. Mercier had a few small orchards and fields, as well, where they organically farmed their own corn and other vegetables to serve in the dining room. They also established a Mercier Cove Trust that contributed a substantial amount of money annually to help farmers, watermen, and hunters maintain local ecosystems. The more I learned from Owen, the better I felt about being a part-owner of the place. My spirits began to lift.

It was a pleasure to be outdoors. Mercier was located on the Delmarva Peninsula, where my mother had grown up. The familiar, perfectly flat landscape was covered with pine trees, fields of tall grasses, and hedgerows, and streaked with creeks and streams. It was like being back near Lewes, Delaware, where Ardis still lived. My whole body softened, relaxing in a way it hadn't for years, and I realized I felt at home in this landscape in a way that I didn't anywhere else.

Owen took us to every attraction on the grounds, and there were so many that I lost track. All of the buildings were of the same Adirondack-style construction as the lodge, with the exception of an ordinary-looking barn where they kept things like riding mowers and maintenance equipment. There were several guest cabins, a clubhouse with a spa, an indoor shooting range, and a smaller hunting lodge stocked with all types of bright orange clothing, overshoes, guns, and several coffeemakers. He also took us through the boathouse, which stored kayaks and canoes along with equipment for the boats they kept docked at the pier. Finally, he showed Ben the garage, so we could see for ourselves that the Jag was safe and well cared for.

With an hour before dinner, I was ready to head back, but Owen wanted to show us more of the hunting amenities. Ben was clearly interested, so I went along. Owen took us out to some deer stands, duck blinds, and what turned out to be my favorite stop—the kennel, which was home to the hunting dogs. The "kennel" turned out to be a small cottage with a loft and a few dog runs built inside the front door. The hunting guides were a young married couple, the Selbys. The dogs, who lived as the Selbys' pets, appeared to be models of good health, happy and content. There had been four dogs—two black Labradors and two Brittany spaniels—until about six weeks prior, when Stella, one of the elegant brown-and-white spaniels, had given birth to two puppies.

Fortunately, the puppies were awake when we arrived. I could have spent the rest of the week right there, absorbing their playful, sweet energy. Owen handed us one each—I got the girl, and Ben the boy. As though she'd intuited exactly what I needed, my puppy just curled up in my arms and snuggled, letting me pet her and tell her how beautiful she was, and what fun she was going to have with Stella and the other dogs.

Meanwhile, before my eyes, Ben transformed. Every tense muscle relaxed and every worry line was erased as Ben rolled around in a pile of shredded newspaper, play-wrestling his delighted puppy and letting it beat him time after time. With a permanent grin on his face, Ben let the puppy bite his fingers, then wailed softly when the puppy made little threatening growling noises. The puppy looked so proud of itself, its tail wagging nonstop.

Every time I thought I couldn't fall any harder for Ben… My heart felt as light as the beams of sun coming in through the window blinds. I thought about how much Ben had loved Tank, the Rottweiler his Marine Corps unit had worked with for a time. Ben's Marine nickname, "Rottie," came from their apparent similarities, and Ben was so fond of Tank that he'd gotten a big tattoo of the dog's likeness on his hip. I wondered if Tank was still in active duty. If so, I hoped he was living a happy life with other Marines who loved him as much as Ben had.

On the ride back to the lodge, Owen chatted away about Mercier's history, but all I wanted was to be close to Ben. I leaned over and pressed my head against his chest, twining his fingers in mine and listening to his heartbeat. Ben wrapped his arm around my shoulders and held me close as we drove over the rough ground. I closed my eyes and pictured him playing with the puppy, and for a few moments, all was right with the world.

After our adventures, we both showered before what turned out to be an elaborate dinner in the dining room with Skeet. We shared our admiration for the property with him, and he rewarded us by telling humorous "tall tales" of hunting and fishing feats that had taken place at Mercier. Skeet was a good storyteller, and after thirty years at the lodge, he had plenty of material. I noticed that he steered clear of stories about my father, presumably wanting to keep the conversation light. But I was there to get answers, and dinner seemed like the perfect time.

The waiter came by to clear away what was left of our appetizers. I took advantage of a pause in the conversation to ask, "Did my father spend a lot of time here?"

Skeet shifted uncomfortably in his seat. "Well, no, actually. Before his last trip here, I don't think he'd been to Mercier in over twenty years. He was very dedicated to his work at NIMH; he practically lived there, in fact. Rarely took a break."

"I hope you don't mind me asking, but what caused the falling out between you two?" In response to the look of surprise on his face, I added, "Ardis told me."

"Of course I don't mind," Skeet said, then took a deep drink of his gin and tonic. "Not long after your mother left Joe, he and I had a professional disagreement. We were unable to reach a resolution. We found a way to keep working together as colleagues, but unfortunately, our friendship never fully recovered."

"Your professional disagreement. Did it have to do with my mother? Ardis told me that she left my father because of something to do with your research."

Skeet appeared to age ten years, his face lined with fatigue and regret. "The two were related, yes. Your mother didn't like some of our research methods. After she left, Joe began to question them, as well. I was confident in our methodology and tried to defend it, but Joe just couldn't make peace with certain aspects. We decided to solve the problem by separating our roles a bit more. I took over the hands-on research in the lab, while Joe wrote all of our papers, took care of the administrative needs, wrote grant proposals—that sort of thing."

My body suddenly went cold. I wrapped my arms around

myself. "What kind of research methods did my mother find objectionable?"

"It wasn't anything out of the ordinary—in our field, that is." Skeet waved his hand dismissively. "But to a regular person, some of what we did might have appeared a bit odd. And we often fear what we do not understand."

That didn't sound like my mother. When something seemed strange to her, she always wanted to learn more, not run away. "I'm surprised to hear that," I said. "My mother was usually pretty open-minded. Was there something specific that worried her?"

I peered at Skeet with intense focus, like I was looking into a microscope. He cleared his throat. "Well, like many people, she was a bit disturbed by our use of sensory deprivation and operant conditioning, and she found it off-putting that we used electric shocks as part of our punishment/reward system—even though the voltage was tiny, perfectly harmless. Everything we did was one hundred percent safe."

Safe or not, I doubted electric shocks could be considered harmless. However, I also didn't think they would have terrified my mother to the point that she would deprive me of a father. I sat back in my chair and folded my arms. "*That's* what made her leave Joe?"

Skeet shifted uncomfortably and cleared his throat. "Well, partly. That, and some of the pharmaceuticals we were experimenting with."

"Pharmaceuticals?" Ben asked, sounding casual. "Psychedelics, perhaps? I know a lot of paranormal researchers were using them around that time."

Skeet's eyebrows shot up. "I'm impressed. Most people believe that research ended in the 1970s."

"I had access to some of the studies in the Marine Corps while I was getting my Ph.D.," Ben said. "Some of the results looked very promising."

Did Ben suspect drugs might be causing the problems he'd seen in Skeet's research subjects? If he did, he was doing a good job of disguising any feelings of concern. I guessed he was trying to put Skeet at ease so he would confide in us.

That strategy seemed to work, at least partially. "Quite promising. And yes, we used psychedelics in some of our research." Skeet turned to me. "Now that we're talking about it, I seem to recall that was where your mother drew the line. She had a very rigid outlook when it came to the use of drugs, even for legitimate research purposes."

I was working hard to conceal how disturbed I was by Skeet's nonchalance. Electric shocks, sensory deprivation, and psychedelic drugs? I was skeptical about *all* of those research methods—and who knew what else they'd done that he wasn't telling us about. "Yeah, she took a pretty hard line. She watched drugs destroy the lives of some of her family members and close friends."

"Joe explained that to me after the fact," Skeet said. "I just wish I'd known it at the time, and I wish she'd given me a chance to explain. I'm sure I could have reassured her. But by the time she and Joe had separated, it was too late. Rhona didn't want anything more to do with us."

Ben placed his hand over mine on the table. "I'm sure having Cate changed the way she saw things, too."

"Of course it did." Skeet smiled, but it didn't reach his eyes. "Rhona had strong, protective maternal instincts. And as far as she was concerned, the sun rose and set over you, Cate."

There was another break in the conversation as the waiter delivered the soup course. Skeet had ordered us the ultimate comfort food: luxurious lumps of backfin crabmeat suspended in a thick cream base. The mood at the table lifted.

After we finished our soup, Ben found my hand on my lap and held it. "Skeet, it sounds like you were doing some pretty groundbreaking research," he said. "Can you tell us more about it?"

"It was groundbreaking," Skeet said, appearing pleased with that description. "We made some fascinating discoveries about how different psychedelic drugs can enhance paranormal gifts."

So the drugs were used to try to pump up sensitives' abilities.

The concept of using mind-altering substances as some sort of paranormal steroids sounded creepy to me. It was becoming clearer by the minute that Ben was right to be worried about Skeet's research subjects.

Skeet continued, "In fact, I'd love nothing more than to share our results with you, but only people involved in our work are privy to that information—which is one of the reasons I wanted to talk to you about the personal project I'm working on. Of course, Harris will insist that everyone sign nondisclosure agreements first," Skeet said, smiling apologetically. "He's a real stickler for things like that."

So Skeet wasn't going to reveal anything more unless or until we officially joined his inner circle. "No problem," Ben said. "I sympathize, being a bit of a stickler, myself. We look forward to hearing more about your work."

"Wonderful! It's a plan, then. This calls for a drink." Skeet energetically waved over a waiter. "Can I get a round of drinks, here? Cate, Ben? What can I get you?"

"Just water for me," I said. "Still in training mode."

"Oh, right. Austerity for you! Ben, what'll you have?"

"Ginger ale," he replied. "In solidarity with Cate."

"Hah! Very well." Skeet flagged down the waiter. "Water for the lady, ginger ale for the gentleman, and another gin and tonic for me."

While we waited for our drinks to arrive, I slipped in another question. "Skeet, I was wondering, if my father had stayed away from Mercier for so long, what made him decide to come that last time?"

Skeet's expression took on a nostalgic glow. "He came to prepare to meet you, actually. You were about to turn twenty-five. It was all he could talk about. And it was important to him that when you met, he had something to give you—something concrete to show that he'd been thinking about you and planning for your future all these years. He came to Mercier to familiarize himself with your inheritance portfolio so he'd have up-do-date information to share with you. Once he got here, he was pleased to see what we'd done with the place. He even talked about getting more involved, especially with the environmental efforts. And as a young man, Joe was an avid outdoorsman; he enjoyed hunting and fishing as much as the rest of us. That's why he got involved in Mercier to begin with."

"Right," I barely managed to whisper. So it was my fault that my father was dead. If he hadn't been preparing to meet me, he wouldn't have come out to Mercier, and he wouldn't have gone hunting...

Ben seemed to sense where my mind was going. He placed his hand gently over mine, which was white-knuckled, clutching the napkin in my lap, and whispered one word: "Don't."

I guess if anyone knew about battling irrational guilt, it was Ben. I nodded and tried to smile as the waiter delivered our drinks. Then I downed half of my water in one go.

Our empty soup bowls were whisked away and replaced with platters of lobster stuffed with crab imperial. We took a few bites and expressed our admiration for the cuisine.

"Skeet, is there anything you can tell us about this personal project of yours—prior to our signing nondisclosure agreements, that is?" Ben asked after a sip of ginger ale.

Skeet smiled. "Sure, I can tell you a few things. I think you'll find it interesting. My project is all about the double kheir."

I nearly choked on a piece of lobster.

"I didn't realize that was an area of interest for you," Ben said calmly.

"Oh, yes!" Skeet leaned toward us as his enthusiasm ticked up a notch. "It's the hottest area of research right now, for those of us who are in the know. Not at NIMH, of course. Our activities there are limited by the needs of our stakeholders and the rigors involved in obtaining government approval. I can just imagine the reaction if we asked Congress for a grant to investigate the spiritual origins of paranormal abilities." Skeet chuckled. "No. In order to pursue more esoteric subjects, I had to establish a private project. It's headquartered here at the lodge, and all of the funding comes from Mercier, so we have complete control—and freedom."

"That's an attractive arrangement," I said. My previous

conversation with Skeet about his research at NIMH had left me with the impression that he chafed under governmental restrictions.

He nodded. "A unique opportunity, certainly. Since you have a double kheir and Dr. MacGregor is involved in the Smithsonian study, I thought you might be interested in joining us."

I glanced sideways at Ben, expecting him to jump in with questions, but he was leaning back in his chair and looking bleary-eyed. It had been a long day for both of us, I guessed, but Ben usually preferred to be the point person in tricky conversations—and this one seemed to be getting tricky. How did Skeet know so much about us? Did Dr. MacGregor confide more in him than I'd imagined? Had she filled him in on our Saturday meeting with the researchers? Smiling, I asked Skeet, "How much has Dr. MacGregor told you about the Smithsonian study?"

Skeet leaned back in his chair as well. "She fills me in here and there. It sounds like they're making great progress translating those kheir tablets."

So he knew quite a bit, but probably not about our visit there. "I'm sorry, I'm just curious—how did you know that *we* had a double kheir?"

"Oh, I'm surprised they didn't tell you," Skeet said. "I walked in on Vani and Kai talking about it while they were planning a ritual last week—something to cure your paralysis, I believe. I wasn't trying to be nosy, but we were all in pretty close quarters." He smiled and shrugged. "Ben's mother and I haven't really had a chance to catch up since you joined the group, or I'm sure she would have told me. At any rate, I'm very excited for you. In our project, we have a couple of double kheirs. Now the trick is figuring out how to make the darn things work. Am I right, Ben?"

If Skeet didn't know that we might be close to discovering how to activate the double kheir, I certainly wasn't going to tell him. And why did he have a *couple* of double kheirs? What was his private project, exactly? I glued a smile on my face and looked over at Ben, expecting him to jump in with an incisive comment. But something was wrong. Ben's jaw was slack, and he appeared to be struggling to stay alert. I put my hand on his arm and gently squeezed. "Ben?"

Thankfully, he rallied. "That's right," Ben said, leaning forward and resting his elbows on the table as if to balance himself. "That's the trick—how to get the double kheir to work," he said slowly, as though it was hard work to articulate clearly. "If we could figure that out, it would be a game changer."

"Indeed. But let's be honest, no one has any idea how long that will take, if we manage it at all. The timeline for decoding ancient rituals is maddeningly unpredictable, is it not?" Skeet smiled and clasped his hands behind his neck. "At any rate, with Team Forward—that's the name of my project—we're doing some unique work that I believe will interest you. Especially now that you're going to be a part owner of Mercier, Cate. I mentioned yesterday that a couple of our NIMH research subjects are spending a few days here this week. They also happen to be members of Team Forward. They can tell you what we're all about, on both fronts."

"That's great!" Desperately, I tried to open up my empathic senses so that I could figure out what was really going on with both Skeet and Ben. But when I focused on my heart, all I could feel was the hard edges of the lockbox into which I'd shoved all of my negative emotions. I couldn't open myself up at all; it was as though my abilities had been shut away as well.

That settled it. I had no idea what was going on in the conversation with Skeet, but it felt like he was probing for information, and I didn't like it. I also had no idea what was happening to Ben, but it was scaring me. He wasn't giving me any indication that he was in distress, though, and if he was faking some kind of impairment as a strategic gambit with Skeet, I didn't want to get in his way. I had to come up with an indirect way of asking Ben if he was okay.

All at once, it came to me. "Well, with a couple of double kheirs, it sounds like you and Team Forward have the best chance of figuring out how they work. Soon, we'll all be turning to you for help." Cheerfully, I added, "Ben, what was that line of Princess Leia's in *Star Wars*?"

Ben's head dropped to one side as though he was a marionette and a thread had been cut. I could tell he was making an effort to focus on my eyes. "'Help me, Obi-Wan Kenobi,'" he said.

"'You're my only hope,' that's right! That's the quote." My heart was in my throat, but I managed to smile brightly at Skeet. "You'll be our Obi-Wan Kenobi!"

"Well, let's not get ahead of ourselves," he said, chuckling.

Skeet was acting as though everything was normal. I started to wonder if Ben's altered state was obvious only to me—not that it mattered. He'd given the distress signal, and I had to get him out of there. "We really do look forward to hearing more about your project," I said. "In the meantime, though, it's been a long day. I think it's time Ben and I called it a night."

"Oh, no, don't leave now," Skeet objected. "We're having such a great conversation. Why don't I have the waiter bring some coffee?" He waved at the waiter.

"No," I said with more force than I'd intended.

Skeet gave me a curious look.

"No, thank you," I said, plastering another smile on my face. "I just think we need sleep rather than caffeine at this point."

He frowned. "If you're sure."

"I'm sure."

"I can't convince you to stay? Tempt you with some dessert, perhaps?"

"No, I'm sorry."

"Well, perhaps Ben would like to stay a while—"

I stood up. "There are some things he and I need to go over before bed. About our clinic patients," I added in an effort to sound convincing.

A current of irritation ran beneath Skeet's expression. "I see. I suppose it has been a long day. I didn't mean to push; I just enjoy your company tremendously."

"The feeling is mutual!" I turned to Ben, who was barely able to get out of his chair under his own strength. "We're so glad to be here. See you tomorrow," I said as I positioned myself next to

Ben, sliding in close so that he could put some of his weight on my shoulder. Then I put my arm around his waist.

Ben's words were starting to slur. "Thank you for your hospitality, Skeet. We'll have to continue this conversation later."

Skeet stood as well and finally seemed to notice the trouble Ben was having. "Ben, are you all right?"

"Fine," Ben said, "just tired. Need to do what Cate says and get some sleep."

Skeet looked genuinely concerned. "If you're sure, but we have a doctor on staff."

I knew it would make *me* feel better if someone looked him over. "Ben, that might not be a bad—"

"*No*," Ben declared.

I took a deep breath and tried to think. I wanted to trust Ben's judgment that he didn't need a doctor, but he was clearly out of it. I also knew, though, that my anxiety had a way of spiraling out of control. Finally, it dawned on me: I could call Pete when we got back to the room. He had been a medic in the Marine Corps, and he knew Ben better than anyone. If anyone would know what to do, he would.

"Yeah, we're okay," I said, trying to sound reassuring. "We just need some rest."

Skeet still looked worried. "Okay, but don't hesitate to ring the front desk if you change your mind, or if you need anything else."

"We will," I promised.

"Goodnight then," Skeet said.

"Goodnight!" I called as we walked out of the dining room—or rather, as I steered Ben out. He leaned on me, shuffling his feet as we walked to the elevator. I managed to get him upstairs and into my room, where he collapsed onto the bed.

I knelt on the mattress next to him as his eyes began to close. "Ben!" I pressed the back of my hand against his cheek. His temperature felt normal, but he looked like he'd done about ten Jello shots in as many minutes.

"I'm okay," he mumbled, this time not trying to hide how difficult it was for him to speak. "I was drugged, but I'll be all right."

"Drugged? *What?*"

"Probably my ginger ale," he said. "It was just GHB. I'll sleep it off." He rolled over onto his side and draped his arm over his head.

"Ben, for the love—argh!" I grabbed my cell phone and called Pete.

It took him several rings to answer; all the while, my blood pounded louder and louder in my ears. "Hey, sis. How's the—"

"Pete!" I cut him off. "Ben was drugged with GHB. He thinks they put it in his ginger ale at dinner."

"*What?*" I was grateful that Pete sounded as alarmed as I felt. "How do you know? And who did it?"

"I know because Ben told me, right before he passed out," I said. "And I don't know who—somebody here at Mercier, though. We were having dinner with Skeet when the drinks were brought out."

"Oh, hell," Pete said. "Let me talk to him."

"Okay." I pulled Ben's arm off of his head and held the phone up to his ear. Pete yelled, "Ben, what happened?"

Ben moaned.

"Come on," he cajoled. "Wake up, it's Pete."

"I know it's you," Ben said. "Somebody slipped me a roofie."

"Scale of one to ten?"

"Three or four."

"Okay. Cate?" I heard Pete say.

I took the phone back. "What do you mean, 'scale of one to ten'?"

"He'll be fine," Pete reassured. "We got trained on this stuff in the Corps. Ben knows what they gave him and roughly how much. He just needs to sleep it off. Just to be sure, though, I'll come check him out."

"But how does he know it's a three or four?"

"Oh, he knows, believe me. Ben got an A-plus in roofies."

I felt the phone fluttering against my cheek and realized that my hand was trembling. "Pete, I'm scared."

"Yeah," he said, his voice gravelly. "I get that. Can you stay in the room with him?"

I watched as Ben threw his arm over his head again, snoring lightly. "Well, yeah, he kind of landed on my bed. I couldn't move him if I wanted to."

"Good. Just keep an eye on him, and let me know if anythin' changes."

"Like what?"

"Any new symptoms. You'll know 'em if you see 'em," he said, and I could tell he was afraid that giving me any more specifics would cause me to worry. "Make sure the door's locked, and don't open it for anybody but me. You listenin'?"

"Yes," I whispered, checking and double-checking the door.

"You sure you can stay awake?"

My nerves were so on edge, I didn't think I'd ever sleep again. "Yes, definitely."

"Okay. When we say goodbye, don't hang up, just put whatever phone you're on by the bed. Plug in the charger if you need to. We'll leave the call active and open until I get there, so if anything happens, I can call in reinforcements. I'm packin' now. I'll be there soon."

"Security is crazy here. I'll call the front desk and tell them to expect you. Do you know how to get here?"

"Yup. Don't worry, okay? Everythin's gonna be all right. I'm sure it was accidental. You know how it is at those fancy resorts; you can order anything you want. Somebody likely asked for a little special something in their cocktail, and their drink got mixed up with Ben's."

I knew Pete was just trying to comfort me, but I decided to let him. "You really think that's what happened?"

"Sure I do. You got a book to read?"

I hadn't brought any reading materials, but I decided to comfort Pete right back. "Yes, I've got something."

"Good. Try to relax until I get there."

"Okay." I looked down at Ben. I couldn't remember ever seeing him so vulnerable. "Is there anything I can do for him?"

"There would be if he'd let you, but knowin' him, he probably won't. Just leave him alone; I'll check him out when I get there. Now say goodbye so I can get on the road."

"Goodbye. And thank you, Pete."

"Sure thing, sis. If I wasn't busy savin' Ben's ass all the time, I wouldn't know what to do with myself. See ya."

I laid the phone carefully on the bedside table. Then I changed into my pajamas, looking over at Ben every fifteen seconds or so, just to check on him. Still asleep. Still breathing. Then I curled up on the bed next to him, wrapped my arm around his waist, and waited for the cavalry to arrive.

Chapter Nine

As promised, Pete arrived an hour and a half after my phone call, medic kit in tow. He said he also brought several steamer trunks and duffle bags full of other equipment, most of which he left in the truck. Pete woke Ben up and gave him a thorough examination, including a rapid toxicology screening. His verdict was that Ben had been right: it was GHB, and not a dangerous amount—just enough to induce a state similar to drunkenness. Pete settled into his room down the hall, and I was able to get a few hours of uneasy sleep before morning.

• • •

ParaTrain Internship, Day Eight

Ben woke up Monday morning with a headache—and quite a bit of embarrassment over having worried me and fallen asleep in my bed—but that was the worst of it. After hovering over me and asking four times in four different ways if I was all right, he went back to his room to shower and dress while I did the same. A permanent fist of tension had taken up residence just below my sternum, and my whole body ached. I took a scalding hot shower and some ibuprofen, which helped a bit. Once I was dressed and my hair was braided, I went over and knocked on Pete's door. We had agreed to have breakfast called up to his room.

Ben was already there. They were both dressed, and Pete was in the middle of repacking his bags.

"What are you doing?" I asked.

Pete grinned at what must have been sheer incomprehension on my face. "Old Marine Corps habit. We like things orderly. You'll see; Rottie here is the same way."

I walked up behind Ben, who was rifling through a duffle bag of equipment on the bed. Sliding my arms around his waist, I clasped my hands in front of him and rested my cheek against his back. Ben paused, dropped what he was doing, and turned around, pulling me close. "I'm fine," he murmured. "I'm sure it was a mistake, like Pete said. We got a call from Skeet this morning; one of his kitchen staff fessed up to putting the drug in my ginger ale. He was trying to play a prank on a friend and got our drinks mixed up. Skeet was apologizing all over himself."

I peered up at Ben. "Do you actually believe that?"

But instead of answering me, Ben looked over my shoulder for a second, presumably exchanging a look with Pete. That told me everything I needed to know. "Do you even remember the conversation we were having with Skeet?" I asked. "It was like he was pumping us for information."

"I remember," he said. "I filled Pete in, and I called my mother a few minutes ago. She confirmed that she *has* spoken to Skeet about her research at the Smithsonian, but not in great detail, and not since we got involved." Ben looked down at me, his eyes soft with sympathy. "She also asked me to extend her condolences on the loss of your father—and to tell you how upset she is on your behalf that Skeet didn't tell you everything sooner."

"That was nice of her," I said. "Please thank her for me, the next time you talk to her."

Ben nodded. "We'll have to ask Vani and Kai if Skeet's story checks out—that he walked in on them talking about our double kheir. Then we'll have a better idea of what we're dealing with."

"Ugh." I buried my face in his chest. "I don't like this."

"Relax, sis," Pete said, chucking me in the shoulder. "We've dealt with much worse. This is nothin'. We'll get it sorted out."

"We will." Ben placed a warm kiss on the top of my head. "The good news is, Skeet seems more than eager to tell us all about Team

Forward and what they're up to. It should be an interesting week, at least."

"Yeah, speaking of which." My hands clenched, digging my nails into Ben's back. I tried to force my fingers to relax. "What did you really think about those research methods he was talking about last night—the ones they were using back when my mom and dad were together?"

"To be honest, they weren't so unusual at the time. And psychedelic drugs are even making a comeback lately, mainly in psychiatry." Ben's brows gathered together to form a dark ridge. "But among people who work with sensitives, it has been common knowledge for more than half a century that mind-altering drugs should *never* be used on people with paranormal gifts. They're known to have bad side effects—the kinds of problems we've seen in Skeet's research subjects. You're a special population, and there are ethical boundaries and protocols that have been set up to protect you. It's clear that even in their early days at NIMH, Skeet and Joe were ignoring those protocols—which is pretty alarming, even if it *was* done with governmental oversight."

"So my mom," I said softly, "she was right."

"Right to be worried?" His eyes searched mine as he rested his hand against my cheek. "Yes, I believe she was. And your mother's concerns stirred Joe's conscience—"

"Triggering the fallout between Joe and Skeet." Skeet had said as much the night before, but as we talked it over, the picture snapped into focus.

"Right," Ben said. "After last night's conversation, it's obvious that Skeet has little regard for the health and well-being of his research subjects. And given the patterns we've observed in our clinic, I'm willing to bet that he's either still using psychedelic drugs, or he's moved on to some other unethical research methods that are hurting his subjects. We still don't have proof, though."

And if we wanted to find any, we had to pretend that nothing was wrong and that we were all still friends—even though, after what I suspected he'd done to Ben the night before, all I wanted to do was wring Skeet's neck.

I would have to curb that impulse, though. Skeet had asked Ben to meet him in the lobby after breakfast so that he could apologize in person. We all went down together. Skeet appeared genuinely horrified by the drugging. He assured Ben that the waiter responsible had already been fired and that they were considering having him arrested. But Ben came to the waiter's defense, saying that it was a mix up; that a safe dose of the drug had been used; and that since Ben wasn't the intended target, he wouldn't press charges. Eventually, Pete brought an end to the conversation by confessing that they'd pulled much worse pranks on one another in the Marines.

I did my best to play along as Ben and Pete worked to convince Skeet that they believed his story and that there were no hard feelings. I managed to keep a half-smile on my face while my stomach busily tied itself in knots.

Vani arrived just in time to join us back in Pete's room for coffee. As usual, she looked like the cover model for a health and lifestyle magazine. Even her pearl-white turtleneck sweater was a step up in elegance from what most people considered casual wear. It was no wonder she attracted admirers like flies to honey.

She wrinkled her nose as she sat down next to me on the couch. "What did you *do* to yourself?" she asked quietly. "Your aura is dim and closed off."

"I don't know what you're talking about," I said, even as my thoughts wandered to the internal lockbox where I'd temporarily confined all of my troublesome emotions. "I didn't do anything to myself. I'm just trying to focus."

"Ah." She pursed her lips. "You shut down your heart chakra so you could think. Not a good idea for an empath, Cate. You can't use your gifts if that chakra's closed down."

I had only used that visualization technique to better cope with what I was feeling. I had no idea it would actually affect my heart chakra. And Vani was right; it had impacted my abilities. "I noticed that," I said, remembering my failed attempt to empathically read

Skeet and Ben at dinner. That settled it; I would have to work on prying that chakra open again and just deal with whatever emotions emerged. Now more than ever, I needed the advantages my gifts could provide.

We spent about half an hour filling Vani in on everything that had happened. I appreciated that she was as horrified as I was by the drugging incident, but she wasn't yet willing to conclude that Skeet was responsible. After all, she pointed out, the other part of what he told us was true: Skeet *had* walked in on Vani and Kai while they were planning a ritual the previous week. There wasn't a lot of space in the sub-basement where we were sequestered, so they had been working in the makeshift staff lounge. Skeet had come in to make coffee—after asking their permission, she emphasized—so he would certainly have heard what they were discussing. She couldn't remember specifically whether they mentioned our double kheir while he was there, but she said they might well have. After all, at the time, they were more focused on curing me than on anything else, and they didn't know of any reason to keep secrets from Skeet.

Still, my instincts screamed that Skeet had been trying to get information out of us the night before, either by debilitating Ben and leaving me vulnerable, or by getting Ben to let his guard down so that Skeet could ply him with questions. Fortunately, we'd left the table before he got the chance to execute either of those strategies.

Ben pointed out that if I was right and Skeet had orchestrated the drugging with ulterior motives, then my idea to create a *Star Wars* distress signal had truly saved the day. He told that part of the story with great relish, and Vani and Pete duly expressed admiration for my "secret agent" skills.

By that point, I was blushing hard. I didn't like being the center of attention, and I'd never taken compliments well. Ben suggested that we take a short break and pulled me into a far corner of the room. He tucked my hair behind my ear and placed his lips an inch away from it. "You were brilliant, by the way."

My pulse skittered. "How so?"

"The way you managed to work that *Star Wars* line into the

conversation last night," he murmured. "Terrific problem-solving, quick on your feet. You got me out of that situation just as skillfully as Pete or anyone else could have. I was too out of it to say it then, so I'll say it now: Thank you."

I turned my head so that our eyes met. A warm wave of emotion crashed through the portal between us, filling me with the pride and love Ben was feeling and cracking my heart chakra open. I blinked back tears. "You're welcome." My voice hitched as I remembered the intense fear I'd felt the previous night. "Just don't get drugged again, okay?"

With his fingertip, Ben traced an arc from my temple to my chin. "I promise," he whispered. Then he pulled me close, holding me until I relaxed into a deep sigh.

When we rejoined the others, Vani gave us each bracelets of braided black leather that Kai had sent with her. Since we didn't know exactly what kind of sensitives Skeet would be bringing in, Kai had woven some crystals and stones into the bracelets that would block any telepaths from being able to read our thoughts. As Ben pointed out, we had to defend against *all* potential methods of surveillance.

Once all of our bracelets were tied on, we went down to the cove. Vani and I sat on a bench along a walkway that led down to the pier, and Ben and Pete went down to look at the skiffs. It was so quiet that we could hear the water lapping against the shoreline. The scent of cattails tickled my nose as the sun drifted higher, taking the chill out of the air. The sound of distant honking broke the silence, and Vani pointed to a double-V formation of Canada geese flying high overhead.

In that peaceful moment, exhaustion began to set in. My worries about Ben combined with poor sleep had done me no favors. When Pete and I had finally gone to bed the night before, I had begged my mother's spirit to appear to me in my dreams, as she had in the past. I had a long list of questions for her. But no dice. It occurred to me that she might be avoiding me for some reason—or worse, that she might have visited my dreams for the last time, then moved on to some other spiritual dimension. But that thought made my throat tighten, and I couldn't afford to panic. I forced the whole subject into the back of my mind.

For Ben and me, the morning was going to be spent meeting with Skeet and Harris, my father's estate lawyer. Skeet's research subjects would arrive that evening, so the afternoon looked like it might be the only free time we'd have for a while.

We had discussed how best to spend those free midday hours. After hearing more about the property, Pete was itching to take one of the boats and "check things out." Ben thought we'd appear more trusting—not to mention trustworthy—if we were seen to be casually enjoying Mercier's amenities, so he and Pete told Skeet that they wanted to take a boat out fishing. Vani and I had decided to do our part by visiting the spa, even though I would have preferred to take a long nap.

But first, Ben and I had to get through our meeting. It wasn't long before we found ourselves in one of the lodge's offices, seated around a small conference table with Skeet and the estate lawyer. Harris appeared to be in his fifties and had a healthy tan, like he spent a good amount of time golfing or playing tennis. Everything else about him was understated and nondescript—his features, his clothes, his mannerisms, and his soft, clear voice. It was as though he didn't want to stand out in any way. However, his light blue eyes were unusually sharp and alert, and his head turned at every sound, like a bird of prey. He greeted Ben and me warmly, and seemed genuinely somber when he extended his condolences about my father's loss.

Harris pulled a stack of papers out his briefcase. "So, Cate," he began, "I guess Skeet gave you the basics. Joe was one of ten founding members of Mercier, so with his passing and no one else having a claim on his inheritance, the ownership of his tenth of the property goes to you."

He slid a copy of some papers over to me and looked at a copy of his own. I moved the papers so that Ben could also see them as Harris explained the details using terminology that was completely foreign to me. I was utterly baffled by the time he asked, "Any questions?"

"I'm not sure," I said, shooting Ben a pleading look. "Ben, do you have any?"

Under the table, he rested a reassuring hand on my leg. "This all looks pretty straightforward. However, Cate will want to have her lawyer review everything, I'm sure—to get a handle on the potential tax implications, that kind of thing. Right, Cate?"

I had no idea who my alleged lawyer was supposed to be, but I trusted that Ben did—and I hoped that it would be someone who could explain everything to me in plain English. "Yes, of course. If you don't mind."

"Not at all." If Harris was the least bit fazed, he didn't show it. "You'll also want your lawyer to look this over, then." He slid another set of papers over to us. "Joe was a passionate philanthropist; he left most of his assets to NIMH. However, he did leave you a small nest egg. In his will, he noted that he wanted to make up for the years your mother refused his offers of child support."

I looked at the piece of paper. There were countless numbers on the page, but one was large and bold in the lower right-hand corner. I rubbed my eyes and looked at it again, then looked at Ben, then at Harris. "I'm sorry, what's the value of this nest egg?"

Harris dropped the news casually, as though he were accustomed to saying large numbers out loud. "Two hundred and fifty thousand dollars, give or take, based on today's interest."

I froze. "Two hundred...*what*?"

Harris clasped his hands on the table and looked solemn. "Joe wanted to meet you when you turned twenty-five. But when he passed away before your birthday, per a prior agreement, this was all left in trust to your mother to handle as she saw fit. The nest egg was meant to be ten thousand dollars for every year he'd been away from you. I'm just sorry Joe didn't get the chance to give it to you himself."

"Oh my goodness." I rubbed my face. "That's just...*incredible.*

I mean, that's...a really big egg—much bigger than I expected. Not that I was expecting anything..."

"Of course," Skeet said, smiling. "We research scientists aren't exactly known for our wealth. But Mercier has become quite a profitable sporting retreat. All of the initial investors receive a monthly income based on Mercier's profits, whether they're active in the business or not—as you will, now."

"Oh." I could only imagine how much Mercier charged for a night at the lodge, and we'd seen so many guests already—people from D.C. who were probably happy to pay a premium to stay at such a beautiful resort, not to mention one that was secure and assured their privacy. And if it was a destination for people to entertain prominent guests... The financial part of things was starting to make sense. "So, you were all fraternity brothers? All of the founding members?"

"That's right," Harris said.

I bit my lip, imagining how much of an outsider I was going to feel like in that group. "Will I be the first female co-owner?"

Skeet chuckled. "Yes, now that you mention it. I hadn't thought of that. But you won't be the last. A few other members have willed their interests in Mercier to their wives and daughters."

"I was just curious." I shrugged. "I don't really know what else... Ben? Can you think of anything?"

"Well, knowing Cate's lawyer," Ben said, flashing Harris a collegial smile, "she's going to want to see Mercier's financials so she can work up an estimated income—give Cate some idea of what to expect—and start planning on how to invest it."

"Certainly," Harris said. I might have imagined it, but I thought a look of annoyance flickered across his face. "I'll put those together and send them to you as soon as I can."

"Thank you." If Harris had been annoyed, it must have been at the prospect of doing more paperwork. After all, there was no reason why they should be reluctant to show me Mercier's financial records, given that I was part of it all now.

Harris tucked his papers back into his briefcase. "I was going to ask you to sign a few things, Cate—you know, to make things official—but that can wait until your lawyer has had a chance to review. Meanwhile," he said warmly, standing and extending his hand to me, "allow me to be the first to welcome you to Mercier, Cathryn Duncan, our newest owner!"

The rest of us stood as well, and I accepted Harris's handshake, followed by Skeet's congratulations. "Though the circumstances are tragic, we're certainly glad to have you," Skeet said. "I know Joe would be incredibly pleased to see you taking your place here."

"He would, indeed," Harris agreed. "If there isn't anything else..."

I glanced at Ben, who shook his head. "I don't think so, not at the moment," I said. "Thank you so much for taking the time to explain everything. I'll get back to you as soon as I've gone over things with my lawyer."

"I'll look forward to hearing from you, then," Harris said, handing me his business card.

"Go ahead, Harris," Skeet said, shooing him towards the door. "I know you have a date with the dogs!"

The two men chuckled. After Harris left, Skeet asked Ben and me to sit for a few more minutes. "Please allow me to apologize again for what happened last night," he said somberly. "Nothing like that has happened before, and I assure you it will never happen again."

Ben gave Skeet a nod. "I appreciate that, but there is no need for any more apologies. It's already forgotten."

"That's very gracious of you," Skeet said. "Since our conversation last night got cut short, I just wanted to reiterate how happy I am that you're here this week, so that you can meet some of the members of Team Forward and learn more about what we do. Which brings me back to your father, Cate."

I tried to maintain my outward composure, but internally, I was steeling myself. "Yes?"

Skeet looked thoughtful as he rubbed his hands together in slow motion. "You know that he wanted you to be involved in our paranormal research studies."

"Yes," I said, "from infancy, apparently."

"Well, I share his desire for you to be a part of our work—you, and the whole MacGregor Group. As the week goes on, I'd just like both of you to remember that you have an open invitation to join us."

"Thank you," Ben said, taking my hand. "That's very generous of you, and we'll certainly keep it in mind. We're eager to meet Team Forward."

"They're looking forward to meeting you, too." We all stood. Skeet shook Ben's hand, and then put his arm around my shoulders and squeezed. "I'm so glad you're on board."

I forced my smile to stay in place. "Thank you."

After Ben and I were a safe distance down the hallway, I allowed myself to shudder.

"Come here." Ben pulled me tightly against his body and squeezed. I clung to him, soaking up his warmth, his scent. Ben's lips grazed my cheek. "You're incredibly brave, do you know that?"

I pulled away. "What are you talking about? I'm a ball of nerves!"

"Which makes how you're handling all of this even more impressive. You've had a lot of bombs dropped on you in the past two days."

"Yeah, well." It was true, I had—and I knew that if we started talking about it, I'd probably end up crying, which I had no desire to do. Instead, I steered the conversation elsewhere. "Some of the bombs have been worth a quarter of a million dollars, so…not so bad."

"Yeah, I guess that wasn't the worst thing that could have happened." Ben's light brown eyes shimmered gold. "So, are you going to quit the MacGregor Group now that you're independently wealthy?"

"Please don't say that," I said, wincing. The truth was that the idea of having money was so foreign to my experience that it seemed surreal. "And of course not. Paying off my student loans alone would take a sizeable chunk out of the nest egg."

"Well, I'm sorry about the loans, but glad to hear that your debtor status means you won't be leaving us."

As a smile crept across my face, I soft-punched him in the arm.

"I will be getting an income from this place, though, and you know what *that* means."

"I do?"

"It means *I* can finally buy *you* some gifts for a change." Ben's family was well-off, having earned a good amount of money in Scottish shipping. He had been extremely generous to me ever since we'd started dating, and it irked me that I'd been unable to return those gestures.

Ben put his hands on my shoulders and held me at arm's length. "What are you talking about?"

"You know," I reminded him, even as I felt a blush creeping up my neck. "I told you how uncomfortable it makes me that you keep buying me things, and I can't afford to buy anything for you. Well, now I can."

Ben tilted his head to one side and said, softly but firmly, "There is nothing I want that I don't have—right here, right now."

I pressed my lips together, trying and failing to suppress a smile. "That's what you think."

"Oh." His brows arched upward. "You have something in mind already?"

"Maybe."

"Hmm. Interesting." He offered me his elbow. "I think it's time for lunch. But after that, I may have to find a way to get this secret gift idea out of you."

"Promises, promises. Oh, hey, wait!" I grabbed his elbow. "Since when do I have a lawyer?"

"Since you joined the MacGregor Group. We keep an attorney on retainer. Danielle works for the IRS, but she also has a private practice."

"Oh. Well, thanks for that. I had no idea what Harris was talking about most of the time."

"No reason why you should; that's why we have Danielle. I can tell you more over lunch. Shall we?"

"We shall." I walked with Ben down to the dining room, smiling to myself as I turned my secret gift idea over and over in my mind.

CHAPTER TEN

Pete, Vani, Ben, and I stood in the hallway. Vani and I had just returned from our ridiculously relaxing afternoon at the spa, where we indulged in hot rock massages that left me feeling like a cooked noodle. Meanwhile, Ben and Pete had already showered and changed after taking one of the skiffs out on their mysterious outing. We were just getting ready to go downstairs for dinner when I told Ben, "You and Vani go ahead. I need a word with Pete."

All three of them looked equally surprised. Ben and Pete exchanged puzzled glances, but no one seemed prepared to challenge my request.

Ben said slowly, "We'll go get a table, then."

"Okay!" I finger-waved. "See you in a few!"

Pete hooked his thumbs into his belt and frowned at me from beneath the brim of his cowboy hat. "What's goin' on, sis?"

"Don't worry, it's nothing to do with your wedding."

"Phew!" Pete stretched his lean frame back and pushed his hat up, rubbing his hairline. "'Cause if you were gonna ask me to do somethin' to surprise Kai... Let's just say I'm doin' as I'm told on this one, down to the letter."

"Very wise." Pete and Kai had just gotten engaged the previous week, but Kai was already in full wedding planning mode. I smiled at the formidable cowboy who was nonetheless cowed by his fiancé's forceful will. "I just wanted to ask if there was any way you could contact Captain Abbott for me."

Pete's look of confusion was understandable. Captain Abbott could only be described as "prickly" on a good day, and since I didn't exactly excel at following orders, our interactions the previous week had been a bit fraught. However, we'd ended things on a note of mutual respect, and I knew how much he liked Ben. "It's about a surprise gift for Ben."

After I explained what I wanted, Pete dropped his chin to his chest and rubbed his eyes for a full minute. Then I saw his shoulders shake with silent laughter. "I'll tell ya what, sis. If you're willin' to ask Abbott for *that*, then you got it *bad* for Ben."

With a sigh, I replied, "Yes, Pete, I got it bad, okay? Are you happy now?"

When he looked up, he was wearing a wide grin. "Yup. You know, Kai's been talkin' about us havin' a double weddin' with you and Ben."

I gave him my driest smirk. "If you talk to Abbott for me, I'll pretend I never heard you say that."

He threw his hands up in surrender. "All right, I'll ask him. Just don't get your hopes up."

I couldn't help it; I kind of *had* gotten my hopes up. Pete's reality check made my shoulders droop. "I know it's a long shot."

"It's a fine idea, sis, and I hope it works out." Pete smiled and pushed his hat back into place. "If that's all you needed to talk to me about, I'd like to get down to dinner. As usual, Ben sat back bein' lazy while I did all the heaving liftin' on our boat trip. I could eat about six steaks right now."

I smiled back. Ben, lazy? That would be the day. I had yet to find out what their boat trip was all about. I'd have to grill them over dinner.

• • •

"*Muskrats*?" Vani made a face like she was sucking on a sour candy. "What are those?"

Ben had requested a table for us in the far corner of the room, away from other diners. The dining room was about half-filled, with a soft candle-and-moonlit ambience. We were in the middle of yet another amazing meal of fresh seafood accompanied by various sauces and local vegetables. As it turned out, it probably wasn't the best time for me to ask about Ben and Pete's aquatic adventures. Then again, I'd had no way of knowing what was coming.

"They're like big rats, only real musky," Pete explained.

Vani's fork stopped halfway to her mouth, then slowly returned to her plate.

"They're just large rodents that live in the marsh," Ben said, trying too late to make the conversation sound normal. "The pelt is quite valuable, actually. They use it to make those Russian ushanka hats."

"Oh." Vani appeared relieved that the topic had shifted to hats. "Those are quite beautiful."

"Expensive, too, so there's a healthy trade in muskrat fur around here," Ben said. "We were out examining the perimeter of the property along the water when we ran into two guys checking their traps."

"From what we could tell, their traps were right up on Mercier property," Pete added. "So we asked how they got past security, and they just laughed it off, sayin' any waterman worth his salt knew how to get around things—an attitude I respect."

I shook my head. "So much for a secure facility."

"Well, if it's just local trappers infiltratin' the place, I'd say they've got nothin' to worry about. Lonzie and Clayton were good guys, and they said they went to high school with some of the guards that work here, so there's probably a blind eye bein' turned. Anyway, they gave us some good intel."

I swallowed a bite of fish. "What kind of intel?"

"They see a lot that goes on around here," Ben said. "Apparently, for the past year or so, there have been a lot of what the trappers referred to as 'outsiders' coming and going under the cover of night. They said that lodge owners bring these people down the bay on their yachts, then drop anchor on the Miles River. Then they use smaller boats to transport their guests down the creek and into Mercier Cove. Their visits always coincide with Skeet being present—along with some of his research subjects."

"Team Forward?"

"I'm guessing."

"That's strange," Vani said, delicately dabbing the corners of her mouth with her linen napkin. "It seems that the owners are going to a lot of trouble to keep visits from these 'outsiders' a secret. Otherwise, they'd just drive to the lodge like everyone else."

"Who are these 'outsiders'?" I asked.

"They're not sure, exactly," Pete said. "Just people they'd never seen before, or since. They said they heard some of them speaking in foreign languages."

"Something's going on," Ben said, "we're just not sure what. We exchanged cell numbers with the trappers; they said they'd give us the heads-up if they saw any of these 'outsiders' coming in. Meanwhile, Vani, part of Team Forward is arriving after dinner. I'm counting on you and Cate to charm some information out of them."

"Nothing like being respected as a professional," Vani said dryly. "But it *is* true that charm is not exactly one of your strengths, Benjamin." She looked me up and down. "Cate, you have that guileless, innocent vibe going on. I think we can manage between the two of us." She flashed me a smile.

I wasn't sure if "guileless and innocent" was meant as a compliment, nor was I thrilled about the idea of trying to wheedle information out of Team Forward without Ben there. I batted my eyelashes at him. "I think you're charming. Why won't you be joining us?"

He reached over and stroked the back of my hand. "I'd love to, but I've got to go to Neavitt to see our Marine buddy, Max. He said he has an office in his garage with a secure phone line; I've set up a call with Danielle."

"Yeah," Pete said, eyes narrowed. "It always feels to me like somebody's listenin' around here—or tryin' to. At least this room has enough background noise so we don't have to worry."

"Oh." I frowned. On the one hand, such concerns about privacy seemed extreme. On the other, our stay so far had given us more reasons to be cautious, not fewer. "What about you, Pete? Are you coming with us?"

"Well, as much as I love interrogatin' people," he drawled, "I gotta get some equipment out of the truck and set a few things up. Besides, I do believe I'd stick out like a sore thumb."

"Don't worry, Cate," Vani said with a confident toss of her hair. "We'll have those birds singing in no time."

• • •

Vani and I went back up to our rooms after dinner to await word of Team Forward's arrival. About half an hour later, we received calls from the front desk inviting us to meet them in the Sanctuary—dressed for "movement." I thought it was pretty presumptuous of Team Forward to assume that we'd be into "moving" instead of, say, getting to know them over tea and scones. Vani, however, was pleased with the idea, pointing out that if everyone's attention was focused on doing some kind of physical activity, she could discreetly check out their auras without being noticed.

The Sanctuary was dimly lit and candles flickered. Sitar music played softly in the background as a man and a woman stood in the middle of the room, holding matching yoga poses. I'd taken yoga in the past—just enough to know what it looked like, and how to do deep breathing. Vani and I stood respectfully by the door and waited.

"Reverse warrior," the man said, and as one, they shifted poses, stretching back to put one hand on their ankles and reaching skyward with their free arms. The man caught sight of us and flashed us a quick smile. After a minute or so, he said, "And release. Liv, our visitors have arrived."

"Oh, great!" Liv straightened up into a standing position and stretched up to her full height, which appeared to be about five feet. She wore her black, curly hair in a bob, and her ivory skin almost glowed in the dark. Her biker shorts and formfitting tank top revealed a wiry physique. Liv pressed her hands together in front of her chest. Wearing a beatific expression, she said, "Namaste."

"Namaste," Vani repeated the Hindi greeting, hiding her almost imperceptible annoyance behind a smile.

They both came over to greet us. "I'm Michael," he said, "and this is Liv."

Michael had shiny, gel-tousled blonde hair and the kind of deep, uneven tan that only comes from spending the majority of one's days in the sun. He had handsome features and a well-muscled, athletic build. They both seemed so self-assured that I decided it had been a mistake to think we could get anything out of them that they didn't want to share.

"I'm Cate," I said, trying to project confidence I didn't feel. I quickly reached out to shake Michael's hand before my palms started sweating. I went to shake Liv's hand, too, but she gave me the "Namaste" greeting. Since I'd never greeted anyone that way before and would have felt awkward reciprocating, I just nodded.

"And I'm Vani." She swept forward and took hold of Michael's hand. Then she covered both of their hands with her free one and gazed up at him, her thousand-watt smile on full display. "We've been *so* looking forward to meeting you."

It was the first time I'd witnessed Vani really turning on the charm. Mild irritation flashed across Michael's face when he saw the telepath-blocking bracelets we were wearing, but once Vani focused her attention on him, his expression warmed. "Likewise," he said, matching her smile. "Skeet has told us such impressive things about you." The way Michael had his eyes fixed on Vani, I got the impression that the "you" he was talking about was her, in particular. "You're an aura reader, correct?"

He obviously knew that somehow, so she just nodded. "And Cate is an empath," Vani said. "She's new to our group, still in training."

"Oh," Liv said with a knowing grin. "Still in monk mode? I guess we won't be doing any tantric sex rituals, then!"

As I tried to reconcile the fact that the words "tantric sex" had just fallen from the same lips that had demurely greeted us with "Namaste," my face fell into an epic gape. Liv's speech was melodic, and she had an accent I couldn't quite identify. As I tried to force my jaw closed, Michael said, "You must forgive *our* aura reader. She may look innocent, but her sense of humor isn't always appropriate."

"Hey," Liv said defensively, "I might as well be myself around these two. It's not like we can hide anything from each other, anyway!" She spread her arms out to her sides like wings.

I recognized her awkward attempt to create camaraderie and decided to play along. "Well, you're right about 'no tantric sex,'" I said. "I *am* in monk mode—for the next week, anyway."

"I was just kidding around." She scrunched up her face. "Sorry you're still on restrictions. We all had to go through that. I hope I didn't make you uncomfortable."

"Oh no, not at all," I reassured her.

Meanwhile, Vani held Michael in the tractor beam of her doe-like eyes. "And what is *your* gift, Michael?"

"Telepath," he said.

"Oh!" I resisted the urge to touch my telepath-blocking bracelet by playing with my pendant, instead. "That's really cool."

Michael pointed at my necklace. "I've never seen anything like that before."

"It's custom made. Kai—our medium—is also an artisan. The pendant protects me from picking up other people's negative energy."

"Very impressive." Michael's appreciation appeared genuine.

"Kai is coming early tomorrow morning, followed by the rest of our group," Vani added. "Is anyone else from your group coming up this week?"

"I think Skeet just needs the two of us for now," Michael said.

"Needs you for what?" I asked.

Michael and Liv exchanged an inscrutable look. Then Liv said, "Well, to show you what Team Forward is all about, for one thing."

"We do some *in vivo* training exercises when we come up here," Michael explained. "We get to practice our skills in real-life situations. I think Skeet wants you to see a demonstration of that—to watch us in action, as it were."

"In action?" Vani asked with a coy tilt of her head. "What kind of action?"

"It depends on who's here," he replied enigmatically. "All of the members of Team Forward rotate in and out to prevent burnout, and also to provide whatever special combination of skills Skeet may need. Skeet brings different parts of the team to Mercier at different times for different reasons. Sometimes there are as many as five of us here—an aura reader and a telepath, as well as a precog, an empath, and a medium."

"A kheir," Vani observed.

"Right," Michael said. "Actually, we have enough sensitives to form a few kheirs—even a couple of *double* kheirs at this point. Skeet tells us you have one, too. I know we're all still trying to figure out how the double kheir works, exactly, but isn't the concept cool? And the possibilities... But Skeet said we'll talk more about that when the rest of your group gets here."

So Skeet had set up these kheirs with what sounded like interchangeable parts—as though he was building some sort of machine. What was *that* about? Was it really just a way to prevent burnout, or was there some other reason? It seemed clear that Skeet was spoon-feeding us information, bit by bit, and there were few things that annoyed me more.

Vani and I exchanged a lightning-quick glance. I could tell that she had as many questions as I did, but judging from Michael's last statement, we weren't likely to get anything more out of the Dynamic Duo that evening—and if we pushed, we might raise suspicions.

"Yes, it's a wonderful opportunity to collaborate," Vani said smoothly. "Maybe even a historic one. Multiple double kheirs—no wonder Skeet wanted to bring us together. We can compare notes."

"And maybe even unlock the secrets together," Michael said. "Skeet is a visionary, for sure. I know he's hoping we can do some joint projects."

The last thing I wanted to do was get involved in any project even remotely related to Skeet, and it was hard work to pretend otherwise. Fortunately, Vani clocked my mood and deftly changed the subject. "That's why we're here, to discuss all of the possibilities. I, for one, am looking forward to it." She sealed her statement with another one of her signature smiles, which she directed at Liv. "So, Liv, you're from Dublin—South Side, maybe?" Vani asked.

"Most people can't guess that specifically!" Liv smiled. "And you're from London, I take it. Have you been to Dublin?"

"I haven't had the pleasure yet, but a good friend of mine at Oxford was from Foxrock."

"Oh, what was her name?"

As Vani and Liv got lost in conversation, Michael turned to me. "So, how long have you been at this empath thing? Before you joined the MacGregor Group, I mean."

I struggled to think of an appropriate response. "That's a hard question, actually. I mean, I was a psychotherapist before, and I kind of used my skills in that role without understanding what I was doing."

"I can see that. I bet it came in handy as a therapist, being able to pick up on what your patients were feeling."

"I don't know," I said. "A lot of therapists are very intuitive; I always figured most of us were good at that. The part that freaked me out was the empath healing stuff. I never told anyone I was doing it with my clients; I didn't even know how to explain it until I met the MacGregors. In my head, I used to call empathic submergence 'mind-melding.'" I rolled my eyes and smiled.

Michael squinted. "Empath *healing*?"

"Yeah," I said, surprised he wasn't familiar with the concept. "First, I use empathic submergence—entering someone else's consciousness through eye contact. Once inside, I locate the source of their emotional wounds and talk to them about it, hoping to gain some insight. Finally, I send them empath healing energy."

As far as I was concerned, my ability to submerge into others offer them healing was my most rewarding gift. It was also what the MacGregors wanted me to do with the clients at their clinic. But as I described the process, Michael looked at me like I was a small child offering him a mud pie—made of actual mud.

"Oh, I know what it is," he said. "I just didn't realize that's what you guys were into."

What the heck was he talking about? "Sorry if this is a stupid question," I said carefully. "I'm know I'm new to this, but aren't we all into the same things, more or less?"

Michael shrugged. "Figuring out what's really going on with people—we all do that—empaths, aura readers, and telepaths, at least. But the *healing* thing isn't a priority for everyone. In Team Forward, we use our gifts for other purposes, and since you all work with Skeet... But I shouldn't have assumed anything."

I began to feel disoriented. What did he mean, the whole "healing thing" wasn't a priority for everyone? I'd been led to believe that was what sensitives were all about. If not healing, then what was Skeet up to? I remembered what Lonzie and Clayton had said about "outsiders" coming to the lodge under cover of night, always when Skeet and some Team Forward members were in residence. What kind of world had we stepped into, exactly? I pulled myself together and went into information-gathering mode. "Well, our group may do things besides healing, but I wouldn't know yet. I just joined, after all, and I'm still in training," I admitted. "What other uses do our gifts have?"

"Oh, you'll see later this week," Michael said. "Like I said, we'll be giving you a demonstration. It's pretty cool, believe me."

"Great," I said, smiling to cover my disappointment that he hadn't really given me an answer. The strain of pretending started to wear on me. I tried to push down a wave of nausea.

"...and Cate," Vani said, finishing a sentence and smiling over at me. But when we made eye contact, she frowned. "We'd both love to stay longer. As you can see, we followed your instructions and came dressed to do some physical activity. But Cate has been suffering from insomnia lately, and I can see that she's fading. I promised Ben I'd get her to bed early if that happened." With great earnestness, she added, "I hope you don't mind."

"No, of course not." Liv looked at me and wrinkled her nose. "I can see the sleep problems in your aura, as well, Cate. During training, it's especially important to get enough rest." She bobbed her head to the side. "Don't worry, though! We have the rest of the week to get to know each other. We do yoga in the Sanctuary every morning after breakfast while we're here, usually around nine. Feel free to join us."

"We'll plan on it. And thanks for giving us a hint of what's coming up this week, Michael," Vani said. "It sounds quite intriguing."

"Well, *we* think it is. We'll tell you more about it later."

"Wonderful!" Vani's faux enthusiasm was so well executed that it was almost contagious.

We exchanged "Great to meet you!"s and goodbyes, then Vani ushered me out the door. Once in the hallway, she held her finger in front of her mouth in a "silence" gesture. We walked without speaking until we were back in my room. After closing the door, we both collapsed into armchairs by the fireplace. Free to talk, we were nonetheless speechless.

Finally, I ventured, "Tea and scones?"

Vani nodded. Gently, she asked, "Are you okay? You look a bit green."

"I feel a bit green," I acknowledged. "How about you?"

"Oh, I'm fine. And definitely intrigued—I overheard a bit of what Michael was saying to you." As I reached for the phone to order our late-night snack, she added, "I wonder what Ben is going to make of all of this."

• • •

ParaTrain Internship, Day Nine

I awakened early on Tuesday morning, around three thirty a.m., and couldn't get back to sleep. It was one of those mornings—all too common of late—when my thoughts marched through my head like a news ticker that I couldn't turn off. I tried meditating, counting sheep, singing myself lullabies, even asking my mother's spirit to somehow force me into a dream state, but nothing helped. I considered climbing into bed with Ben, but the night he was drugged had been an exception. He had since renewed his devotion to the program rules, advising that we stay in separate bedrooms. *Goddamned rules.*

I tossed on some clothes and wandered around the lodge a bit. But the combination of darkness, eerie quiet, and animal trophies on the walls drove me outside. Owen was watering the planters at the building's entrance. When asked why he was up so early, he said the water soaked in better if he gave it to the plants before the sun came up.

Owen asked me the same question, and I admitted I couldn't sleep. I mentioned offhandedly that I wished I were at the kennel playing with the puppies. That had been the first time in a long time that my mind had truly been at peace. Owen offered to drive me over to the kennel, explaining that while the rest of dogs would be on their way out to hunt, the puppies and Stella would still be around to give me some good canine company.

It occurred to me that by going to the kennel, I would be separating myself from Ben, which I'd promised not to do. But the puppies hardly posed a threat, and besides, I'd be back before Ben woke up. And I just couldn't face going back to my room, staring at the ceiling and waiting for sleep that never came. With only a slight twinge of guilt, I took Owen up on his offer.

As we drove to the kennel, I thought about the discussion Vani and I had with Ben and Pete before bed the previous night. We'd filled them in on our conversation with Liv and Michael. Since it had turned out that Michael was a telepath, we were all relieved that Kai had sent the bracelets ahead with Vani. But Ben's whole body became taut when Vani told us that in a preliminary scan of their auras, she had seen the energetic residue of recent drug use—something similar to Ecstasy, she guessed.

"I'd be willing to put down money that their drug use is part of Skeet's experiments trying to 'enhance their abilities,'" Ben grumbled.

Then Ben and Pete both went on high alert when we told them about the mysterious *in vivo* training exercises we were supposedly going to witness—which had nothing to do with healing, apparently—and about Skeet's double kheirs with interchangeable parts. "Sounds like he's workin' with military-style efficiency," Pete said. "I wonder what that's about."

Vani was particularly disturbed by Michael's declaration that healing wasn't a priority for Team Forward. She argued that while some sensitives chose to use their abilities for other things—most often, accruing money or power—the true purpose of our gifts was to heal humanity. "In essence, sensitives are spiritual beings," she said. "Those who turn their backs on that fact eventually become lost and twisted up inside. They usually end up self-destructing. I've seen it happen all too often."

I didn't yet share Vani's certainty about our nature and purpose in life. Still, we all agreed that the evidence seemed to indicate Skeet and Team Forward had headed down a dark path. The more we spoke, the quieter and more grim Pete and Ben became, exchanging meaningful looks and muttering to one another in Marine-speak. I wanted to question them about what they'd been up to and what they were thinking about what we'd told them. But every time I opened my mouth, I yawned. My recent poor sleep was catching up with me. After Ben assured us all that we'd sit down and talk through everything the next day when the rest of our crew arrived, I had decided to shelve my questions for the moment.

Now, I tried to push all of that drama and intrigue out of my mind and enjoy the fresh morning air as Owen and I headed across the property. On our tour the day before we had meandered, but it turned out that as the crow flew, the kennel wasn't far from the lodge. When we arrived, it was a busy scene. The Selbys and several guests were on their way out to go hunting with the father of the puppies. The Labradors had already gone with some other guests. Owen and I set a time for him to come pick me up and take me back to the lodge. The sun was barely kissing the horizon when I found myself on the couch in the kennel, petting Stella while her two pups climbed all over us.

The truth was, I just wanted to stay at the kennel with the dogs all day, and by the looks of things, the dogs felt the same way. Stella immediately melted into my lap and fell asleep, and the puppies appeared thrilled to have a visiting playmate. Eventually, though, they wore themselves out, too. I carefully shifted myself out from under Stella and put the sleeping pups back in their dog run.

I found myself at a loose end, since I wasn't expecting Owen for another half hour. As busy as I expected he was, I decided to walk back to the lodge, spending some time alone in nature and getting to know Mercier's land more intimately. Once I got back, I could have the front desk radio Owen and tell him that he didn't need to pick me up after all.

Fortunately, with the sun rising, I was able to get my bearings pretty easily. Outside the kennel was a field of grass a few inches taller than I was. I jumped up a few times and caught sight of the lodge and the field adjacent to the one I was in—a harvested cornfield. I would have loved to keep taking in the scenery, but I had to watch where I stepped to keep from turning my ankle on the rough ground. I stopped for a moment, closed my eyes, and inhaled deeply, enjoying the poignant scents of plants, earth, and marshy water. That's when I heard voices coming from the direction of the cornfield—two men speaking in low tones, and close by.

I was about to call out a greeting—if for no other reason than to make sure they knew I wasn't a deer or something—when I heard one of the men ask in a low southern drawl, "Did you hear something out there?"

There was something cold and menacing in the man's voice. Like some unseen hand pushing me downward, a deep instinct told me that it would be safer to conceal myself. Careful not to make any noise, I lowered myself into the grass until I was squatting on the ground.

"Yeah, it was old Joe's ghost," a second man said mockingly in a broad New Jersey accent. "No, I didn't hear anything—and we won't *see* anything, either, if you don't sit down and stop talking."

Old Joe's ghost. Was he talking about...? But I couldn't even think it. I forced myself to focus on keeping quiet and listening.

I heard an irritated sigh. "We never see any damn geese. We should have brought Selby with us."

"He put out corn and decoys," Jersey said. "They'll show eventually."

"Just don't try to call them again, for God's sake," said the Southerner. "You'll scare them off."

"I paid two hundred dollars for this damn goose call."

"It looks like a bong."

There was some low laughter. "How would *you* know?"

"Remember, I roomed with Skeet in college."

"That's right," Jersey said. "He probably doesn't even remember the seventies."

The Southerner chuckled. "I'll bet he *still* smokes. He uses all kinds of designer drugs on those so-called research subjects of his. You think he's not taking some of that stuff home?"

I clamped my hand over my mouth to silence a gasp. So our suspicions had been right; Skeet *was* still using risky drugs on his subjects.

"Not famous for his good judgment, our Skeet," Jersey replied.

"Yeah, like deciding to bring *her* here," the Southerner muttered.

Somehow, I knew that "her" meant me. A cold, slimy sensation wormed its way into my stomach.

"You don't believe she's on our side?"

"I don't know," the Southerner said. "Skeet's always overstating things. Besides, she's with that Marine."

"I heard he left the Corps."

"Come on; you know they never really leave. And Harris said he asked for our financials."

"Nothing unusual about that," Jersey said. "Could just be a sharp guy looking out for his girl. They'll get a nice, cleaned-up version, I'm sure. As long as they don't know what they're looking for, they won't find it," Jersey said. "Besides, Harris is on it. Now quit worrying until there's a reason."

"There's always a reason," came the Southerner's dry reply.

"You're paranoid. Skeet seems pretty sure of her."

"Well, this *was* her daddy's place," the Southerner acquiesced. "Blood's thicker than water."

"Good thing we kept Skeet in the dark, then," Jersey said. "He's never been good at keeping his mouth shut."

It sounded like the men must be co-owners of Mercier. What on earth could they be keeping from Skeet—and why? More secrets. I shuddered involuntarily.

"Quiet—I think they're coming."

I heard the men rustling around, then faint honking in the distance. I looked up to see a V-formation of Canada geese heading in our direction, dropping altitude as they dipped toward the cornfield. They rotated their wings and flapped, slowing as they approached. Knowing what was about to happen, everything in me longed to jump up, yell, and wave my arms, scaring them away. But I suspected that if I gave away my position—and what I'd overheard—the consequences could be dire.

The week before, my mother had come to me in a dream and told me that Ben and I were mated Canada geese in a past life. She said that I'd got goose-Ben killed when I flew into a suspicious-looking field and he'd come after me. She also told me that geese mate for life. I'd never been anti-hunting, but my mother's story had given me a new feeling of kinship with the geese, and it sickened me to think I was about to witness some of them losing their mates in the very next field—and at the hands of those shady-sounding men.

I balled myself up even more tightly, biting my sleeve to keep from making any noise and squeezing my eyes shut against the tears as a volley of shots tore through the air. My heart shattered like a dropped glass at the sound of alarmed, desperate honking and the rustle of birds flying away. Then came the hunters' hoots of victory. I heard the men scrambling out of wherever they had been hiding and charging through the field, presumably to retrieve the dead geese.

Finally, Jersey boasted that they were over their limit and declared that it was time to get back. It seemed to take forever for them to leave. My muscles burned, and I trembled with the effort to remain completely hidden. On top of that, everything I'd overheard was making my head pound. Finally, the men headed out. I waited until I hadn't heard a sound for a full five minutes before I forced my stiff body into a half-standing position, peering through the thin grasses. I saw no one. Ever so slowly, I rose up to my full height—then proceeded to bend over again as I lurched forward and vomited. I wasn't made for espionage, apparently—or goose hunting, for that matter.

I couldn't remember ever feeling so miserable in every possible way. I urgently needed to get back to my room, preferably unseen and unnoticed, so I could shower, get dressed, and generally pull myself together. I trudged through the field toward the lodge, trying to make sense of what I'd heard. Two things were certain: the secrets were flying thick and fast, and there was a lot more going on at Mercier than hunting and fishing. I was glad the rest of the MacGregor Group was arriving that morning. We were going to need all hands on deck.

Chapter Eleven

Any fantasies I'd had about quietly slipping back into the hotel were ruined when I emerged from the tall grasses and stepped onto the large circular driveway. Ben and Owen were standing on the lodge's front deck, scanning the horizon. Ben spotted me first. He barked something at Owen before he took off running, covering ground at a surprising clip as he headed in my direction.

Oh, hell, I thought. I had figured that if he woke up before I returned, Ben would've assumed that I was sleeping and left me alone, rather than checking on me. No such luck, evidently. I had no idea what I looked like, so I just tried to straighten my clothes and remove any large pieces of grass from my hair in the few seconds before Ben reached me.

"Cate!" he called out as he approached, his voice taut. I tried to smile so he'd know I was all right, but since I could feel my mouth twisting into some tortured expression, I gave up. All at once, Ben was there. His presence was like a wall of highly focused energy slamming into me. His hand lightly caressed my cheeks, my arms, while his sharp gaze evaluated the rest of me.

"I'm fine," I insisted. "I'm absolutely fine."

Ben's eyes met mine. The portal between us burst open, and a potent mixture of love and concern shot through it like a missile. "You don't look fine."

He spoke with the quiet intensity of a ticking bomb. I knew he meant that I looked *upset*, which was true. But I couldn't discuss that at the moment, since Owen was rapidly approaching in his Jeep. I looked myself up and down and muttered, "I'm just a little dirty."

Ben took firm hold of my hand. "You know what I mean."

Owen pulled up in his Jeep. He looked unreasonably happy to see me. "I went back to the kennel and you weren't there! What happened?"

I pulled a bright smile out of somewhere. "It's a nice morning. I just decided to walk back. It took longer than I thought, though. I'm sorry."

Ben let go of my hand. He began rubbing his forehead as though trying to release a band of tension.

"No problem. It is a nice morning," Owen said, scratching the back of his head. "A nice morning for hunting, too, though. You shouldn't go out walking around here until a little later in the day—especially not without a safety vest on." He jumped out of the Jeep and walked around to the back, rummaging until he produced a bright orange vest. He jogged back and handed it to me. "Here, you keep this one. Just in case."

"Right, of course. Thanks." I patted the vest. "I guess I should have thought of that."

"Yeah, well, all's well that ends well. Right, Ben?" But Owen's attempt to sound cheerful was clearly strained.

Ben gave a quick nod. "Can we get a ride back?"

"Sure! Hop in."

I felt a little ridiculous to be riding such a short distance, but my muscles ached so much that I didn't object. As soon as I sat down in the Jeep, my eyes closed of their own volition and my body groaned with relief.

When we reached the lodge, Ben walked me up to our floor with great care, as though I were an invalid—one arm around my back, the other holding my hand. I tried to hide the wave of sickness that hit me as we passed a stuffed Canada goose mounted on the wall. *Someone's lifelong mate*, I couldn't help thinking.

Once inside my room, I took Ben's hand and led him over to the bed. I sat down and gestured for him to do the same. "I have to tell you something," I said in a near-whisper. "Something that happened out there."

Every muscle in Ben's face was contorted with worry and

concentration. I could tell that he was fighting the urge to interrogate me about my well-being before anything else happened. Finally, he seemed to reach an internal compromise. "Okay, but first, you look like you need some water."

Hearing the word "water" made me realize how incredibly thirsty I was. "Okay."

Ben went into the bathroom, and I heard the tap running. He brought me a glass and took his seat next to me on the bed. I practically chugged the water and placed the glass on the bedside table.

"I *knew* something happened." He took one of my hands and began stroking the back of it with his thumb. "When you came out of the field, you looked distraught."

"I'm sure I must have." I rubbed my eyes. "Honestly, I don't even know where to start."

Brow furrowed, Ben suggested, "How about why you got up at four a.m. and ran off to visit the dogs—by yourself?"

I shook my head. "It wasn't like that. I was up; I couldn't sleep. It was driving me crazy, so I just started walking around the lodge. Then I ran into Owen. I told him I wished I were with the puppies, because they helped me relax. He offered to take me to the kennel."

The muscle in Ben's jaw was ticking double-time. "So you just decided to go. Didn't even leave a note."

He sort of had a point. "Okay, yes, a note might have been a good idea, in retrospect. But I expected to be back before anyone woke up. And a trip to the kennel seemed totally harmless."

Ben held his hand over his eyes, and I sensed he was trying to decide how to respond. "You had me worried."

I winced as the pain in his voice pricked my heart. "I know. I'm so sorry. I didn't mean to."

Ben took a deep breath and exhaled slowly. Finally, he dropped his hand from his face. "So did the puppies help you relax?"

Thank God, I thought, relieved that he had forgiven me, and that the conversation hadn't turned into an argument. "Yes, actually, they did. But then, when I was walking home, I heard voices nearby. I knew I should have announced my presence because there were hunters out, but I just…I can't explain it. It was like some invisible force pressed me to the ground and put its hand over my mouth. I felt *compelled.* No matter what my head was telling me, I *had* to follow that instinct."

Ben's eyes searched mine like he was sweeping a minefield. He gave my cheek one soft caress, as though reassuring himself that I was really there in front of him and that I was safe. "Okay, what happened next?"

I described everything I'd overheard to the best of my recollection, making several tries to be sure that I recounted the conversation between the two men as close to word-for-word as possible. As I spoke, a bone-deep chill settled into my body. And the more Ben heard, the darker his expression grew.

When I finished, he again pulled me to him, and I burrowed in. Although his muscles were hard with tension, he cradled me gently.

I could have stayed there forever, the two of us like nesting dolls sitting on a shelf, forgotten by the world. But after several moments, Ben let out a hard sigh. He pulled away from me just far enough that his eyes could meet mine.

"Okay then." He glanced around the room. "Let's get packing."

"What?" I asked, disoriented by the abrupt change of subject.

"I'm always packed, and so is Pete. Vani's accustomed to travel, I'm sure she can put her things together quickly. So I'll help you."

I followed his glance, a little embarrassed by the fact that the few things I'd brought were already scattered around the room. Then I gave my head a hard shake. "Wait—pack for what?"

"Well, we can't stay."

"Why not?"

He looked at me in disbelief. "Cate, what you just told me—it's not safe here."

"You mean because I wasn't wearing an orange vest?"

"No. Although yes, that was very unsafe, but that's not what I meant." He took my hands in his. "Judging from what you overheard, there's something sketchy about Mercier's financials—something big that they want to keep hidden—and your presence is perceived as a potential threat to their secrecy. Meanwhile, we have no idea who or what we're dealing with, and until we do, we can't protect ourselves."

I marveled at how quickly Ben had shifted into security mode. Yes, the hunters' conversation had creeped me out, but it seemed unreasonable to think that our actual *safety* might be at risk. At least I thought it did. Ben had worked pretty hard to convince me that even the drugging episode hadn't put him in any real danger. Then again, he had probably been minimizing that situation so that I wouldn't worry. I swallowed hard. "What exactly are you afraid might happen?"

"We don't know—and that's the point. We're in a remote location with water access and a lot of guns and ammunition lying around. Besides, we still don't know anything about the people who own and run this place, except that they work in D.C. That could mean nothing—or it could mean that you might be in danger."

"*I* might be in danger? *You're* the one who got drugged!"

Looking down, he pressed his lips together. "Probably to incapacitate me so you'd be left alone and vulnerable for a while. You're the one they have to win over here, Cate. If you accept your inheritance and become an owner—even better, if you convince the MacGregor Group to be part of Skeet's project—then your fellow owners won't care if we uncover whatever shady activities they're up to. You'd be an official member of the Mercier family by then, so exposing them would expose you, too. Who knows what kind of evidence they could manufacture to 'prove' that you'd been complicit in their activities? I'm sure they'd do their best to set it up so if they fell, you'd fall with them—and they know we would never do anything that might hurt you."

"Well, if they know *that*," I argued, "then why do you think I could be in danger?"

"Because they're not *going* to win you over, and at some point, they're going to figure that out. Once they do, given how much you already know, you could be viewed as a liability—and we simply don't know what they're capable of."

There was something in his voice—an unspoken thought. I was willing to bet it was the same thought I'd had, but hadn't had the courage to say aloud. "Ben, you don't think...my father's death?"

Instantly, his hand was cradling my cheek. "I have no more information than you have, but after what you heard this morning..." He folded one of my hands between his. "All I know is that we're dealing with some bad people here, and we don't know how bad. Until we do, we're safer in our house than in theirs."

"But wait a minute!" I stood up and began to walk back and forth, shaking my hands out. That week at Mercier might be my only chance to get the answers I needed about my father—and I strongly suspected that if we left, Ben would move heaven and earth to make sure that I never returned to the lodge. And Ben was right; it made sense that if Mercier was going to target anyone, it would be me—and only after they concluded that I wasn't going to go along with their shenanigans. I could live with that risk, as long as I was the only one in jeopardy. I focused on sounding calm and rational. "Look, I hear what you're saying, and I'm not dismissing your concerns. But if we leave now, how will we ever find out what's going on? If whatever they're doing is so secret, and they've managed to keep it hidden this long, I doubt we'll be able to uncover anything from a distance."

"That may be true," Ben said, "but on the scale of priorities, your safety far outweighs figuring out what these jokers are up to."

His expression hardened, and I could see that he was getting ready to dig his heels in. I had to think fast. "But what if my safety and what's going on at Mercier are related? Thanks to Joe, I'm tied to this place now. If the other owners come to see me as a threat, it's possible that I won't be safe anywhere! Like you said, we don't even know who these people *are*." I turned to face Ben, folding my arms across my chest. "If you're so hell-bent on keeping me safe, it seems to me that the best way to do that is to stick around long enough to figure out what's going on and who we're dealing with."

I was relieved to see that my argument gave him pause. Ben rubbed his jaw and regarded me intently. I could tell that he hadn't missed a trick. "You're right about one thing," he said. "I am hell-bent."

Oh for God's sake, I thought. At least he was considering. I just needed to give him a final push. "I want to find out exactly what happened to my father. And what about Skeet's research subjects? Their safety is important, too."

He raised an eyebrow, and I knew that my strategy had been seen through. Nonetheless, I managed to stand there, still and silent, as my argument hung in the air between us. Finally, his eyes softened a bit.

"All right, you win this one, Trouble." He gave me the grudging look of someone who had just been bested at poker. "We'll stay—for now. With new security protocols in place, which you will follow. Without exception."

I stepped forward and stood between his knees, smirking down at him. "I knew my 'win' would come with list of terms and conditions."

Ben's eyes flashed with amusement as he slid his hands around my waist. "And I'll tell you what they are after I consult with Pete. For now, though…" He shifted me to one side, then got up and walked over to the couch, producing a duffel bag. He pulled out a small, black cylinder that I recognized. It was a panic button like the one he'd given me when I was being stalked by a former client's ex-boyfriend. "The panic button is connected to my cell and Pete's," he said, placing it on the bedside table. "Keep it with you at all times." Then he produced something that looked like a misshapen electric can opener.

"What is *that*?"

"It's called a portable door jammer. Whenever you're here in your room by yourself, you can put this against the door and no one will be able to get in—not by using a key, and not by pushing. Here, I'll show you how to use it. It's easy."

Ben led me through the simple installation of the door jammer and watched me do it a few times to be sure I had the hang of it. "I want you to use this whenever you're alone in the room, okay?"

"Okay." A ball of nerves swirled around in my stomach. "I know you're not sure, but what do you suspect is going on with Mercier's financials?"

"I don't know, but we're going to find out. And I'm going to start by telling Danielle what you overheard. Since she works for the IRS, she's good at finding 'things that aren't there' in financial records."

"Okay. Good." My nerves calmed a little. Ben was in problem-solving mode, and Danielle was on the case. There was no way I wanted to sign any papers with Harris until I knew what the hell was going on. I stepped towards Ben, and as he took me in his arms, I closed my eyes. We stood there in silence for several moments. "Thank you," I said softly, my face pressed against his chest.

"For what?"

"For not telling me that I was an idiot for taking a walk with hunters all around and no orange vest on. Or telling me how miserable I make you whenever I make you worry."

"Cate," he scolded, "you could never be an idiot." He kissed the top of my head before carefully continuing, "Your natural spontaneity just takes over at times."

"My…natural spontaneity?" I marveled at his creative, diplomatic reframing of the phrase, "idiotic impulsivity." "You make that sound like it's a *good* thing."

"Oh, it can be." An unmistakable vein of carnal intent ran through his voice. "It depends on the situation."

My imagination sprang to life. It was all I could do in that moment to keep a lid on my "natural spontaneity." I bit my lip until I tasted blood.

"And you could never make me miserable. I guess I have to work harder to make that clear." He pulled away and looked down at me, taking my chin gently between his finger and thumb. "Any moment spent not knowing whether or not you're safe is hell on earth for me. But that's because you make my life more wonderful than I ever imagined it could be, *not* because you make me miserable."

"Oh." Ben's words nestled into my heart. If he kept saying things like that and looking at me like that… But before I could even attempt a transgression, the adrenaline roller coaster I'd been on for the past hour took a serious dive, and my energy crashed. Once again, I dropped my head against his chest.

Ben bent over me, his worry lines deepening. "Look, you need a break, and I need to talk to Pete about what you heard in the field. I'm not sure I'll get the details right, though. I'll tell you what." He led me over to the bed. "I think Pete and Vani are at breakfast. I'll join them, then take them to Pete's room for an overview. In a little while, I'll come and get you so you can give them the full version. And I'll bring up some breakfast for you. How does that sound?"

I looked down at my muddied, grass-sticking-out clothes. "Do you think I'll have time for a bath?"

"Sure."

Bath and breakfast sounded like the two most beautiful words I'd ever heard. "Coffee, too?"

Ben cracked a smile, and I saw that for the first time since he'd learned I was gone that morning, he was genuinely convinced that I was all right. "Of course, coffee."

"Sounds perfect."

"Good. I'll wait outside the door until you've locked the jammer in place."

I groaned. "Are you serious? You think someone is going to attack me in my room now, in the middle of breakfast?"

"You're right, that's very unlikely. Still—indulge me?"

I sighed. "Okay, under one condition."

"What is it?"

"This level of worry you carry with you all the time—it's not healthy." I spoke softly, sliding my hand into his. "Promise me again that when we get home, you'll let me help you with this overprotective streak of yours?"

The gold flecks in his eyes lit up like flares. As we looked into one another's eyes, the portal between us opened, and I was slapped by a surge of Ben's emotions—anger and irritation for the most part, but also elements of embarrassment and fear. After what seemed like hours, he said, "I object to the term 'overprotective.'

In this case, my level of caution is completely appropriate. But I did promise last week that I'd let you help me work through a few things, so yes. When we get home. I promise."

"Okay, then." Thinking it might be wise to lighten the mood, I smiled and said, "Now get out of here so I can show you my mad door-jamming skills."

Ben grinned as he let himself out. Before he closed the door behind him, he said through the gap, "If you need any help with your bath..."

"Go!" Laughing, I put the door jammer in place. "It's done, okay?"

Ben tried the door. Apparently my work satisfied him. "Okay. I'll be back soon."

"Bye!" I called after him, then immediately began shedding my clothes, anxious to immerse my aching body into some scalding hot water. I couldn't wait to replace the smell of wet marsh with vanilla bean bubble bath to forget the hunters just for a few minutes and lose myself in the intoxication of sensation.

• • •

I was bathed, dressed, and feeling more like my usual self when Ben came to get me. We all gathered in Pete's room, which was very similar to mine, but a bit larger to accommodate two.

Not only was Pete there, but Kai had also arrived. I tackle-hugged Kai, who squeezed me until I could feel my ribs rearranging themselves. When I asked where Vani was, Ben said they'd decided it would be safe for her to join Team Forward for yoga after breakfast, to see if she could glean any more information.

We sat in front of the fireplace. Kai took the space next to me on the couch. He grabbed my hand and patted the back of it. "You okay, baby?"

I smiled, grateful that I could always count on Kai to be sympathetic. "Yeah, I'm fine."

"Good, glad to hear it." Then Kai turned to Ben and said

sharply, "I hope you didn't invite me down here to *mind* her. I've got a wedding to plan, and I know what kind of chaos she creates!"

I snatched my hand away from Kai. "What the…? No one is *minding* me! And you're here because there are all kinds of crazy things going on, and we need you!" I peered at Ben. "Right?"

"Absolutely," Ben said without hesitation.

Kai turned a doubtful eye on me. "Well, forgive me for thinking you need to be put on a leash or something! What in God's name were you thinking, running around in a cornfield in the middle of hunting season? And in your *skivvies*, no less?"

"My *skivvies*?" The look I shot Ben was hotly accusatory. "What have you been telling him?"

Pete drew his hat down over his eyes, but it didn't hide the upturned curve of his mouth. "Ben told me what happened, then when Kai got here, I filled him in. I may have embellished a little."

"You don't say!" I glared at Pete, then at Ben. "And you didn't *correct* him?"

"I didn't think your wardrobe was the important part of the story. Besides, I brought them both up here so that you could tell them what happened yourself." Ben made a sweeping hand gesture. "Please, in your own words. And you can start with this morning's adventure. Vani already filled Kai in about your meeting with Team Forward last night."

They all looked at me expectantly, so I regaled an amused Pete and a horrified Kai with the details of my morning's hunting story as Ben paced the room, hands clasped behind his back.

When I finished, Pete gave a low whistle. "You mean to tell me…" He blew out a breath through puffed out cheeks. "You seriously mean to tell me they were shootin' over *bait*?"

I blinked. "What?"

"You said they put corn in the field."

"They said the guide had, yeah."

"Well, that's shootin' over bait, and it's illegal." Pete frowned resolutely.

I dropped my head into my hands. "Do you mean to tell me

that after everything I told you, the stand-out fact for you is that they were shooting over *bait*?"

Pete shrugged. "Well, it's just not very sportsmanlike, is all I'm sayin'. I mean, they're shootin' for fun, not survival."

I was gearing up to full-tilt incredulity when Ben jumped in. "Pete's right, and the fact that they hunt over bait tells us something about how they approach things."

"Yeah. They like to take shortcuts, and they don't fight fair," Pete said. "Put that together with the rest of it, and I'm not likin' what I'm hearin'."

"Pete and I will work on an action plan," Ben said. "I'll call my mother, as well, and get her take on the Skeet aspect of this. We'll reconvene when Eve and Asa get here."

"You got it, Big Dog," Pete said.

Kai jumped up, smiling brightly. "Cate, that means we have a few minutes of down time! Which is perfect, because I need to run some wedding stuff by you. Let's leave these boys to it and go to your room."

All I wanted to do was lie down for a few minutes in peace and solitude and try to pull my thoughts together. "I don't know, I'm really tired—"

"We're all tired, but I'm only getting married once." Kai snapped his fingers and grabbed a large leather tote. "Now, let's go. No arguing."

Pete stood and offered me his hand and a crooked smile. "Come on, sis, we all got jobs to do."

As we headed for the door, I cast a pleading glance over my shoulder at Ben, but he just smiled and waved. Evidently he only felt the need to protect me from certain things, and wedding planning wasn't one of them.

Chapter Twelve

"So we're going to do the whole thing on New Year's Eve at the American Visionary Arts Museum—you know, the AVAM, down by the Inner Harbor. I know a druid who can do the ceremony in the museum itself, followed by a dinner reception in their top floor restaurant, which is divine. We can also watch the fireworks from there. Afterwards, we'll send both sets of parents home and have an off-the-hook after-party on the *Spirit of Baltimore*. You're not afraid of boats, are you?"

"No…"

Delighted, Kai clapped his hands. "So what do you think?"

I shook my head slowly. "I think it sounds amazing, honestly. I'm just stunned! When did you *plan* all of that?"

"Well, if you must know…" He pursed his lips and glanced at the ceiling. "I sort of knew we would get engaged; it was just a matter of when. I have friends who work at the AVAM, and I know the guy in charge of booking the *Spirit*, so I put them on standby a while back. Then it was just a matter of making a few phone calls over the weekend, and voilà! The machine was set in motion."

"Wow, I'm impressed!" I wondered if Pete had been as surprised as I was by Kai's efficiency. "And the plan sounds beautiful. I mean it."

"I'm glad to hear that, because I wanted to ask—" he grabbed my hands— "would you be in our wedding party?"

"Really? Are you sure?" Then, not wanting to offend, I added quickly, "I only ask because we all haven't known each other that long…"

Kai dramatically rolled his eyes. "Don't be ridiculous. We've known each other through many lifetimes. We only just met in this one."

I knew he meant the "many lifetimes" thing literally. "Well in that case, of course, I'd be honored!"

"Excellent!" He gave my hands a squeeze. "We haven't had a chance to ask Ben yet, but it's not like he has a choice. We're counting on him to keep an eye on the Marines at the reception. Lord knows we don't need a repeat of the Fried Turkey Limousine Catastrophe of '09. But I digress." Kai grinned. "Oh, you two are going to look so delicious together! And I have a special job for you, too, if you're willing. I need someone to act as a buffer between my cousins Alexys and Petra. Otherwise, there will be a full-on catfight. And you have such a peaceful energy…"

I had to smile. People often said my presence was calming, but beneath the surface, I was usually a churning sea of anxiety. "No problem."

"Oh, thank you. I'm so happy!" He clapped again, and then pulled a notebook out of his tote. "Okay, here's your next job. I need your opinion. I've got my eye on this stunning Vera Wang gown—column-style, off the shoulder. But it might be a little much for the parents' generation if I wore *white*-white, given that Pete and I have been living together for years. So fortunately, it also comes in ecru, champagne, and ivory. What do you think?"

I stared hard at the collected swatches, but they all appeared to be the same color to me. "Um…" As I marveled at Kai's unique take on blending the traditional and the unconventional, I struggled to come up with an answer that would show I was treating his gown dilemma with the appropriate gravitas. "I guess…I'd have to see them *on* you?"

Kai nodded and, with a flourish, closed the notebook. "You are *so* right. It's all about what goes with my skin tone, and that is just too hard to judge in the abstract. I'll make an appointment to try these on. And we'll have you try on some potential dresses, of course." Then he added dryly, "As much as I'd like to force Alexys to wear something hideous, I would never do that to you, so don't worry. It'll be tasteful."

I smiled hesitantly. "Thank you."

Once those major decisions were made, Kai folded his long, lean frame onto the couch. "All right, give me the scoop. Did someone *really* drug Ben?"

"Oh god, yes—and it was awful!" I proceeded to fill Kai on everything that had happened over the past few days. Apparently, Ben and Pete had left out quite a few details. Kai said the two of them told stories "like they're reporting on a mission—just the facts, ma'am."

When I'd told him everything I could think of, Kai leaned back, his face a mask of cold anger. "So in other words, we're dealing with a rare class of bastards, here."

"Yeah." I sighed heavily. "So it would seem. You didn't have to come, you know."

"Please, as though I'd be anywhere else. Pete had to threaten to call off the wedding to keep me from coming down here with him the other night." Kai gave me a gentle smile. "We'll figure all of this out, don't you worry. In the meantime, though, you want to tell me how you're handling all of this?"

If he was referring to the chaos of emotions I was feeling about my father, my mother, Skeet, and everything that was going on at Mercier—and I was fairly sure that he was—then the answer was definitely no. "I'd really rather not talk about it—at least not right now."

Kai sighed and shook his head. "Ben said you would say that. Okay, honey. But whenever you're ready, I'm right here. Right across the hall. And it doesn't have to be me, but don't wait too long to talk to somebody. We don't want you to start having random anxiety attacks or something."

My indignation stirred. "*Ben* told you to talk to me?"

"Oh for goodness' sake, no. I asked if he'd talked to you about how you were coping, and he said he'd tried but you didn't want to talk about it, so I said I wondered if you'd talk to *me* about it, and he said, 'good luck with that.' So in this one unusual case, Ben is not to blame. I am, for being nosy. And I'm going to continue to be nosy, because I care about you. So deal with it." He punctuated his speech with a huff.

"Kai, I'm sorry..." The last thing I wanted was for Kai to be upset with me, but I was in no mood to open up, either. I closed my eyes and turned inward, commanding myself to appear calm and in control. Emotion had no place in figuring out what was going on at Mercier, who my father really was, and what had happened to him. "Thank you for caring so much, Kai. I care about you, too, and I will talk through everything, I promise. It's just that now's not the time."

"All right, fine. But I believe it's you therapists who are always saying, 'what you resist, persists.' It's not good to suppress your emotions—especially for an empath."

Vani had said the same thing. I was going to work on opening my heart chakra back up as soon as I got the opportunity, but we'd been a bit busy. "I agree. I'll try."

"Okay," he said, clearly doubtful. "As long as you know I've got your back. I need my wedding party to be in tip-top shape."

I started to laugh, but then covered it quickly by clearing my throat when I realized that Kai wasn't joking. I decided it was a good time to ask him for the one favor I really *did* need from him. "Listen, I don't know if this is appropriate to ask—I mean, maybe you just do it during rituals—but I was wondering, anyway..."

"Let me guess." He made a sweeping gesture towards my head. "Either you want me to finally help you put some shape on that mess of hair, or you want me to make a person-to-person call to your late parents."

I knew that my long, curly hair was always a bit rebellious, but I hadn't realized Kai thought it needed an intervention. That would have to wait, though. "The latter."

He slapped his thigh. "Just as I suspected. Well, your mother has been really reliable about coming through strongly in the past, and I felt her presence constantly for a while, but she's pulled back over the last couple of days. As for your father, I don't know. We'll have see what happens. But just so you know, the afterlife is a busy place. I don't know what they do up there exactly, but I *can* tell you that they're not sitting around on clouds playing harps and eating bonbons. So I can reach out to them, but I can't guarantee that they'll come through. Sometimes I try to open a connection to one person, and someone else entirely answers; you never know who it's going to be. Also, we'd need to find a place where we won't be interrupted."

Something electric snapped through me; I couldn't tell if it was excitement or fear. All I knew was that Kai had said yes. "Okay, I totally get that," I said, trying to downplay my sense of urgency. "It might not work, and that's fine. But I really appreciate your willingness to try."

"Of course." Kai smiled and patted my knee. "Let's run it by Ben and Pete when they get back and ask them to find us an appropriate venue."

"Umm, about that." I felt a strange possessiveness about my potential conversation with my parents. I didn't want to share it with anyone. "Can we keep this just between you and me? For now, I mean." I hoped my request wouldn't sound too strange.

He eyed me carefully. "You know I don't remember much of what's said when I'm talking to the other side. Are you sure you don't want someone else there as a witness? You'll probably be emotional; you might forget some things, or hear something wrong."

I considered. "Can I record it?"

Kai smirked. "No, dear. Whatever a spirit has to say to you is very personal. They have no desire to have their visits turned into podcasts. Except in very special circumstances, they won't come through if you've got a recording device. But I'm sure any one of us would be willing to be there with you—that is, if you don't want Ben for some reason that I couldn't possibly begin to understand, since that would make the most sense, *hello*."

I couldn't help smiling a little. "I'll think about it."

"Very good."

He held up his arm and adjusted the silver cuff around his

wrist. I realized for the first time that Kai wasn't wearing a leather bracelet like the rest of us. "Hey, thank you for the telepath-blocking jewelry, by the way! Why aren't you wearing any?"

"Oh, but I am," he said, holding out the cuff, which was embedded with small rocks and crystals. "I made this a long time ago, so it's a little bit fancier than y'all's, which I had to throw together in a hurry." His eyebrow pulsed upward. "You never know when you might have to guard your thoughts from intruders."

"Very wise. And the cuff is gorgeous."

We heard Pete's boots clomping down the hallway.

"Oh, well, playtime's over," Kai said, rising from the couch. "Let's see what the boys came up with."

It was all about to begin—ready or not.

• • •

Ben stood toward the bow of the boat. "Everybody ready to get started?"

The entire MacGregor Group was together again. Eve and Asa had arrived mid-morning. We were all crowded onto the skiff, sitting on the small benches that lined it, and we were twice our usual sizes thanks to the puffy life jackets Ben and Pete had insisted we wear. Kai gave Asa and Eve their telepath-blocking bracelets. Asa put his around the wrist opposite his hemp band. Then he held up his arms in an "X" formation, noting cheerfully that now, he could "block thoughts coming *and* going."

Pete manned the outboard motor in the back of the boat while Ben sat on a crate in the front. Having left Mercier Cove, we were slowly humming down Broad Creek. The boat had been scanned for listening devices, and there wasn't a building or another boat in sight, which was how Ben wanted it—total privacy for our meeting.

We started out by catching each other up on personal things, mainly on Kai's wedding planning and Asa and Eve's midterms. Asa's shaved head was covered with a fluorescent orange cap—evidence that he was much more aware of hunting zone safety than

I was. He and Eve were kidding around as usual, taking advantage of opportunities to splash water onto each other, and I felt a surge of gratitude that they had come. Their playfulness added a bit of cheer to an otherwise grim situation.

Then Ben launched into the briefing, filling the group in on everything we knew so far. Some of the information was even new to me. Ben said that after examining Mercier's past tax records, Danielle had noticed some discrepancies that weren't adding up. Multiple accounts in the Caribbean suggested possible money laundering, but she needed more time to figure out the details.

Pretending to be a novice hunter looking for experienced partners, Kai had turned to Owen for suggestions, and eventually got the names of the two hunters I'd nearly encountered that morning. Ben suspected that Mercier might be monitoring our phone and Internet activity, so to avoid being caught snooping around, he had asked his friend Max to research those two men first, then the other owners. Max learned that the man with the New Jersey accent was Paul Tucker, a long-time congressman from New York, and the Southerner was Bertie Hencock. He was from Northern Virginia and worked as a lobbyist for the country's largest defense contractors.

That news hit me harder than I expected. I clutched at the shoulder pads on my life jacket. "Are you telling me that I could have been shot by a *congressman*?"

Asa and Eve exchanged an alarmed look. "*Who* almost shot you?" Asa demanded.

"Wait a minute," Eve said, "I heard you were just running around naked in a field. Which, I mean, if that's your thing, that's cool. But there were *guns* involved?"

I lurched up to stand, but sat back down quickly when the boat rocked and everyone grasped at the sides. "I was not *naked*!" I lanced Pete with a sharp look, but he just shrugged.

"Well, you may as *well* have been naked, for all the protection you were wearing," Kai said. "Naked as the day you were born. And if a congressman shot you, you know they'd find a way to cover it up. The truth would go with you to the grave."

"Oh, for the love..." I threw my hands up. "Just forget I said anything. Ben, please proceed."

"Wait a minute, Cate," Ben said, prompting me to imagine pushing him overboard. "It is worth noting that we're dealing with formidable individuals. If the rest of your co-owners are heavy hitters like Tucker and Hencock, we need to find out who they are. If there's a congressman involved, that opens up a lot of new possibilities in terms of what these people could be into."

Ben had also spoken to his mother. Dr. MacGregor was shocked to learn that Skeet was giving his research subjects psychedelic drugs and that he might be involved in illegal financial dealings. She wanted to call and confront him, but Ben convinced her it would be counterproductive. He argued that she would be better off doing a little digging of her own—with great care, so as not to raise any suspicions. After all, we still didn't know yet what exactly was going on at Mercier or how deeply Skeet was involved. There was nothing to be gained by Dr. MacGregor damaging her friendship with Skeet and possibly losing his trust.

"All right, enough about Mercier," Kai said. "What about these sensitives of Skeet's? What are their names, again?"

"Michael and Liv," Vani said.

"Personally," Kai said, "I think whatever they're up to is much more interesting than money laundering. And they've alluded to some pretty juicy stuff they want to show us this week. I think we should get right on that, not let the grass grow."

"Agreed," Ben said. "I think it's best if the five of you are seen as mainly interested in learning what you can from Michael, Liv, and Skeet about their research and whatever they're doing here at the lodge—as well as getting in some R&R, which is why Skeet allegedly invited us in the first place. Make a point of taking part in some of the recreational activities around here. Just don't go too far afield, and don't do anything involving firearms or take any unnecessary risks."

"The spa is nice," Vani contributed.

"And Vani did yoga with Skeet's subjects this morning, which was a great idea," Ben said. "As for the rest of today, Skeet has invited us to have lunch with him so everyone can meet Michael and Liv. Then our group will convene for a conference call with my mother and the research team at the Smithsonian."

"Cool!" Asa exclaimed. "What about?"

"They have an update for us regarding our meeting last Saturday. Tomorrow, Skeet and his subjects want to give us the demonstration they've been talking about. Until then, have some fun, get to know everyone, try to pick up whatever you can. We'll likely need to bring all of your abilities into play at some point, but right now we're just in information-gathering mode. Got it?"

We all nodded. Ben paused and rubbed his jaw.

"What is it?" Pete asked.

"I don't know," Ben said, "I just have a feeling... My gut is telling me we should all be ready to pick up and leave at a moment's notice, so don't unpack completely. Which brings me to security."

All of us would carry the panic buttons that were connected to Ben and Pete's cell phones, and we were also to use the buddy system whenever we stepped outside of the lodge. If we went anywhere alone *inside* of the lodge, we were supposed to make sure another member of our group knew exactly where we were going, for what purpose, and for how long we'd be gone. Any suspicious activity we observed was to be immediately reported to Ben or Pete.

"Also," Pete said, "make sure you only order drinks that you can see are being poured for everyone from the same container, like coffee, or that can be ordered still in the bottle, like soda. I don't want to have to deal with any more drugged-up patients this week."

"Which brings us to Cate," Ben said, locking his eyes with mine. I sensed that I was about to get the list of terms and conditions I'd been expecting. "We have no reason to believe that you're in any danger right now, but as we've discussed, there are plenty of reasons why Skeet or others might want to isolate you in order to manipulate, influence, or pressure you in some way. Obviously, we can't have that, so you won't be going anywhere alone, even inside the lodge. I spoke to Skeet this morning; he's going to have a cot brought up to your room so that I can sleep in there with you."

Since we were far from alone, I refrained from commenting about how ridiculous it was that he had ordered a cot when I had a frigging king-sized bed. Instead, I asked, "And what reason did you give him for *that*?"

"I told him you've been having insomnia and that you have a history of sleepwalking," Ben said matter-of-factly. "Owen told him about the 'walk' you took through the field this morning, so Skeet very quickly saw the benefit of having someone keep an eye on you during prime hunting hours. Whatever else he might be up to, at least Skeet appears to share our interest in keeping you alive."

A hot blush bulldozed its way up my neck and blasted across my face. I thought briefly about dropping backwards off the side of the skiff and swimming back to the lodge. "All right, fine. I'm a sleepwalker now. Anything else I should know?"

Ben looked up into the distance for a moment, considering. Finally, he shook his head and said, "I think that about covers it."

Eve leaned over and murmured, "Sleepwalking? That's awesome. We can totally use that to go raid the kitchen at night—using the buddy system, of course." She grinned.

"Oh, yeah!" Asa's eyes lit up. "Vani said the food here rocks! We can totally sneak some midnight snacks."

Ben smiled and shook his head. "We'll meet twice a day in my room, after breakfast and dinner, but if anything happens in between, be sure to touch base. Any questions?"

There were none, so Pete turned the boat around. In ominous silence, we headed back in the direction of Mercier Cove.

Once we were docked and walking back towards the lodge, Pete made a point of falling in next to me. "Hey, sis, can I talk to you for a sec?"

I whispered, trying to conceal a sudden rush of excitement. "What is it? Do you have news from Captain Abbott?"

Pete grinned. "Yup. The package is available and will be delivered to Mercier this week."

"Here? This week?" My mouth dropped open. "Really? I mean, that's great, I just wasn't expecting it to happen so fast!"

"Yeah, well." Pete slid his fingers across the front brim of his cowboy hat. "As it turned out, the timing was good. Also, it would seem that Abbott's got a soft spot for you. Or for Ben. Either way, you'll have your hands full soon."

I felt a surge of anticipation, imagining what Ben's reaction to his surprise gift would be. "That's great, Pete. Thank you so much!" I threw my arms around his neck.

Pete tentatively patted me on the back. "No problem, sis. It's the least I can do for one of our *wedding wranglers*!" He said the last two words loudly as Kai approached, looking curious.

"Wedding wranglers? Really?" Kai scowled at Pete. "For your information, the members of our wedding party are our most honored guests. And you're not giving her extra work, are you? Because that girl is going to have *enough* to do!"

Then Kai launched into a monologue about what party favors he might give guests at the reception. Ben came over to see what the ruckus was all about, and I was grateful that Kai's single-minded obsession with wedding planning had shifted the focus away from my conversation with Pete. I didn't want anything to ruin my surprise.

CHAPTER THIRTEEN

The waitstaff had to push two tables together to accommodate our group when we joined Skeet, Michael, and Liv for lunch. Skeet had ordered a number of local specialties to welcome us, followed by huge slices of Smith Island cake. Each slice was a tower of ten thin layers, and we were all full to bursting by the time we finished.

The mood was relaxed and congenial. Still, by the end of the meal, it seemed to me that Skeet and company had extracted a lot more information about us than we had about them. They managed to appear friendly and open while keeping their cards close to the vest. Meanwhile, we were a pretty sincere bunch, and aside from Ben and Pete, unused to subterfuge. Not that we'd divulged anything we shouldn't, but it was obvious that everyone at the table had an agenda.

After lunch, Liv and Michael said they needed some study time to prepare for the demonstration they were going to give us the next day. Skeet said we could use the round meeting room for our conference call, which we told him was with Dr. MacGregor about clinic business. We all agreed to meet later for a game of paintball before dinner—with the exception of Skeet, who managed to duck out of it by playing the age card. Getting shot with high velocity balls of paint didn't exactly sound like my idea of a good time, so I tried to back out, too, with the excuse that I'd never played before. But after Asa and Eve basically shamed me into it and Kai promised to watch my back, my fate was sealed.

Ben came to join me as I lagged behind the rest of the group on the way to our conference call. "Look, Cate," he murmured, "I'm sorry if I made you uncomfortable on the boat earlier, singling out your safety as an issue. I wanted to run it by you first, but other things kept taking priority."

With chagrin, I said, "Like me running around naked in a field?"

His eyebrows slowly lifted. "If you ever want to do that, by the way, I'm all for it, as long as nobody's around but me."

I fake-punched him in the arm. "Thanks, good to know."

He slid his fingers up and down the inside of my forearm. A familiar tendril of heat wound its way through my body. "Seriously, though, I know this has been a lot for you to deal with," he said. "If you need to step out of the conference call, or take a break from any of this, or go home, anything—just tell me."

I knew I wouldn't. The rest of the group had accepted me without question, and seemed to be confident in my abilities. I didn't want to ruin any of that by appearing weak and unable to handle things. But I didn't want to give Ben anything else to worry about, either, so I said, "Okay, I will."

He tugged at my hand, pulling me to a stop. His eyes were penetrating as he looked down at me from beneath the dark ridge of his brow. The portal between us slid open, and his concern wound its way through to me. "I mean it, Cate," he said softly. "Bad things happen when you get overwhelmed."

I sighed; I couldn't argue with him there. After all, when we'd first met, my emotions had overwhelmed me to the point where I was practically a shut-in. "If I feel like things are getting to be too much, I'll let you know. I promise."

He stared at me a few seconds longer, and I had to resist the urge to squirm. I could see the memory of every promise I'd made to him and subsequently broken flash across his face. Finally, he brushed his lips across my temple. "All right, then."

We filed into the conference room. Those who were seeing it for the first time were duly impressed. Skeet had set us up with an octopus-like phone featuring a round module in the center of the table. Wires led from that module to small microphones sitting in front of each chair. Pete set up a "scrambler" device on a table near the window, while Asa clipped something on to the wire leading from the phone to the wall jack. "To keep the line from being tapped," he stage-whispered. Then the rest of us settled in as Asa showed Ben how to dial out and put us in conference call mode.

They answered on the first ring. We heard a chorus of "hellos," and the Smithsonian researchers did a roll call. We did, as well. Then Dr. MacGregor spoke. "We've been looking into all of the information you gave us on Saturday and your demonstration," She said. "We were struck by the similarities between the way Eve described Ben's role in the circle and the information we received from the Chinese team on Monday. They've been working on some tablets that refer to the palm of the hand, the center of the kheir, and they came up with a new translation: 'a steadfast heart,' or 'one with a steadfast heart.' That doesn't refer to a *paranormal* ability, but I think everyone who knows Ben will agree that that accurately describes my son. However, it also describes Pete, so we are left with more questions."

"Yes, it certainly fits you both," I said, reaching under the table and laying the back of my hand on Ben's thigh. He reached down and took my hand in his, intertwining our fingers.

"Dr. Byrne here. The word 'one' would seem to suggest a person, rather than a theory or a concept," Dr. Byrne said. "And if that person is 'with a steadfast heart,' that would be consistent with Eve's observation that the light came from Ben's heart chakra—the light that seemed to be 'charging' the rest of you, as she put it."

Eve grinned. "That's because he's the Energizer Benny!"

"The...what?" Dr. Morgan asked.

"Nothing!" Ben shot a warning glance around the table. "Sorry, side conversation. You were saying?"

Dr. Morgan continued. "If these interpretations are accurate, then Ben is the key to activating your double kheir. Of course, as Dr. MacGregor said, this raises more questions for us to answer, such as what is unique about Ben's 'steadfast heart.'"

"Yes," Dr. Singh chimed in. "As far as we know, there has never been another incidence of double kheir activation—at least not in the modern era. If we could find out what it is that makes you special, Ben, well—not to sound too dramatic, but it could lead to a sea change in the field of paranormal research."

Dr. Abera couldn't conceal the excitement in her voice. "It could save us decades of study—centuries, even! Having the means for sensitives to access their gifts fully and instantly..."

"Let's not get ahead of ourselves," Dr. Morgan said. "There are many more experiments to be run before we can draw any conclusions. In the meantime, MacGregor Group, have you had any additional insights?"

Ben looked around the room full of shaking heads. "Nothing here, I'm afraid."

"At any rate," Dr. MacGregor said, "I'm sure it's obvious that we'd love for you all to return and do some additional work with us. I know that you have your own work to do this week," she said discreetly, "but we hope you can pencil us in after your return."

"Absolutely," Ben said, and we all voiced our willingness. We all said our goodbyes. Then Ben nodded at Asa, who pushed a button on the center phone module.

We all sat in silence for a moment, taking in what had just happened. Finally, Vani mused, "Well, that seemed to go well."

"Yeah, that was super cool, Ben," Eve said. "The 'steadfast heart' part gave me chills."

Kai cocked an eyebrow. "Well, I know Pete's heart is steadfast. But the question remains: is Ben's heart steadfast *in general*, or just steadfast toward a certain empath with curves that won't quit?"

At that, everyone chuckled. As a blush worked its way up my neck and into my cheeks, I tried to kick Kai under the table, but it was so big that I couldn't quite reach him.

Ben squeezed my hand and deadpanned, "I guess we'll have to leave that question up to the experts."

Pete kicked back in his chair, pushed his cowboy hat up, and rubbed his hairline. "Well, Big Dog," he said to Ben, "good to hear you don't have any special powers, at least. I wouldn't want you to have an unfair advantage at paintball."

Ben broke into a half grin. "I don't need an unfair advantage to take you down."

"Oh lord," Kai moaned, "the trash talk's already starting. I'm going to take that to mean this meeting's over. I don't know about everybody else, but I need a coffee and another piece of that Smith Island cake before we go anywhere *near* paintball."

The mention of cake caught everyone's attention. As the rest of the group stood and filed towards the door, I pulled Ben back so that we could have some privacy. I slid my arms around his waist and pulled myself close to him. "That was pretty amazing stuff, Mr. Steadfast Heart," I said. "How does it feel to be the key to the whole thing?"

Ben sighed and kissed my forehead, then smiled. "It feels like we shouldn't jump to conclusions. It's all still theory, interpretation, and translation. And if it turns out that I am transmitting energy to the rest of you somehow, I think that Kai was right; it must be because of the way I feel about you."

Heat tingled in my cheeks. "That's very romantic, but it's not just *me* you have a heart for," I pointed out. "You love everyone in this group! I know you'd lay down your life for any one of them."

"As would Pete. Like Dr. Morgan said, we shouldn't get ahead of ourselves. I suspect further experiments will show that it's you and the others who are making things happen. There's nothing special about me, Cate."

With a surge of emotion, I squeezed him as tightly as I could, pressing my cheek against his chest. "Oh, Ben, there's so much!"

He held me in his arms for a moment, then pulled away, smiling down at me. "Well, there is one thing. I have you."

Clearly, he didn't want to discuss his profound role in the double kheir any further. But his romantic words made me want to push up onto my tiptoes and kiss the side of his neck—which I promptly did.

"So," Ben began, but his voice caught. He cleared his throat. "What *are* skivvies, exactly?"

I tried not to laugh. "You don't know?"

He shook his head.

"Well then, I'll just have to show you. When this damn internship is over, and I don't have to act like a nun anymore, I will show you." Then, in my best seductive voice, I added, "You'll like them, trust me."

"Oh really?" His scandalous tone sent shivers all the way to my toes.

"Yes," I whispered. "I even have some extra-special skivvies in mind."

It was true. There was a sweet-but-sexy purple lace chemise with matching lace-up panties that I'd bought on impulse one day from a department store clearance rack—then never worn, not even for Sid. The set had been a real find, since my curves were too copious to look good in most clothes off the rack, and I'd wanted to save it for a really special occasion—or person. The thought of wearing it for Ben had been flitting through my mind ever since we'd started dating. I would have Ben wait on my bed, then I'd go into the bathroom and change, unbraid my hair and fluff it out, maybe even put on some cat-eye make up…

And all it took was one sexy "Oh really?" from Ben to make my mind wander from all the worries we were facing to my stupid chemise. I closed my eyes in an attempt to bring myself back into the moment, but when I opened them again, Ben's expression was candidly ravenous. "You are very distracting," he said in a sensual rumble.

"Oh, please," I snapped. "Pot, kettle!"

"Tryin' to get out of paintball?" Pete called from just outside the doorway. "'Cause if you're scared I'm gonna kick your ass, that'd be totally understandable."

Ben gave me a smoldering "we'll finish this later" look, turning my knees to jelly. I clutched his arm for support as we walked toward the door.

"I'm ready," Ben called back at Pete. "Bring it."

"Oh good grief," I muttered to myself, knowing that for the next couple of hours, I was going to feel completely out of my element.

• • •

"Rule number one. Always wear your mask when you're on the field."

Randy, our paintball safety instructor, was a no-nonsense retired state trooper with a commanding presence. He towered over all of us, even Pete. We were standing in a line near the entrance to the paintball field, all trussed up in protective gear, with our facemasks pushed up on top of our heads. The only person missing was Vani, who'd beaten the rest of us to claiming that she had a headache and needed to rest. I was still kicking myself for not thinking of it first. Our paintball guns lay on a table in front of Randy.

"What's rule number one?" he asked.

"Always wear your mask when you're on the field," came our scattered mumbles.

Eve raised her hand. "What if the mask fogs up?"

"Double layer lenses," Randy said. "They won't fog."

Liv wrung her hands. "What if a bug crawls in it?"

"Hold your gun in the air, yell 'time out,' leave the field, and then you can take off your mask and remove the bug." He scanned the group. "Any more questions about rule number one?"

We all shook our heads.

"Rule number two. Always put your gun sock back on before you leave the field." He demonstrated how to slide the cover over the muzzle and secure it. "We don't want anybody outside the field getting shot. What's rule number two?"

There were mutterings about gun socks. That seemed to satisfy Randy.

"Okay. When I call your name, come up and get your gun. Ben, Pete, and Michael are paintball veterans, so they've already selected their weapons. For the rest of you, I chose what I thought would suit you best. All of the rifles have been looked over and tested for velocity, but I still want everybody to shoot off a couple of rounds on the test range before we begin. If you don't like your gun, we'll find you another one."

Before I knew it, I was toting a paintball rifle towards the shooting range. We all stood back and watched as Pete, Ben, and Michael took a few shots, and I was shocked to find that the rifles were rapid-firing and sounded like machine guns. Then Randy and our three experienced team members helped the rest of us figure out how to hold the guns, aim, and fire.

I normally would have enjoyed having Ben stand so close behind me, but the idea of paintball made me too nervous. I'd always been horrible at athletics—team sports in particular. Also, my hand-eye coordination had never been great, which I was pretty sure would make me useless at hitting a target. The first time I took a shot, the loud noise and the kickback from the gun made me scream and jump backwards, nearly knocking Ben over. He tried valiantly to conceal the doubt that flashed across his face and encouraged me to try again. Once I managed to get off a few shots without losing my balance or injuring Ben, Randy declared me ready for battle even though I still hadn't managed to hit any part of the target.

The paintball field was simply an area of the pine forest that had been cordoned off by white netting and fluorescent orange flags tied every ten feet or so to make it visible to hunters. Man-made obstacles of various types had been placed around the playing field, such as old farm equipment, tractor tires, and overturned workbenches. We were playing capture the flag, and a scarf with the Mercier logo was tied to a stake in the middle of the field, surrounded by twelve-foot mounds of earth.

I was on the Red Team with Ben, Kai, and Eve. Pete, Michael, Asa, and Liv made up the Blue Team. Randy led us to an opening in the netting, and as each of us walked through, he repeated, "Mask on, mask on…" One by one, we obeyed his instructions. Then he pointed the Blue Team to a shed that would be their home base, and led the rest of us across the field to another shed.

"Everybody remembers what to do if they're hit? How to surrender? How to give someone the option to surrender if they're at close range?" Randy quizzed us on all of the rules before leaving to give the Blue Team the same final exam. We sat around in the shed waiting for the air horn to blow, signaling the start of the game.

Ben leaned against the wall next to me. He bent down close and murmured, "If you're too nervous, you can always hang back from the action. But you never know, you might have fun if you give it half a chance."

I wished he could see the smirk beneath my mask. Just in case the shed was bugged, I whispered low. "I don't want to have fun. I want to figure out what the hell is going on here and go home."

"I know," he said, placing his lips close to my ear and speaking so softly I could barely hear. With care, he brushed the tail of my braid back from where it had fallen over my shoulder. "But this is part of it. Playing along, showing interest, building relationships and trust. All of these things will help us get the answers we're looking for as quickly as possible."

"I know." I sighed hard. Speaking in a normal tone again, I said, "It's just that I've never enjoyed this kind of thing. I never even liked shoot-'em-up video games."

Eve overheard me. "That's because you've never played with *me*!" she said gleefully. "We'll fix that when we get home."

Kai's reply was stern. "You'd better get your head in the game, Cate. If Pete gets to that flag before we do, we'll never hear the end of it."

"Okay, okay." Awkwardly, I adjusted all of my protective gear and hoisted my gun up against my shoulder. "I'll try to channel Princess Leia."

Ben's low chuckle melted me.

"Whatever does it for you," Kai said.

Then the air horn sounded.

"Gun socks off!" Ben barked. "Red Team, ready?"

"Ready!"

"Okay, let's go!"

The next few minutes were a blur as we rushed out of the shed, and I tried to remember the strategy Ben had laid out. I was supposed to stay a little ways behind Eve, who claimed to have "mad sniper capabilities," and to cover her as she picked off the opposition. But I soon lost her among the trees and found myself wandering around aimlessly while trying to get my bearings.

I heard a burst of intense gunfire to my right, so I headed that way, figuring that was where the action was. I felt ridiculous moving from tree to tree as Ben had instructed, knowing that I was about as stealthy as a rhinoceros in my protective gear and that very few of those pine trees were wide enough to conceal my bulk. There was more gunfire slightly off to my left, so I changed direction.

In the distance, I saw an old tractor that I recognized as being somewhere near the stake with the flag on it. I made my way over, then ran and crouched down behind the tractor, listening for voices, more gunfire—anything that would give me a clue as to where Eve was.

That was when I heard it. There was a single burst of gunfire, then a sharp shout followed by Ben letting flow a stream of curses I'd never heard him utter before. Without thinking, I dropped my gun and ran in the direction of his voice. "Ben!" I cried out.

"I'm hit!" Ben managed to spit out before resuming his blue streak.

Eve yelled, "Cate, what are you—"

Pow, pow, pow! Several forceful blows to my protective vest knocked me off balance. I fell onto a soft bed of pine needles. *Goddammit,* I thought as I scrambled back to my feet. "I'm hit, I'm hit!" I remembered to shout as I stumbled into a run, charging headlong toward Ben.

I found him sitting behind a round wooden tabletop that was partially buried in the ground. By the time I reached him, he had stopped cursing and was just moaning, holding the side of his head.

"Oh my god, what happened?" I crouched over him, trying to see what his hand was covering.

"I don't know," he growled. "Somebody shot me from behind."

Pete's voice grew quickly closer as he shouted, "Cease fire, cease fire!" I backed up as he leaned in to look at Ben. "Damn," he exclaimed. "We better get you off the field."

Ben must have been in pain, because he didn't object. Pete and

I helped him up, and it took him a moment to steady himself. Then, leaving our rifles behind, we walked towards the entrance, where Randy was holding the netting open for us. Once we were off the field, Ben pushed his mask up onto his forehead; we could see he was wincing in pain. Meanwhile, Pete and I removed our masks completely as we all headed toward the paintball headquarters. Randy stayed behind and gave some instructions to the remaining players, then followed us.

Pete led Ben to a stool while Randy retrieved the first aid kit. When Pete explained that he'd been a medic in the Corps, Randy let him take over. I'd never seen Ben snarl before, but he was none too pleased at the idea of letting Pete look at his injury, insisting he was fine and didn't need any "nursing." Pete cleverly appealed to Ben's protective side, instructing him to look at how worried I was. I must have looked pretty bad, because Ben's objections immediately softened.

"Now, the only way we're gonna get the color back in Cate's face is if you let me at least look at your damn thick head," Pete said, then threw me a forceful glance. "Am I right?"

Obediently, I nodded. "Please let him look at it, Ben."

Expressions of pain and irritation creased Ben's face in equal measure. Slowly, he removed his hand from his head. Pete was standing in my line of vision, so I couldn't see what was wrong, but I saw how gingerly he removed Ben's mask. Someone had shot him just below and behind the ear—right where the protection of the facemask ended.

There was some cotton, some alcohol, and more cursing, although Ben tried to keep it under his breath that time. Finally, Pete gave the verdict. "I'll give you a more thorough once-over when we get back to the lodge, but you're gonna live. You'll have one hell of a goose egg, though."

Suddenly, the door to the shed swung open and three men in EMT uniforms burst in. "Medics," their point man shouted as they all rushed towards Ben.

But before they could reach him, Pete and I both had placed

ourselves between the door and where Ben was sitting. I was just stunned and wanted to find out who they were, but I could feel aggressive energy radiating from Pete. Still, his voice was calm as he said, "Hello, there. Can we help you?"

The medics looked at Pete, then at each other, appearing confused. Their point man said, "We're here to help you. We heard there was an injury."

"I'm fine," Ben called out. "How did you get here so fast?"

"There's a clinic on the premises," Point Man said. "Someone here pushed the emergency button. We move pretty fast. We brought a stretcher," he said, gesturing to the other two men who carried it forward. "We can get you back there in no time, check you out."

Pete held up his hand. "Don't worry, we got this. I'm a medic, too, and I've looked him over. He'll be fine."

Point Man craned his neck, trying to look beyond Pete and me at Ben. "I'm afraid we have to take him in for an exam—Mercier policy."

Pete clearly didn't want these other guys to get their hands on Ben. I wasn't sure why, but I did what I could to back him up. "Well, I'm one of the owners," I said, "and I'm giving you permission to waive that policy this time." I smiled and put my hand on Pete's arm. "Pete here is a highly trained Marine Corps medic. I have every confidence in his decisions."

Point Man scowled at me. "Nice to meet you, ma'am, but you must be new here if nobody's explained to you yet that the policy can't be waived."

Randy came around from behind Ben, where he had been conspicuously silent up to that point. "Look, guys," he said, "if anyone comes down on you, just send them to me. I'll take the heat."

The medics consulted with one another briefly. "All right, Randy," Point Man said, "if you say so. I hope your man there is okay."

"He'll be fine, thank you," Pete called after them as they turned and left the shed.

Once they were gone, Ben said, "Thanks, Randy. I hate medical exams—even from this one," he said, pointing his thumb at Pete. "Two in one day would have been too much."

Randy chuckled. "No problem—and I feel the same way."

"Yeah, thanks," Pete said. "They were persistent."

"They were just doing their jobs," Randy said. "Someone on the field must have hit the emergency button."

"They didn't seem impressed by my 'I'm an owner' speech," I observed.

"No offense, but if they said that they waived policy because the pretty new owner told them to, it wouldn't impress anybody," Randy said, grinning. "What they really needed was a blame hound."

"Oh, I see," I said. "So once you offered yourself up, they felt free to go."

"Well, if anyone tries to come down on *you* over this," Ben said, "you send them to me and Pete, okay?"

Randy nodded. "Got it."

Ben sucked in air and held his hand to his head as a fresh flash of pain hit.

"The shot got you right behind the ear," Pete said. "It's already swellin' up, so whoever hit you must've been close. Did you see who it was?"

"No," Ben grumbled.

"Well, I'm sure they're feelin' pretty bad about it right about now," Pete said, gripping Ben's shoulder and giving Randy a reassuring smile.

"That's right," Ben said, pulling himself together enough to realize what Pete was doing. "Accidents happen. I'm just glad you're here, Pete, so at least I know *you* won't capture the flag."

Randy, who had been visibly tense since the incident, finally began to look more at ease. "You sure you're all right, Ben?"

"Oh, yeah," he said. "I just got soft, being out of the Marines for too long."

"Soft is right," Pete cajoled, "but your head's as hard as ever."

The three of us forced a laugh, and Randy relaxed a bit more. "I should probably go check and see how the game's going."

"Yeah," Pete said. "Make sure Kai hasn't got everybody hogtied. He gets a little carried away."

Randy gave us the thumbs-up. "Good to know. Feel free to wait here until the game is over, or you can take one of the ATVs back to the lodge."

"Probably the latter," Ben said. "We'll see you later. Thanks for everything, Randy." He stood up, and they shook hands. "It's been a great afternoon."

"Even with the goose egg?" Randy asked.

"Sure," Ben said with a smile. "Reminds me that I'm alive!"

Randy said his goodbyes to Pete and me and headed out. Then we turned back to Ben, who listed slightly to one side. Pete and I each grabbed one of his arms.

"Okay, Big Dog," Pete said, "Let's get you back to the lodge so I can check you out properly."

Chapter Fourteen

We took Ben to my room, where Pete gave him a thorough medical examination. He declared that Ben was all right, but told me not to let him fall asleep for a while and said he'd come back and check on him periodically. The bump on Ben's head was large and angry-looking, but visible only when his hair was smoothed back. That was a relief to Ben, who didn't want anyone worrying about him—including Pete and me, but that ship had sailed. After the crisis had passed, I asked Pete why he had been so dead set on keeping Mercier's medics away from Ben.

"Somethin' was off," Pete grumbled. "They got there too fast, first of all. And they brought a stretcher into the shed before they even checked Ben out to see how bad it was. Then they tried to steamroll me…" He pushed his hat back and rubbed his hairline. "Maybe Randy's right, and they were just doin' their jobs, but my gut told me somethin' wasn't right."

"They got there too fast?" I asked, my nerves set on edge. "You mean, you think they were waiting—like they knew ahead of time that Ben was going to be injured?"

Pete pushed his hat back into place. "Well, unless the clinic's right next door to the paintball field, it sure looks suspicious."

"It isn't," Ben said. "I remember seeing the clinic while we were on our tour—a small, white building with a red cross on the roof. It's on the far side of the property."

"But why would they do something like that?" I jumped up and began pacing the room. "What would they have to gain by hurting you?"

"Cate, it's okay," Ben said. "It's just like when I was drugged.

Their objective seems to be to put me out of commission or get me out of the way for a while. It looks like they're trying to isolate you, probably so they can talk to you alone, try to manipulate you somehow. But just like before, no harm was actually done. I'm fine."

He wasn't fine, though. He was hurt, no matter how minor the injury. And he'd been drugged into unconsciousness, even if he'd only needed to sleep it off. "But I thought—" I covered my hands with my face.

"You thought what?" Ben asked.

I sat down on the edge of the bed next to where Ben was lying and rested my hand on his leg. "Back at the bed-and-breakfast, you said that *my* safety might be a concern. I never would have come, if I thought you or anybody else..." Tears choked off my words.

Pete headed out the door. "I'll give you two a minute."

Ben pushed himself up on his elbows. "So, what you're saying is, you get to put yourself at risk, but no one else does?"

"Basically, yes." I pulled my hand back into my lap and looked down. "Well, not on my behalf, anyway."

"I see," he said somberly. "Well, in that case, we may have a serious dilemma, because I'm in love with you, so I reserve the right to do whatever's necessary to protect you—including putting myself at risk."

My head snapped around. "No one is putting themselves at risk *anymore*, is that understood?"

I must have spoken more loudly than I'd intended, because Ben grimaced. "Believe me, I'd prefer that, as well. But sooner or later, you're going to have to come to terms with the fact that you're dating *me*. And you know how hard-headed I am." He pointed to the swelling on his head and grinned.

"That's not funny."

"Humor an injured man."

"Oh for God's sake." He had managed to wheedle a smile out of me. "I'd better bring Pete back in here before he starts thinking we're canoodling."

After a while, Ben was a little steadier on his feet. We were able to meet the others in the lobby upon their return to the lodge. Given everything that had happened, it brought us great satisfaction to hear that Eve captured the flag for the Red Team, even with two of us gone. Apparently, Kai had proven to be a formidable opponent. While that came as no surprise to anyone in the MacGregor Group, Michael and Liv hadn't been expecting Kai to be much of a challenge since it was his first time playing. That gave Kai and Eve a tactical advantage, and they were congratulated by winners and losers alike on their unexpected victory.

As for the question of who had shot Ben, no one fessed up. Publicly, Ben showed no surprise about that, saying that it must have been a stray paintball, it happened all the time, it was hard to keep track with those rapid-fire guns, et cetera. Pete played along, so by the time we all parted ways, it was with warmth and high spirits.

Once back in my room, however, Pete and Ben discussed in low tones how it was impossible that someone had shot him in the head at close range without realizing it, particularly since he had immediately started shouting and cursing. They couldn't be sure who had done it, but Pete said that given where everyone had been positioned, his money was on Michael. Ben was inclined to agree, but they stopped discussing it when room service arrived—dinner for Ben and me, and a note from Skeet sending Ben good wishes and saying he hoped we'd be able to join the rest of them downstairs for breakfast. Ben bristled at Skeet's presumptuousness, since Ben had been planning to have dinner in the dining room so he could show everyone how "fine" he was. But Pete pointed out that it would be rude to let the room service meal go to waste—then gently added that as a medic, he recommended Ben stay in the room for the rest of the night, "just to be safe, no point getting yourself worked up." Pete said he'd come back later to check on Ben again, and to let us know when it was safe for him to go to sleep for the night. Until then, if Ben fell asleep, I'd have to wake him periodically to make sure his symptoms hadn't worsened.

Once we were alone in the room, our tension slowly began to

ebb. I pulled the room service cart over to the mini-living room and convinced Ben to have some dinner.

Skeet certainly hadn't spared any expense. It was surf and turf with filet mignon, crab cakes, and scallops, not to mention an assortment of vegetables and breads with two kinds of soup. After about ten minutes, Ben started to look a little better, relaxing and giving me a genuine smile. "He may be crooked, but I've got to give it to Skeet—he knows good food."

My shoulders dropped with relief, and I smiled back. "He does, that."

We finished the meal mostly in silence, only talking to request the butter or salt. I guessed that neither of us wanted to talk about the immediate concern, which was Ben's injury. After dinner, Ben managed to get up off the couch without any assistance. I wasn't sure if it would help or hurt for me to say it, but I couldn't stop myself. I went over and took him by the hands, gave him the brightest smile I could muster, and said, "I'm glad you're okay."

Ben's expression softened, and he pulled me into a tight embrace. I slid my arms around his waist and squeezed, needing to feel his body against mine like I'd need water in the desert.

I could have stood there like that forever, but I remembered that Pete had wanted Ben to rest. "I'm kind of worn out after that meal," I said. "What do you say we go over to the bed and play cards?"

I should have known Ben would immediately grasp the real motive behind my suggestion. "I'm okay, Cate. Really. But if it will make you feel better if I lie down, and you want to play cards, *and* you don't mind losing—then I'm game."

The daring grin he gave me made me want to throw him down on the bed and kiss him until all of our clothes came off. It also inspired an overwhelming urge in me to find whoever had shot him and mete out some kind of draconian justice.

Even though I picked Rummy 500, my best card game, Ben made good on his promise. I was just starting to get tired of losing all the time when there was a knock at the door. Pete led the rest of the MacGregor Group into the room for our nightly meeting.

First, there was a lot of teasing about the paintball game. Kai and Eve gloated shamelessly, and Pete accused Ben of getting injured on purpose to distract the Blue Team and secure a pity win for the Reds. Everyone wanted to see the bump on Ben's head. He reluctantly complied, which led to much ribbing of Vani for claiming earlier that *she'd* had a headache (which had magically disappeared right before dinner). When we ran out of things to say, everyone settled into a seat. Clearly unused to being fussed over, Ben awkwardly thanked everyone for their concern, reassuring us that he was fine.

Meanwhile, Pete told us about a call he'd received from Max with more information on Congressman Paul Tucker and Mr. Bertie Hencock. Apparently, both men were Washington fixtures known for quietly making deals while keeping out of the spotlight and away from scandals. Max had also found out about Mercier's other owners. They were all movers and shakers of various types, headquartered in the D.C. area. Congressman Tucker was on the Ways and Means Committee, and they had a Senator on the Foreign Relations Committee. There was also a high-powered lobbyist for the IT industry, someone at the Federal Reserve, the owner of a private security firm staffed by former military, and two think tank types who were connected to politically oriented private foundations. All had indeed been members of the same fraternity in college, and Tucker had been their president. But according to Max, it wasn't an officially recognized fraternity—more of a secret society that had since been banned from campus for reasons unknown.

After Pete finished, Eve cleared her throat. "So, while we're sharing information, I don't know if this means anything or not, but while Asa was talking to the front desk, I saw Michael duck into the nook of one of those wide hallways. I followed him and hid behind a tree-pillar. Then another man joined him, and I heard Michael call the man 'Hencock.' They started talking really low. Eventually they shook hands and took off in opposite directions."

We discussed the possibilities. It seemed odd that Michael and Hencock would be so familiar with one another. On the other hand, if they'd both spent a lot of time at the lodge, maybe they'd become friends. But since Hencock had spoken derisively about Skeet's "so-called research subjects" when I'd overheard him in the field, I didn't imagine he held Michael in very high regard. Hencock had also expressed concern about Ben being at the lodge. And what was the handshake for? Had Hencock put Michael up to shooting Ben with the paintball?

"Whatever the answer to that question may be," Ben said, "in light of the paintball incident today, let me be clear: anyone who wants to leave—now, or at anytime, for any reason—has my blessing. No questions asked."

There was absolute silence. Eve and Asa looked off into the distance as Vani contemplated her fingernails.

"I can't say for sure," Pete said in his slow drawl, "but I think that means they're stayin'."

I could see from Ben's clenched jaw that it was taking a great deal of effort for him to refrain from ordering everyone to go home immediately. "Okay, then. As long as we're here, we stick to our safety protocol. No exceptions."

With those two final words, Ben gave me a meaningful look. I suppressed a smirk.

"Thanks, everybody," Ben said. "I know this situation is strange…"

Asa guffawed. "Please, we're used to strange. We were *born* strange."

At that, everyone smiled, if uneasily.

"Well, I still appreciate your willingness to help out. Tomorrow we'll see this demonstration by Team Forward. That should answer a lot of our questions. In the meantime, get some rest."

As everyone said their goodnights and filed out the door, I saw Ben pull Kai aside. Their expressions were grim as they exchanged a few words. Then everyone was gone, leaving Ben and me alone in my room again—this time with the addition of a cot and his bags. Ben sat on the couch and gingerly touched the swelling on his head.

I sat on the chair nearest to him. "You okay?"

"Hmm? Oh yeah, I'm fine. Just tired." He forced a smile. "Pete finally gave me the okay to go to sleep for the night, though, so—problem solved."

"Good." I tried to smile back. "I'm impressed that you're letting everyone stay."

"That's because I'm experimenting."

"With what?"

He took my hand in his. "With that thing you wanted me to try—what was it? Letting people take more responsibility for themselves, instead of taking everything on myself?"

A rush of warmth melted my insides. I'd thought those words had fallen on deaf ears. But Ben had listened to me; he was even trying something new at my suggestion. "I'm impressed. You've assembled a pretty incredible group of people, here. They won't disappoint you."

"Well, don't get too excited. If the experiment goes badly, I'm going right back to the way I'm used to doing things."

"It won't go badly." I squeezed his hand. "What were you talking to Kai about, anyway?"

"In case things go sideways, I want him to be ready to take Vani, Eve, and Asa out of here at a moment's notice."

So Ben hadn't fully abandoned his way of doing things, after all. "I bet he wasn't happy about that. I imagine he wouldn't want to leave Pete."

"No, but he understood. He wants to keep those three safe, and they listen to him. He knows Pete can take care of himself."

"What about me?" I asked, surprised that Ben hadn't included me in the list of Kai's potential evacuees.

"If you're in danger, *I'll* get you out of here."

I smirked. "You trust Kai to take care of the others, but not me?"

"I trust Kai to take care of you," he said matter-of-factly. "But I can't be sure you'd go along with Kai without giving him any problems, and that could cause dangerous delays."

Well, hell, I thought. That didn't sound very complimentary, but he was probably right. I wouldn't go willingly with Kai if it meant leaving Ben behind. Kai might trust Pete to take care of himself, and intellectually I knew that Ben could do the same. But my heart… well, that was another matter. "I'm glad you realize I'm not going anywhere without you."

Ben gave me a wry half-smile. "I did pick up on that, yes." Then he began to tug at the corner of his shirt. "I'm beat, Cate. I hope you don't mind if I just hit the sack."

"No, of course not." I'd never seen Ben look so worn out. There were dark circles under his eyes, and his shoulders slumped. I tried to busy myself, getting a few things out of my bags, so I wouldn't stare as Ben stripped down to his boxers.

He lay sideways on the cot and faced the wall. "Goodnight, Cate," he murmured.

"Wait," I objected, "you should take the bed! I'll take the cot."

"I'm already asleep," he murmured.

"But Ben—"

He made a loud, fake snoring sound.

"Fine," I said with a heavy sigh. "Goodnight."

Even though I knew he wouldn't turn around and look, I was gripped by a sudden sense of propriety. I grabbed my pajamas and went into the bathroom to change.

Chapter Fifteen

In my dream, Mom and I were on the Delaware beach, enjoying the mid-morning sun. We lay on towels under our umbrella with a cooler of sodas and a box of saltwater taffy positioned between us. Both of us wore sunglasses and were reading books in our bathing suits, trying to absorb as much vitamin D as possible without burning. It was just warm enough that we felt sun-kissed, but a nice breeze kept the heat from becoming sweltering. It must have been a weekday, because there weren't many other people there, just some couples walking along the sand and a few kids squealing as they jumped in and out of the foam left behind by the waves.

Out of the corner of my eye, I noticed a group of three men who looked to be in their mid-twenties kicking a soccer ball down the beach. They were athletic and tanned, as though they'd spent the whole summer doing nothing else. They stopped in front of the spot where my mother and I were sunbathing and formed a triangle, making a game of trying to keep the ball from touching the ground.

"I think they're trying to impress you," Mom murmured.

"How do you know they're not trying to impress *you*?" I countered. My mother was older than they were, but she had a natural beauty that had only deepened with time.

"Please, Miss Monroe," she teased, "with *your* figure, I'm surprised they're able to concentrate on their game at all."

"When was the last time you had your eyes checked?" I asked dryly.

Mom laughed, and the sound was light and musical. "Cheeky. You're gorgeous and you know it."

I most certainly did *not* know it. I'd never felt completely comfortable in my body, which stayed soft no matter how hard I worked to tone it up.

"Ben certainly can't keep his eyes off of you—or his hands, from what I've seen. He's always finding some excuse to hold your hand or put his arm around your waist."

Oh, I thought, *so this isn't just an ordinary dream. Mom's spirit is visiting me in the present—otherwise she wouldn't have mentioned Ben.* I said a silent prayer of gratitude. Maybe I could ask her some questions.

"So, Mom," I asked, trying to sound casual. "How does this double kheir thing work, anyway?"

She reached over and slapped me lightly on the arm, laughing again. "You know I can't do your homework for you. There are some things you have to figure out yourselves. Otherwise, there would be no mystery, no challenge!"

Clearly I wasn't going to get any help from her. I was gearing up to ask about my father when we heard a frantic scream. The soccer players froze for a second. Then all three of them ran at full speed toward the ocean. Mom and I scrambled to our feet as the men ran and leapt through the waves until they reached a woman. She cried out desperately as she plunged her arms down into the water, over and over again.

The scene seemed to play out in slow motion. We watched as the men dove down into the water a few times. Finally, one of them came back up, holding a listless child in his arms. The whole group rushed as quickly as they could back to the beach, and the man laid the child down on his back. We went over to see what was happening. The child looked to be about six, and he didn't appear to be breathing.

Whistles blew shrilly. A lifeguard arrived. He checked the child for a pulse, tilted his head back, and swept his mouth with a finger before starting CPR. I became aware that my whole body was trembling when I felt Mom's arms around me. Tears flowed down both of our faces, as well as those of many who had gathered.

We stood in silence as the lifeguard did his work, and two more lifeguards arrived to assist. It felt like whole hours were crawling by, days, months… Finally, the child coughed violently, expelling an impossible volume of water as the lifeguards turned him on his side. The mother wailed, and two of the soccer players held onto her, lowering her gently to her knees. After a few moments, the child was sitting up, nodding and shaking his head in answer to their questions as his mother wrapped herself around him. Those of us who had gathered around sighed in relief as though we were one being, physically connected to this boy and his mother. The lifeguards spoke to the mother as they wrapped the boy in blankets. Then they had him lie down on the stretcher they'd brought.

My mother and I clung to each other—both still crying, me still trembling. The beach scene began to swirl around us as though we were standing in the middle of a turntable, and everyone else was on the surface of a vinyl record that began spinning faster and faster. "It's okay," Mom whispered. "He'll be okay."

All at once, my vision went black, and the dream was gone—the beach, the people—Mom. All gone. My eyes flew open, and I found that I was sitting bolt upright in my bed at the lodge, drenched in perspiration. I touched my cheeks; they were soaked with tears. *What in the heck kind of dream was that?* I immediately thought, *Is Ben okay?* Was the dream some kind of warning? Was his head injury worse than Pete had thought?

My heart kicked against my chest like someone buried alive trying to break out of their coffin. As quickly and quietly as I could, I scrambled out of the bed and stepped close to Ben's cot. He was lying on his back. I watched his chest to see if it was rising and falling with breath, but the room was too dark. I couldn't see a thing. I wanted to press my fingertips to his neck and find a pulse, but I knew how badly he needed sleep, and I didn't want to wake him. Besides, if he was fine, how much of a basket case would I look like? I grabbed my purse from the bedside table and took out my cell phone and compact mirror. Then I scrambled back to Ben, kneeling next to the cot. Turning my phone on for ambient light, I opened the compact and carefully lowered it beneath his nose—then swallowed a cry of relief when his breath fogged the mirror.

Quietly, I closed the compact, turned off the phone, and slid them to one side as I dropped cross-legged onto the floor. I held my head in my hands, realizing that I was trembling, just as I had been in the dream. "He's okay, he's okay," I whispered to myself, swallowing down the sobs rising in my throat.

Ben's rich voice vibrated through the air and touched me like a divine reprieve. "Cate?"

"Yes," I managed to whisper.

He shifted onto his side. Dark as it was, I could feel his eyes on me. "What are you doing?"

I scooted closer and leaned my head against the side of the mattress. "Checking to make sure you're still breathing."

"Oh," he said casually, as though that weren't a totally crazy thing to be doing. "Well, I am."

"Yeah, I figured that out," I said. A light laugh escaped me as I realized the absurdity of the situation.

He rested his hand gently on my head. "I'm not planning to stop, either, if that helps at all."

"Yeah, well." I reached up and gripped the frame of the cot. "You weren't planning on getting shot in the head, either, but that happened."

"True," he said thoughtfully. "But only with a paintball."

I sighed as he began stroking my hair, soothing my jangled nerves. "Your point being?"

"My point being that it's extremely rare to stop breathing because of a paintball injury."

Was that actually supposed to make me feel better? All of the worries I'd had about Ben from the drugging and the paintball incident mixed with my fear from the dream, triggering an explosion of emotion inside of me. I pulled my head away from beneath his hand and turned to face him. "Well, you'll have to forgive me for being less than comforted by that statistic! I mean, it's *extremely rare* for me to fall in love, but *that's* obviously happened, too, so 'extremely rare' clearly doesn't mean 'impossible.' And when it comes to worrying about whether you've stopped breathing, 'impossible' is the only standard I'm comfortable with! Understood?"

Ben's face was entirely in shadow. There was a long pause, during which I replayed what I'd just said in my head. *Oh my god,* I thought as my hand flew up to cover my mouth. Had I just admitted... Had I really just said...?

The previous week, Ben had given me a miracle—he had told me for the first time that he was in love with me. But I hadn't been ready to say it back, and he had been so understanding, seemed so unconcerned. Now, without intending to, I had told him that I felt the same. It had just slipped out, and maybe because of that, there could be no question in either of our minds that it was true.

Slowly and deliberately, Ben pulled off his blanket, sat up, and planted his feet on the floor. Then he leaned down and cupped my cheeks in his hands. I still couldn't see his expression, but I could feel his eyes searching mine, feel the pressure of his energy as it surrounded me. Finally, in a voice rough with feeling, he said, "Understood."

I inhaled sharply as he lowered his face towards mine, pausing just long enough for us to look at one another as our eyes adjusted to the dark. He kissed me gently at first, over and over again, until I was straining towards him. Then his mouth pressed against mine with urgency and his tongue forged its way between my lips, plunging in desperately, like he was a man returning home from a long and brutal war. As though I was floating, I rose up on my knees, answering his kiss with intense yearning, as though I'd been awaiting his return. Involuntary, primal sounds rose into my throat, and Ben took them into his body as though they infused him with life.

The need to be close to him poured through me like warm honey. Ben spread his knees apart as I slid closer, leaning into the cot and combing my fingers through his hair, careful to avoid his injury as I gripped the back of his head. We had both finally declared our love, and I felt it in the way he kissed me—the sense of wonder, the quiet confidence that he was mine and I was his. I never wanted it to end.

His fingertips slid down the sides of my neck to my shoulders. His hands made their way to my waist, which he gripped with unexpected strength. He stood and lifted me to my feet, his mouth never leaving mine. A soft moan emanated from somewhere deep inside of me, and my hands grasped at him, wanting to touch him everywhere at once. He held me so close against him that I had to settle for digging my nails into his shoulder blades. I heard him grunt softly as I pressed myself against the hard muscle of his chest. The center of my universe was the exact spot where his lips devoured mine, and nothing existed beyond our two bodies. There was only the languorous sensation of his mouth claiming my expression of love, his form stamping its shape onto mine, and the heat of his skin searing mine, even through the cotton of my pajamas.

I placed my foot between his feet, sliding my leg up along the inside of his. *We love each other,* I thought. *Nothing else matters.* But as soon as my thigh reached the bottom of his boxer shorts, Ben's whole body froze.

No, I thought, mewling desperately into his mouth. But Ben used his leg to gently push mine aside. He wrapped one arm around my back and the other under my knees, lifting me up and carrying me over to the bed.

The brief thrill of hope I felt died quickly as he laid me down on the covers and pulled his mouth away from mine. He just stood next to the bed, looking down at me. My body went weak with disappointment. Letting go of Ben, my arms flopped to my sides, and I turned my head away from him. My mouth felt abandoned, my body betrayed.

Finally, he spoke. "The answer is, I don't know."

My frustration spiked. "You don't know what?"

"I don't know where I keep finding the willpower to stop myself from making love to you, every moment of every day." Desire infused his voice, making my blood heat up all over again. "It has something to do with wanting what's best for you, wanting you to be able to get the most you can from your training, wanting to make sure that you're as prepared as you can be for everything that's to come. But how that part of me manages to dominate the part of me that wants to make you dissolve into pleasure over and over again, I have no idea."

His words affected me even more profoundly than his kisses. Keeping my face turned away from his, I folded my arms across my chest, trying quite literally to hold myself together. "That's not helping."

"I know, and I'm sorry. But I felt it was important for you to know that in spite of how it may seem, following the program rules isn't easy for me, either."

I knew what he was saying, and I appreciated his intentions, but I didn't want to acknowledge that just yet. My body still felt the sting of rejection. I remained as I was and focused on trying to breathe rather than pant.

The mattress dipped as Ben sat next to me.

"That's very daring of you," I remarked.

"I know, but I want to ask you about something."

"What?"

"Why were you afraid that I'd stopped breathing?"

"Oh." I frowned. "I just...I had a bad dream."

"Hmm." I heard him rub the rough surface of his jaw. "About what?"

I flashed back to my mother and our perfect day at the beach... the child coughing up water...my mother's arms holding me as I trembled. "I really don't want to talk about it."

"You sure? It might help."

As much as I didn't want to relive it, I knew that he was right. "It was just—my mom was there. And then she wasn't." I shrugged. "I know she's gone, but she does come to me in my dreams sometimes. Which is great, but when she leaves...that part never gets any easier."

"I'll bet." His hand came to rest on the small of my back. "I'm sorry, Cate."

"Thank you."

We sat together in silence for a while. Ben seemed to recover from our kissing session more quickly than I did, but with concentration,

I too was eventually able to return myself to a somewhat normal physiological state. My frustration ebbed as I ran over Ben's words in my mind—his confession that he wanted me as much as I wanted him and that his self-control came from a place of deep caring. I could hardly fault him for that.

I rolled onto my side, facing him. "I'm sorry I woke you up."

"I'm not. I couldn't be happier about it, in fact."

"But you need your rest."

"You said you're in love with me," he said softly. "That's all I need."

My eyes closed as my heart swelled. It was too perfect—so perfect that I knew I'd spend the rest of the night lying awake, staring at the ceiling, worrying about losing him.

I felt his fingertips trace a line down my temple. "What is it?"

Opening my eyes again, I looked up at his face—his perfectly Ben face, the face of the man I loved. "I don't think I'm going to be able to fall back to sleep."

He nodded. "Insomnia?"

"Yeah."

"Well, what helps?" He smiled. "Want me to get you some ice cream?"

I couldn't help smiling back, remembering that night when we'd only known each other for a couple of days, and Ben was guarding my house, and I'd been unable to sleep. I'd had ice cream, but he had refused any—then confessed his phobia of eating in front of other people. That had turned out to be a memorable night. But the emotions keeping me up this time were too agitating. Ice cream wasn't going to do it.

I knew what *would* help, though. "There is one thing that always works," I ventured, "but I'm not sure you're going to want to do it."

"Why not?"

I blushed hard, reluctant to bring up my former friends-with-benefits, but feeling obligated to do so. Finally I confessed, "Because Sid used to do it."

There was a moment of hesitation from Ben—whether from

surprise, or jealousy, or what, I didn't know—but it was just a moment. Then he said, "Cate, if it works, we're doing it. What is it?"

And all at once, I wanted to kiss him again. But if we started, that would go on for ages, and I wanted him to get back to sleep as soon as possible. And I knew he wouldn't go back to sleep until I was asleep. "Okay, if you say so."

"I do."

"It would probably help if you sat on the bed and held me until I fell asleep."

Before I even finished my sentence, Ben was in motion. He lifted me up and moved me to the middle of the bed, then climbed in and sat with his back against the headboard. He pulled me into his lap, cradling me and helping me shift into a comfortable position. "Is this good?"

I closed my eyes and smiled. Curled upon the bed, half of me resting on top of Ben, his bare arms wrapped around me… "Good isn't the word," I sighed.

"All right, then." He leaned down and placed a chaste kiss on my temple—then, without even having to be asked, began stroking my hair. "I'm staying awake until you're asleep, so you better get started."

I placed a kiss on his sheet-covered knee. "Sleeping now."

"I'm in love with you too, Cate," he whispered.

My whole body fluttered with pleasure. "I know," I whispered back, awestruck by the power and simplicity of that exchange. Within moments, I sank into a warm and dreamless sleep.

Chapter Sixteen

ParaTrain Internship, Day Ten

Kai and I sat cross-legged, facing one another on the flat stone circle in the middle of the Zen meditation garden. We'd asked Owen where we could go for some privacy, and he'd pointed us toward the large, round garden-within-a-garden that was carefully designed as a walking maze. The brick tile walkway was laid out in spiraling circles leading to the center. It was edged with large stones and small, fern-like plants. Owen explained that walking the garden was supposed to aid in meditation, but he admitted that it was only ever used by a few groups of Buddhists who came to Mercier for summer day trips. He guaranteed that we wouldn't be interrupted—and added that we were in the "safe zone," far away from the hunting areas, so we wouldn't get shot, either.

We'd gone to breakfast as a group, with Ben making a point to show that he was hale and hearty in spite of the paintball incident. Pete and Ben were quick to spot a new group of guests in the dining room. There were six men dressed in black athletic gear with some kind of gold logos on their shirts. Every one of them was huge, like massive brick walls challenging the strength of the dining room chairs. Pete nodded in their direction and asked Skeet who the rugby team was.

"They would make a good rugby team, wouldn't they?" Skeet chuckled. "That's the security detail for some of our new guests, a group of businessmen from Russia."

"What kind of business are they *in*?" Asa asked, casting a wary look at their table.

"They do quite a variety of things," Skeet said. "You'll learn more this afternoon. They'll be part of our demonstration."

Skeet explained that Team Forward would be in the domed conference room, and we would be watching the demonstration on a live feed video in the movie viewing room. With everyone's curiosity piqued, Skeet then invited us to spend the morning exploring the game room, which featured pool, ping pong, and video games. He promised there was zero chance of injury, and in keeping with our goal to look like innocent recreational guests, we accepted his offer—with the exception of Kai and me. Kai begged off, claiming that he was an amateur botanist and would like to tour the gardens. He said that I should come along, too, since this was my *place* now and I should know what grew there. Kai had that sort of presence that made people reluctant to contradict him, so even though we got some questioning looks, Skeet arranged for Owen to take us out.

Kai ran up to his room to gather a blanket and a couple of other small items. Once we were in the Jeep, he explained to Owen that while we'd love a tour of the gardens, what we *really* needed was some time alone to do a cleansing ritual to treat my insomnia. He told Owen we hadn't told anyone else, not wanting them to be concerned. Fortunately, Owen had witnessed my insomnia firsthand *and* had seen Ben in full worry mode, so he understood immediately. Also, with Skeet and his research subjects around, Owen had enough familiarity with the "woo-woo" that he didn't bat an eyelash at the concept of a cleansing ritual. He swallowed Kai's fabrication hook, line, and sinker, and agreed without hesitation to keep our secret.

As Owen drove us to the Zen meditation garden, I stared out at the passing landscape—forest, outbuildings, fields with hedgerows—and let my mind wander back to the exquisite moment that morning when I'd awakened to find myself still in Ben's lap. Apparently, he'd fallen asleep in my bed, collapsing sideways onto a bank of pillows. I was lying with my body positioned between his outstretched legs and my head resting on his stomach.

I'd never felt anything so divine as being wrapped in Ben, inhaling his scent, which was trapped in the bedclothes—all while he was still sound asleep. It felt deliciously intimate. Longing spread through me, building like a crescendo—a desire to wake up just like that, surrounded by Ben, every morning for the rest of my life. I didn't want to be anywhere else, ever, or do anything else. Well, maybe *some* other things, but only if they involved staying in bed with Ben.

I figured that the whack on the head he'd received must have still been affecting him if I'd awakened before he had. Ever so carefully, I had turned and shifted in micro-movements, trying not to disturb him. But in a few seconds, he was awake and alert, looking down at me with such intense affection that I thought he was going to take me into his arms right there.

Instead, he brushed a stray piece of hair off of my forehead and asked softly, "How did you sleep? Any more bad dreams?"

"No," I admitted. "I slept beautifully."

"Glad to hear it." But after we stared into each other's eyes for a few more moments, I could almost see his brain clicking into pragmatic mode. Shifting out from under me and throwing his legs over the side of the bed, he apologized for falling asleep there instead of returning to his cot. I curtly observed what an absurd thing that was to apologize for, and asked to look at his injury. He lifted his hand to feel it, and winced. After some hesitation, he let me examine it. Not that I had any medical training, but as softly as I could, I smoothed his hair away from the bump. Even I could see that both the swelling and the redness had gone down.

"It looks better, really." I teased him, holding up three fingers and asking, "How many?"

He teased me back by kissing each fingertip, my eyelids, my cheek, the edge of my mouth…and then getting up and heading to the bathroom, casting a devilish look over his shoulder.

It was *that* look I kept picturing over and over in my mind during my Jeep ride with Kai and Owen. I knew I must have been grinning like a bear with her paw in a honey jar the whole ride over, but Kai opted to leave me undisturbed with my thoughts. He just kept shaking his head at me and smiling knowingly.

Once we arrived at the Zen garden, Kai adjusted the blanket he'd brought for us to sit on and pulled a tea light and matches out of his tote bag. Then he produced a cup-like candleholder made of rough crystals. A light fog clung to the ground, softening everything around us. Kai lightly drew his fingers across his forehead and down to his lips, looking at me intently. "You sure you want to do this, honey? Really sure?"

"Yes, I'm really sure." Kai had warned me that the attempt to contact my parents' spirits might result in disappointment, but I had to try. I had too many questions, and they were the only ones who could answer them.

"All right, then." He took a deep breath, then released it and placed the tea light in the holder. "What I need you to do is—well, ordinarily, I'd ask you to say a prayer, but I still don't know where you stand on that. So just try to concentrate on what your intentions are for this reading. Then send that intention out to God or the universe or nature, whatever feels right to you. Let me know when you're done."

"Okay." I rested my hands on my knees and closed my eyes. What *was* my intention for contacting my parents? There were a million reasons I wanted to talk to them, but Kai had warned me that the spirits usually stayed for a limited period of time, and that I shouldn't overwhelm them with too many things, instead focusing on one or two of the most relevant. I decided that I'd better find out what I could about our immediate concern, the situation at Mercier. I could always bug Kai to help me contact my parents again once we were safely home.

Mom, Joe, please help me, I thought, visualizing my words reaching them. *I need guidance. What's going on here, and what do you want us to do?* Then I imagined the love I had for my mother flowing from my heart to hers, wherever she was. I didn't know what else to send out to the universe, so I said, "Done."

Kai lit the tea light, and the crystal cup flickered. "The candle is their invitation," he explained. "It lets the spirits know I'm open for business." Then he rested the backs of his hands on his knees, holding the tips of his forefingers and thumbs together to form circles. Kai pulled himself up into a straight posture with his head tilted slightly backwards. After a few moments, he said, "Oh, okay. Cate," he said, "we have a visitor. Someone I know, but you don't."

I blinked. "What?" Then I remembered that Kai had told me anyone might come through, not necessarily who I asked for. "Um, who is it?"

"Hi, Malcolm," Kai said. "Thank you for being with us today." He opened his eyes. "Okay, Cate, so whatever intention you put out there, your mother felt she wasn't the best person to address it." As he spoke, Kai alternated between looking at me and looking up and to the side, as if speaking to the sky. "Joe can't come through yet. He's still working through his emotions about crossing over. Oh." Kai nodded. "He didn't shoot himself, after all; someone else pulled the trigger. His anger is blocking him."

My stomach lurched. So my worst suspicion and Ben's had been right: the hunting accident hadn't been an accident, after all. "Does he say who did it?"

"No," Kai said, "but Malcolm is here to address your questions. He says it's nice to meet you. Cate, Malcolm is Ben's father."

"What?" Ben's father? What was *he* doing there?

Kai rolled his eyes at me. "He's asking why Ben isn't here." Then he looked up again. "Malcolm, Cate wanted to do this on her own. Yes, we'll fill Ben in. What do you want to tell us?" He nodded slowly, eyes closed, and murmured, "Mm. Mm-hmm," as though he were in fact responding to someone else's voice. Experience had led me to believe in Kai's abilities, but it still freaked me out to watch him in action. "Ah, okay. This has to do with that." Finally, Kai opened his eyes and said, "Cate, Ben told you that a few weeks before you joined the MacGregor Group, Malcolm came to me for the first time. Malcolm predicted your arrival at the church, and he also said that we would all need to stick together, since we'd soon be facing a rising darkness. Apparently, that rising darkness is centered here. Mercier is the head of the snake, he says, and we've been sent here to deal with it, to cut off the head."

"*What?*" I thrust my hands into my hair and gripped it by the roots. How could my father's lodge possibly be related to predictions Malcolm's spirit made weeks before I even knew Ben existed? A snake, a rising darkness? "Um, can he be a little more specific?"

Kai resumed his sitting mediation pose, closing his eyes and tilting his head back. "He says not to be afraid, that our group has everything it needs to complete the task. We're the guardians of the kheir, which means we've been given stewardship over the gifts of light—the gifts that illuminate the unseen, the unknown."

It felt as though the Zen meditation garden was spinning around me. "Given stewardship by *whom*—to do *what*, again?"

Apparently Malcolm didn't feel the need to answer my questions, because Kai just shook his head and continued. "He says it's important that we keep our eyes open, trust our instincts, and believe in each other's gifts. We also have to be willing to fight for what we value. If we do those things, he says that by the end of the week, we will be the victors—oh, great." Kai broke his posture and smirked at me. "He says what we do here is very important, because if we don't cut the head off the snake, its venom will poison the whole world." He held a hand up to the sky and called out, "Thanks, Malcolm! No pressure!"

"What snake?" I pleaded, desperate to find out what Malcolm's spirit was talking about. "What darkness? How do we fight it?"

Kai shrugged. "Sorry, he's pulling his energy back. I think that's all we're going to get... Oh wait!" He tensed for a moment. "No, that's it. He had more that he wanted to say, but only directly to Ben." Flipping his hair back, he murmured, "I *told* you we should have brought him."

"Well, if I had known his *father* was going to come through, I would have!" I chewed on my lip.

"Okay, calm down." Kai led us both through a deep, slow inhale-exhale. "So like I told you, I don't remember everything from my readings. Go over it with me—tell me everything I said."

Since the reading hadn't been that long, I was able to recite

Malcolm's words back to Kai. When we'd finished, Kai shook his head slowly. "That is some kind of messed up."

I flopped into a slumped position like a deflated balloon. "Yeah."

Kai reached out and took my hand. "So your daddy was murdered."

I stared into the flickering candlelight. "I guess so."

"You don't seem surprised."

"Ben and I had talked about the possibility."

"Hmm." There was a somber moment of silence. Then Kai continued, "And we're here to stop this snake of rising darkness from poisoning the world."

"Apparently."

"A snake named Skeet, maybe?"

"Maybe. Or maybe there's more than one. Maybe it's not a person at all, but something else entirely. It would have been nice if Malcolm could have given us a few more details, for God's sake!" I stood up abruptly, forgetting that the blanket we were sitting on covered a smooth stone surface. As it slipped out from under me, in spite of Kai's efforts to grab my arm, I executed a perfect pratfall, landing on the soil. Fortunately, I fell into the space just between a rock and a plant, so neither the foliage nor I were injured.

"Good grief, honey! Are you all right?"

"Fine!" Too embarrassed to accept Kai's offer to help me up, I stood awkwardly, brushing the dirt from my clothes.

"Look," Kai said gently, "I told you, when you ask for a reading, you never know what the Other Side is going to send. You just have to have faith that whatever you get, that's what the Divine needs you to know right now. I don't know what intention you sent out, but clearly someone up there felt we needed some light shed on what we're doing here and how to proceed."

"I know." The sun had risen high enough in the sky that it had burned off the fog, revealing a perfect, crisp autumn day. The touch of warmth on my face was soothing. "I'm sorry, I'm just—frustrated. It's not your fault. And I'm sure that whatever Malcolm told us is important. I was just…I don't know."

"You were hoping for your mom."

"Yeah."

"I know. I get it." Kai wrapped his long arms around me and squeezed. "I'm sorry it didn't turn out the way you wanted, honey. But given the way it *did* turn out, I'd say we should get back to the lodge and fill the others in ASAP."

"You're right. We should." I did my best to shelve everything I was feeling as I helped Kai pack his tote, and we headed back to the lodge.

• • •

Unfortunately, there was no way to drag our crew out of the game room without raising suspicions, so we'd have to wait to share Malcolm's message. I joined Eve and Asa, who were embroiled in a tournament at an old fashioned *Asteroids* arcade game. Kai sidled over to the pool table where Ben and Pete were locked into a battle with Skeet and Michael. Kai stood there twirling a pool stick and trying to look interested until Skeet sank the eight ball, and there were simultaneous cries of delight and defeat. Once congratulations had been good-naturedly doled out, Kai pulled Ben aside for a moment. Then they both spoke to Skeet, and after some kind of agreement had been reached, everyone went back to playing their games.

Kai wandered around the room, looking nonchalant, then finally made his way over to our *Asteroids* game. "Working lunch, kiddos," he said, loudly enough to be overheard. "The back-up team at the church needs our input on some cases. Ben says we'll meet in Pete's and my room and conference them in from there. Skeet's having food sent up."

Eve and Asa nodded and muttered their slightly irritated assent as they concentrated on destroying the asteroids with their tiny ships.

As lunchtime neared, the game room emptied out and we all returned to our rooms to freshen up—which meant Ben and I were alone in my room for a few moments. I tried to avoid making eye contact with him as I grabbed some non-dirt-stained jeans and a fresh cotton tunic and headed for the bathroom to change. But before I could reach the door, Ben said, "Sounds like you and Kai had an eventful morning."

I had no idea how much Kai had told him, but since they'd only spoken for a few seconds, I guessed it couldn't have been much. I plastered an untroubled expression onto my face and turned around. "In a sense," I said, keeping it vague, then pointed to the dirt stain on the seat of my jeans as though to indicate that falling down had been the height of our adventures.

"Hmm." Ben covered the space between us in a few steps. He put his hand on my shoulder, turned me to the side, and flagrantly stared at my rear end. "I didn't realize you'd fallen." The gold flecks in his eyes flashed as he pointed at the stain. "Do you need me to examine that for you?"

"Very funny." I twisted away from him. "Sorry to disappoint you, but I'm *fine*. I just need to put on some clean clothes." Then I marched into the bathroom and closed the door.

"Good," he called through the door. "That means we can get right to the point—how you and Kai snuck off and had a secret conference with my father this morning."

Good God, I thought, *Kai managed to squeeze a lot of incriminating information into a few seconds of conversation.* Ben still harbored a lot of anger towards his father; I knew he'd be less than thrilled that we'd connected. "That's *not* how it happened…"

"How *did* it happen, then?" he asked, his voice taut.

Guilt washed over me, but I knew there was no point trying to either explain myself or apologize through a bathroom door. "Is this what we're going to talk about at lunch?"

"Yes. As you can imagine, I'm anxious to hear all about it."

"And I really want to tell you, as soon as possible. So." Pulling together the threads of my courage, I opened the bathroom door and headed straight for the door to the hallway. "Let's get going, shall we?"

But Ben came up behind me and placed his hand atop mine as I grasped the doorknob. "Cate," he murmured, his tone unexpectedly gentle. "Everyone has things that are private, sacred. But you and I, we can't keep secrets from each other—not here, not now, and especially not about something like this." I bit my lip as he palmed my hip with his free hand. "We have to work as a team, unified."

I knew what he wanted me to say, but my mouth was too dry. I swallowed hard. "I understand that. I just…the morning didn't go the way I was expecting it to."

He pressed his lips against the top of my head for a long moment. When he spoke, his words were heavy with sympathy. "I know. You were probably hoping to talk to your parents, right?"

Barely, I nodded.

"And my father barged in, instead. Typical. I'm sorry about that."

"Good grief, it's not *your* fault!" I covered his hand on my hip with mine and squeezed. "I'll talk to my parents sooner or later. Today just wasn't the day."

"Still, I'm sorry they didn't come through. You must have been disappointed."

Not trusting my voice, I only shrugged.

Ben seemed to take the hint. He didn't dig any further—just pressed me to firm up my promise. "So, no more secrets—and no more secret missions?"

"Didn't I just say yes?"

"You did." He leaned over, brushing a kiss along my hairline. "All right, then. Let's go talk about your first meeting with my father. Allow me."

I slid my hand off the doorknob, and Ben opened the door. I walked through, tucking my head to the side to disguise the blush making its way rapidly across my face.

• • •

At our lunch meeting, the mood was heavy—especially when Kai shared Malcolm's confirmation that my father's death had not been an accident. I was glad that Ben and I had taken one of the love seats. He seemed to sense that while I didn't want to attract attention or sympathy, I could still use some comforting. He slid his arm around my shoulders and began to run his fingers along my braid, soothing me.

Ben and Pete both sat at attention, though, when Kai told us we had been named the guardians of the kheir. I knew the two of them took duty and responsibility very seriously. But the bit about having to cut off the head of the snake at Mercier to stop the rising darkness—that rendered everyone speechless. We decided the best way to find out what Malcolm meant by that was to keep playing the role of innocently curious colleagues, staying upbeat and even exchanging some harmless information with Skeet and Team Forward to establish trust.

Ben remained remarkably unemotional during our discussion, in spite of the strong feelings I knew he had about his father. He still harbored a great deal of anger towards Malcolm, which I suspected stemmed somehow from his father's struggles with addiction. But Ben had never discussed it with me directly. He had only shared how devastating it had been for him to find his father's body after he accidentally overdosed. I knew that incident had kicked Ben's excessive over-protectiveness into high gear. Once again, I felt a surge of relief that he had agreed to let me work with him on that issue when we got home. I couldn't bear the thought of Ben carrying around so much unresolved pain. And whatever wounds I couldn't heal with my empath skills, I hoped Ben would consider talking through with a therapist. But as resistant as he'd been so far to accepting any help, I knew we'd have to take it slow.

When our meeting came to an end, we all tried to set aside the weight of everything we'd just discussed as we put on our game faces and made our way to the movie viewing room. Skeet dropped in to make sure we were all situated. A man in a crisp, blue suit, who was introduced as "one of Mercier's lawyers," came in and passed out the nondisclosure agreements. Skeet must have told him that we'd all been given top-secret military clearance the previous week, because he used that as an analogy for the level of confidentiality that applied to everything we were about to witness. Once the lawyer took us through the agreements in detail, he collected our signed copies and disappeared.

Skeet reminded us that the Russians were clients of Mercier's and would be joining him and Team Forward as part of the demonstration.

Tentatively, Asa raised his hand. When Skeet nodded at him, Asa asked, "Just wondering—do the Russians know we're going to be watching?"

"They are aware that all of their activities here at Mercier may be monitored internally by our team members. And by signing those non-disclosure agreements, you all became team members—at least for today. No worries." Skeet smiled broadly. "If there isn't anything else?"

There were no more questions, so Skeet left us to go to the domed conference room.

A technician was in the viewing room with us, which meant that we couldn't speak as freely as we would have liked. Once we had all taken a place in the stadium-style theater seats, the tech turned off the lights and turned on the viewing screen. It was divided into four parts, all with different angles on the conference room, where Skeet, Liv, and Michael were setting up. Even watching from a distance, we could tell the atmosphere was alive with anticipation. Michael and Liv turned to one of the cameras in the room and gave us smiles and waves.

Eventually, the Russians arrived—or we assumed that was who they were. A number of men and women, all in dark suits, sat at the conference table while their security team stood against the walls of the room, still dressed in their signature athletic gear.

Skeet was at the head of the table with Liv and Michael sitting on either side of him. "Welcome," Skeet said, bringing the meeting to order. "I can't tell you how honored we are that you chose to take a detour from your D.C. trip to join us here at Mercier."

"The honor is ours," one of the Russians said with a mild accent. He stretched his arms out in front of him and clasped his hands on the table, revealing cufflinks that looked like large rubies.

"We have heard a great deal about Team Forward, and we have been eagerly anticipating this demonstration for some time. We have also been enjoying your facilities. Excellent hunting."

"I'm pleased to hear it!" Skeet smiled proudly. "As you know, Team Forward is a large group with a variety of abilities, but we have brought two individuals here today who we thought would interest you. Liv is an aura reader."

Liv smiled and raised her hand.

Skeet then gestured toward Michael. "And Michael is a telepath—who is fluent in Russian, by the way."

That news was greeted with anxious murmurs around the conference table. In the viewing room, Ben asked if anyone had known that Michael spoke Russian, but no one did. Clearly, Skeet had decided to save that piece of information for a potent "reveal," perhaps to create some drama while impressing both us and their Russian guests.

"As I said, a variety of abilities," Skeet continued. "We've been recruiting the best sensitives from around the world for years. Most of them jump at the chance to come to Washington and work with NIMH. And when they learn about the exciting work Team Forward is doing, well—let's just say we don't have a problem keeping ourselves fully staffed."

He paused long enough for the Russians to speak among themselves for a moment. When the conversation quieted down, Skeet went on, "You have already been briefed on what Mercier and Team Forward have to offer. But there is quite a difference between hearing about something, and experiencing it directly. The purpose of today's demonstration is to give you a taste of what you would gain by partnering with us. Ilya," he said, turning to the man with the ruby cufflinks, "would you care to choose someone in the room for Liv to read?"

Ilya, who was apparently the boss, looked around, finally pointing to a member of his security team. "Maxim."

Liv stood and gave the fidgeting Maxim a reassuring smile. Then, just as Vani did when she was reading auras, Liv closed her eyes. "Maxim," Liv began. "Your aura is strong with loyalty. You are a man who can be counted upon."

Maxim nodded modestly, while Ilya looked pleased.

"However," Liv continued, "the one thing you cannot be counted upon to do is to refrain from smoking. I see you are trying very hard—the effort you are making shines brightly—but this vice keeps getting the better of you. I don't see any permanent health effects yet; your fitness level is high. But there is some fraying around the edges. You should find a way to quit soon, before it causes you irreversible harm."

"Is she right?" Ilya demanded. "Is it true?"

"*Da*," Maxim said, hanging his head.

We all jumped as Ilya pounded his fist on the table. "Maxim, I *told* you!" Then he turned to another member of the security team who was standing behind him. "Get him the nicotine patch. I don't want to hear any more excuses." With a pained look, Ilya said to Maxim, "If not for me, then for your wife and daughter."

Maxim nodded. "I will use it, I swear. I will stop."

"Good," Ilya said, settling down.

I shuddered as Maxim shot Liv a malevolent look, but she just smiled graciously.

"And whose thoughts would you like Michael to read?" Skeet asked Ilya.

At that point, everyone in the conference room looked like they wanted to bolt. After scanning his employees, Ilya said, "Me. Have him read me."

Ilya fixed Michael with a challenging, intense gaze, but Michael appeared unfazed. "There may be a slight time delay while I translate," Michael said.

Ilya nodded.

Michael crossed one leg over the other and slung his arm over the back of his chair. "Sir, you are thinking about your business, Opretec, and wondering whether it would be worthwhile for you to hire the services of Team Forward."

The people around the table exchanged unimpressed looks.

"You are also thinking about the fact that Opretec may soon be merging with a Ukrainian company," Michael said, "but you don't trust the leaders of this other company to deal honestly with you. You also suspect that someone in this room is on their payroll, and is feeding insider information to the Ukrainians."

Suddenly, everyone in the room was sitting or standing at attention. "Very good, young man," Ilya said. "Now, if you can tell me which of the individuals in this room—if any—is acting as a double agent, so to speak, I will be very grateful."

"I'll do my best," Michael said, then looked one by one at each of the people seated around the table. "There are many loud thoughts, so I am not sure which person this is, but he is in his room, and he is betraying you. Right now he is worrying about his wife, Natalya, and his twin boys, and what will happen to them if he is found out."

Very slowly, all of the Russians turned to look at someone seated toward the back of the room, a handsome man in his fifties who appeared shocked by the accusation. "That's outrageous," he said with a guffaw. "Ilya, surely you aren't going to listen to the ramblings of this American boy."

"That test was not for you, Anton," Ilya told the man, his voice chilling. "That test was for Michael. I already suspected that you were feeding information to the Ukrainians, but I did not know for certain until now."

Anton's face reddened. "You are setting me up! You are afraid I will challenge your leadership, so you told this boy ahead of time what to say. This is all smoke and mirrors!"

"That is a fair challenge," Ilya said. "Anton, think of a secret—something about you that no one in this room knows. You are so mentally undisciplined, I know that you won't be able to resist my suggestion." He smiled maliciously. "Michael, what is Anton thinking?"

Michael looked at Anton for a few moments, then spoke to Ilya. "He is thinking that his mother once told him that his father was not his biological father. He is the product of an affair his mother had.

Anton kept her secret even after her death, because he feared being dropped from his father's will."

Anton stood and shook a fist at Michael. "That's a lie! You blacken my name!"

Ilya nodded at two of the security team members, who took Anton by the arms. "This is easy enough to prove," he said. "We will speak to your father. A paternity test will tell us whether your name is being blackened or exposed." Ilya waved his fingers and the security team removed a struggling Anton from the room.

"Oh my god," I heard myself whisper. I looked around the viewing room. Everyone looked as stricken as I felt, except for Ben and Pete, who remained intensely focused on the screen. The Russians were having mixed reactions. Some appeared upset, others nodded knowingly as though their beliefs had just been confirmed.

"Michael," Ilya said, "an excellent job."

"Thank you," Michael replied, "although I'm sure you will feel even more secure in my abilities once you get the results of the paternity test."

"Indeed," Ilya agreed, "although now that I reflect on it, Anton never looked anything like either of his parents. Still, Skeet, we would like to get those results before we make a final decision about entering into a partnership with you—just to confirm. You understand."

"Of course," Skeet said. "That's not a problem. But before we conclude, I do have one more thing to share with you." He pulled a piece of paper out of his shirt pocket. "A message from one of our precogs—sensitives who can see the future. She asked me to share something that she saw about Opretec in a vision this morning."

Ilya leaned forward, listening intently. "Please, do share."

Skeet opened the paper and read. "She says that late tomorrow night, there will be a major tunnel collapse in your Chu-Sarysu uranium mine in Kazakhstan. Before the end of business tomorrow, you should evacuate the mine and close the entrance or there will be multiple fatalities, as well as a release of radiation."

The conference room fell completely silent for a few moments.

Everyone was looking at Ilya to see how he would respond to the precog's prediction. Ilya narrowed his eyes at Skeet, then Liv, then Michael. Finally, he turned to the man sitting on his right and said, "Do it."

There was an explosion of activity as everyone jumped up, presumably to get started following Ilya's instructions. Opretec's employees left the room briskly, leaving behind only Ilya and two of the security team members. Ilya went to the front of the room and took Skeet by the arm. Liv and Michael quietly slipped away, giving them some privacy. Ilya spoke into Skeet's ear, so quietly that we could not hear. Skeet nodded a few times, then smiled and extended his hand, which Ilya shook.

The tech turned off the viewing screen and turned on the lights. There was a collective sigh as many of us released the breaths we'd been holding. As we began exchanging astounded looks, one of the waitresses from the dining room popped her head in the door. "Skeet and the others would like you to meet them in the living room next door," she chirped.

I steeled myself, sensing that our already-interesting afternoon was about to get a lot more interesting.

Chapter Seventeen

We slowly filtered into the large living room. It felt a little bit like a cushy cave. The walls were covered with dark wood panels and wine-colored brocade fabric, and there was a rich, forest-green carpet. The pleasantly sweet smell of cigars hung in the air. We arranged the soft leather club chairs and love seats around a few antique coffee tables.

Skeet, Liv, and Michael arrived at around the same time as a server wheeled in a beverage cart. Skeet's smile was triumphant. He waited patiently for us all to get settled with our drinks, then pulled up a chair and sat on its edge, facing us. "Well, MacGregor Group, I hope you enjoyed our demonstration!"

We dutifully smiled and nodded. We had decided ahead of time that no matter what happened in the demonstration, we would act impressed and agreeable in the hopes of encouraging Skeet to be more open about his activities.

"Allow me to give you some context," Skeet said, leaning back in his chair. "As I'm sure you gathered, the Russians represent a company called Opretec Corporation. They found out about Team Forward by way of their connections with Congressman Tucker, who is also visiting this week. They've been involved in some international development projects together. But as you know, there is a lot of uncertainty in the world today, particularly after the recent global economic collapse. Like many companies, Opretec Corp. is trying to find ways to position themselves optimally for whatever might come down the pike."

The waitress brought Skeet a whiskey on the rocks. Skeet took a sip. "Ah. Thanks. So as you now know, one of the things they mine is uranium. But we have a precious resource here, as well—Team Forward." He gestured Michael and Liv, who beamed. "We have developed a unique business model, using paranormal gifts to provide information to our clients that will help give them an edge in the international marketplace. In turn, they provide us with a percentage of their profits."

Skeet took another sip of whiskey and scanned our faces for reactions. Vani jumped in first. "That is so creative!" she cooed. "You've found a way to monetize paranormal gifts in the modern global economy."

"Exactly!" Skeet glowed in the light of Vani's understanding and apparent approval. "And our income is used for other purposes, in addition to developing the Team Forward business. We maintain and keep expanding Mercier's property; we donate generously to the paranormal research projects at NIMH; and of course, we're able to make the lives of our sensitives much more comfortable than they would otherwise be."

Liv nodded. "Which is a welcome change. As you all know, we're so often mocked or distrusted by society in general. And I had a decent job before I joined Team Forward, but I never could have made this kind of money as an accountant."

"And why shouldn't we build some security for ourselves by using our gifts?" Michael chimed in. "We have special abilities, and they come with special risks. We should be compensated accordingly."

Eve raised her hand. "Wait, so—what Team Forward does, it doesn't have anything to do with healing?"

Skeet put his whiskey glass on a table and pointed at Eve. "A very astute observation. Michael, Liv—Eve here is a talented acupuncturist, so naturally, healing is her main focus. Eve, we are committed to healing, as well, but we've decided to separate that from our commercial enterprise. At NIMH, most of our research is about healing. Through Team Forward's work at Mercier, though, we give sensitives an opportunity to secure their financial future.

Now more than ever, we have to use every advantage we can to take care of ourselves and each other."

"Sure, that makes sense," Pete drawled. "I can see the attraction for the sensitives. But how do your clients know you're not turnin' around and sellin' information to their competition?"

"Another excellent question," Skeet said, appearing pleased that we were so engaged in the discussion. "We sign noncompete clauses with each contract, of course. But each time we deliver some information, the clients put their payments into escrow accounts. If the information proves useful within the relevant time frame, the money is released to us. If not, the client would get a refund—if that were ever needed, that is. So far, all of the information we've provided has been right on the money, so to speak."

Ben leaned forward and rested his elbows on his knees. "With such an impressive track record, Skeet, Team Forward must be growing."

"At a healthy rate, yes," Skeet acknowledged.

"And do you have any competition?" Ben asked. "Are there other groups like this one?"

"Well, as I mentioned," Skeet said, "we've been recruiting the most talented sensitives from around the world for decades to come and work at NIMH. We have eyes and ears everywhere, telling us when new talent is emerging, and we work hard to tempt them to come to Washington—to consolidate the talent, you could say. Others may try to form groups like ours, but we're so far ahead of the game, we don't think we'll ever have any real competition."

"Impressive," Ben said. "I can see why you're keen to crack the mystery of the double kheir, as well. If it operates as some people believe it does, not only would you be able to increase your output dramatically, but you'd be light-years ahead of any potential competition—untouchable."

"Absolutely—if, as you say, it operates as expected. In fact, I'd like to talk to you more about that. I have a follow-up meeting with Ilya in just a few minutes here, but perhaps tomorrow would be a good time."

Ben nodded. "I look forward to it."

"Before I go," Skeet said, drawing an arc with his hand, taking in the room, "any other questions? Overall impressions?"

As we had planned, all of the MacGregor Group members smiled and made approving noises. But we all knew that what Skeet really wanted was Ben's response.

Eventually, Ben said, "I agree with Vani. It's a very creative idea, and the demonstration was impressive."

Michael and Liv exchanged satisfied smiles, but Skeet's reaction was more measured. He pressed his lips together and nodded. "I'm glad you think so."

"I have one last question," Asa ventured. "What's going to happen to Anton?"

The silence that fell over the room told me everyone had been wondering the same thing. "I sense your concern and respect it," Skeet said, "but whatever happens to Anton is not our business—and not our doing. As Ilya said, they knew ahead of time that he was a corporate spy. It's up to Opretec and the Russian legal system to deal with that situation."

"Every business has to deal with ethical concerns," Ben said thoughtfully. "But it does appear that the way you've arranged things, Skeet, it's a three-way win—for the owners here, for your clients, and—most importantly, of course—for the members of Team Forward."

While his words were positive, it was clear from Ben's tone that he was still holding back his full approval. Skeet seemed satisfied for the moment, however. "Indeed," he said, standing and extending his hand to Ben, who in turn stood and shook it. "I'm glad you see it that way. Until we meet again, everyone relax and enjoy yourselves. Excellent work, Michael and Liv!"

The rest of us seconded that sentiment, and the debriefing transformed into a cocktail hour. On his way out the door, Skeet asked if he could talk to me in the hallway—and since Ben was standing right next to me, I asked if he could join us. Skeet didn't object.

Once we were outside of the room, Skeet laid a hand on my shoulder and gave me a warm, paternal smile. "Cate, a couple of the other owners are here visiting this week, and we were hoping that you could join us tonight for a dinner cruise on the Bay. Congressman Tucker has plenty of room on his yacht, and it would be a good opportunity for you to meet people who were friends of your father's."

His invitation shot straight to the pit of my stomach and sat there like a cube of ice. The last thing I wanted to do was to spend an evening with Mercier's shady owners. On the other hand, we were there to gather information, and a dinner cruise might be the perfect opportunity to learn things we couldn't otherwise.

Ben laid his hand gently on the small of my back, and I felt instantly reassured. I wouldn't be alone—or would I? "That sounds lovely," I said tentatively. "You're free, aren't you, Ben?"

"Oh, I'm sorry," Skeet said. "I should have made it clear—the cruise is only for owners and their families, although no family members are here this week that I know of. It's for privacy reasons. I'm sure you understand, Ben."

A bolt of panic shot through me. There was no way on God's earth I was going out to that aquatic pit of vipers alone. Fortunately, my anxiety led to a sudden inspiration. I gave Skeet a shy smile, slid my arm around Ben's waist, and asked, "Do fiancés count?"

Skeet and Ben both looked at me with equal degrees of shock, then looked at each other. "Ben, you look more surprised than I am!" Skeet said.

Ben recovered quickly and kissed the top of my head. "I am, a bit. Cate said she wanted to tell Ardis before anyone else."

"Wait a minute," Skeet said. "You weren't engaged last week, were you? When did this happen?"

"Friday night," I said dreamily, "on the way home from that lovely banquet you hosted for us."

Skeet looked perplexed. "But didn't you just meet a few weeks ago?"

"It's true, we haven't known each other long," I admitted,

stepping closer to Ben and sheltering myself in his arms. "But when something's *right*..." I leaned my head up to look lovingly at Ben, even batting my eyelashes a few times.

"You just *know*," Ben said, the picture of charm. "We figured, why wait?"

"Well, then!" Skeet smiled indulgently. "I think you make a wonderful couple. I told Cate as much last week, didn't I, Cate?"

I grinned like a fool and nodded.

"Oh no!" Suddenly dismayed, Skeet slapped his forehead. "You were probably planning to tell Ardis last Saturday, weren't you? But I was there, ruining the moment."

"Oh, don't worry about it!" I reassured. "I'll tell her next weekend. We were planning on stopping by her house before going back to Baltimore."

I was a little alarmed by how fluidly I was able to fabricate lies, but Ben kept up beautifully. "That's right. But if you wouldn't mind just keeping it between us for now..." He cocked his head back toward the living room.

Skeet nodded solemnly. "Oh, of course. Mum's the word. Well, a *quiet* congratulations, anyway! And yes, of course fiancés count. Ben, you're welcome to join us on the yacht. I'm sure the other owners will be anxious to meet you."

Anxious is right, I thought, remembering the conversation I'd overheard between Tucker and Hencock. They already had their eyes on Ben and me, and were trying to gauge us both. But I just kept a crazy-in-love smile on my face.

"Thanks so much," Ben said. "I'd like to meet them, as well."

"It's settled, then." But Skeet looked a bit *un*settled. "As I mentioned, I have some things to take care of. You two go back in and enjoy yourselves. We'll meet a smaller boat at the dock around four thirty. It'll take us out to the yacht."

I felt a twinge of nerves. I'd never been on anything even close to a yacht before. "Um, is there a dress code?"

Skeet waved his hand dismissively. "Oh, don't worry about it. We usually wear business attire to these dinners, but everyone knows you didn't come out here expecting to attend any special events. Wear whatever's comfortable."

"Okay," I said, already thinking about begging a dress from Vani. "Thanks again for the invitation." I grabbed Ben's hand. "We're looking forward to it!"

"So am I. See you soon!" Skeet walked off down the hallway.

Ben and I just stood there for a moment, perfectly still. He still had his hand on my back, I was still leaning into him, and we were still holding hands. In the silence, I reviewed the implications of what I'd just done. Guilt pricked at me for having acted so impulsively without first considering Ben's feelings. I cleared my throat. Staring down at our hands, I said, "Ben, I'm sorry—"

"Sorry? For what?" he murmured, twining our fingers together. "That was some quick thinking. This dinner is bound to be highly educational, but there is no way you could go out there by yourself."

"Well, that's what I was thinking. But engagement, commitment—I know they're not things either of us take lightly. It's just the first thing I thought of..."

"Please stop apologizing." Ben placed his finger under my chin and tilted my face up until our eyes met. "It was a brilliant solution. I have to admit, though, I was surprised by how naturally you took to the idea of our engagement—like a duck to water."

I conjured up my best deadeye stare.

He grinned roguishly. "Maybe we should think of this as a practice run. Speaking of which, there's a jewelry store in St. Michaels where my mother is a regular customer, and she's very picky. We could go look at rings this week."

I flattened my palm against his chest and shoved. "Very funny."

Ben pulled back, but only slightly. "Hey, and we should talk to Kai and Pete about that double wedding idea."

That was a step too far. It was one thing for us to pretend we were engaged for the owners, but I didn't want to get anyone else involved, even as part of the subterfuge. They might get their hopes up, and who knew where that would lead. Besides, according to the lie we'd told Skeet, none of them were supposed to know. I tilted my head back and opened my mouth to object, but Ben mirrored me, opening his own mouth ever so slightly—sensually, as though he thought I had been coming in for a kiss. But I could tell he knew I had been gearing up to speak, not lock lips. His eyes darkened, holding my gaze for a few beats before flickering over my mouth, my cheeks, my neck… The air between us crackled like lit kindling.

Dammit, I thought as warmth prickled in my cheeks. My mouth was still open, but I'd forgotten what I was going to say.

Ben took advantage of my dumbfounded moment to wrap his arms around my back and slide his hands down lower than they'd ever traveled before, holding me firmly in a way that was borderline indecent for a public hallway. His voice was scandalously low. "You were about to say…?"

I tried to ignore my increasingly rapid breathing and played our conversation back in my head. "Oh, right!" I whispered. "Don't even *think* about telling anyone in our group!"

One of his eyebrows lifted as his hands drifted down. "You can't police a man's *thoughts*, Cate."

Smartass. Part of me wanted to reach up and push him away—but it was doing battle with the part of me that didn't want his fingertips to move from where they were pressing, just firmly enough to make themselves known. "You know what I meant. Things have a way of snowballing—especially where Kai's involved. If he got wind that either one of us had even uttered the phrase, 'double wedding'—"

"He would do his best to make it happen, and you'd be my wife by the New Year." The gold flecks in his eyes shimmered. "That's one of the things I like about Kai. When he puts his mind to something…" Ben tilted his head down, moving his lips a quarter of an inch closer to mine and holding my gaze prisoner.

The portal between us opened, and his frank desire burst through, bathing my body in a flash of intense heat. I either needed to find a fire extinguisher ASAP, *or* I needed Ben to take me upstairs so we could finally consume one another. My pulse pounded through my body like the Kentucky Derby. "Which is why we can't tell anyone," I said in a small, strangled voice.

"Hmm." He tilted his head to the side. He was so close, I could feel the warmth radiating from his lips. "So you don't want to marry me, you just want to kiss me—unless I'm reading you wrong."

Under normal circumstances, I was sure I could have thought up a clever, pithy comeback, but my brain was as overheated as the rest of me, and those two words, "kiss me," reverberated through my head. Finally, I exclaimed, "Oh, hell!" I jumped up onto my tiptoes and pressed my lips against his with a great shudder of satisfaction.

Ben's mouth answered immediately, his audacious tongue exploring as his hands took advantage of my upward slide, gripping the fleshiest curve of my bottom and pressing my hips against his.

I couldn't stop myself from wriggling into his hands. Between his grip and his mouth, he was turning me into a human flame. My very bones seemed to melt, and a deep longing arose—a raw desire for Ben to lift me into his arms, carry me to my room, and do all of the things a real fiancé would do to the woman he loved.

But I knew that wasn't going to happen. The realization hit me like a bucket of cold water, allowing a rational thought to break through. *Good grief, Duncan, what is wrong with you? You keep letting yourself get worked up when you know you're only going to be frustrated.*

Fortunately, before I could scrutinize my self-control any further, Eve popped her head into the hallway, gasped, and retreated back into the room. We broke our kiss as she called softly from inside the doorway, "Sorry, guys! We were just wondering what happened to you."

I pushed myself away from Ben so hard that I stumbled. He reached out and grabbed my hand, steadying me until I'd regained my balance.

Ben leaned towards me and quietly asked, "So, just to be clear—you *don't* want me to tell them?"

In answer, I glared at him and stalked back toward the room. But my body still smoldered everywhere he'd touched me. I took in a deep breath and exhaled slowly, trying to cool myself off before we rejoined polite society.

CHAPTER EIGHTEEN

In light of Skeet's dinner invitation, our group spent the next couple of hours in Kai and Pete's room putting together a game plan. Eve asked Ben to allow her to go into a trance to see if she could glimpse anything useful about the future. He was hesitant at first, since Eve was still new at using her precog gift, and he worried about the toll it took on her. But she was so insistent, and we had so many unanswered questions, Ben finally agreed to let her try.

Eve sat cross-legged on the bed and closed her eyes as she began to chant something in a language I couldn't quite place.

Seeing my confusion, Ben whispered, "Cantonese—one of her first languages."

"From Hong Kong?" I remembered that Eve's family had moved from there to the U.S.

Ben nodded. After a few moments, Eve lifted her arms in front of her, palms out, as though she was preparing to catch a ball. She continued to chant, but her voice became lower and softer until there was no sound at all. The room was dead silent and tense with anticipation.

After a few minutes, Eve sighed heavily and rubbed her eyes. "I don't know what's going on," she said. "It's like I can open the doorway to the trance, but something is stopping me from stepping through—a sense of doom, almost. And all I can see are dark clouds swirling on the other side."

"Well, you gave it a shot," Ben said. "Thanks for trying."

"I'm not giving up yet!" She rolled her eyes at him. "I just need to think of some way to push through the door. Does anyone have any ideas?"

Vani tapped her finger against her lips. "Well…"

"Well, what?" Kai asked.

"Given that we have what appears to be a functioning double kheir…"

Kai smiled at Vani. "I like where you're going with this. Maybe if we all support her with our energy…"

"Or," Ben said pointedly, "the sense of doom she felt was a warning that should be heeded. I don't think we should risk it."

There was a pause. Then Eve held her hand up. "I'm the one who would be at risk here, and I vote we do it. We need this, Ben."

"She has a point," Vani said. "We need as much information as we can get. And we can monitor her carefully. If things get too intense… Kai, is there a way you can pull her out of there?"

Kai had walked across the room and was rifling through his suitcase. "Way ahead of you." He pulled out something wrapped in a black velvet cloth. It turned out to be a small crystal ball on a wooden platform. "Eve, could you try using this ball to go into your trance? I know you usually do this with your eyes closed, but if you can use the ball, then I can end the trance anytime by covering it with the cloth."

Eve shrugged. "Sure, I can give it a try."

Everyone looked expectantly at Ben. He looked as uncertain as I felt about the wisdom of pinning Eve's welfare to the powers of a crystal ball. On the other hand, Kai and Vani knew what they were doing, and people who questioned them typically ended up looking foolish—just as I had earlier in my training. Finally, Ben relented. "All right. Eve, if you're sure, we'll give it a try. But at the first sign of a problem—"

"We'll pull her right out, don't you worry." Kai set up a folding tray in front of Eve and put the crystal ball on it, with the cloth to one side. "Okay, everybody form a circle. Come on, hold hands, just like in kindergarten. That means you, too Ben, remember? Mr. Palm?"

"Oh, right." Ben placed himself between Asa and me. Only Pete stood off to one side, watching.

Eve wanted to leave her hands free, so Vani and Kai stood on either side of her with their hands resting on her shoulders. Eve took a few slow, deep breaths, then focused on the crystal ball. She began to chant again, this time with her eyes open, staring into the ball. She held her arms out in front of her again. Then, just like it had the previous two times we'd activated the double kheir, the air in the room began to feel as though it was pulsing, vibrating against my skin and throughout my body, bringing everything into unison.

"It's working," Vani murmured.

Suddenly, Eve's arms dropped into her lap. She began to make soft sounds of distress, shaking her head and crying, like someone who was asleep and having a nightmare. She reached up and fisted her hair, rocking back and forth. I looked over at Kai, but he was focused on Eve. A glance around the circle told me that everyone else was as concerned as I was—especially Ben.

Vani spoke again. "Everyone visualize sending Eve some positive energy."

I wasn't great at visualizing, but I did my best. All at once, I felt a crackling surge of warmth shoot from Asa's hand through my body and into Ben. Asa and I exchanged curious glances, but Ben didn't seem to register that anything unusual had happened.

Eve stopped moving and fell silent. We all held our breath. Suddenly, her body jerked as though she was startled by something. Then her back straightened and she stared at the crystal ball, wide-eyed, and howled, "Noooo!" Kai quickly broke the circle and covered the crystal ball with the cloth while Vani hurriedly began rubbing Eve's arms.

"Come back, Eve," Kai said loudly. "You're done, baby. Come back now."

Eve's breathing was fast and labored, her eyes open but unfocused. She reached out and clutched at Vani and Kai. Asa got her a glass of water and encouraged Eve to take a few sips.

Meanwhile, Ben hovered in the background, the knuckles on his fists turning white. "Is she all right?" he barked.

"Yes. She's fine, as promised," Kai said pointedly. "You know the drill. Just give her a minute."

Ben retreated to the window, looking outside as he raked a hand through his hair. Meanwhile, Pete's expression was stony, but it was obvious they'd been through something similar with Eve before, and everyone had their roles to play. Ben was so wired, I knew it probably wouldn't be a good idea to touch him, but I walked over and stood near him. I leaned against the wall and tried to look calm. His grip on the windowsill loosened.

"Is it always that hard to watch?" I whispered.

"Yeah," he muttered. "When someone inexperienced goes into a precog trance, there's always a risk that they'll have trouble coming out of it, or that it will harm them somehow. The risk is slight, and we always take precautions. But with that sense of doom Eve said she was feeling… Let's just say it was especially hard to watch this time."

Thankfully, Eve recovered quickly. Kai and Vani helped her off of the bed. She appeared tense, but otherwise fine. "Ben," she said.

He was at her side in an instant. She tugged at his sleeve and took him over to sit with her on the couch. She tapped the coffee table. "Does anyone have a pen and paper?"

Kai produced these, and Eve leaned over the table. We all gathered nearby to watch. She drew a large circle and put several dots on it. "Okay," she said. "This is the earth, and these dots, these places—they're toxic, like black mold. This one—" she tapped one of the dots with her finger— "this one is Mercier."

My hand flew up to cover my mouth as she continued. "I saw thin lines of black smoke rising from these dots. Most faded into the atmosphere; some connected with each other. But a huge cloud of smoke rose up out of Mercier, and it drew in all of the other thin lines like a magnet. The more lines that connected with Mercier's cloud, the bigger it grew, until it was covering the whole earth." Eve shuddered. "I think it was the dark cloud I saw through the door on my first attempt at the trance. It's bad, Ben. It's…it's destructive, evil. It blocked out the sun's light."

"The rising darkness Malcolm warned us about," Kai whispered.

Eve nodded. "I focused in to try to see what was underneath the clouds, but it was so thick. I did catch a glimpse of something, though." She began to draw squiggly lines leading away from each of the black dots. "I heard a bunch of loud pops—like fireworks, or maybe gunshots. Then I could see rivers flowing out of each of these places, but…" She paused and swallowed hard. "The rivers were red."

Pete's eyes narrowed to slits. "Well, that can't be good."

"Yeah. It didn't feel good, that's for sure." Eve flopped back against the couch. "And then I thought the vision was over, but it zoomed in on Mercier, and—oooh!" She squeezed her eyes shut.

"It's okay, Eve," Ben said. "What is it?"

She turned and looked at him, taking his hand in hers as though Ben were the one in need of comforting. "I saw you. You were lying on the floor in some kind of shed. You weren't moving and…and your head was bleeding."

A rivulet of tears slid down Eve's cheek. Ben tucked his thumb beneath the cuff of his shirt and used it to dry her face. Both his voice and his smile were filled with warmth as he said, "Eve, listen. What you just did was incredibly brave. You need to worry about yourself right now, not me—especially because the last bit of the story sounds an awful lot like my paintball accident. I'd wager that your vision ended exactly when you thought it did, and then a frightening memory intruded into your thoughts. But the rest of what you saw is so valuable. Thank you so much for doing that."

Eve didn't appear convinced, but she smiled. "You're probably right. I hope it helps. Just promise me you'll be careful?"

"Always." He spoke with a depth of conviction that seemed to calm her.

It didn't calm me, though. First of all, I knew that Ben put his own safety pretty far down on his priority list. Everyone else in that room came ahead of him, as far as he was concerned—along with his mother, our patients, and innocent bystanders, for goodness' sake. Secondly, in Eve's vision, he was lying on the floor of a shed, not moving, bleeding from the head—none of which had happened when Ben got shot with the paintball. Cold dread wound its way through my body.

We talked about the significance of what Eve had seen and how it fit in with what Malcolm's spirit had told Kai and me. Whatever this rising darkness was, it was scattered around the earth, but Mercier—the head of the snake—was the center, and was going to draw in the rest somehow. The meaning of the cloud blocking out the sun's light wasn't as clear, but we connected it with Malcolm's pronouncement that our group had been given stewardship over the "gifts of light," or paranormal abilities. Kai guessed that somehow, by stopping whatever was happening at Mercier, we would be protecting sensitives, or at least keeping gifts like ours from becoming weapons of evil. And we all agreed that only something truly evil could make the rivers run red, even if that image turned out to be just a metaphor.

The whole room fell into a torpor. There was a long silence as everyone felt the weight of the responsibility we suddenly bore. It was too much, too big—almost paralyzing.

"All right," Ben said, breaking the spell. He stood and began pacing the room. "What else have we got? Any new information?"

Vani went first. She had been quietly reading as many auras as she could. She sensed that Michael and Liv were excited to be a part of Team Forward, but assuming their drug use was part of Skeet's research, there wasn't anything unscrupulous about them, aside from perhaps a willingness to overlook suspicious events if it meant getting a bigger paycheck. Skeet was more complex. Vani said his aura revealed genuine passion and feeling, both for his work and for the people he cared about. He was also concealing a lot, and had been infected with some dark energy, but it hadn't yet penetrated to his core. She got the sense that his morals had stretched to fit whatever corrupt activities he was involved in, to the point that he really didn't believe that he was doing anything wrong.

Hencock and Tucker were another matter. Vani said that their auras were so full of rot that she couldn't bear to read them for long.

She was able to tell that they were the reverse of Skeet—corrupt at the core, but with well-developed exterior shells of civility and charm. Like most people, she said, they weren't entirely evil; on some level, they had convinced themselves that whatever they were doing was right. But they were mistaken, and the evil had formed such deep roots that she warned us to assume the worst and not to trust one word that came out of their mouths.

Asa didn't have much to report, since Ben had put him under strict orders not to use his telepathic skills. Unless Kai put him into an elaborate trance, reading minds gave Asa serious migraines. Asa did say that Skeet, the other owners, Team Forward, and the security staff all must have donned telepath-blocking devices, because he had done some preliminary probing, and their minds appeared to him like closed books. However, he had spent some productive time with Michael, who had been quite happy to share some techniques for reading minds without getting headaches. Asa had been practicing a little—"just on Owen, and he's easy to read, so don't get mad, Ben"—and he was getting better at it. Asa offered to jump in and help "when things go sideways. I mean *if*," he added quickly. Asa had proven to be a valuable asset in dicey situations in the past, so Ben said they'd discuss later how he might put his new skills to use.

Then Pete gave us his update. He'd been making some plans with our contacts outside of the lodge to keep eyes on Ben and me during our yacht trip. The muskrat trappers, Lonzie and Clayton, said they and some of their waterman friends would be scattered throughout the area, keeping us in their line of sight while we were on the water.

"Just out of curiosity, what's in it for them?" Kai asked.

"They know something shady is going on in Mercier," Pete said. "This is their backyard, remember, so they want to find out what exactly the deal is just as much as we do." He tipped his hat back and rubbed his hairline. "Of course, even though they're helping us out for their own reasons, they're also doing us a favor, so it's only right that we should show our appreciation. I managed to strike up a conversation with one of those Opretec bodyguards at the bar downstairs. Turns out they're into those ushanka hats, and would love to get their hands on some muskrat skins wholesale."

Kai rolled his eyes and said, "I should have known you weren't over there trying to learn some romantic phrases in Russian." Everyone grinned.

"Moving right along," Ben said. He had heard from Danielle, and she'd confirmed that the owners were using the Mercier Cove Trust to launder money. To keep their transactions away from prying eyes, clients like Opretec would anonymously deposit payments into escrow accounts in Switzerland. Then the money would be broken into smaller amounts and sent as payments for imaginary business services to any one of a number of shell corporations Mercier had set up in the Caribbean. Finally, the shell corporations would give the money to the Mercier Cove Trust in the form of charitable donations. This process greatly reduced the amount of taxes being paid, but more importantly, it allowed transactions to go through while keeping the clients' identities secret. Mercier could use Team Forward to sell information to whomever they liked and do it in complete privacy.

And Ben and Pete didn't like who Mercier was selling information to that week. Max had done some research into Opretec, and while the corporation appeared to be aboveboard, they were indeed heavily invested in uranium mining in Kazakhstan. Max's sources inside the military told him there were rumors that Opretec was taking the ore back to Russia, where they were enriching bomb-grade uranium-235. If true, Ben said, that was a serious violation of several nuclear nonproliferation agreements and treaties—and the members of Team Forward might be inadvertently violating the Espionage Act, depending on the content of the regular updates they were giving to Opretec and other international clients. Pete thought the "inadvertently" part was probably optimistic, but Ben didn't want to jump to any conclusions until we had evidence. We hoped our dinner that night would shed some light on the owners' true motives.

Armed with as much information as we were going to get, it was finally time for Ben and me to get ready for our trip out to the yacht. Although Vani was petite and I was decidedly *not*, she had brought a sundress that sort of fit me, although she'd had to use considerable force to pull up the back zipper. It was white and dotted with yellow daisies. Fortunately, I had some white sandals to match. Ben had a suit with him, of course, but he decided to match the formality of his outfit to mine, opting for slacks and dock shoes with a sports jacket over his dress shirt—top button undone as usual.

The week before, I'd been outraged when Ben secretly planted a GPS tracker in my bag—but it had ended up saving my life. This time, I immediately agreed to wear the tiny, stick-on device. We decided to put my tracker inside the waistband of my dress, and Ben wore his in the pocket of his sports jacket. Also the previous week, their friends in Yankee Company had gifted Pete and Ben a couple of cell phones that also worked as single-channel radios. That meant Ben would be securely transmitting every sound within shouting distance to Pete, even if there was no cell phone reception or the phone was turned off. Pete wanted Ben to carry a gun, but Ben was fairly sure that bringing a weapon to an intimate dinner on a congressman's yacht would send all the wrong messages.

Talk of bringing a gun made my stomach churn. Ben took my hand lightly in his and reassured me that we were talking through all of the options "just to be thorough," and that everything would go smoothly. We'd have a chance to take the measure of some of the other owners, and hopefully convince them that we were eager to be a part of Mercier—and benefit from it financially—without worrying too much about how the profits were made. Then, hopefully, they'd be willing to open up and answer a few questions for us.

Chapter Nineteen

It was almost four thirty. Ben and I waited for Skeet on the pier. We admired one another for how well we'd cleaned up, but he voiced a concern that the bust of my dress might burst at the seams any moment. At least that was the excuse he gave for glancing at my chest repeatedly.

"Cut it out," I said with a laugh. "You're going to distract me, and I need to focus on our plan. Otherwise, I could blow it."

Playful Ben disappeared, replaced immediately by all-business Ben. "Cate, you're not going to blow anything." He touched my elbow and slid his fingers down my arm until his hand was holding mine. "We both know the plan backwards and forwards. If by some chance you say or do something that doesn't fit, I'll find a way to cover. And since I have every intention of talking you into marrying me one day, the engagement part should be easy to fake," he teased, trying to put me at ease. "Besides, we're not going to be alone out there. There's nothing for you to worry about. Understood?"

I nodded and squeezed his hand, forcing myself to smile back.

Skeet joined us on the pier, dapper in a light gray suit. He reiterated that there had been no need for us to go to the trouble of dressing up, although he appeared pleased that we'd done so. He explained that the other owners had spent the day on the yacht and were waiting for us there. We boarded a large speedboat and enjoyed the warmth of the late afternoon sun. The boat's captain, Phil, was a local with extensive knowledge of the area. He helped us pass the time by pointing out landmarks, plants, and birds.

Eventually we reached the open waters of the Chesapeake Bay, falling into a comfortable silence as we savored the feel of the breeze and misty sprays of water. Once Phil spotted the yacht, I ducked down into the covered section of the speedboat and undid my tight braid, giving my curls a quick fluffing. Vani had said it would make the sundress look better if I let my hair fall down and cover my shoulders, and since I had no clue about fashion, I took her word for it.

As we drew closer to the yacht, I realized how massive it was—a floating mansion. There was some awkwardness climbing the stepladder in sandals and a dress, but Ben had encouraged Skeet to go up first to give me a hand in. Then Ben brought up the rear so that if I fell, he could catch me—and if I flashed anyone, it would be him.

Congressman Tucker and Mr. Hencock were there to greet us, also wearing suits and with cocktails in hand. Apparently, it was just going to be the five of us for dinner. Greetings were exchanged, and Ben and I behaved with due deference and humility as we were introduced to the congressman. I noticed two men trying to blend into the background, but they looked an awful lot like security guards or Secret Service agents. They wore black suits with bulges at the hip, earpieces with wires that went down into their shirts, and they carried themselves like big cats—loose but ready to attack.

A crewmember approached us with a small metal lock box and held it open. Several cell phones were inside.

"I hope you don't mind," Tucker said. "We figure there's no point being out on the water if we're going to stay tethered to land. We have a policy: all cell phones go in the box until you leave the vessel. That way, we're all living in the moment, and not tempted to check messages constantly."

I hadn't brought a cell, but I tensed, knowing the significance of Ben's. If he was concerned, though, he didn't show it. Ben pulled out his cell, turned it off, and dropped it in the box. "I like that policy," he said, sounding sincere. "I may have to experiment with instituting it at our clinic."

A ripple of approval passed through the owners. "Don't worry,"

Skeet added. "The staff at the lodge knows where we are, and they'll contact the captain if anything requires our attention."

"So let's hope it's a quiet night—aside from the celebration, that is," Tucker said, winking at me. He gestured to one of the uniformed, white-gloved members of the waitstaff, who brought forward a bottle of champagne in an iced silver bucket. Another waiter appeared with a tray of empty glasses.

"To Cate," Tucker said as the glasses were filled. "Your father was a dear friend of ours, and we feel his loss keenly. But we know that he would be more than pleased to see you take your place as an owner of the property."

The waiter distributed the glasses and we followed Tucker's lead, holding them aloft. "To the newest owner of Mercier!"

Smiling, the others toasted, "To Cate!" Everyone took a drink except for Ben and me.

"You two don't drink?" Hencock asked in his smooth southern drawl.

Skeet smacked his forehead. "Paul, I forgot to tell you! I'm sorry, Cate, Ben."

"Not a problem. Cate is still in training with the MacGregor Group," Ben explained. "As part of our protocol, she can't have alcohol. I don't want her to feel like the odd man out, so we'll both just have soda, if you don't mind."

"Oh, I can do you one better!" With a flick of his finger, Tucker ordered us new glasses. "Sparkling cider for our guests."

"We also wanted to celebrate you two kids," Hencock said. "Skeet tells us you're getting hitched!"

"That's right," I said, not even having to fake my happiness as Ben put his arm around my waist and kissed the top of my head.

The waiter popped the cork on a bottle of sparkling cider and poured our drinks. Then we all raised our glasses again. "Nothing could bring me greater joy than to see the daughter and son of two of my dear friends fall in love," Skeet said, his eyeglasses misting. "Congratulations on your upcoming nuptials!" To that, we all drank.

Tucker then took us on a tour of the yacht, which was even

more spectacular than I had imagined. There were two entire floors above deck with walls of glass. The first housed a dance floor that could be converted into a large dining room, professional audio/visual equipment, and a lush living area with the largest flat-screen TV I'd ever seen. A conference room and an office space on the top floor both provided a breathtaking view of the Bay. We paused there long enough to finish our drinks and take in the sunset. Everywhere we went, the two black-suited men shadowed Tucker, confirming my guess that they were some type of security detail.

One of the black suits touched the com device in his ear, then spoke briefly to Tucker, who announced that dinner was ready. He assured us that the best parts of the yacht were below deck. Once we got down the stairs, I understood why. The floors and walls were made of dark wood, complemented by furniture covered in soft leather and richly textured fabrics. An enormous stuffed swordfish hung on one wall, but the rest were decorated with photographs of the local area. At one end, doors lead off to other rooms—bedrooms, I guessed—and at the other, a door bore the sign, "HEAD," indicating the bathroom. Just in front of the bedrooms was a large dining table. While the men settled in around it, I excused myself to wash my hands.

Though small, like everything else on the yacht, the bathroom was nicely appointed. Once inside, I ran cold water over my hands and tucked them around the back of my neck. Everything seemed to be going well, but my nerves were still on edge. It was easy enough to make admiring noises while Tucker showed us his yacht, but once we sat down to dinner, I knew the dynamics would change, and Ben and I would be put under a magnifying glass. And with Ben's phone shut away, we truly were on our own.

No point worrying now, I told myself. *You have a job to do.* I closed my eyes and tested my empathic senses, trying to transform myself into an energetic satellite dish so that I could catch all of the emotions that would be flying around the dinner table. Knowing that I would have to be in top form, I had allowed Vani to perform an aura cleansing-ritual to open up my heart chakra as much as possible.

From my work as a therapist, I knew how to subtly reach out and empathically sense another person's feelings while keeping my facial expression neutral. But this was a whole *group* of people, and they were all trying to conceal things. It was going to be a challenge, to put it mildly. I took a deep breath, plastered on a smile, and headed back to join the dinner party.

When I returned, classical music was playing softly in the background. *So civilized*, I thought, a few drops of bitterness rising in my throat. I remembered what Vani had said about Tucker and Hencock, that beneath the surface, their auras were rotten to the core.

As I predicted, the owners had already started in with the questions. Ben was handling everything smoothly, of course—a little too smoothly for my taste, in fact, as he described where he was taking me the next day to pick out my engagement ring. They all stood as I approached, and Ben pulled out my chair. Unused to such formality, I just smiled, nodded, and let him push my chair in.

"So when's the big day?" Hencock asked.

"Oh, we haven't set a date yet," I said.

"That's right." Ben caressed the back of my hand with the pad of his thumb. "In fact, we might not set a date at all, and elope instead."

Somehow I managed to keep my smile plastered on and refrain from kicking Ben under the table.

"I like that," Tucker said. "A man of action."

"Well, what do you know," Hencock added, "we might have an old-fashioned whirlwind romance on our hands!"

Skeet wagged his finger at Ben. "I know you're telling Ardis about your engagement this weekend, but I hope you'll tell your mother too, Ben—sooner rather than later. Especially if you're considering eloping. You know Angeline will be mad as a wet hen if you leave her out!"

"Sound advice!" Ben and Skeet exchanged knowing smiles.

A mild headache started behind my eyes as the discussion about our pretend marriage continued over appetizers. There was some discussion of the tax benefits, interest rates on mortgages, and various other mind-numbing financial subjects that I had no desire to even think about, let alone talk about over dinner with a group of unscrupulous businessmen. Fortunately, Ben seemed energized by the conversation and was more than able to hold up our end. *At least we're actually in love*, I thought as I dug into the shrimp cocktail and crab dip. *That's one thing we don't have to fake.*

The appetizers were cleared away and the main course was brought out: plates of grilled bluefish, accompanied by wild rice, a squash casserole, and delicious mango chutney. Salad and a few other sides were served family style. As we began to taste the various dishes, I voiced my admiration of the superior cuisine. Tucker explained that he and Hencock had caught the bluefish earlier that day, and Skeet had brought the squash from Mercier's farm. As for the chutney, Tucker said that he'd attended a White House dinner recently. The President had a chef who was a chutney expert, and if he liked a particular guest, he'd send them home with a few jars.

For a moment, I felt like I was outside of myself, watching someone else have dinner with these men—one of whom was a congressman who had recently dined with the President. Who was I to be there in the first place—and who was I to even think about trying to extract secret information from such powerful individuals? I suddenly felt the weight of the task Ben and I had set for ourselves—the impossibility of it. I was on the verge of losing heart when Ben prompted me, giving me the code phrase we had practiced.

"Cate, you mentioned earlier that you wanted to tell Skeet something," he said.

"Oh, that's right!" I dabbed the corners of my mouth with my napkin and turned to Skeet. "My lawyer looked over the papers. You can let Harris know that I'll sign them whenever he likes." Then I cast my eyes downward. "Sorry for bringing up business at dinner…"

"No, not at all! That's great. Gentlemen, we're talking about the papers that'll make Cate official as an owner," Skeet explained. "How long are you staying?"

"Cate and I plan to stay until Friday," Ben said. "The rest of our group may have to head back Thursday. We, on the other hand, have some ring shopping to do, and I know Cate wants to spend more time getting to know Mercier."

"Perfect," Skeet said. "I believe Harris will be back Friday morning, so we can take care of it then."

"Wonderful," I said.

"It's good to hear that you want to get to know Mercier better," Hencock said. "There's a lot going on, a lot to learn."

"Speaking of which," Tucker said, "what did you think of Skeet's little demonstration this morning?"

Skeet winced at the phrase, "little demonstration," but only for a second. "Yes," he said, leaning back and clasping his hands behind his neck. "We talked a little bit about it immediately afterwards, but I promised we'd discuss it more later. Now's the perfect time, and I'm very interested to hear what you thought—both of you. After all, as a sensitive and a manager of a paranormal clinic—and also as outsiders—you have unique perspectives."

Ben mirrored Skeet, leaning back in his chair, and rested his arm along the back of mine. He gave me an encouraging look. "You go first, Cate. What did you think?"

I tried to channel Vani and be as charming as possible as I responded. "Well, I thought it was very impressive. Michael and Liv are so good at what they do—and Michael speaking Russian, that surprised everyone! I think our group could learn a lot from the training you're providing to your sensitives, both at NIMH and as part of Team Forward." I looked to Ben, who nodded. "Also, it may be because I'm new to the world of sensitives, but it had never occurred to me that our gifts could be used for anything other than treating patients. Your demonstration really opened my eyes to the possibilities."

Skeet rubbed his chin. "It's not just because you're new, Cate. Most people think of using paranormal abilities in terms of healing, treating people. The government used to be interested in potential wartime applications such as spying, but they lost faith after some poorly designed experiments in the 1970s ended badly. We've been able to keep our research going at NIMH, but only because a few members of Congress have championed us. They're viewed as eccentrics, though, and as I mentioned to you last week, we have to operate outside of the public eye and under strict constraints." He gestured toward Tucker. "Paul here has been the only one on the Hill keeping us alive at times."

"I do what I can," Tucker said, "but at NIMH, Skeet will never get enough money or enough freedom to really move things forward. As usual, it's up to private industry to make something happen."

"So you started up Team Forward as a business?" I asked, trying to sound innocent.

"Exactly." Skeet leaned forward and tapped his finger on the table. "We all know that there is a stigma around paranormal abilities. No one wants to admit to believing that they're real, for fear of not being taken seriously. That applies to governments, businesses, investors—everyone. However, no one can argue with the kind of results we produce—the unique edge we can give to our clients. And in today's world, even a marginal advantage is highly sought after."

"And like Ben said earlier, it's not only a win for them. It's a win for you, and for the sensitives," I said. "The training you give them must be amazing. Asa said Michael was able to teach him how to read minds without getting headaches. You've found some real answers."

"Yes!" Skeet smiled across the table, taking in both Ben and me. "With the exception, of course, of the elusive secret of the double kheir. But we're working hard to crack it."

"That's an elusive one, all right," Ben said without even a whiff of insincerity. "I have to say, I'm impressed with the way you've set up Team Forward. How you've recruited sensitives with a variety of paranormal gifts and other skills and enabled them to move in and out of activity, depending on what you need—that's military-style efficiency. It must be a big selling point for your clients, to know that your team will never be out of commission."

"It is," Skeet acknowledged. "You can't very well sell a service to powerful global interests, and then not deliver one day because your telepath has the flu."

All of the men chuckled, so I joined in, even though I could feel the tension in the room rising. There was a pause. Finally, Tucker broke the silence. "Speaking of military-style efficiency, Ben," he asked casually, "why is it that you left the Marine Corps? A man with your training and a Ph.D. in organizational psychology—Skeet told us—I'm sure they didn't let you go without a fight." He smiled broadly, and I could have sworn his teeth had sharp tips.

Ben had hoped that question would come up. It gave him the perfect opportunity to mislead them. "It was a tough decision. I love the Corps, and as I'm sure you know, once a Marine, always a Marine. I left when I did because my father died, and my mother needed my support." He paused as everyone nodded respectfully. "But the deeper reason—well, to be honest, Congressman, I just got tired of taking orders and following rules that didn't make sense to me, particularly when no one would explain the reason behind them."

"You wanted to be your own boss," Hencock summarized.

"Yes." Ben rubbed his jaw. "But not *just* that. The way the world is now, the only constant is change, and it's accelerating. You have to be able to make your own judgments, to act without wasting time on bureaucracy and red tape."

"Well, we certainly agree there," Tucker said. "Do you have any concerns about Team Forward giving information to foreign clients?"

Wow, he gets right to the point, I thought, trying not to hold my breath while Ben considered the question.

"Certainly not as long as you're involved, Congressman."

"Oh? And what have I done to earn your trust?" Tucker asked, once again donning his crocodile smile.

"You've dedicated your life to serving our country," Ben said, smiling back. "A man like you would never be a part of anything that was contrary to our national interest."

"I appreciate that." Tucker nodded slowly. "But let's say for the sake of argument that you became involved with Team Forward, as I believe Skeet would very much like you to. As you're now aware, one of our international clients is involved in uranium mining. Do you have any concerns about that?"

"About Opretec?" Ben shrugged. "I have no doubt that you have a reliable vetting process in place. Although if I *were* involved with Team Forward, I'd probably want to know more about that process. As I mentioned, I like to know the reasons behind things."

"Of course," Hencock said lightly, as though Ben had just asked if we could have mint juleps on the veranda. "Cate's an owner, and as her husband, you'll be on the inside, as well. You'll quickly find that we like everyone to be fully informed about what the various branches of Mercier are up to. We prioritize openness. No secrets."

I pressed my lips together hard, fighting a wave of nausea. I knew very well that there were secrets. One was about my father's death. And Hencock and Tucker were keeping at least one secret from Skeet. The air around me suddenly felt heavy.

"Cate, are you all right?" Skeet asked.

Ben turned to look at me. "You do look a little green around the edges. She used to get seasick," he explained to the table. "She's been all right lately, though, so we didn't think it would be an issue. Plus, she didn't want to take a Dramamine; they make her drowsy."

"What would help?" Tucker asked. "Some fresh air?"

The thought of fresh air was extremely tempting, but I didn't want to leave Ben alone in the shark tank. "Maybe a Coke on ice, with some lemon?"

Tucker snapped his fingers. In less than a minute, the waiter was pouring my soda into a glass and squeezing in a fresh-cut slice of lemon. "Thanks." At least the distraction had eased the pressure in the room a bit. The waitstaff also took advantage of the pause to clear away our dinner plates and deliver after-dinner drinks. I began to sip my soda quietly. "Feeling better already."

"Glad to hear it." Tucker smiled, then refocused on Ben. "Well, you're right; we do have a robust vetting process for our clients. I'm on the Ways and Means Committee, and some of the other owners are well placed in the government, so we have access to privileged information, which helps. And of course, we're careful never to take on clients whose work could undermine our national interest—although as you said, the world today is in a constant state of change. Some of those changes mean that there are often disputes over what is or is not in the national interest at any given moment."

"Hell, that's always been the case," Hencock said.

"True, but now more than ever." Tucker eyed Ben carefully. "What's your take on that, Ben?"

"To be honest, sir, since leaving the Corps, I've been focused on helping my mother set up the clinic. But from what I hear, the geopolitical landscape has grown so complex that it's nearly impossible to get a handle on what's what. I don't envy you your responsibilities, Congressman."

That answer appeared to satisfy Tucker. He leaned back in his chair and idly rubbed his belly. "Well said—at least I think so. Cate, do you share Ben's viewpoint?"

I laid my hands on the table, palms up. "I don't really know enough to say. I mean, everything that's been said makes sense to me, but politics isn't really my area." There was enough truth in that for me to say it with some sincerity.

"Of course; your focus has been elsewhere," Tucker said indulgently. "Well, you two won't be in the dark much longer—any more than you want to be, that is." He leaned forward. "I know you like to know what's going on behind the scenes, Ben, and as a Marine, I know you can handle anything we've got to tell you. And Cate, you clearly have a keen mind. But I'll warn you both, the kind of knowledge Mercier has access to can be a heavy burden to bear. There are limits to how much some of us can share, of course. Ben, you understand; there are things that are top secret, confidential. But we'll always tell you as much as we can."

"Of course." Ben flipped me a thumbs-up sign under the table, indicating that he had all of the information he'd come for. That meant that if I still wanted to, it was my turn to play investigator.

The truth was, I had heard all I wanted to hear, and my

tolerance for tension and subterfuge was reaching a breaking point. But I knew it might be my only opportunity to get answers, and that I'd hate myself later if I passed it up just because I was feeling overwhelmed.

Allowing my genuine emotions to show on my face, I said, "I don't mean to change the subject, but I just wanted to say, it's so nice to get to know you—friends of my father's." Everyone visibly relaxed; apparently, I wasn't the only one who was grateful that the conversation was shifting to a new topic. "It's a source of great sorrow to me that I never knew him, especially since I found out that he wanted to be a part of my life all those years."

"He truly did," Hencock said. "And it was *his* greatest sorrow that he had to wait so long to reconnect with you, but looking forward to that moment was also his greatest joy."

"Thank you; I appreciate that. And I feel that by getting to know you and becoming a part of Mercier, I'm finally making some connection with him, after all."

Tucker lowered his chin to his chest. "Your father's death—it was terrible. A great loss."

Hencock nodded. "Terrible, indeed. We couldn't quite believe it when it happened."

When it happened...? I blinked. "Were you there when he died?"

"The three of us had gone out hunting together," Tucker said, nodding toward Hencock. "It was the damndest thing. You hear about these hunting accidents, but you never think it could happen to you. The tragic truth is that it can happen to anyone."

They're admitting they were the only other people there when he died, I thought. *And someone shot him. That means they did it. They murdered my father. I just ate dinner with murderers.*

I nearly fainted from the combination of fear and fury that blasted through me. My head started to fall backwards, but Ben was there, sliding his fingers up the back of my neck and into my hair, supporting me. He rested his other hand on my forearm and squeezed gently. "Cate?" I could sense that he was feeling the same thing I was: the horror of realization. "Congressman, can we trouble you for a fresh drink?"

No sooner had he said it than a new drink appeared. I took a moment to gather myself as I sipped the soda. "Thank you," I whispered. I couldn't look Hencock or Tucker in the eyes, but I managed to ask, "Can you tell me what happened?"

Hencock began softly, "We were goose hunting early one morning at Mercier. I'm not sure how much you know about hunting, but we were down in a pit, like a trench, with all our equipment and the dogs, waiting for the geese to fly over."

I thought back to the morning I'd overheard them in the field. Icy tendrils trickled along my arms.

"When the geese came, we all jumped up and grabbed our shotguns, the way we always did..." Hencock choked up with what appeared to be real emotion, unable to continue.

"Like we'd done a hundred times before without incident," Tucker confirmed. "But Joe hadn't been hunting in years; he must have forgotten that you're not supposed to lean your gun up against the wall of the pit. Anyway, he had just leaned it up there so he could tie his bootlace when the geese came. I don't know if the barrel was slippery from the fog, or if he tripped on a root, or what happened." He hesitated. "Are you sure you want to know this, Cate?"

Not trusting my voice, I just nodded.

He sighed heavily. "When Joe reached for his gun, he stumbled, and ended up grabbing it by the trigger while the barrel was pointed at him." Tucker tried to reach across the table for my hand, but pulled away when he realized I wasn't reaching back. "I'm so sorry, Cate. There are no words."

The only words I could hear echoed through my head, and they were spoken in Kai's voice: "He didn't shoot himself, after all; someone else pulled the trigger." I knew if I stayed there much longer, I was either going to pass out or lunge across the table at my father's killers. It was time to find a path to the end of that conversation so we could get the hell out of there.

I forced my eyes to flit upwards long enough to meet Hencock's and Tucker's. I could sense their genuine regret, although for what, I couldn't say. Maybe they had really liked my father, and were sorry that they'd felt the need to kill him—why, I might never know. But sorry or not, they'd done it anyway. I worked to unclench my teeth. "Thank you for telling me. I know that was hard, but it helps me to know."

"Of course," Skeet said, his voice raked with sadness. I looked over at him and saw the grief of a man who had truly lost a friend. Suddenly, it dawned on me: *Skeet doesn't know. He still believes it was an accident. This is the secret they've been keeping from him.*

In spite of myself, I suddenly felt sorry for Skeet. I wanted to say something to ease his pain. "I'm glad he had you—that he had such good friends."

His grateful smile pinched my heart, and I knew I couldn't take much more. It was time to give Ben my five-minute warning. I leaned over and whispered, "Ben, what time is it?"

He met my eyes, and his told me silently that he understood: I needed to leave. "I don't know," he admitted. "I didn't wear a watch tonight, and my phone…" He looked around the table.

Skeet checked his watch. "Well, look at that. It's eight thirty. I hadn't realized it was so late. Phil is probably outside with the speedboat already." He stood, and the rest of us followed suit.

"Unless you'd like dessert?" Tucker asked. "Phil can wait. We have some homemade ice cream—"

I managed a light laugh. "After that amazing meal, I can't think of eating another thing. Don't forget, I have to fit into a wedding dress soon."

"You have nothing to worry about," Ben said, giving me a broad wink.

I knew he was trying to help me relax, but with every passing moment, I felt even more urgency to get off the boat and away from those people. We all filed up to the deck and said our goodbyes and thank yous. If Tucker and Hencock suspected that we'd been less than genuine, they didn't show it. Instead, they warmly reiterated how glad they were that we would be joining Mercier. It took everything I had left in me to smile and shake hands with them before we departed.

While a crewmember gave Ben back his phone, Skeet announced that he was spending the night on the yacht. They had an early morning fishing adventure planned. "I was right," he said, "Phil is here already. You two have a pleasant trip back, and good luck with the engagement ring search tomorrow!" He pulled me into a hug and pumped Ben's hand. "Congratulations again!"

"Thanks!" Ben and I called out, joining Phil near the stepladder. We climbed into the speedboat, and I pulled Ben to the bench in the back. I wanted to be able to bury my head in his chest and cry without Phil overhearing.

Chapter Twenty

Ben took off his jacket and draped it over me, holding me against him as I let the tears fall. I didn't even know why I was crying. Was it just from relief that we'd managed to get away, safe and sound? Was I releasing the rage and horror I'd felt while sitting at that absurdly fancy dinner, surrounded by murderers? It couldn't be grief over losing my father, a man I'd never even known. But I had *wanted* to know him, and now I would never have the chance—all due to a combination of greed and whatever Machiavellian philosophy Mercier's owners embraced.

There on the water with Ben's arms wrapped around me, the tears slowly grew lighter, and my heart calmed. Once we returned, we'd meet with the others and put a plan in place. I closed my eyes and felt the cool breeze, listened to the way sounds were dampened as they were absorbed by the wide water and the even wider sky. Ben produced a tissue from somewhere. But as I dried my cheeks, I noticed the mascara stains on his shirt. "Oh!" I quickly straightened. How many of Ben's shirts had I ruined in the past few weeks by crying on them? "I'm so sorry," I said, pointing to the stain.

"About what?"

"I ruined your shirt again."

The sky was completely overcast—we couldn't see any stars, and just a soft glow from a cloud-covered moon—so Ben had to lean down close to see the stain. He chuckled, then looked over at me, the affection in his eyes visible even in the dark. He tucked his mouth down near my ear and murmured, "Never apologize. All I want to do is be here for you, and those marks on my shirt mean I've done my job. I consider them badges of honor. Besides, with that big nest egg you're getting, you can buy me a new shirt."

"Oh, please," I moaned. "I could never accept that nest egg. It's probably made up of illegal gains that will end up with the IRS anyway. I'm going to stay poor forever."

"Then I'll buy *myself* some shirts, and you can work off the cost by picking them out for me."

I felt the beginnings of a smile tugging at my mouth. "That's a very brave offer. Vani says I have no fashion sense."

"I trust you."

"Hmm." I slid down the bench away from him, handing him back his jacket as I looked him up and down. "How do you feel about plaid?"

"I'm a MacGregor. Our clan has its own tartan, so I'm pro-plaid."

"You're kidding, really?" I'd never seen him in plaid, so I'd been hoping to shock him.

"Yes, really. You have your own tartan, too—Duncan."

"I do?"

"You didn't know?"

My mother and I weren't big into family history, so I'd never given it any thought. I shook my head.

"Are you saying," he teased, "that I have to show you yours *and* show you mine?"

At that, I laughed my first real laugh in ages. The boat lurched slightly, tossing me back towards Ben. He caught me handily around the waist and swooped in for a kiss. I started to get lost in the dreaminess of kissing him on a boat as we sped across the Bay in the dark, but then we heard the engine sputter and go silent. Phil cursed up by the steering wheel. With reluctance, Ben stood and hitched his thumb toward the front of the boat. "I'd better check it out."

"You do that," I said breathlessly. It looked like we were getting closer to the shoreline. I could see the contrast between the moving shadows of the water and the consistent dark line of the land. We would be back at the lodge soon, and the murderers would be far away, asleep on the yacht. I closed my eyes and imagined being locked in my room with Ben, with that stopper device against the door—temporarily safe, at least.

I opened my eyes when I heard Ben say, "Phil, you got a flashlight?"

Ben was crouched on the deck near the steering wheel, trying to get a look at the engine. Phil had lifted up one of the benches and was rummaging around in the storage area beneath. He produced a thin, cylindrical object. I guessed it was a small flashlight, until he pulled a cap off of its top and I saw that there was no beam of light coming from it.

What's that? In my confusion, time slowed almost to a stop. Phil wasn't handing the object to Ben, either. Instead, he appeared to be aiming it at Ben's neck.

Time rushed ahead again at full speed. I leapt off of the bench and charged toward them, yelling, "Ben, look out!"

When Ben turned, Phil stuck the object into his shoulder, pressing in a plunger at the end. I heard a plastic-sounding *click*. Ben crumpled to the ground like a sheet torn off a clothesline.

"Ben!" I screamed, lunging forward. But Phil was ready for me. Simultaneously, he threw his arms around me in a vice-like hold and tripped me. He lowered me onto the deck, sitting on me with his knee in my back. I turned my head and saw Ben just a few feet away, barely awake, eyes glazing over. Desperately, I fought Phil, kicking, clawing, and writhing with all my might. He must have had some kind of special training, though, because my wrists and ankles were tied together in no time flat.

Phil stood up and touched his face; his hand was bloody when he pulled it away. "Dammit, Cate, I'm not going to *hurt* you! I'm just going to stick you with a needle."

With some satisfaction, I saw that I'd managed to make a couple of deep scratches on his face. But that wasn't going to help Ben. "Phil, what is going on? What have you done?"

"Don't worry, you'll be fine. Damn, they're here already."

I heard the sound of another engine approaching. "*Who* is

here? And how are we going to be fine? You just knocked Ben out! What did you give him?"

"The same thing I'm gonna give you. It's just a sedative. Once these guys pick up Ben and are well on their way, I'll take you back to the lodge. Hey!" Phil called out to the approaching vessel.

"Hey, Phil!" someone called back in a thin, reedy voice. "You ready for us?"

"Yup!" They threw Phil a rope and he caught it, tying it to a metal fixture.

I took advantage of Phil's absence, inch-worming my way over to Ben so that our heads were nearly touching. His eyes were closed. "Ben! Ben! Wake up!" He moved slightly, and I heard him moan. He was alive, at least. My heart thudded hard. "Ben, wake—aarrrgh!" I groaned as Phil grabbed me by the feet and dragged me away to the far side of the boat.

Two burly men in baseball caps climbed aboard. Panic crept up my throat as they shifted Ben out from behind the steering wheel and put plastic ties around his wrists and ankles. Could these men be Lonzie and Clayton? Had they betrayed us? If so, that meant no one was coming to our rescue.

Ben must have cut his head when he fell. Bright red blood was dripping down his cheek and onto his shirt. "Ben!" My call came out as a strangled cry. "Phil, he's bleeding!"

"What, you didn't drug her yet?" asked one of the men.

"I was about to when you rolled up!" Phil replied, then turned to me. "It's only a little cut. Head wounds just bleed a lot."

Rage bloomed inside me as the two strangers lifted Ben, one at his shoulders and one at his feet, and carried him toward their vessel. He moaned again, but didn't show any other signs of regaining consciousness. "He better not be injured!" I yelled. "I swear to God, Phil, if you know what's good for you, you won't be around when these ropes get untied!"

"You'll be knocked out cold when that happens!"

Helplessness clawed at me as the men laid Ben down on a thick net and used it like a stretcher, lowering him from the speedboat into their vessel. "And *you* bastards!" I screamed at them. "If you harm a hair on his head, I will hunt you down and kill you myself!"

The reedy voice called from the other boat, "Would you shut her up please? She's gonna wake up Sleeping Beauty, here."

"That's it. Where'd that other needle get to?" Phil went back and rummaged around in the storage bench.

"All right, we got him," one of the men yelled. "Unhitch us."

Phil gave up his search for the second syringe, untied the other boat's rope, and threw it down to them. "Go, get outta here!"

"I just hope you gave him enough. He looks like a mean bastard."

"Don't worry, he won't wake up for a while." Phil waved as the other boat's motor revved. The sound faded as they headed away from us.

I tried to fight through my desperation so that I could think clearly about the situation. Phil began rifling through the storage bench again. I reached out to him with my empathic senses. I picked up that while he wasn't uncomfortable with violence, in that moment he felt a pang of regret. I got the impression that he liked Ben and me. We'd had a good conversation on the way out to the yacht. Phil was following someone's orders, but I could tell he was ill at ease. Maybe his usual violent activities didn't involve women.

I decided to stay still and silent for a little so he would think he'd scared me into submission. As the minutes passed, his discomfort grew. He gave up his search for the syringe and began pacing around the boat. He lit a cigarette and only smoked half, tossing it into the water. Then he took his seat by the steering wheel and opened a compartment near the engine. "*There* it is!"

"Phil?"

"What?" he snapped.

"I don't understand what's happening. Aren't you going to be in trouble when we get back to the lodge and everyone finds out about this?"

His laugh was small and bitter. "That won't happen."

I swallowed hard. "I thought you said you weren't going to hurt me."

"I'm not," he said defensively. "I'm just giving you the same drug I gave Ben. When you wake up, you'll be in your bed at the lodge, and you won't remember this at all. Your trip to the yacht might even be a little foggy. Aside from a headache, though, you'll be fine."

Oh no, no, no, I thought. That would *not* do. I had to keep him talking. "What about Ben?"

"He'll live. Far as I know, they just want to ask him some questions."

"Who does?"

Phil leaned down and squinted at me. "Honestly? I got no idea. I just do what my boss tells me, like everybody else in this world."

"Your boss—Skeet?"

Phil spit on the floor. "You ask a lot of questions. Look, Ben'll be fine—as long as he doesn't try to kill somebody, that is. Beyond that, there's nothing I can tell you." He reached down and pulled a first aid kit out of the compartment.

I was running out of time. "How are you going to explain the bruises on my ankles and wrists? There are going to be rope marks."

He took a syringe out of the kit and pulled off the plastic cap. "I guess they'll be looking to Ben for answers about those. After all, he's your fiancé, right? Who knows what kind of crazy shit you two got up to out there in the woods." Phil held up the syringe and stood. "You might feel a pinch."

"So help me, Phil, I swear to God, if you touch me, I'll kill you!" I rolled away from him and towards the back of the boat, then twisted around so I could track his movements.

"Would you please stop movin' around, already?"

Suddenly, a third voice pierced the night air. "Hey, Phil!"

Phil jumped, looking around. "Who's there?"

"It's just us, Lonzie and Clayton."

Lonzie and Clayton? So they hadn't betrayed us! I prayed that I'd heard correctly.

Phil held the syringe behind his back with one hand and waved to them with the other. "What, did you row up here? I didn't hear you coming."

"We're trying not to scare the fish," one of the voices said. "Unlike you—I heard somebody shouting up there. Is that Cate Duncan?"

"Yes!" I cried out. "It's Cate!"

"Shut up!" Phil hissed, kicking the bottom of my foot.

"Are you Pete's friends?" I called.

"Yeah," one of the voices said. "I'm Lonzie. He told us to come get you."

"Who's Pete?" Phil was beginning to look extremely annoyed. "And how do you know Cate? Look, you guys, I was just getting ready to take her back to the lodge. Following orders, you know."

"Yeah, we know," Lonzie said, "but unlike you, we don't answer to Tucker." This statement was followed by the distinctive click of a gun being cocked.

Phil froze. "You're not gonna shoot me, Clayton. We're family."

"Not by *my* choice. But you're right. I'm not gonna shoot you—long as you hand the girl over."

"Don't let him get close to me," I pleaded. "He has a syringe, he's trying to shoot me up with something!"

"You heard her," Clayton said. "Back away, Phil."

I could see in Phil's face the very moment he decided that he didn't really want to hurt me, and that it certainly wasn't something he wanted to risk dying over. He held up the syringe, showed it to Lonzie and Clayton, and tossed it into the water. I breathed for what seemed like the first time in ages. "I wasn't going to hurt her," he said.

"Good. Still don't move, though."

I heard a loud clunk as two multi-pronged metal hooks flew over the side of the boat and onto the deck, then slid back until they were gripping the railing. A few minutes later, a man's head appeared. He looked at me, scowled, and said with disgust, "You tied her *up*? Not cool, Phil."

"Just take her and get out of here," Phil muttered.

"Keep the gun on him, Clayton." Lonzie climbed into the speedboat and came over to me. He had a hard, lean look about him, but his voice was kind. "Hey, Cate."

"Hi." My heart skittered—was I really going to be rescued? I thought I could trust Phil. How did I know I could trust Lonzie and Clayton? "I'd shake your hand, but…" I smiled and wiggled my fingers.

He chuckled. "All right, look. I'm gonna pull out a knife, but just to cut off these ropes. I know you don't know me from Adam, but Pete told me to tell you, he's been listening to everything that's been happening since you left the yacht on that high-tech radio phone Ben's got."

"Oh, thank God!"

I felt the back-and-forth tug of the knife as Lonzie worked to free my hands. "We got a little confused when it sounded like Ben was being kidnapped, but his GPS tracker stayed put."

My heart sank as I looked up and saw Ben's jacket still sitting on the bench. "It's there, in his jacket," I whispered, trying not to cry. "Can't you use his phone to track him somehow?"

"Calm down, now," Lonzie said. I rubbed my wrists and pushed myself into a sitting position as he made quick work of the ropes around my ankles. I saw that his hands were gnarled, probably by arthritis, but it didn't seem to slow him down at all. "They disabled the GPS on his phone, but we were expecting that. Don't worry, we'll find him. Stay here for a sec."

Lonzie walked towards the boat's engine.

"What the hell do you think you're doing?" Phil cried.

Pulling open the panel door, Lonzie said, "We can't have you following us." He reached in with his knife and appeared to be slicing a few things inside. "And I wouldn't call the maritime police if I were you. We know the guys who are on duty tonight."

"Goddammit, Lonz!"

"Consider it payback for marrying my sister!" Clayton shouted from the other boat.

Lonzie grinned as he came back to help me up. "C'mon, Cate, let's go."

Looking over the side of the speedboat to the skiff rocking below, I suddenly felt dizzy. Lonzie seemed to know enough about Ben's kidnapping that I could trust him. But the fact was, I couldn't be sure I wasn't jumping from the frying pan into the fire.

"Hey, Cate!" Clayton called. He had a round, boyish face, and he smiled warmly—even as he kept his eye and his shotgun trained on Phil. With his free hand, he held up a walkie-talkie.

"Cate, honey!"

I nearly fell into the water with relief at the sound of Kai's voice.

"Are you okay?"

Clayton pushed a button and spoke into the receiver. "She's scared to get in the boat with us—not that I blame her."

"Oh, lord," I heard Kai say. "Cate, get in the boat already. We need you back here. Pete and Asa have gone off looking for Ben, and Eve, Vani and I are having a hell of a time here at the lodge, trying to make it look like everything's normal!"

They were out looking for Ben. That was all I needed to hear. I climbed down the ladder as fast as I could in my sundress and sandals. "Phil!" I yelled up as Lonzie followed behind me, carrying Ben's jacket. "You'd better pray that I never see you again!"

Phil just cursed, shook his head, and slunk back away from the side of the boat.

Clayton kept his shotgun trained on Phil as Lonzie started up the outboard motor. It roared to life, and before I knew it, we were speeding towards the shoreline.

CHAPTER TWENTY-ONE

Pete's blue eyes shined brightly under the brim of his camo baseball cap. "Well, would ya look who's here."

"Hey, Cate!" Asa scrambled to his feet and gave me a quick squeeze.

With my arrival, it was crowded in the small lean-to shed, which looked like it was about ready to lean all the way over. There was no floor, but the bed of pine needles beneath us was dry. A couple of large canvas bags lay on the ground, filled with equipment. Pete had set up a small radio, and he was listening to its output through a pair of headphones pressed against one ear. Pete and Asa wore full camo and had applied some kind of black makeup to their faces. Asa handed me a small jar and indicated that I should put some on, as well. I'd changed into a black sweater, jeans, and heavy duty hiking boots before leaving the lodge—as close to camo as I could get.

"How'd you get away from Kai?" Asa whispered as I smeared the makeup all over my face.

"After Lonzie and Clayton dropped me off at the lodge," I whispered, "I joined the others upstairs. They tried to get me to stay, but they seemed to be handling things just fine. Obviously, I was going to come look for Ben. When they realized I was leaving, they wanted to come with me, but I told them that we needed someone to stay at home base. Kai was really angry. He couldn't come out because Ben made him promise to evacuate Eve and Vani if an emergency came up. And while we're not to the point of evacuating yet, this is definitely an emergency."

Pete shook his head. "I shoulda known you wouldn't stay put at the lodge—*like I asked*."

I glared at him. "Like I told you early on, I'm *not* a Marine, and I *don't* take orders."

"No kiddin'," he said, grinning. "So you found us here, how?"

"Well, you gave your location to Lonzie. I just convinced him that I needed it, and then asked Owen to bring me over." I smiled. "I told Owen we were playing a secret midnight version of capture the flag, since we had to leave the paintball game prematurely the other day. He totally bought it."

"He did," Asa confirmed. "I made a point of listening in on his thoughts when he dropped you off outside. But he doesn't know *we're* in here."

I shook my head. "I told him this was my hiding place until I got the 'go' code."

"Good thinking," Asa said with a grin.

"Oh, and Lonzie said you might need this." I pulled Ben's jacket out of my bag and handed it to Pete. "I don't know why. It has Ben's GPS tracker in the pocket." I blinked back tears, remembering how my heart had been sliced out of my chest as I watched Ben's kidnappers lower him into their boat.

"Hey, Cate," Pete whispered, "Isn't Harris that lawyer guy? One of the owners?"

"Yes—why?"

"He's with Ben, him and some other guy who's takin' orders from him."

"Are you kidding me? Harris?" I had a hard time imagining the mild-mannered estate attorney involved in something as gritty as a kidnapping. "What are they saying?"

"Harris hasn't said much yet, but this other guy's a real weasel. They're trying to get Ben to talk."

"Ben's *awake*? Why didn't you say something?" I jumped up on my knees and reached for the headphones.

But Pete moved away quickly. "Hey, take it easy!"

I sank onto my heels and pleaded, "Can't you put it on speaker or something?"

"I *can*," Pete said, "but I gotta keep the volume down, so stay quiet. And if I need to listen closer, I'm puttin' the headphones back on, no arguin'. Got it?"

Asa and I both nodded. Pete flipped a switch on the radio and twisted a knob.

There was nothing but light static for the moment. Pete leaned over to me and whispered, "Is Ben hurt? I only ask 'cuz he sounds a little…tired."

I closed my eyes and tried to keep panic at bay. "Our speedboat captain drugged him with something. He cut his head when he fell, but I'm not sure how badly." The memory of that moment made my stomach lurch.

"Was he unconscious?"

"It was hard to tell. He moaned and moved his head, so I knew he was still…you know."

I looked up at Pete, and he nodded. I figured that as a medic, he was trying to determine how bad Ben's situation might be. He and Ben had fought closely together in the Marines. If anyone could tell how Ben was really doing just by listening to his voice, it was Pete. But that didn't do us any good if we didn't know where he was. Despair howled through me, threatening to bring me to tears. "I could check on him—through the portal, I mean."

"No, no," Pete said. "Probably best you don't. You need to stay focused."

"You mean calm."

"Look, we're gettin' all the information we need over the radio. Just sit tight."

I was about to object when we heard Ben speak.

"It's a little hard to be intimidated by someone who crashed out of boot camp."

It was his angry voice. His injured voice. His working-hard-to-stay-in-control voice. But it was his voice, crackling over the radio. A rush of lifeblood pumped into my heart.

"For your information, I didn't *crash out*," a thin, reedy voice said. I recognized it as the voice of one of the men who had kidnapped

Ben. "I decided to leave all on my own, once I found out all you military types are just a bunch of pricks!"

"I'm sure that's *exactly* how it happened," Ben said dryly.

"Son of a—" We heard something that sounded like an empty metal container being kicked across a hard floor. "You know what? I don't give a damn what you think!" The reedy voice reached a high pitch. "Say what you want! I'm in charge, now!"

"You keep letting him change the subject," Harris said. I recognized his voice at once—soft but clear, and given the situation, infuriatingly unconcerned. "Would you like me to take over?"

"No! No. I got this," Reedy said. "Now tell us the goddamned secret to the double kheir so we can beat you to death and throw you in the creek for the crabs to eat!"

"Tempting," Ben replied.

"Jesus Christ, can I please cut this guy loose and let him take a swing at me? All I need is one excuse—"

"Why are you letting him wind you up?" Harris asked. "Look, Ben, we already know that you're the key to making the double kheir work."

"And you know that, how?" Ben asked.

"Because we have people everywhere—including at the Smithsonian. For example, Dr. Morgan, the head of your mother's research team, is married to Senator Johnson, one of our owners. She's a big supporter of Team Forward, so it's been handy having her in charge of the double kheir project, where she can control what information gets shared with other research institutions, and what stays quiet. Needless to say, she's been keeping us updated on the MacGregor Group's activities, including your little meeting with them last Saturday. Good job blocking our bugs in the conference room during your call with the Smithsonian, by the way. Didn't do you much good, though; Dr. Morgan filled us in."

Asa and I looked at each other, wide-eyed.

"Holy hell," he whispered. "Dr. *Morgan*?"

"Oh my god," I murmured. So they knew *everything*. They had just been playing with us all week—and it was Ben they wanted, not me. I felt the blood draining from my face.

Pete held up a hand to silence us as he squinted at the radio.

"Then what you *know*," Ben said, "is that we had a couple of rituals that were unusually effective. That's it. We have no idea if we actually activated the double kheir, or if we did, how. So you're wasting your time, and what's worse, you're wasting mine."

"What the fuck?" Reedy sounded even more annoyed.

"Shut up," Harris snarled in a menacing tone I'd never heard him use before. "We know that Cate said the double kheir started working for her only when you joined the circle, and we heard about Eve's heart chakra charging theory. The researchers at the Smithsonian were sufficiently impressed that they want to bring you in for more experiments. But even Dr. Morgan has to follow meticulous scientific protocols, so it could be years before they reach any conclusions, and we don't have that kind of time. Meanwhile, you claim you don't have any special gifts, but that's obviously not the case. Unless, of course, Cate was lying. Should we bring her down here and ask her?"

I seethed. They were trying to use me to get to him. I squeezed my eyes shut and tried to transmit my feelings through the portal to Ben, even though I knew the flow of emotion only went one way—from him to me. *I'm fine, Ben,* I thought at him. *I'm with Pete. Don't let them use me against you.* But I knew that might be too much to ask. The last time he'd seen me was on the boat. Ben had no way of knowing what had happened to me after that.

When he spoke again, Ben's voice sliced through the air like an icy blade. "Nice try. But if you had permission to kidnap her, too, you would have brought us here together. I don't know who's calling the shots here, Harris, but my money's on Tucker, and I'm certain he's clear on what the consequences will be if any harm comes to Cate."

"Ooo, scary!" Reedy guffawed. "So what if we don't have your girl to use as leverage? We still have you—and permission to use any means necessary to make you talk." There was a sharp slapping sound, like a fist punching the palm of a hand. "Unless you just want to tell us what we want to know, that is."

"He's really bad at this," Ben said.

"You're telling *me*," Harris said. "It's like watching a B movie."

Reedy yelled, "Hey! He's the one going all Liam Neeson with threats about consequences!"

"I was just stating a fact," Ben said.

"Oh yeah? What are you gonna do?" Reedy taunted. "You're tied to a chair, you stupid son of a bitch!"

"Quiet!" Harris shouted. Reedy mumbled something under his breath.

"I don't get it, Harris," Ben said. "If you think I know something I'm not telling you, why not just bring your telepath, Michael, down here?"

Softly, Harris spoke again. "You know how these 'sensitives' are. They don't have the stomach for this kind of thing. Bertie practically had to talk Michael off of a ledge after he shot you; he didn't know a paintball could really hurt anyone. As a rule, we give Team Forward the minimal amount of information they need to do their jobs."

"What was that about, anyway?" Ben asked. "The paintball, the medics. We thought you were trying to get Cate alone."

"Well, that would have been a secondary benefit," Harris said. "But primarily, the medics were planning to give you a brain scan, take some blood and tissue samples, things of that nature. Hencock thought you might have some unique physical trait that makes you the key to the double kheir. If that were true, and we had been able to isolate that trait, we could've avoided *this* little intervention. But you didn't play along. It's just as well; I didn't think that approach was going to work anyway."

"And when you drugged me—the first time, with the ginger ale?"

"Oh, that. Skeet just wanted to ask Cate a few questions," Harris said. "He was sure that without you hovering, he could get her to tell him what she knew about how you worked as the key. Skeet figured with some GHB in your system, you'd just get tired and go to bed.

Best case scenario, Cate would get worried and make you see our medics. Then we could've taken care of that part of the plan right out of the gate. I thought Skeet's approach was ham-fisted. After all, it depended on both of you trusting him. I told him that between an empath and a Marine, at least one of you was likely to catch on pretty quickly that something wasn't right. But he insisted on giving it a try."

We heard Reedy mutter something again, and Harris hissed, "Shut up, damn it!" Then he spoke solicitously. "All we want to know is how you activate the double kheir. It's that simple. So you tell me, Ben. What's it going to take for you to tell us?"

Another moment of silence. "A fair exchange of information—and since I don't trust you, I want to ask my questions first," Ben said. "There's no reason why you should object to that. After all, you're holding all the cards. As your crack assistant here pointed out, I'm the one tied to a chair in this rickety shed of yours. What is it, an old mechanic's garage?"

Pete picked up his cell phone. "Max, you hearin' this? Rickety shed, old mechanic's garage, sounds like a concrete floor. Corrugated tin, the way the sound echoes. Okay."

So Max was out there, too, looking for Ben. I whispered, "How many people are helping?"

Pete counted off on his fingers. "Max, Lonzie, and Clayton, a whole slew of watermen searchin' the Bay and the creeks. And some reinforcements are comin'."

My heart fluttered. "Reinforcements?"

Pete held his finger up to his lips. Harris was laughing. "I don't know who you think you're feeding information to. You're phone's turned off, and the GPS is disabled. I'm hoping to pull some good information off of there later, by the way. But let's be clear: no one can hear you out here but us."

"That's what he thinks," Pete said with a wry half-smile.

Ben was quiet for a long moment. Finally, Harris said, "All right, look. I'll answer your questions. Although with all of the research you've been doing on Mercier, I'm not sure what else I can tell you.

Oh yes, we know you've had your friend Max sniffing around for you. After one of our drones followed you to his house, we started monitoring his activities. I want your word, though, that after I answer your questions, you'll answer *mine.* If you don't, I reserve the right to let my assistant here do what he wants to you."

"Fine," Ben said. "You have my word."

"Good. Go watch the door," Harris said. We heard footsteps walking away from Ben. "Ask away."

"You're right; we did some research, so I know the basics. Mercier's founders, you all went to college together, part of a secret fraternity. Some of you decided to stay in D.C. and what, run the world? Which you're close to doing, it sounds like, with your people high up in important places—the House and Senate, ties with the military and security forces, connections with various global power players. Right so far?"

"So far, yes." Harris sounded mildly amused. "Please continue."

"But at some point, you realized Joe and Skeet had the golden goose. They'd developed a unique product—something no one else could offer, something that could give its users an unprecedented edge over their competition. They found a way to use paranormal gifts to deliver intel on a reliable basis—intel that could be obtained in no other way. Who could turn that down? And clients could pay for it securely, privately. No one would ever have to know how exactly they were getting their information."

"So what's your question? It sounds like you've got it all figured out."

"Most of it—except for the end game." I could hear in Ben's voice that he was fighting pain and fatigue. My fists tightened until my nails dug into my palms. "It can't just be money and influence. You already had that. And with Team Forward, you could be risking everything. Your involvement with Opretec, for example. They're mining uranium, taking it home, refining it into weapons-grade, and none of you bats an eyelash. But if the wrong people find out you have clients like that, you could all get thrown in jail, or worse."

Pete, Asa, and I all leaned in closer to the radio.

"Ben, I'm surprised at you, buying into such slander. Opretec is a well-regarded company with a spotless reputation." Harris's faux indignation transmitted clearly over the radio. "But even if it weren't, it wouldn't matter. Things like countries, borders, and national loyalty—they've all been rendered meaningless. Your cell phone was made in China with materials mined from Africa and sold to you by an American company that just moved its headquarters to Denmark. Multinational corporations and the people whose wealth is behind them—they're the ones really running the show today, not governments. We would be foolish not to form relationships with those 'shadow rulers,' no matter whose national interest they're serving this week."

"You're describing an international oligarchy."

"It's inevitable. That's what we're moving toward—rule by the few. And the few will decide what happens when the *big* global economic collapse comes—and make no mistake, it's coming," Harris said. "Now, we at Mercier—we're realists. None of us are members of the global elite. But the next best thing is to being a member of the elite is to be indispensible to them. And that's exactly what Team Forward is allowing us to do—make ourselves indispensible. Then, no matter what happens in the future, we'll be taken care of. Security in an insecure world."

"And if Opretec makes a nuclear missile, and it falls into the wrong hands—gets dropped on Hencock's house in Arlington, for example?"

"Well, that would be a great tragedy," Harris said with all the sincerity of a snake oil salesman. "But Opretec would have given us plenty of advance warning, and we would have moved our whole operation to a safe location well ahead of time."

"So all of that destruction, all of those lives lost—no skin off your nose."

"You make us sound like madmen," Harris said defensively. "We're just pragmatists. Of course we'd regret collateral damage, but as you well know, people die in war—and the world is in a constant state of war. Now more than ever, it's important to be connected to the right people so we can look out for our own and protect the ones we love. Cigarette?" There was a pause. "Suit yourself." We heard the soft *whoosh* of a match being lit. "Look, I know our philosophy, our methods—they might take some getting used to. But as someone who has people depending on you, I thought you'd understand the sentiment behind what we're doing. Any other burning questions?"

"Well, Skeet did say something that didn't scan for me," Ben said. "He said they're consolidating paranormal talent here by attracting sensitives to NIMH. But I find it hard to believe that so many sensitives from all over the world would be willing to leave their homes and come work for the U.S. government. After all, some people do still care about national loyalty—not to mention staying near their friends and family."

"Oh, right," Harris chuckled. "Yeah, Skeet actually believes that he's something like 90% successful as a recruiter. The truth is, if he tries to recruit someone and it becomes clear that he's going to fail, we simply make sure that person disappears, or has a tragic accident. One of Mercier's owners operates a private security firm with offices all over the globe; they take care of those things. After all, we can't have competitors cropping up all over the place." We heard him take another puff of his cigarette. "It's a dangerous world out there."

I covered my mouth to silence a gasp. They were actually *killing* sensitives to get rid of Team Forward's competition?

Asa, Pete, and I exchanged wide-eyed looks. Then Asa whispered what we all were thinking. "Eve's vision—the rivers running red with blood."

"Bastards," Pete growled.

My stomach lurched as I thought of all the sensitives who might have been murdered, just because they didn't want to come to Washington and work for Skeet. I closed my eyes and tried to breathe as nausea threatened to overtake me.

Pete squeezed my arm. I looked up and met his eyes, which were even steelier than usual. "We'll get 'em," he said in a tone that left no doubt. I nodded and took a deep breath as he turned back to the radio.

"Skeet really doesn't know the truth?" Ben asked.

"He's mastered the art of denial," Harris replied, "which is fine with the rest of us. He has his uses, but in this area, he's never had the stomach to do what needs to be done."

"Like with Joe?" Ben asked. "Cate bought the hunting accident story, and I'm glad she did, for her sake. But if I don't buy it, do you really think Skeet does?"

"I think deep down in his subconscious somewhere, he knows. But his conscious mind bought the story. I don't think he has enough steel in his spine to face the truth."

"Which is?"

"Well, since you're not going to remember any of this, anyway..." We heard Harris draw in, then blow out a long drag of his cigarette. "We all started college as patriots; that's only appropriate when you're young. But Joe, he never outgrew that phase. He saw what was happening in the world, just like the rest of us did. But he couldn't let go of the notion that we should try to fight it somehow, take back our democracy, that kind of thing." Harris's tone was mocking. "Since he was relatively harmless and good at what he did, we humored him. Joe and Skeet worked out a division of labor at NIMH. That worked for a long time, everybody giving each other space. But a few years ago, Skeet formed Team Forward, and they started taking clients. Skeet asked the sensitives not to say anything to Joe, but they'd known him for years. After a while, a few of them confided in him about some of their less savory clients. They were troubled by the intel they were getting. They didn't realize that by telling Joe, they were lighting a fuse."

My muscles went limp and trembly. I scooted over to the wall and leaned against it to hold myself upright. Asa joined me.

Pete held up the headphones and threw me a questioning glance, offering to take Harris off of speaker. But I wanted to know the truth. I needed to know. I shook my head.

"Joe figured out that Skeet had been shielding him from

whatever Mercier was becoming, so he bypassed Skeet and went straight to Tucker. He was brave, I'll give him that. He came to the lodge to confront Tucker, threatened to go to the FBI, the CIA, Homeland Security, report him to Congress, all of that, unless Mercier quit working with clients whose activities could be damaging to U.S. interests." Harris paused to clear his throat. "What can I say? Joe was a good guy. We all liked him. He should have just let things be. But as it happened, he never even made it out of that conference room—got the same drug you got, but a stronger dose."

"So Tucker made up the hunting accident story."

"Tucker and Hencock staged the accident the next morning, then brought in some friends Skeet had been cultivating in local law enforcement…the usual."

"For some, I guess," Ben murmured.

"Fine; be self-righteous. But whatever shape the future takes, we're coming out on top."

"As long as I tell you the secret to the double kheir, that is. If some upstart group of sensitives somewhere in the world gets it before you do, then you could have that competition you've been working so hard to avoid."

"Like the MacGregor Group, you mean?" Harris asked. We heard the creak of a chair, then footsteps slowly pacing. "Frankly, we were shocked that you solved the problem first. You were barely on our radar. You didn't even have a full kheir until a couple of weeks ago, and we thought all you cared about was your alternative healing clinic. The fact that you found the key was quite a wake-up call for us. We have to lock this information down now, before anyone else does. All we want is to control the knowledge, keep it under tight guard and make sure it doesn't fall into the wrong hands."

"And your hands are the right ones?"

"Our hands are the only ones we can control—which is why we're so pleased that you and Cate will be joining us."

"You think that after this kidnapping stunt, we'll still want in?"

Harris barked out a laugh. "Oh, don't worry about that. Pharmaceuticals are amazing things. We'll dose you again later and, like I said, by tomorrow morning, you won't remember any of this. Neither will Cate. She'll wake up in her bed, safe and sound in the lodge, but Phil will be found unconscious on his speedboat, floating around in the middle of the Bay, and you'll be missing, presumed dead. Cate won't remember what happened. She'll blame herself for that—for forgetting."

A whirlwind of rage kicked up inside of me. My hands fisted. "Pete—"

Pete shushed me, but he looked as outraged as I was. Then he mumbled into the cell phone again and nodded at the reply.

We heard the pacing start again—this time slower, more deliberate. "She'll be devastated, of course. Naturally, her new family at Mercier will take her under our wing, with the blessing of Skeet's good friend, Ardis—all the people she trusts. With you gone, the glue that holds the MacGregor Group together will dissolve, and everyone will go their separate ways."

"Only *presumed* dead?"

"I thought that part might interest you," Harris said, and I could hear the sick smile in his voice. "Yes, you'll be fine—just locked away in a secret facility while we figure out how to use you to activate the double kheir. And you'll cooperate, because Cate will be with us at Mercier, her safety guaranteed as long as you do what you're told. We'll need you to do a few highly illegal favors for us, of course. That'll give us enough blackmail material to keep you loyal after your release. Once we get the information we need, we'll arrange for you to wash up somewhere—alive, if somewhat worse for wear—and you'll return to a joyous Cate. And if it turns out that you can't activate the double kheir on your own, once we bring you back, we can test the theory that your special relationship with Cate is the key. You'll never tell anyone what happened, and you'll convince Cate to stay with Mercier, if any doubts remain."

"And then you'll have us right where you want us."

"Where we want you isn't a bad place to be, Ben. You should count yourself lucky. Once you and Cate are in with us, you'll be protected from the winds of global change. A lot of people would kill to be in that position." The pacing stopped again. "So there you have it. I believe I've told you quite enough. Now, it's your turn."

Ben coughed, and it sounded labored. "Give me a minute?"

"Fine," Harris said, "but then I'm getting *my* answers." We heard Harris's footsteps walk away from Ben.

They were going to interrogate him next. Every cell in my body screamed, and I felt as though I was about to fly apart, a trillion atoms exploding. I leaned my head against the wall and closed my eyes. *Just keep breathing,* I ordered myself. *You have to stay alive if you're going to save Ben, so keep breathing.*

CHAPTER TWENTY-TWO

Suddenly, we heard a lot of rustling outside the lean-to. Pete pulled out a gun with a silencer and gestured for Asa and me to stay still. He crouched down and slowly made his way out of the shed and around the corner. We heard muted voices arguing, but it sounded like a friendly disagreement. I wondered if Lonzie and Clayton had arrived. Much to my shock, however, the faces that appeared outside of the opening to the shed belonged to the Marines of Yankee Company.

Asa and I jumped up. I threw myself at Hector and Kevin, two of the men I'd spent a lot of time with the previous week, and squeezed them until they coughed. So that was what Pete had meant by reinforcements. The Marines were in full combat gear, ready for action. For the first time since Phil had knocked him out, I allowed myself to believe that Ben was going to be all right, after all.

Pete was still outside talking to someone. From the few words I caught, it sounded like he was filling them in on what was happening. Then Pete rounded the corner with a man wearing casual sporting attire. "I'm Max," he said, extending his hand. "You must be Cate and Asa. Hi."

"It's great to meet you," I said as we each shook his hand. "I understand you've been busy behind the scenes this week, helping us out."

"A bit. Then I called these mutts in," Max said, punching Hector in the chest. "I hope they don't disappoint us."

"Did you say 'mutt'?" From around the corner came none other than Captain Abbott. Wearing combat gear, he resembled a tree trunk even more than usual. "I'll have you know," he barked, "that this is a purebred Rottweiler. Cate, here's the package you requested."

Sure enough, at the Captain's feet sat a dog the size of a footlocker. He appeared to be all muscle. Even though he was panting, Tank sat at attention, as though waiting for an order. His coat was mostly black, but he had two brown spots above his dark, soulful eyes. He seemed almost human, and I understood immediately why Ben loved him. I stepped forward, then hesitated.

"Hey, Tank!" Pete said jovially, earning him a soft but heartfelt *ruff.* "You look good, boy! Show him the back of your hand, Cate."

I did as instructed. Tank leaned forward and sniffed.

"That's Cate," Pete said. "She's one of the good guys."

Tank responded by giving my wrist an enormous lick. I couldn't help but smile. "It's nice to meet you too!" I whispered, scratching the top of his head. I knew that Captain Abbott wasn't much for public displays of emotion, so I just gave him the most grateful smile I could muster. "Captain Abbott, I'm so glad to see you. And thank you for going to all the trouble of getting Tank. I can't believe you brought him here yourself!"

"Well, I heard there was good hunting here," he said, "and it was no trouble getting him. He's retired, and his foster parents were happy to get rid of him. They said to warn you that when he's bored, he eats everything—furniture, walls, vehicles. Sit." Captain Abbott pointed to a spot outside the shed, and Tank obediently walked over and sat. "What's the latest?"

Max produced a tablet computer and pulled up a map. The Marines gathered around. "Okay, so this is us. Given the parameters, we've got Ben narrowed down to two possible locations, here and here."

"Two teams, then," Captain Abbott said. "Hector, take Tank. If anyone can find Ben quickly, it's him. Do we have anything we can use for tracking?"

Pete grabbed Ben's jacket. "This." Then he held up his hand, and everyone fell silent as we heard a voice come over the radio.

"Break time is over," Harris said menacingly. "No more

excuses. I want my answers—and if you don't give them willingly, my assistant here will gladly beat them out of you."

"I've heard enough," Captain Abbott said, nearly spitting with anger. "Let's go get our man. If you can capture any of these bastards, do it. If not, shoot to kill." He turned to Asa and me. "I assume we can't keep you from joining us."

"No, sir," Asa and I said together.

"All right, then. Go with Hector and Kevin. Let's move, let's move!"

We ran outside to find another four marines waiting. Several of them followed Captain Abbott in one direction, while Asa and I ran to keep up with Pete, Max, Hector, and Kevin—and of course, Tank. Fortunately, it wasn't too far to their Jeep. We all climbed inside. Hector started the engine while Kevin shouted directions.

Pete ended up in the far back with Asa and me. He gave Asa a com device with an earpiece and microphone, and put one of his own in, as well. "Once we get there, go wherever Hector and Kevin tell you to go, get low, and don't move. Asa, if you can pick up anybody's thoughts, talk to me. But if you can't, it's okay—we're gonna get him out of there, one way or another. Do *not* put yourself in danger, either one of you. Got it?"

Asa nodded so vigorously that he had to readjust his com.

Pete gave me a hard look. "Cate, we both know the only reason you're here is that you're safer with us than alone back in the lean-to. After all, Owen knows where he left you, and he thinks you're just playing a game, so if someone asked him where you were, he'd have no reason not to tell them. Frankly, you're a liability on this mission. The best thing you can do for Ben is exactly what I said to Asa—go where you're told and stay there. Is that clear?"

I reached out and clutched Pete's forearm. "I'll do whatever you say," I said, my voice breaking. "Just get him out of there."

Pete covered my hand with his. "Don't worry, sis. I'll bring him home."

I just nodded, not trusting myself to speak without crying.

"Put these on." He handed us some bulletproof vests and

helped us strap them on. A flash of terror threatened to push me into a panic attack, but I ordered it to retreat. *Later,* I promised myself. *You can fall apart later.*

The Jeep slowed to a stop. Kevin turned back and put his finger in front of his lips. We all stayed silent as Hector got out of the car and made a hand gesture that brought Tank immediately to his side. Tank whined softly when Hector gave him Ben's jacket to sniff.

Kevin nodded at us, passing out flashlights as we all got out of the Jeep. "Don't turn these on unless you really need to," he said. "Just stick close to us. We'll make a path."

Hector crooked his finger, and Tank leapt into action. At first, he walked around quickly in circles, sniffing. Gradually, he moved more slowly, spending more time at each spot he was investigating. Finally, his whole body tensed, and he began to strain against the leash. We all followed as he dragged Hector through the forest—and that was no small feat, since Hector was somewhat tank-like, himself.

It was so dark, I could barely see a few feet in front of me. I grabbed a strap that fell across Pete's back, and Asa held on to the edge of my bulletproof vest. We ran in convoy, concentrating on not tripping each other or ourselves.

Suddenly, the pace slowed. I saw light ahead. We drew closer and ended up gathered together behind Tank, who had stopped dead in his tracks. Still concealed by the forest, he was staring at a large shed in a dirt clearing just ahead. Light poured out of the building from an opening the size of a garage door. I didn't know if he had stopped on his own or on Hector's orders, but Tank didn't look happy. He was snarling, revealing large, white teeth.

Hector approached Asa and me, and pointed to the base of a wide tree trunk. "You two," he whispered, "sit behind that tree with your backs to the clearing. Don't make a sound. Tank will guard you."

We nodded and did as we were told. Hector unhooked Tank's leash and pointed at us. Before I knew it, Tank had bounded over and was sitting directly in front of Asa and me. He appeared relaxed—maybe because his tracking job was done—but there was a commanding quality to his presence, and I didn't want to find out what would happen if Asa or I tried to leave that spot.

Even with Tank there, though, we couldn't resist peeking around the tree trunk to watch as the Marines made their final approach. Tank didn't seem to mind us turning to look, as long as we didn't try to get up. Quickly but silently, the men closed in on the shed, using things like trashcans, discarded boxes, and piled-up tires for cover in what could have been a choreographed dance. Using only hand signals, they moved as a unit with an intuitive ease that could only have come from years of practice.

Ben's in there, I thought, my heart pounding into my throat. *Please, God, let him be okay.* I turned back to Tank and smiled as best I could. "Thank you, Tank," I whispered softly. "You're a good dog. Good boy."

I'd seen that he only had a nub of a tail, but I heard it wagging, swishing against the pine needles and dried leaves on the ground.

Asa elbowed me. I turned to look. We held our breaths as Hector and Kevin flanked the open doorway. All at once, they burst inside, followed quickly by Max and Pete. We heard yelling and sounds of a scuffle, but no gunshots—*Thank God*, I thought. The sounds of fighting went on for some time. With my stomach knotting, I turned back to look at Tank. His ears were pointed forward, and he was snarling again. I got the feeling that he wanted to be in on the action.

Asa was concentrating, trying to use his telepathic skills to listen in. "Anything?" I whispered.

Looking despondent, he shook his head, then turned back towards the shed. I felt his hand grip my arm hard. "Oh no," he whispered.

I peered back around and froze. Max, Pete, Kevin, and Hector were being slow-marched out of the shed with their wrists tied behind their backs. At least ten men in Mercier security guard uniforms surrounded them, holding them at gunpoint. Another dozen security guards in ATVs kicked up clouds of dirt as they roared into the clearing from an access road. They formed a circle, trapping the Marines in.

Reedy turned out to be a slimy-looking guy whose every movement was jerky. He stood in the doorway of the building, looking back and forth from the scene outside to the scene inside. "Four guys?" He made a point of bending over with laughter. "Seriously, Ben? Four guys? This is your rescue squad? Jesus, you're pathetic!"

Blood pounded in my ears. If Reedy was talking to Ben, that meant Ben must still be conscious, at least—didn't it?

But there was no sound from inside the shed. The hairs on my arms stood on end. Reedy sauntered into the yard and stood in front of the Marines. "Okay you guys, here's the deal. We're not going to kill your friend. He's just going to have a bad night. Meanwhile, if you swear you won't come back, our guys'll take you to Annapolis and drop you off on the front steps of the Naval Academy. The midshipmen will love that. What do you say?"

"Pete, he's lying," Asa murmured into his com. "They're going to drive you out to the marsh and kill all four of you. And yes, they're going to keep Ben alive, but this guy plans to do him some grievous bodily harm as soon as Harris's back is turned."

Pete took a step forward from the line of Marines and addressed Reedy. "Well, I'll tell you what I say." He looked at the ground for a moment, as though carefully considering his next words. Then he locked his gaze on Reedy's. "I say you're feedin' us not just one, but several lines of bull. You're gonna drive us outta here, all right—then kill every last one of us. And you're gonna find a way to do Ben some serious damage, too, even though you know it'll piss off your boss. You just tell me if I got any of that wrong."

A long, thin shadow appeared in the doorway. "So?" we heard Harris ask. "Did he get any of that wrong?"

"Of course he did!" Reedy blurted out. "I mean, yeah, we're gonna kill *these* guys. But I know the plan is to keep that Ben bastard alive. I'm not gonna hurt him bad, much as I'd like to."

"Just cut off a few fingers, right?" Pete asked in his gravelly voice, repeating another prompt from Asa. "Maybe gouge out an eye? Break his back so he can't walk anymore?"

Reedy's jaw dropped. Then he ran up and sucker-punched Pete in the gut. Pete bent over a little and grunted, but then straightened back up.

"What do *you* know about it?" Reedy screamed at him.

"Quite a bit," Pete said. "I'm a telepath."

"No you're not!" Reedy's eyes darted around. "What? You're lying!"

As Asa murmured into his com, Pete grinned. "I know that right now you're thinking, 'Holy shit, he's reading my mind. I better get out of here.' I'd say that would be a very wise move."

Reedy stepped in one direction, then another, appearing confused. Finally, he spat a couple of epithets at Pete, then turned and ran around the outside of the shed, disappearing behind it.

I jumped as I heard a soft *thwap* nearby. Tank yelped and twisted to one side. He looked up at me as his eyes glazed over, the bottom half of a dart sticking out of his haunches.

I lurched forward just in time to put my arms around him as his whole body relaxed and fell onto the ground, pulling me over with him. In an instant, Asa was by my side, stroking Tank's head. I pointed at the dart, and Asa nodded. With great care, I grasped the edge and pulled. Fortunately, it slid out easily. But we were too late; whatever tranquilizer he'd been given had already taken effect. Tank was sound asleep, tongue lolling out of his mouth.

Asa and I exchanged horrified looks. We couldn't see or hear anyone, but whoever had shot Tank couldn't be far off. Asa hooked his thumb in the direction of the Jeep. I nodded, and we got to our feet, crouched over and ready to run. Was it possible that Tank's shooter hadn't seen us yet? If we could radio Captain Abbott—

"That's far enough," a gruff voice said. We looked up to find ourselves surrounded by four of Mercier's armed security guards. Two of them grabbed us by the elbows and pushed us towards the clearing. "Let's go."

My heart sank as we were taken toward the shed. As we drew closer, I could see the determined rage burning in the Marines' eyes, and I knew the battle wasn't over yet—at least not as far as they were concerned. I cursed inwardly as the security guards stopped us just before the point where I would have been able to see inside the door to the building.

Harris stepped out of the shed to greet us, moving with easy confidence. Dressed in khakis and a golf shirt, he stood out among the uniformed men.

"Cate, what a nice surprise." He smiled, but had the sense not to try to shake my hand.

"Cate! Are you okay?" Ben shouted from inside. He made the question sound like a threat to anyone who might cause me to answer in the negative.

"Yes, I'm okay!" I managed to shout back before a security guard came up behind me and clapped his hand over my mouth.

"Congratulations! I hear that you and Ben got engaged. What happy news. And this is Asa, right? The *real* telepath. I don't believe we've had the pleasure. Two syringes," he said to one of the security guards, who disappeared into the shed. "Phil radioed us that you'd managed to escape, but the story was so far-fetched, I didn't quite believe it—something about you being rescued by his brother-in-law, who is also a muskrat trapper. And yet here you are, so it must be true. Don't worry," he said loudly, turning so that his voice could be heard inside the shed, "I have no intention of harming either you or Asa. We'll just give you a little injection and put you to bed. You'll wake up in the lodge tomorrow with no memory of any of this. Much more pleasant that way, trust me."

"He's telling the truth—and your reinforcements are coming," Asa whispered into his com. But the guard holding him saw Asa's lips moving. He spotted the device in Asa's ear, dropped it on the ground, and crushed it under his heel.

Harris shook his head. He walked over and removed Pete's com device, bending and crushing it with his hand. Then he returned to where Asa and I were standing. "Reading minds—that's quite a useful gift, Asa. You could be a great addition to Team Forward." He turned to address the Marines. "You four, on the other hand—I don't give a damn what happens to you. Killing you and dropping you in the marsh sounds much cleaner than finding some way to keep you alive. At least you'll have the satisfaction of knowing that you died trying to do something *worthy*," he sneered.

Despair chilled me. I knew the Marines were itching to fight, but I didn't see how they could. They were outnumbered and outgunned. And I'd heard Asa say reinforcements were coming, but I didn't know what that meant, exactly—or if they'd make it in time. The security guards tied my wrists and Asa's with plastic zip ties, then covered our mouths with wide strips of cloth, knotting them tightly behind our heads. Tank was down, and Ben was presumably still tied to a chair—in what shape, I had no idea.

Tears burned behind my eyes. Maybe everything would come to pass just as Harris had said it would. After all, if Mercier's security team had got the jump on our unit, what was to say they didn't also have Captain Abbott and his crew in their custody? Would they kill them, too? Or let them go, since they hadn't actually seen Ben on the property? Or call the police and accuse them of trespassing? Or drug everyone into oblivion?

Panic tightened my throat as the tears began to fall. I turned to look at Asa. His eyes were moist too. But I was *not* going to stand there and just let everything unfold the way Harris wanted it to—not without putting up a fight.

I tried to yank myself out of the grip of the security guard behind me, catching Harris's eye. The guard held my wrists tight, but Harris motioned for him to release me.

I straightened my back and walked quickly toward Harris. There was surprised amusement on his face as I approached. I stopped right in front of him, but when he reached out to pull my gag down, I used the only combat move I could use with confidence—one that I'd perfected over years of self-defense on the playground. I drew my leg back and kicked him squarely in the shin, as hard as I could.

"Ah!" Harris cried out, stumbling backward and grabbing his leg. I went to kick him again, but a guard grabbed me. I tried to kick the guard, as well, but he was too close for my foot to connect.

For a few seconds, all eyes were on us—and that was all the

time the marines needed. They took advantage of the moment, attacking the nearest guards with body slams, martial arts-style kicks, and head-butts.

"Get them!" Harris shouted. A few shots were fired, and I screamed as I saw Pete fall to the ground. I tried to tear myself away from my security guard, but he held me fast. Hope began to melt away like a dusting of snow under the morning sun.

Then, in a flash, everything changed. It was like we were on the set of a war movie during the scene of an invasion. At least a dozen Jeeps and armored cars peeled into the clearing and skidded to a stop, surrounding us. We heard the *chop-chop* of a helicopter overhead, and it shone a blinding spotlight down on the yard as soldiers jumped from their vehicles and flooded the area. A loudspeaker sounded from the helicopter. "This is the United States Marine Corps! Drop your weapons!"

Asa was right—reinforcements! My guard let go of me, presumably to follow their orders. With everything in me, I wanted to run to Ben. But out of shock or fear—I didn't know which—I fell to my knees, unable to stand. A group of medics swarmed around Pete, and more Marines than I could count ran into the shed.

I turned to check on Asa. He was standing, wide-eyed, talking to a Marine who had removed his gag and was working to free his wrists. Then the soldier took off into the woods with a few others. Asa turned and caught my eye. "They're getting Tank!" he shouted.

I tried again to stand, but failed. *I can walk on my knees,* I thought, and started to crawl towards the shed. It was slow work, because the clearing had become a chaotic obstacle course. The air was thick with dust. Everywhere I looked, Marines were holding security guards on the ground, handcuffing them and barking instructions. Harris was there too, his face pressed into the dirt. I heard Reedy before I saw him, pleading his innocence as he was dragged into the courtyard by a quartet of soldiers.

Tears wet my face, but this time it was from the sheer intensity of the hope I felt. I was still forty feet or so from the entrance to the shed when two large boots blocked my path.

"Miss Duncan, are you injured?"

Captain Abbott's voice was gruff, but genuinely concerned.

I looked up at him, and his eyes widened. He reached down and pulled the cloth off of my mouth.

"Thanks," I said in a small voice. "No, I'm fine—but Pete?"

"Just a flesh wound. He'll live. Why are you walking on your knees?"

Pete was okay. *Thank God.* I said a silent prayer of gratitude and weakly smiled up at the Captain's frowning face. "I'm just tired, I guess."

He bent down and put his hands under my shoulders, lifting me up as though I weighed nothing at all. He put me in a standing position but kept his arm around me, holding me up as he pulled a knife from somewhere and cut the tie off of my wrists. "Now?"

I put weight on my legs, but my knees still wobbled.

The Captain huffed. "Let's go." He lifted me into his arms as though he was about to carry me over the threshold—and so he did, right into the shed.

Ben had described it well. The rickety shed looked like an old garage that had been out of commission for twenty years at least. My eyes scanned the room and found a large group of Marines gathered around one spot.

"Make way," the Captain said. At the sound of his voice, the sea parted.

Ben lay on a stretcher, eyes closed. A medic was dressing his head wound, a cut several inches long. Ben's shirt had been torn open, and it was clear that Reedy had roughed him up. Ben's stomach and chest were covered with red marks, some of which were already darkening. There were new bruises on his face, too, and one eyebrow was cut and swelling badly. His knuckles were bleeding, which meant that at least one of his kidnappers hadn't escaped unscathed.

Seeing him like that made everything in me hurt. I tried to roll myself out of the Captain's arms to get closer to Ben, but he held me firmly, apparently not yet trusting my ability to stand on my own.

"Benjamin," the Captain barked.

Ben's eyes flickered, and my heart opened like a flower.

"I have Cate here."

In response, Ben forced his eyes open. "Cate," he said softly. He tried to push himself up on his elbows, but couldn't quite manage it. The medic lowered him down. "Are you hurt?" Ben demanded, his voice getting stronger.

"I'm totally fine," I said, smiling so wide that my face hurt. "I'm only being carried because the Captain insisted."

"It's not safe for civilians to be walking around," Captain Abbott declared, winning my eternal affection. "It's dark, and there's debris everywhere."

Ben squinted up at me, looking as though he was wavering between disbelief and confusion. "You're really okay?"

"Yes, really!"

"Are you questioning my assessment, MacGregor?" the Captain barked.

"No, sir," Ben said, his words starting to slur. "I just want to get up," Ben growled at the medic, trying again, and failing. "Why can't I get up?"

"We gave you a sedative," the medic said. "I guess you're both getting carried out of here."

"In that case," I suggested, "can we be carried out together?"

The medic looked skeptical.

"Get another stretcher, soldier," Captain Abbott said. "For these two, we can make that happen."

CHAPTER TWENTY-THREE

Miraculously, no one had been killed that night at the shed, and Pete and Ben were the only ones injured badly enough to need a hospital. I'd ridden in the ambulance with Ben, while Max went with Pete. Asa stayed behind to tell Kai, Vani, and Eve what had happened—and to call Dr. MacGregor, fill her in on the night's events, and warn her about Dr. Morgan.

By the time we reached the hospital, I had regained my strength and could walk on my own again. Pete was put on a fast track. He'd been shot in the side, but Captain Abbott was right—the bullet had ricocheted off of his rib, taking a chip out of the bone, but no organs or arteries had been hit. He would be in pain for a while, but he would make a full recovery. I could tell where Pete was by listening for the grousing: "I'm a medic! I'll tell you what I need!" I reveled in the sound.

I was allowed to stay with Ben in the ER until he'd been fully examined, including X-rays, a CT scan, and an MRI to check out his paintball injury. The doctor said he might have internal bleeding from the beating he'd taken, so they wanted to keep him overnight for observation. Pete was staying the night too.

By the time they were admitted and settled in their rooms, the rest of our group had arrived. Pete had been heavily sedated and was already asleep, so everyone piled into Ben's room. There was some crying, and everyone took turns holding Ben's hand or squeezing the life out of me. I spent a long time talking to Kai, who was beside himself. There was the terror of Pete getting shot, compounded by the fact that Kai hadn't been allowed to join the fight, but instead had waited helplessly at the lodge until he got the awful news. One minute, he was crying; the next, cursing about how much he wanted to go kill everyone at Mercier; and the next, scolding Ben for letting himself get kidnapped and beaten up. Vani and Eve stayed on either side of Kai, each with a hand on his shoulder or his arm.

Not wanting to ruin the surprise for Ben, Asa subtly pulled me aside, whispering that Tank was okay and resting at the kennel. Then he took center stage, describing what happened after we were taken away. Apparently, there were four or five times more Marines there than we had seen, along with the FBI, who raided the lodge and made several arrests. Max had also been listening in on Ben's radio frequency and recorded the whole conversation between Ben and Harris. That gave law enforcement enough evidence to bring in every one of Mercier's founders on suspicion of treason, not to mention a whole slew of other crimes. They were even able to get an arrest warrant for Dr. Morgan at the Smithsonian. Thanks to the watermen keeping watch on the yacht and hemming it in, Tucker, Hencock, and Skeet had been taken into custody, as well. Asa said that by morning, I would be Mercier's only owner who wasn't behind bars.

That news seemed to cheer Ben considerably. "I wish I could've seen their faces. I guess we'll all get to see them in court."

"That will be one *awesome* day," Asa agreed.

Eventually the nurse came in and told us that everyone had to leave—except for Kai and me, of course. She said we could stay overnight in the reclining chairs in our fiancés' respective rooms.

I sucked in my cheeks and looked at the floor as several stares landed squarely on me. After the nurse left, Kai arched a well-groomed eyebrow. "Your *fiancé's* room?"

Ben and I exchanged a glance. He was trying to smile, but his face was too messed up. "Go ahead, Cate," he said, "tell them."

Of course I wanted to set the record straight that we weren't actually engaged, but Ben had enjoyed the ruse so much, and there he was, lying in the hospital bed, looking like hell… I bit my lip.

"Uh, yeah," Asa said, "I wasn't going to say anything, but did I hear Harris congratulate you on your engagement?"

"Oh my god!" Eve exclaimed, grinning. "And the nurse knows, too!"

No. I couldn't do it. I couldn't let everyone get excited for us over nothing, whether it put a damper on Ben's mood or not. But I would try to be gentle. "Look, the dinner on the yacht was owners and family only, so we told Skeet—"

"You told *Skeet* you were engaged," Kai said, counting on his fingers as he spoke. "You told *Harris* you're engaged. You probably told your *hairdresser* that you're engaged. You just didn't see fit to tell *us*." He flipped his hair back.

"Because we're *not*, that's why." I felt the need to defend myself, but I tried to pick my words carefully, knowing that Kai was very fragile at the moment. "Seriously, you guys, we just met a couple of weeks ago; we're still getting to know each other. I promise, though, that if we *do* get engaged, you'll be the first to know."

"Make it official whenever you like—or never, if you don't want to," Vani said, glancing between Kai and me. "But I just have to tell you, the words coming out of your mouth do *not* match your aura."

Sometimes I didn't know whether to love Vani's blunt honesty or hate it. "What do you mean?"

"I *mean*," she said, "those men believed you when you said you were engaged because it's already true on some level. Your aura is like a big, blinking neon sign that says, 'I'm getting married!' and Ben's already clearly states, 'I'm a married man.'"

Kai threw his hands in the air. "There you go."

No one was going to rush me into marriage, least of all my aura. "I don't just do whatever my aura tells me to!"

"She doesn't get it yet, does she?" Kai murmured to Vani, who shook her head. "You do whatever you like, honey," Kai said, patting my hand. "You just might want to pick a different *excuse*, at least around us. We all know you and Ben have submerged into each other, so even though you've only known each other 'a couple of weeks,' you already know each other better than most people who've been married fifty years."

I couldn't argue with him there. I had empathically submerged into Ben my first week of training to help heal his phobia of eating in front of others. And even though he wasn't an empath, thanks to the ritual Vani had designed, Ben had been able to submerge into me the previous week as part of the effort to unparalyze me. I had entered his consciousness, and he had entered mine. We'd spent time exploring one another's innermost selves. As a result, we knew all of the important things about each other. But that wasn't the point. I wasn't sure what the point *was*, actually, but I knew *that* wasn't it.

Before I could come up with a reply, though, the nurse popped her head in the door. "It's nice that you want to be here for your friend, but it's time to go, everyone!"

"Okay!" Eve seemed eager to escape the tense conversation we were having. "Let's leave these two lovebirds alone. See you tomorrow!" She grabbed Asa and Vani by their jacket sleeves and dragged them out the door.

Kai stayed just long enough to toss me a conspiratorial look. "Cate, I guess it's time you and I were each with our *fiancés*."

"Right," I said, smiling. "Go be with Pete. We'll see you in the morning."

"Goodnight, you two." Kai closed the door behind him.

My shoulders slumped with relief. Finally, it was just Ben and me—safe and sound.

"Hey."

I turned at the sound of his voice. He patted the bed next to him, but I hesitated. He looked like one big bruise, and I was afraid that even the slightest touch would hurt him.

"Come here," he said. "Lie down with me."

"But there's no room," I objected.

Ben painstakingly shifted over a bit, grimacing as he did so. "Now there is."

Well, I couldn't disappoint him *then*. Ever so carefully, I lay on my side next to him and slid into the narrow space between his body and the bedrail. I tucked one arm under my head, but I didn't know what to do with the other one. I held it aloft, trying to figure out where to put it.

Ben's body shook with silent laughter. "What are you doing?"

"I don't want to hurt you."

He reached up and took my hand, then guided it gently down until my arm lay across his stomach. He moved it up a little, then down a little. "That's a good spot."

"Okay," I whispered, blinking back tears.

"Hey, no crying," he said, trying to inject some command into his exhausted voice. "I'm going to be fine, remember? Full recovery. They're just keeping me for observation—and I really like who they've chosen to observe me."

I smiled weakly. Having Ben so close to me was heaven. I could smell him, touch him, watch his chest rise and fall, even feel his heartbeat. Every second, I had some way of reassuring myself that he was there, that he was alive, and that no one was going to disappear him to some secret facility and make me believe that he was dead. My stomach clenched at the thought, but I forced myself to take a deep breath and relax.

Ben's usual scent was masked almost entirely by a chaotic mess of other smells: antiseptic, chemicals, the harsh detergent they used to wash the sheets and Ben's blue hospital gown. But it was still there, clinging to him, just barely. I drank it in. My body felt content only where it touched Ben's. Every other inch of me ached with longing. I had to keep telling myself to be patient, because Ben would never be able to touch me everywhere at once.

"I know I must look scary," he said, "but I'd like it if you looked me in the eyes, even just for a few seconds."

Immediately, my eyes locked onto his. "You could never look scary," I insisted. "You just look…rugged."

He chuckled, and the sound lit my heart up like a supernova. "Rugged?"

"Yeah, like a rugged outdoorsman who had a disagreement with a tree trunk, and then a grizzly bear."

"And I won? I guess I'm pretty impressive."

I swallowed down a sudden urge to sob. I didn't know what I would have done had he *not* won.

Even in his weakened condition, Ben managed to sound stern. "You know, at some point, we're going to have to talk about what you were doing out there in the woods, instead of staying at the lodge. I'm willing to bet Pete didn't approve that idea."

"At *some* point," I said, trying to sound equally stern as I changed the subject. "Right *now*, though, I want to know why you didn't use our distress code."

"What?"

"At *no* point during this ordeal did you say, 'Help me, Obi-Wan Kenobi. You're my only hope.'"

His shoulders shook as he laughed, then coughed. "The situation was never that dire. I knew help was on the way."

"How did you know? *I* didn't know!"

"I'll tell you the whole story later, I promise. But the basic reason is that Pete's never let me down." Reaching over, he touched the tip of his finger to my forehead right between my eyebrows. "And I have you, now, so I knew I couldn't let myself down, either." He trailed his finger down my nose to my lips. Then, softly, he began to trace the outline of my mouth.

A blush started in my cheeks and raced all the way down to my toes. "Cut that out," I whispered, gently removing his finger.

"What?"

"Making me want to kiss you. I have a feeling Nurse Killjoy would object."

"Mmm. Now I can't think of anything else."

I untucked my hand from beneath my head and ran it carefully over the outer edges of his hair—the wavy part on top that never stayed quite where he put it. "I love you," I whispered. "Please don't ever let anything bad happen to you ever again. I mean it."

Ben reached over and touched my cheek. "I'm sorry, Cate."

I shook my head. "That's not what I meant—it's not your fault. *I'm* the one who should apologize. If it weren't for me, you would never—"

"Stop," he gruffed. "The only people at fault are the people currently under arrest. End of discussion. What I meant was, I'm sorry that you had to go through this—all of it—and that you had to spend even a minute worrying about me. I don't like that. *I* want to be the one worrying about *you.*"

I turned my head and kissed his fingertip, which appeared uninjured. Then I looked him in the eyes again. "Too late. I think I'm going to worry about you forever, now."

Gold flecks glimmered in his eyes for the first time that evening. "I know it feels that way, but your anxiety will fade, I promise. And when we get back to our normal lives, I'm going to do my best to make sure you never have to worry about me, or anything else, ever again. I'll even wear a GPS tracker if you want me to."

Smirking, I said, "You'd only do that as a way of talking me into wearing one too."

"That sounds fair." The eyebrow that wasn't swollen up like a golf ball arched upward. "Wait a minute, did you say you thought you were going to worry about me…forever?"

"After what happened tonight? Yes, probably."

"Hmm." He took his finger back and used it to stroke my cheek. "You do realize that would require spending the rest of your life with me."

The gold in his eyes was sparkling and jumping, so I knew he was only being half-serious, not trying to pressure me. What unsettled me was the absolute calm I felt when he said those words. Nothing inside of me tensed up from anxiety, or shouted in objection, or felt even the slightest bit uncomfortable. Rather, the deep sense of rightness I felt lying there next to him in the hospital bed grew stronger, infused with joy. I already knew that my heart called out to his, and his to mine, every moment of every day. The portal that connected us was strong and primal. I didn't want to do anything except be with him, just like that, lying in bed, talking. We could have been floating in space for all I cared. Being there with Ben felt like home. In just a short time, he had become the best part of my life—and the best thing I'd ever known.

I wished my mother were there, so I could tell her everything I was feeling, explain all that was happening, and ask her—is this love? Is this what people feel when they decide to commit to one another? How do you know?

I felt her voice resonate through my chest: *Yes, Cate. This is love. This is what you're supposed to say "yes" to.*

I didn't know if it was really her voice, or if my heart was making itself sound like her so I would listen to it. But as always, my anxiety also had to have its say. Could I believe what my heart was telling me, or was it playing a trick on me? Would I dive in and get used to a life of magic with Ben, only to have it all snatched away?

Again, I felt my mother's voice in my heart. *It's real, Cate. It's not a trick. And it would be absurd to give up something this precious just because you're afraid of losing it.*

I had to admit, she—or I—had a point. I felt like I was swirling down the inside of a happiness funnel, traveling ever closer to the hole at the bottom—the wonderful point of no return. I wasn't ready to go there yet, but I didn't see any point in keeping Ben in the dark about what was I was feeling, especially when he had consistently displayed so much openness and emotional courage. I knew he was patient; I knew he would wait for me as long as it took. But I didn't want to make him wait any longer.

I willed the portal between us to open, bathing in the love that flowed freely from him to me—always strong, always true. "If I tell you something," I whispered, "will you promise not to tell anyone?"

"Of course," he whispered back.

"I *love* the idea of spending the rest of my life with you."

His hand froze where it had been stroking my cheek. "You do?"

Trying not to panic at what I'd just said, I played with his hair some more. "Yes."

"What does *that* mean?"

A smile stretched all the way across my face. I should have known that he'd want more. He always wanted more.

Sounding suspicious, he asked, "What are you smiling at?"

That was it; the time had arrived to get down to brass tacks.

I cleared my throat and said firmly, "Okay, look. This should go without saying, but just in case, I do *not* want to have a double wedding with Kai and Pete. I want that to be their day, and besides, New Year's is way too soon. Simone would kill me, and Ardis would have a heart attack."

Keeping his eyes locked on mine, Ben nodded. "Fair enough."

"And I don't want to get publicly engaged until well after their wedding, like February or March. Kai is so happy; I want him to enjoy the spotlight for a while without having to worry about being happy for anyone else. You know how he is; he goes all in on everything. I think it would be overwhelming for him, and he has enough on his mind, especially with Pete…"

Ben nodded, saving me from having to say anything about Pete's injury. "Got it."

I narrowed my eyes at him. "You're being extremely agreeable all of a sudden."

"I'll agree to anything you want—as long as you agree to marry me, which it sounds like you might be on the verge of doing."

My god, he's right, I thought, swallowing hard. "It does sound that way, doesn't it?"

The passion pouring from his eyes tripled in strength, so powerful that it knocked the breath out of me.

"I'm in love with you, Cate," he said, softly but with great intensity. "That will never change. Forgive me; it's been a rough day, so I'm not much for speeches right now. But I hope I don't have to say much. Hopefully, you already know. You're my life now, so my life is yours to make or destroy. Either way, I'm yours, and I'll wait as long it takes to hear you say that you're mine forever, too."

He coughed again, and I could see how much that short speech had taken out of him. My heart did an Olympic flying leap, trying to jump out of my chest and join his. And in that moment, I knew—I *was* his. I'd fallen headlong into love with Ben, and it was a love that would never go away. I knew it as surely as I knew that we were lying together there in the bed. There was no point keeping the truth from him anymore—or from myself.

I rested my hand gently on the uninjured side of his head, the only part of him that I could be certain I wouldn't hurt, and tried my best to let my heart speak through my eyes as I said, "I am."

Hope flashed across his bruised and broken face, and I could see that he hadn't actually been expecting an answer right away. "You're what?"

I turned and kissed his finger, then once again joined my gaze with his. "I *am* yours forever."

Ben's eyes fell closed, as though he'd been forcing them open all evening, and he could finally let them rest. His whole body seemed to relax, and his hand flattened against my cheek. "That's all I needed to hear. That's all I ever need to hear, for the rest of our lives."

"Good," I whispered, stroking his hair again, marveling at how peaceful I felt in spite of having said and done something so momentous. "Then I'll just keep telling you over and over."

"I won't try to stop you." His attempt to smile cracked my heart in two. "I hate to say this, but I seem to be falling asleep whether I want to or not."

"Please sleep," I whispered, my whole body swimming in warmth. "Nothing would make me happier. I'll be right here when you wake up."

• • •

ParaTrain Internship, Day Eleven

Ben slept so soundly that I couldn't stop checking to make sure that he was breathing. It was such a relief to see him resting peacefully after all he'd been through, even though I knew it was probably only thanks to the medications he'd been given. He barely stirred the few times the nurses came in to check his vitals and adjust his IV.

I had stayed on the bed until he'd fallen asleep, then moved to the recliner to give him more room. In the morning, Ben looked both worse and better. His bruises were getting darker, and he seemed more stiff and pained when he moved. But he was awake and alert, his mood was clearly brighter, and he seemed back to himself in every way but physically. The doctor stopped by early to examine him, and said that Ben looked as she had expected. She also said that although they wanted to run a few more tests, he didn't appear to have any internal bleeding, and she agreed with Pete's assessment that Ben hadn't suffered a concussion from the paintball. If all went well, she told us, Ben could probably leave that afternoon.

Soon after, the nurses brought Ben his breakfast. As he took the lid off of the tray, the look on his face told me the hospital food wasn't exactly stimulating his appetite. I decided to slip down to the cafeteria for fresh coffee and egg sandwiches. Thankfully, they proved more tempting, and I was happy to discover that Ben was still comfortable eating in front of me. I'd been a little worried that the trauma of the night before would have reactivated his phobia.

Once we finished eating and were relaxing with our coffee, I couldn't help asking a question that had been nagging at me. "Last night you said you'd tell me how you knew that help was on the way."

He managed a teasing half-smile. "No rest for the weary, huh?"

"I'm sorry," I said, immediately regretting bringing it up. "I was just so scared for you, and I wondered why you didn't seem scared. Or *were* you scared, and you were just hiding it? But we can talk about it later."

"No, I'm the one who's sorry," he said, pushing the rolling tray away from his bed and scooting over to make room for me. "You're so resilient that sometimes I forget you're not used to this kind of thing. Of *course* you were scared; you must have been terrified. Forgive me, Cate. Come over and sit."

I sat and let him pull me down onto the bed until I was molded next to him again. This time his arm was wrapped around my waist, holding me. "The first thing you should know is that you were safe at all times," he said. "That night after he invited us to the lodge, I made a phone call to Skeet and explained that you were very precious to me, so while we were at Mercier, I would hold him and our other hosts personally responsible for your safety. I reiterated this after he invited us to dinner on the yacht. Skeet reassured me that he understood."

"Understood what, exactly?"

"That his safety and that of the other owners were directly tied to yours."

"You *said* that to him?"

"I didn't have to. He knows that whatever happens to me, Yankee Company will always have your back. We not only watch out for each other, but also for one another's loved ones—even those of us who aren't active duty anymore."

"Wow," I said, duly humbled. "That's reassuring, believe me—but it didn't stop you from getting kidnapped. I knew Lonzie and Clayton and the other waterman were keeping an eye out for us on our trip to the yacht. Why did they let you get taken?"

"Eve's vision tipped us off that I might find myself in a hairy situation. We figured that if Mercier planned to grab me, and I went along with it, there was a chance we could get the information we needed to take them down. So we told everyone that if anyone tried to separate us, they shouldn't interfere, just let me go and stay with you, to make sure you got back safely."

"But… How could you…? That doesn't…" I sputtered, trying to contain my fury. I tried to prop myself up on my elbow, but Ben's arm around my waist wouldn't budge. "That is *not* okay! You getting kidnapped—that's the part *I* was worried about! How could you be sure that we'd find you before—" I blinked back tears— "before they made you *disappear*?"

Ben cupped my cheek, staring at me intently. "That was never going to happen, Cate."

"But how did you *know*?" I pleaded. "Because *I* didn't know!"

He leaned over and kissed me on the forehead. Then he began stroking my hair, no doubt trying to relax me. "Pete and I had put a few key people on alert—Max, Yankee Company, the FBI."

I gaped at him. "And you didn't think to mention that to me?"

"I didn't want to worry you."

"But you told Eve that when she saw you on the ground,

bleeding, it was just her memories of the paintball incident intruding on her vision!"

"I didn't want to worry her, either."

"Okay." I took a deep breath, gathering my patience. "I understand not wanting to worry Eve, but you said we were going to tell each other things from now on, remember? No more secrets?"

"I didn't know for sure what Eve's vision meant," he said. "I just had my suspicions, so we took some precautions. What I did know for sure was that you had a demanding role to play on the yacht, and I didn't want you to be distracted, worrying about things that might never even happen. Besides, I knew that if things went sideways, you could always check on me through the portal and put your mind at ease. As it turns out, my kidnapping *was* the break we needed. We've got everything we need now to hang these guys."

It was clear that Ben believed his rationale was sound. It was also clear that at some point in the future, we were going to have a serious conversation about what the term "keeping secrets" meant—not to mention the term "double standard."

"Okay, yes," I conceded. "If I had thought that you were going to be in danger, I would definitely have had trouble play-acting at dinner. But we also could have just *not gone to dinner*! We could have just gone home, and none of this would have happened, and you wouldn't be in the hospital right now!"

At that, the tears I'd been holding back began to flow freely. Ben pressed my head against his shoulder and kept stroking my hair. "It's all right Cate," he soothed. "Everything's okay now. It's over, we're all safe, and the mission was a success. And if Eve's vision was right, what we did was of crucial importance, with much broader consequences than we had imagined. If Mercier had been allowed to continue accumulating power and influence, with murderous men running the organization, there's no telling how much harm they could have done."

My body shuddered. "I can't believe—oh god. They were killing sensitives, Ben. Hunting them down and killing them in cold blood."

"I know."

"Do you think—do you think we actually did it?" I whispered. "Cut the head off the snake, stopped the rising darkness? Do you think it's over?"

"I'm sure of it," he said. "And we couldn't have done it without you—any of it. You were amazing, Cate—so brave and quick off the mark. And you fought like a true warrior. You should feel incredibly proud."

My trust in Ben had grown to the point that I just opened up and let his words flow through me, let him soothe me without fighting it. Slowly, my tears ebbed and finally stopped. Ben loaned me his hospital blanket to dry my face, then I tucked my head into his shoulder again. We fell into a peaceful silence, cradled together in the knowledge that we had accomplished something meaningful, and that now we could rest.

I did allow a small bit of pride to break through all of my other emotions. After all, Ben, a Marine, had said I'd fought like a true warrior. I was a little surprised that he was praising me for fighting, instead of going on about how I shouldn't have put myself in danger by attacking Harris. Maybe he was learning to trust my judgment. I smiled into his shoulder. "Who told you about my warrior moves?"

"Max did. He heard about it from Lonzie."

"Lonzie?" I frowned, sifting through my memories of the night. "But Lonzie wasn't there."

"He was. Lonzie was one of the men who rescued you from the speedboat, remember? He told me how fearless you were with Phil—and that you scratched him up pretty good, too."

"Oh, *that*." Ben was referring to how I grappled with Phil. Max had probably left out the part about how I'd kicked Harris, and it was just as well. If Ben knew I'd stood in the middle of a bunch of armed men and attacked their boss, I was sure that every last one of his overprotective buttons would get pushed.

"I'm going to kill Phil, by the way," Ben said, his tone hardening. "I still can't believe he dared to put his hands on you. Apparently Tucker didn't think having someone tie you up and drug you constituted a risk to your safety. I think I'll kill him too, while I'm at it."

The pain meds had clearly compromised Ben's usual restraint. I tried to cool him down. "I'm sorry, but you're going to have to curb your vengeful impulses. I suspect both of them are in custody by now."

"Hmm," he said with troubling vagueness. Then he shifted onto his side, forcing me to lift my head until we were face to face. Even with the bruises and swelling, I recognized that he suspected he'd missed something, and was going into interrogator mode. "What did you mean, Lonzie wasn't there? Something else happened, didn't it?"

In my whole life, I had never been so grateful for a surprise explosion of chaos. The door flew open, and a cannonball of black and brown fur burst through, heading straight for the bed. Instinctively, I lunged forward onto my hands and knees, covering Ben's bruised body. But I was no match for the unbridled love of the Rottweiler who leapt up onto the mattress. He landed near Ben's feet and drilled his way up, nose first, pushing me off of the bed. With a loud, "Ooof!" Ben swerved onto his side and threw his arms protectively over his torso as Tank began a relentless assault, licking every inch of his face.

Finally, Ben managed to open one eye and take in the dog's adoring gaze. "Tank?" he asked, his tone awe-filled.

Tank barked and resumed his face-licking project.

"Tank!" Ben gingerly removed one arm and slung it around Tank, who at that point was in a full-body wag. "Hey, buddy! It's good to see you! What are you doing here?"

"Ask your *fiancée*," Kai said, pushing Pete in a wheelchair. Asa was close behind, grinning from ear to ear.

Ben looked incredulous. "Cate?" he asked as he wrestled with the dog. "*You* did this?"

"I told you I had a secret gift idea." I smiled tentatively, hopeful that he'd be pleased.

"I can't believe it!" Ben guffawed as he tried to dodge Tank's slobbering tongue. Even with his injuries, Ben's face took on a boyish delight I'd only seen hints of when we'd visited the kennel.

"We told the nurse he was your service dog," Pete said.

Satisfied with his licking job, Tank settled down on the bed, half lying on the mattress and half on Ben, who shifted to make room. Ben didn't seem to mind the inconvenience, though. He was smiling as much as his face would allow and enthusiastically petting Tank. Then he saw Pete. "What's with the wheelchair? I thought you were okay."

"I am," Pete growled. "Hospital policy."

"Oh," Ben said. "Well, enjoy it while it lasts."

"I'm enjoying it," Kai said. "He has to stay where I put him. Good morning, you two. Benjamin, how are you feeling?"

"Fantastic," he said, and at the moment, he clearly meant it. Tank appeared to be a miracle drug. "Cate, how did you get this big, dirty old mutt over here for a visit?"

"I asked Pete to ask Captain Abbott," I explained, unable to stop smiling as Ben wrestled with his dog. "And he's not just visiting; he's yours. He retired not long ago and he was being fostered, but they've been looking for a permanent home for him."

"He's mine? You mean, I can take him home?"

"Yes."

Ben gave me a look so full of affection and gratitude that it made me melt into my shoes. "You've given me so many wonderful gifts. I wanted to get you one."

"Oh, Cate." Ben scratched the big dog on the head and closed his eyes. "This is the *best*." Tank nuzzled under Ben's arm, as though echoing the sentiment.

I walked over to the bed and held the back of my hand out to Tank, as Pete had told me. Tank immediately licked it, then burrowed his head into the palm of my hand, asking to be petted. I immediately complied.

Ben chuckled. "So you two have already met."

Pete nodded. "We used Tank to track you last night. He sped the search up a bit, probably saved you a few knocks."

"He did? Thanks, boy."

"And somebody shot him with a tranquilizer gun," Asa added. "He was guarding Cate and me in the woods, and then *bam*, he just went over."

"Oh, buddy!" Ben said, sympathetically rubbing his side. "You took a bullet for me." Then Ben's expression sharpened, and I could tell he was thinking back to the conversation we'd been having before our guests arrived. "What happened then?"

I didn't want to be around when Asa told Ben that I'd kicked Harris. "Kai," I said, smiling innocently, "any chance you'd like to come downstairs with me and get coffee for everyone?"

"Absolutely," Kai said. "Let the boys bond for a bit."

Slowly and deliberately, Ben said, "Cate, I don't need any more coffee."

"Selfish much? I could use some," Pete said.

"Me, too," Asa admitted. "Thanks."

"No problem," I said cheerily, ignoring Ben as Kai and I headed for the door.

"Asa," Ben said, "you were saying?"

"Oh, yeah," Asa continued, his voice alive with excitement. "So then these Mercier security guards took us down into the clearing. That was when it was just Pete and the other three Marines out there, and that asshat Harris came out and started flapping his gums."

"I see," Ben said. "And when did Cate break out her 'warrior moves'?"

Fortunately, Kai and I were already in the hallway when that question was asked. We heard Asa speaking indistinctly, then Ben's raised voice demanding, "She did *what*?"

Kai gave me an intrigued side eye. "What did you *do*?"

"I just asked myself, 'What would Kai do?' and did that."

He winked down at me, linking his arm with mine. "That's my girl. *Somebody's* got to keep Benjamin on his toes."

Chapter Twenty-Four

ParaTrain Internship, Day Fourteen

Once Pete and Ben were released from the hospital, we returned to Mercier, spending one more night there and most of the next day. Yankee Company and the FBI were still there, making sure they nabbed any and all corrupt individuals at Mercier and collecting evidence. Apparently some of the guilty parties had tried to escape on boats, but Lonzie, Clayton, and a small army of watermen had closed off the waterways leading out of Mercier Cove. We all gave witness statements, and Max and Danielle shared their research with the FBI agents.

Meanwhile, the remaining staff, led by Owen and the Selbys, asked if I would take responsibility for the place, since all of the other owners were "indisposed." Our lawyer, Danielle, had come down to help with the investigation, so with her approval, I signed papers accepting ownership. But since I lived in Baltimore and had no idea what it took to manage the place, we needed to appoint someone on site to be in charge. Then the staff took a vote, and it was decided that Owen would run things.

Vani, Eve, and Asa spent their time helping the investigators as much as they could, while Kai and I had our hands full making sure that Ben and Pete rested and recuperated. That involved a lot of time lounging in front of the television, so we four were among the first to see on the news that there had, in fact, been a tunnel collapse at the Chu-Sarysu uranium mine. Fortunately, they had evacuated the mine ahead of time—thanks to "warning signs in our geological data," an Opretec spokesman said.

"Well, I'm glad Team Forward did *some* good, at least," Kai said.

But there was unanimous agreement when Ben replied, "Not enough."

Friday night, we'd headed back to Baltimore. On the ride home, I texted Simone from the car, letting her know that I was finally on my way back. She said she was glad I'd contacted her, because she had been about to put out an APB on me. I refrained from telling her how appropriate that would have been just a couple of days earlier. Instead, I told her Ben was "under the weather" and I was taking care of him, so it would still be a few more days before we could get together. Reluctantly, she acquiesced, but with the promise that if another week passed without her laying eyes on me, there would be "serious consequences." Her confidence was restored when I gave her my solemn word and sent her another "proof of life" selfie.

It felt wonderful to be home again, away from all of the drama. Ben's bruises looked worse, but he said they were less painful, and the swelling on his face had gone down. His color was improving, and he was moving around a little more easily. Ben's mother offered to let us stay at her house so she could help take care of him, but Ben was anxious to get Tank settled in at my place, where we planned to stay for the immediate future. Kai called me periodically to complain that Pete spent most of the time arguing that he wanted to get out of bed and do something. But since Pete was fighting Kai, we all knew he would lose that battle.

By Sunday, both Ben and Pete had been cleared by their doctors to go on short outings, and they were champing at the bit. Our whole group was anxious to get together to celebrate and debrief. Kai and I thought that since Ben and Pete were still recuperating, something low key would be best. We decided to meet at MacGregor Group headquarters and order lunch.

Our headquarters was a beautiful old abandoned church in East Baltimore that had been renovated into offices and the clinic. We convened in the lounge, a majestic room in the office wing with tall ceilings, furnished with a few coffee tables and an assortment of comfortable couches and armchairs. Vani ordered in Thai food—a staff favorite—and Asa and Eve brought "Get Well Soon" balloons and a Smith Island cake that the Mercier kitchen staff had made. Ben raised a few amused eyebrows by ditching his usual suit for jeans and a T-shirt, but he pointed out that technically, he was still on sick leave.

Dr. MacGregor even joined us to check on Ben and Pete, and to congratulate us on what we had accomplished. She could barely contain her rage when she spoke about Dr. Morgan, who had been arrested at her office and taken into custody. But Dr. MacGregor assured us that the rest of the Smithsonian team was continuing their research, and that they still wanted us to be a central part of their studies moving forward. With enthusiasm, we all agreed.

"Incidentally, we received a new batch of information from China," Dr. MacGregor said. "Dr. Abera has translated more of the tablets, and the team has a theory as to why Ben is the key to activating the double kheir."

While Dr. MacGregor sipped her tea, the rest of the room stilled. Such a revelation hardly seemed incidental to *us*—not after what we'd been through over the past week. Finally, Ben asked, "So what's this theory?"

"Well, they've been puzzling over why your participation in the ritual worked, but Pete's didn't—particularly given the similarities you two share," she explained. "As you all know, the symbol of the kheir is the hand, and the palm of the hand has been translated to mean the 'heart of the kheir.' Meanwhile, an empath's powers are rooted in the heart chakra. The team has theorized that while Ben, the palm, functions as the key, it is Cate, the empath, who functions as the lock. Therefore, the palm and the empath must share a love bond in order to unlock the energy of the double kheir, thereby activating it."

"Interesting," Ben said, shifting closer to me on the couch and draping his arm around my shoulders. As my nerves kicked in, I dug my fingernails into my thighs.

"That is fascinating!" Vani exclaimed.

Kai sighed, beaming at Ben and me. "Not to mention *romantic*!"

"Yes, I suppose it is," Dr. MacGregor said, smiling warmly. "Of course, it's just a theory."

"But it's obviously *correct*," Kai argued. "I mean, it makes perfect sense—right, Vani?"

"Well, yes," Vani replied. "Not only does it explain our experiences so far, but it fits in with the spiritual school of thought, which holds that all paranormal gifts are a manifestation of divine love. Given that, it makes sense that a love connection would be the key to maximizing the use of our gifts. And of course an empath, with her abilities seated in the heart, would be the perfect instrument."

I couldn't deny that what Dr. MacGregor and Vani were saying made sense, but I would never get used to being the center of attention—and all eyes were turning toward Ben and me.

Fortunately, Dr. MacGregor seemed to sense my discomfort. "That's an excellent analysis, Vani. But there is much more research to be done. Meanwhile, I have other news." She paused to sip her tea again, heightening the drama. "Apparently, word of your activities over the past week has spread. I've been getting phone calls from various people asking if they can use the MacGregor Group's services."

Ben frowned. "What kind of people?"

"People who introduce themselves using acronyms," she said dryly. "FBI, CIA, NSA…"

"Oh, good lord!" Kai threw his hands up. "After this week, what we need is a *vacation*, not a bunch of suits running around, looking at us funny!"

Ben squeezed my shoulder. "I agree. I think everyone here has more than earned a break."

"Well, I'm glad to hear you say that, because that's exactly what I've been telling everyone," Dr. MacGregor said. "Besides, I know that's not what any of you signed on for. We'll have to talk it over and decide as a group before making any changes to our mission statement."

There were general murmurs of agreement. Meanwhile, the

thought of working for law enforcement or intelligence agencies had me chewing on my lip.

"Psst! Cate!"

I looked around and found Eve trying to catch my eye and smiling brightly. "Don't stress out," she murmured. "We've all got each other's backs."

If the events of the previous two weeks had taught me nothing else, they'd certainly taught me that I could count on everyone in that room—and I'd do anything to make sure I never let them down, either. It felt new and familiar at the same time, the sensation that I was a part of something—something a lot like a family. I returned Eve's smile. "Thanks, I know—and I'm grateful."

Dr. MacGregor left to spend the afternoon at her private practice. The rest of us took advantage of being together, safe and in our own space, to start processing what Malcolm's spirit and Eve's vision had told us earlier in the week.

Ben's mother had originally started the MacGregor Group as an alternative healing clinic, a paranormal skills training program, and a center for her own research. But like the tide coming in, the realization was slowly washing over us that some greater force—whether we called it the Divine Source, God, the Universe—might have other, broader plans for us. At Mercier, we had stopped the threat of the "rising darkness" in its tracks. But Eve had seen other sources of that same darkness dotting the planet, so it seemed likely that it would rise again at some point. And according to Malcolm, we had been appointed stewards of the "light," guardians of the paranormal gifts. That meant we would have to stay on top of any potential threats to sensitives and prepare ourselves to deal with them. Although that level of responsibility seemed overwhelming, no one even suggested the possibility of backing out. Instead, we buoyed our courage by reveling in the success of the victory we'd achieved at Mercier.

The week had taken its toll on all of us, though, and eventually, everyone began to look wiped out. One by one, Eve, Asa, and Vani said their goodbyes and headed home. Kai asked Ben and me to stick around for a moment.

Once it was just the four of us in the lounge, Kai said, "I had a few visitors last night."

Pete nodded. "He did—the dead kind."

"Oh," I said, reaching over and taking Ben's hand.

"That's right," Kai said. "Both of your parents, Cate, and Malcolm. I asked them to wait until today to talk to me, so that they could address you live, as it were, but they said they had a thing." He shrugged.

"They have 'things' on the Other Side?" I asked, incredulous.

"Apparently," Kai said. "At any rate, since I never remember anything, Pete took down some notes."

Pete pulled a folded-up piece of paper from the pocket of his jeans and smoothed it out, then handed it to Kai.

"Okay," Kai said, squinting at Pete's handwriting. "So first Joe came through. He wanted to thank all of us for figuring out that his death wasn't an accident, and for putting his killers behind bars. He'll be able to find peace now. And he wanted you to know, Cate, that he believes your mother was right to take you away from him. She was already getting ready to leave him over his research with Skeet when they introduced her to Tucker as the president of this business venture they'd started—Mercier. She immediately sensed how evil Tucker was, and tried to convince Joe to separate himself from the whole thing. But Joe thought she was being paranoid. He didn't see them for who they really were until years later. Now, he's grateful that she kept you safe—and that your new friends are doing the same. Both of your parents send their gratitude to our whole group."

"Thank you," I said, warmth radiating through me. Both of my parents were okay; they were together, and we had managed to do something good for them. I turned to Ben. "We should pass their message along to the rest of the group."

"Agreed," Ben said.

"And your father, Ben," Kai said, "he was very determined that I give you a message."

I felt Ben tense up beside me and instinctively slid closer to him. "Go ahead," he said.

"Malcolm said to tell you that he's sorry."

I glanced sideways at Ben, but his expression was stoic.

Kai flipped over the notepaper and continued reading. "He's sorry for all the pain he caused your mother and you. He said that he knows words don't count for much, but he had to say them anyway. And he wanted me to tell you that there was nothing you could have done to prevent his death." Kai looked up, puzzled. "Do you know what that means?"

Ben cleared his throat. "I think so."

"Okay, good," Kai said, "because we need to talk about this last part." He read the paper silently, then glared at Ben. "He says he thinks that Cate is wonderful, and he wants to *congratulate* you on your *engagement*!" Kai slapped the notepaper against his knee. "Do you mean to tell me that you are engaged, after all, and that you told your *dead father* before you told *us*?"

"Umm…" Ben looked at me, flummoxed.

"Uh, no," I jumped in. "We're *not* engaged, Kai. We told you that! But Vani said it's written all over our auras, right?" I smiled brightly. "I'm supposedly wearing a neon sign saying 'I'm getting married'—remember? Malcolm must have seen that. Or maybe he even saw us pretending to be engaged on the yacht. But we're not engaged, I swear."

Kai folded his arms across his chest and eyed us both. "You *swear*?"

"It's true," Ben said. "You and Pete are the only engaged couple in this room."

Thankfully, Pete stepped in, draping his arm around Kai. "See? I told you."

"Well." Kai appeared somewhat placated. "I'd be overjoyed for the two of you if you were; that's why I wanted to know. And of course I'd try to talk you into a double wedding."

I tried to include Pete, Kai, and Ben in my epic eye roll. "Oh, for the love of—"

But Kai held up his hand to silence me, and continued. "But if you're waiting, you're waiting, and I guess there's not much I can do about it but get back to wedding planning. Oh, and Cate," he said excitedly, "that reminds me—dress fitting, this Wednesday at noon. Put it on your calendar." Then he scanned my outfit with a scowl. "We'll do some other shopping, too. I'm sorry, honey, but I just can't let you live in tunic tops and yoga pants forever."

"Got it," I said, smiling. But I was conscious of how tired Pete looked, and I was anxious to talk to Ben about the message from his father. "For now, though, I think we should get our two patients home."

Kai agreed, so we all headed out to the parking lot and said our good-byes. Ben and I had taken a taxi to the church, but Max had arranged for Ben's Jaguar to be dropped off in the parking lot. Unsurprisingly, even though he wasn't supposed to drive yet, Ben insisted on taking us back to my house himself.

Before he pulled the car out of its parking space, I laid my hand over Ben's on the steering wheel. "Do you want to talk about it?"

He shot me a rakish smile. "About the fact that our love is the key to activating the double kheir, and possibly saving the universe?"

I narrowed my eyes into slits. "You *know* that's not what I meant."

"Hmm." Ben gazed at my hand. "You mean, what my father told Kai."

Gently, I intertwined my fingers with his. "Yes."

He rotated slightly in the seat so that he could look at me as he spoke. "It was good," he began. "It was good to hear those things. But you have to understand, there's a lot of pain there, a lot of history. It's going to take quite a bit more than a few words."

I squeezed his hand. "Of course. I totally understand."

"He can't be all bad, though," Ben said with a glint in his eye. "After all, he was able to see how wonderful you are." He lifted my hand to his lips and kissed the back of it. "And that's all the talking I'm going to do for now. It's time to get home."

I didn't object. I assumed Ben was anxious to get home because he was tired and sore, and needed some rest. But as soon as we left the lot, he began to drive like he was in a racecar time trial. Ben sped through the streets, careful as always over potholes and at intersections, but making up time where he could as though we were late for something incredibly important. His face showed pure focus and intense anticipation.

Maybe he's excited to see Tank, I thought, smiling to myself. Tank had made himself perfectly at home in my house, and he was delighted every minute that he got to spend with Ben. He had warmed to me, as well, but it was clear that Ben was the alpha dog of Tank's heart.

I grabbed the hand rest as Ben took a hard right, pealing down an alleyway that we sometimes took as a shortcut. "Good grief," I said, "you really want to get home to Tank!"

Ben stared straight ahead and took a hard left at the end of the block. "Tank's at my mother's house."

"What? Why?"

"I told her I thought they should get to know each other, so she agreed to dog-sit. Her dog walker picked him up this morning."

"But—" My eyes widened as Ben tore down an empty boulevard. "Then why are you driving like a madman?"

"Because it's day fourteen—the last day of your internship."

Oh my god, I thought, *he's been keeping track.* I'd kept count too, of course, but I figured that with everything that had been going on, Ben would've been too distracted—or at least that it wouldn't matter, given the physical state he was in.

"This morning at the church, my mother and I spoke in the hallway, and we made it official: you've successfully completed your training, Cate. That means restrictions on all activities are hereby lifted."

My heartbeat made its presence known so strongly that I was sure Ben could hear it.

"So…" I was too nervous to say anything serious. "You're taking me to a steakhouse?"

One corner of his mouth rose. "Later, if you like. First, we're going back to your place. A special maid service came in while we were at the church."

"Oh? Special how?"

"They prepare bedrooms for special occasions—clean and straighten everything, put out fresh flowers, chill some champagne."

"Oh!"

"They also put a few meals in the refrigerator so we don't have to go out if we don't want to. I believe our order included steak, now that you mention it."

I was nothing short of astonished. Ben had been planning this. He had taken steps. True, I'd made it clear more than once that I wanted us to make love at the first possible opportunity. But now that the moment had arrived, I felt strangely unprepared.

He shot me a concerned look. "You don't mind, do you? About the maid service?"

"How could I possibly mind?" It was the most thoughtful, romantic thing I'd ever heard of. But Ben had taken charge again, and I had the feeling of being swept along by a strong current—a really romantic, sexy current, but still out of my control.

We arrived at my house. He swung the Jaguar into a space along the curb and turned off the engine. "Don't move," he said as he got out of the car, came over to my side, and opened my door. Not even the remaining cuts and nasty bruises could hide the fierce hunger on his face. His eyes flashed gold as he held his hand out to me. "Allow me?"

The rough passion in his voice made my stomach flutter. I held out my hand and he helped me out of the car, then closed and locked the door. Before I knew what was happening, his body was pressed against mine, pinning my soft body against the hard metal of the Jaguar as his hands slid up the back of my neck, trapping his fingers in my braid. He leaned in and placed a gentle kiss on my earlobe, whispering, "I love you, Cate, and I'm sick and tired of just *telling* you. I want to *show* you."

Ben's first declaration sent sweet tendrils of joy curling around my heart. His second made heat splash up my neck, and within seconds, my face was on fire. With my chest pressed up against his, I knew that Ben must have noticed my breath turning fast and shallow. "But your injuries..." I could only whisper. "You must still be so sore and tired."

"I feel no pain right now, and I'm definitely not tired."

I yelped as he nipped at my earlobe. Lava swirled in my belly, then quickly spread to every other part of my body, swallowing up my hesitations as it went. "Di—did the doctor clear you for this?"

Ben gave my neck a greedy, wet kiss. My knees went weak. His arms slid around my back, holding me up. "There's only one question that matters here," he growled into my ear. "And that is, may I take you inside?"

Sensual images flooded my mind. All of the things I'd fantasized about doing to Ben...all the things I craved for Ben to do to me... and now, with one word, they could all happen. My physical self was just about done waiting for the rest of me to make up its mind. Of their own accord, my eyes closed and my mouth opened. Ben didn't hesitate. His lips were on mine in a fraction of a second, his hands cradling my head, the length of his body taunting mine as we stood pressed up against the car and each other.

The portal between us flew open, and the torrent of Ben's feelings for me crashed through, threatening to drown me—and all I wanted was to drown in him. My heart keened with longing, and the more we kissed, the louder its cry became. I had to be closer to him, to be under his skin, to feel him under mine. With sharp urgency, I needed to be one with him, to coalesce as much as any two separate beings possibly could. I pulled my mouth away from his, gasping in air, and whispered, "Yes."

I barely had the word out before Ben leaned down and wrapped his arm around the back of my knees. As he stood up, he hoisted me over his shoulder like a duffel bag. I yelped in surprise as his arm gripped my thighs, holding them against his chest like an iron bar, while the top half of my body hung upside-down behind him. He had lifted me without a single wince or grunt. As my worries about his injuries faded, I grasped at his shirt, trying to find something to hold onto—but I only succeeded in pulling it up, baring his back.

"At least wait until we get inside," he said, chuckling. "What will the neighbors think?"

"They'll think I'm being kidnapped by a Neanderthal!" I couldn't help laughing. "What the heck are you *doing*, anyway? I can *walk*, you know!"

Ben marched up to the front door and deftly unlocked it with his free hand. "If Captain Abbott gets to carry you, then I certainly get to carry you."

"Oh, for God's sake! Don't tell me you're jealous of Captain Abbott!" I reached down and pinched him on the derriere—lightly, so he wouldn't drop me.

Ben groaned. "You're going to kill me, Cate. But I'll die a happy man."

"No dying allowed," I declared, grabbing his belt for balance. "Not until *after*, anyway."

"Yes, ma'am." He stepped inside and closed the door behind us.

But as we reached the foot of the stairs and began to climb, my anxiety kicked in. Ben was about to see me naked—*all* of me—and under my tunic and yoga pants, I was wearing an equally unenticing beige bra with purple polka-dot granny panties. Also, I hadn't looked in a mirror in ages. My hair was probably a chaotic mess, and I wasn't wearing any make up. I needed a few minutes to freshen up, but Ben didn't seem to be in the mood to wait.

We'd almost reached the top stair when I began to stammer, "Wait, Ben, I have to—first, before we—I mean, I need—"

Ben stopped on the landing in front of my bedroom door. "What do you need, my future fiancée?"

"Um, remember those special skivvies I told you about? My fancy undergarments?"

"What?"

"I want to put those on."

"*Now?*"

Good question, conceded the part of me that had been fantasizing for weeks about this moment. My conviction wavered. "Well, yes—and I want to do my hair."

There was a brief, uncomprehending pause. "Cate, I hate to break it to you, but whatever you put on is just going to come right off, and your hair is going to get messed up." With a note of concern, he asked, "Is that a problem?"

"No, not at all," I reassured, suddenly feeling ridiculous. "I just wanted to get *ready*—"

"Hmm." Ben shrugged his free shoulder. "Well, it sounds like a waste of effort to me, but if that's what you want—" In preparation to lower me down, he reached up and gripped the sensitive juncture where my bottom and thigh meet. As he leaned forward, his hand slid in a scandalous direction, and his touch was like a flint sparking a wildfire. Flames engulfed me, licking every inch of my skin and burning off my insecurities. I gasped as my desire came rushing back.

"Wait!" I cried.

Ben stopped in mid-lean. "Yes?"

"I changed my mind," I said breathlessly. "You're right; it *does* sound like a lot of unnecessary work."

"You're sure?" He asked, sounding entertained by my torment.

"God, yes!" I half-snapped, half-moaned as I dug my fingernails into his T-shirt.

"Well, I'm glad to hear that." He straightened up, shifted me back in place, and grabbed the doorknob. "After all," he said in a low rumble, "as your boss, getting you ready is *my* job. And as you know, I take my work very, very seriously."

If you or someone you know needs help, you may find information and resources, including links to immediate help, on the following website from the U.S. Department of Health and Human Services:

www.mentalhealth.gov

The National Suicide Prevention Lifeline has trained crisis workers available to talk 24 hours a day, 7 days a week:

1-800-273-TALK (8255)

www.suicidepreventionlifeline.org

If you are outside of the U.S., a database of international resources can be found on the website of the International Association for Suicide Prevention:

www.iasp.info

ACKNOWLEDGMENTS

As the Healing Edge series draws to a close, I would like to thank my wonderful agent, Andrea Hurst, for her incredible support and mentorship, and for believing in and championing my writing. Deepest gratitude to my brilliant editors at Diversion Books, Randall Klein (*All the Broken Places*) and Eliza Kirby (*All the Wounds in Shadow* and *All the Light There Is*), for their masterful work in shaping this trilogy. I am so grateful to Laura Duane and Diversion Books for taking a chance on a new author's offbeat stories, and to every member of the Diversion team who has worked so hard to bring this series to life. Much appreciation to Sarah Masterson Hally for her beautiful art direction, and to Nita Basu and Christine Saunders for their exceptional work in publicity and marketing.

I have been overwhelmed by the generosity of the many people in the writing and publishing communities who have assisted me along my creative journey. With respect to this series, special and heartfelt thanks to Rosanna Leo, Shannon Roan, my Online Coven, and the ladies of the Life Raft for their extraordinary friendship, help, and support.

Much gratitude to my parents, Amy, Keith, Carol, Nuala, and all of my dear friends and family who have shared their feedback, subject matter expertise, and encouragement. Profound thanks as well to my first book's first reader, Adrian, without whose extraordinary kindness and insights I may well have given up before I started.

And finally, to my husband. No words are sufficient to express how lucky I am to have you, and how grateful I am for the countless ways in which you bring joy to my days and breathe life into my hopes and dreams. You are my whole heart, and every expression of love on these pages is a tribute to you.

Thank you for reading *All the Light There Is*. For more of the Healing Edge series, look for *All the Broken Places* (Book One) and *All the Wounds in Shadow* (Book Two).

There are many ways to spread the word about books you love! If you enjoyed the Healing Edge series, please consider telling a friend, recommending to your library or book club, or posting a review on Amazon or your favorite bookish website.

You can connect with Anise Eden, sign up for her newsletter, and learn more about her work on her website:
www.AniseEden.com